The Nine Lives Prophecy

By Siaom L.B.C. Strawberry

9/23/19

To Peter,
Thanks for helping me on
my way! Best,
Brett Bagley

The Nine Lives Prophecy

Book design by Donnie Light at eBook76.com

Cover art and internal images by Brett Dylan Bagley

Preface:

I write this book in an aesthetic form that renders the expression like poetry. I am aware that the rules of writing and further syntax are challenged and also semantics seem to confront the traditional method used in writing. I will not defend my book, but claim that in regard to the areas in question, it is, in the end, my intention. My suggestion is to read the book in a way that you may gain something in this unorthodox approach and this will lead to a richer sentiment that you may take from it as well. Sometimes, a question may take the form of a picture and this hopefully will lead you to a sort of slide show that, when united as one, fruitfully denotes a combination of this in a still life that is my life. I am not willing to defend this style in your own writing, though it seems that if you manage to take away something in the process, I am compelled to commend you for the effort. Do not challenge me, as this is not my intention. I think the greater meaning, in this case, is more important than the parts. It may be an art piece in progress, and you may continue, here, what I started. I think you will find that in places where there seems to be no meaning, there is still meaning. I am well aware of the challenges of pre-conceived notions in writing. I wrote this book to express something that I need not defend now. Most simply said, I have something to say, and that is all. I think a picture without an audience has no soul. And so in this process, I must thank you as well, if not only to enrich my endeavor through your critical eye, which I respect.

Author's Note:

Truth manifests itself in the heart of someone's soul. This does not mean that one person's "truth" is the same as another person's "truth"? In this book, I attempt to reach inside and express my truth. If this conflicts with your beliefs, or "truth," I must apologize, as this is not my intention. Instead, I encourage you to find the truth inside yourself as well. If this book helps you to make this journey, then I think it is a success... The book is also referred to as "Adam and Eve Hotel Theater Production," and I consent for you to use it in your art; may it be theater, dance, or whatever? I had something to say and I said it, so thank you! Take every grain of salt with a diet Doctor Pepper. God lives forever in this vein. Remember, "The past has no future, which is not the present either." This book has no scientific basis.

—Siaom L.B.C. Strawberry (pen name for Brett Dylan Bagley)

Adam and Eve Hotel Theater Productions:

The Nine Lives Prophecy

By Siaom L.B.C. Strawberry

To all the muses who contributed...thank you!

Dark Star in Nine Parts
who are you? One: man
(Jason Whitney)

In the hollow bunt of what was a tree.
Where someone returns to the beginning
and where redemption mocks the hope and pride
of a predecessor who does not know himself.
A picture taken of his shadow
and only God reveals such color.

Part One: The Diagnostic Wall of Lepure

"The Exploding Whale"

The exploding whale in Taiwan happened to me first. It did not proliferate with expanding tissue and blubber, but rather resonated in my posterior (exterior behind) like the prior explosion in China with my innocence terminated at this point. The face of the explosion that would recede it, is important because it is a solution to an enigma of God on that day as Simon confronts me on Tenth Avenue, two blocks north of Dykman Street. If I could see Simon, I could see God too. I am reverent to this play. It is the beginning of what is innocence lost thereafter. At such times, I think "Old Faithful" might be a metaphor for a whale trapped in the earth millions of years ago. I know we are from "before the stars and after the dinosaurs."

Simon's brother Mike is different. He represents the sun of yesterday ending his rein with the rising of the thirteenth sun, and the killing of the czar and his family in Russia at the early part of the twentieth century. Really, Stalin knew the Oklahoma City bombing incident was not necessary. With one crash of its tail fin, Simon resounds mightily like a prior explosion and with this it welcomes the beginning of time in 1952. The time ends with Will smashing a glass façade of a courtroom some time in the 1960s in protest of the Vietnam War. At such times, America is at a peculiar crossroad when its innocence is lost and regained at the same time. Then, sharks blow bubbles to signify to God and (Mt. Fuji, who fears the sun) that it is time to leave the ocean.

Mike is a lizard and sits on his cactus patch in Malibu overlooking a mirage of what is there, the Pacific Ocean. The decedents of the Maya (I think) form a circle burning effigies of what is God's waste which is Satan, and he rests unaware of the ritual on the boardwalk of Venice Beach. A parallel universe may be seen then when the sharks, twenty-four to be exact, form a circle and swim on their backs while Lily shows she has projectiles.

1

She leaves her lover behind in the form of Fidel Castro, but too old to show its face in history books at such times. She swims away in a teasing fashion which might be, in actuality, Will's mom in the form of an octopus.

Lily, however, may be remnants of the old world and the fall of Man, but is left as a remnant of God's rage in the ocean as a tiger shark with jaws crooked representing that she has had many lovers since.

Castro stays out of the ocean in fear that his lover might consume him out of shear jealousy that he might be with another.

The rage she feels is different than that of God and is way too physical in nature. Still, more like the effigy deep in the rainforest which defines the predisposition, she is woman thereafter the fall of Man. Yet, she remains in the ocean still, and will never leave, unlike the tiger lost at sea, who escaped this fate.

Like the burning of God's feces, that which is Satan deep within the rainforest, this is symbolically her feminine order. Maybe her existence might not be without some purpose. Her lack of existence here allows for Will's mother to release her tentacles from her son to be free from the maternal feelings she harbors. Stalin's millions were lost in the process, though.

So, as Will crashes through the glass window of the courthouse that might be a metaphor for his father, two worlds divide forever and this exonerates him of what Adam claims to be his innocence in temptation. Will is the brother I never had? What he cannot understand either, that which is Eve, and he leaves behind Lily; the end of God's wrath of yesterday and Will joins God on a path leading to heaven.

Simon, on that day, might be the end of Will's wrath, thereafter. He rides his fancy Mercedes Benz to leave his brother then, which is mostly the fire left in a dying sun. The wrath of Will is no more. The whale or Simon, exists in the water of the ocean, the same way it would exist on land. Castro waves to his lover as a tear drops in the ocean from his eye and it resonates with Simon's fist.

When the explosion expands outward, Rocky Raccoon exists only in the folklore of what is the Beatles. My behind experiences a great blast and John Lennon may be a sacrifice to such a notion. The Chinese would resound the beginning with a test explosion of an atomic bomb in 1952. Prior to this, Ziggy Stardust flies through space in a rocket not knowing where he is really going? Simon uses a crowbar to slam the window of a perfect yellow taxicab. At such times, the children are told it is polite to smile at the sun or so Mike, his brother, says? The cars around Manhattan burn fossil fuels profusely, and this is a beginning and it represents healing agents, I think. (I am told Jesus will return in about two hundred years.) There might be more than one double-entendre in this segment.

"Mt. Fuji"

Mt. Fuji, for selaphobia of the sun, hid in the ocean nearly one thousand years ago. At this point in time, a mid-point of a natural cycle occurs and the Dalai Lama "179" might relay the cruelty of the sun. Will's mom became obsessed with her son after this and he fell in the ocean and was not released until Lily's tempestuous affair that would resound allows his mother to release him. A tiger lost at sea, in essence, he might understand what God's love is better than anyone I know. God may be, historically, "a gorilla that screwed a bear" before the fall of Man whom he will forgive like a verisimilitude to his end. This is way before Mt. Fuji, who enters the ocean's domain? Also, God may have eaten a pineapple and his remains, metaphorically Satan is left in the ocean? Thereafter, Lily and Satan will remain in the ocean forever more. (until he could rectify Man as innocent and Eve tempted by the serpent to eat the forbidden fruit.) Lily finds in time, this to be a punishment at best. Without the love of God, she shares the ocean with Satan.

Adam is a man who is considered weak and there is no reward for this either. The serpent's skin was like leather which might be a sign of abuse? Through the guise of my tail which parted like the ocean, she bore me immaculately, a cow on a hill. But, she would not forgive those who would leave her behind like remnants of a dying sun. Those who feared her would confront her and she would hold her ground. She would become a realtor, later on, but her existence denotes a woman who would obey the word of God and not man. By contrast, Man feared her primal sin, in which she was enamored and she held on to it as though gold. It is all that was left of her and God forgave her for nothing anyway and in the end, she is friend to man, too.

God, thereafter, metaphorically entered the ocean and only he knew our sun would eventually subside into a different domain. When it was time to leave, Satan entered this domain never to leave again. Will's mom lived in the form of an octopus and through her eyes, I could see him before Eve left the garden of Eden, I being one of the animals, I think. Will's mom might have played with him in the darkest areas of the ocean.

My mother was the serpent of yesterday left to watch the tree so that no one would eat the forbidden fruit. Maybe, men would come see her daughter, who forbade her to leave her post as God allows things to continue like they were after the fall of Man. Knowing that Man was innocent, Adam, may be Will in hindsight? When his mother in the form of an octopus released him, God too was freed to enter his domain in heaven.

My mom watched over the garden and she was aware that the land was valuable, and collected trinkets out of boredom and her other daughter became a phoenix who swallowed the sun, as a result of Eve's blatant act that forbade the word of God. The trinkets which had no value may have made men jealous and they took sides with Eve until God would return.

Mt. Fuji is a good man, but feared the sun so much he hid in the ocean. He should tempt the conquistadors to seek the gold of the Incas and Lily, who loved a man (not God) and allowed for a perfect flower (somewhere else) to be picked. Lily is a pun and the flower not hers. Mt. Fuji remains in the ocean until after two atomic bombs landed on his homeland and he thinks he saw Ziggy Stardust's rocket blast off in the night sky. What is left of Eve might be the explosions of these unprovoked menaces and the deterioration of man's fruit is their legacy thereafter.

"In Search of Benny: (Benny the Fly)"

Benny is my Israeli friend. I met him in Washington Square Park when I was sixteen. He lived in Greenwich Village and would surely share his weed, but I do not think I did (it is just not me!) He might have been ten years older than me and he inspected my photographs that I would have a show down the street. I met him one day at a café after our first introduction, and told him he looked like Cat Stevens, which he denied. Really, it was surprising to me that aborigines seek him out as far as from Australia and they consider him their brethren. Within a fly lies the mystery of the mustard seed? He was a pacifist and did not believe in the cause of his homeland to fight the Palestinians. If you should ask, he was hiding in New York City to avoid mandatory service in the Israeli military. I think he thought the Jews and Palestinians should live in peace there. Lily, Benny, and I were going to travel on my spring break from boarding school to the Mississippi Delta Blues Festival, but we never made it.

The aborigines in Australia consider Benny family like their own. They make a sound through a long horn which Benny might hear from far off. I think for a time, they were separated, and they would make timely ceremonial sounds with their instrument for him to come home. Through the slipstream, Benny should deplore the life he once lived as a Jew. Still, on Fifth Avenue, he buzzes about some WASP's upper east side apartment and wordify vaguely the schediasm. The verbatim may have been prolonged over a week though?

*

"What?" "Nothing" "Why did you tip the cab driver so much?" "Tennessee Jed was a great man!" "To be or not to be?" "What?" "Nothing, just testing." "You eat it with your hands." "I know how to eat pizza, I just like to eat it with a fork and knife." "Have you ever eaten calamari?" Jamie asks her father. "No salt or pepper on my eggs...(etc., etc.)" "Wouldn't it be nice if the squirrel smiled once in a while when you feed it nuts?" "Did you remember to send Mother an invitation for our dinner party?" The homeless guy said, "Just a quarter sir, I have not eaten for three days" Continued to daughter Jamie in tangents; "you failed the written part of your driver license test." Someone says out of the blue, "that is all or I will have to call the authorities!" "The street stinks like urine!"

"I know, someone should clean the street up!" "I know!" " Barbados looks so nice in the brochure, I bet it is even better in person!" "Did you say we would be late for the show?" "No dear, I will have a gin and tonic..." "Would you like nuts with your drink?" "How expensive could your suit's dry cleaning cost?" "...then it started raining, Mother, it was awful!" "You don't say?" "...the cheeseburger is more expensive than a Big Mac with an extra-value meal!" Jamie tells her father. "...and then Edward told the chef that he would complain to the maitre d' if they did not cook the fish better." "You don't say?" "...maybe the drinks are more profitable with a value meal than with a separate fries or cheeseburger, without the drink?" "...what about the cruise, how was the cruise?" "You don't say?" "...I know there must be some sort of marketing strategy behind the French fries sale?" "I know, it's the oil for the fries that is so expensive." "...no dear, I am still working on this word puzzle, what is four letters 'to smoke' and rhymes with fag?" "...so, I brought the book back and they said the crease is bent and they would not refund me the money!" "The worse part of the movie is coming..." "What?" "You know, when the cat burglar falls from the scaffolding." "Oh, I have not seen this movie before." "So, I woke up this morning and they were playing that song, you know..." "It was like Simon and Garfunkel's 'Homeward Bound,' I couldn't get it out of my head." "You are still talking to your mother?" "And then the green monster gobbled up the toad..." "No, it's our nephew Matthew. Now, oh, he wants to know then who eats the green monster?" "Tell him he will find out when he grows up." "Funny thing about the dream..." "Tell him that the policeman eats the green monster..." "...and then there was some sort of three dimension to the poster that I am looking at and the man is fishing and he begins to bleed and then I realize that I am the one bleeding!" "How freaky..." "Yea!" "How would some of those black shingles look like on the window sill?"

"Then I say, 'have faith, Mother, and you will be delivered.'"

"Mercury Records"

Mercury is a land without borders, like a never-ending porno film. Like ancient remnants of early earth, it spawns from a fire from one side to another, again and again. The sheep with red glowing rutilant eyes are its brethren, but exist here on earth without any regard to the pundits segue who say otherwise. Jason exists here too without any disturbance of what is the tribulations of sirens on neighboring Venus, and their callings which are a timely disturbance for those on earth. Jason and Lindsay make the transition of bootleg music from Jason's collection on Mercury, similar to the way that Will would leave it, allowing Jason to enter the inner circle in a vestibule of his space-time. It is Venus Pools Inc. that cause the disturbances. They, all women, offer a service, to clean pools and cars when not in their own sump, calling out to those who would rather not hear it. Such esoteric disturbances are best heard in California, and Jason provides a buffer to fight noise with noise. I think he was looking for a way out and found himself somewhere else on Mercury. While Will found a way out to escape the noises that had enthralled him prior? The Mercurian reprisal left him on Mars, which is too far away, and he says the noise does not transcend his realm. But, he still sees the red eyes of sheep as they sleep in green pastures, allowing him to forget the world Jason adopted on Mercury.

"Venus Pools Inc. and the Sect of the Mercurian Reprisal"

Jason's tape collection of bootleg memorabilia, mostly from the sixties, is with substantial allure except for the freaked-out zombie-like aboriginal devil invocation of Venus Pools Inc. How two inordinate injections should compel the two factions to cross the lines from one to another and rarely back again, leaves Jason restless. This time, he reaches for some rare "Mercurian" bootleg and hands someone (waiting in the car with him who is black, but I cannot make out his face) and he hands him the Jimi Hendrix "special." Without any regard to Venus Pools Inc., the transition might be made. In this world of token transactions, the commodity is not money, but rather noise. The scene is just this. Jason waits in his rusted copper-colored Trans Am for a sacerdotal contact who purchases his tapes; Jason being the provider and the contact his distributor. His car rather resembles that which is reminiscent of the seventies. And, at this injection, Jason listens to The Doors bootleg of Fillmore West '68, I think. The medley is "Love Me Two Times," and this leads into "Rider On the Storm." At which time, a girl at the car wash across the street is listening to Enya and would rather counter the Trans Am's pounding blare of The Doors with pink undertones of the Go-Go's "Vacation" etc., etc. You would know this is L.A. despite Myra's Australian accent who started Venus Pools Inc. and since then brought the business here. It is an all-women car wash and pool service too, dedicated to anything feminine for that matter.

Jason is tired of waiting for another contact and calls Lindsay in Philadelphia or a suburb of it rather, and asks, "Where is this guy?"

Venus Pools Inc. might be just a mirage at such times and Lindsay answers the phone where he lies by the pool with some fly zipping around his face and responds to Jason (Ray Bans on of course) "...so I thought you were still in Ireland? And thanks for the sweater you sent me."

"It is 100% wool," Jason responds.

"I know...it will be great this winter," Lindsay adds, "Okay, try this number, 222-7171, his name is Jerry." Jason responds thanks and goodbye. But, what is Venus Pools Inc. really?

Venus Pools Inc. is the belief that women may exist in a society without the penetration of their male counterpart which is a false sachem. On Venus it exists as a strain of megalomania and women would rather dismiss men as a sexual object which backfires, making those who participate as gigolos or tools to their greater objective. It began with three women, with its origin at three different points in time. It is a lesbian society which claims Alison, Ilona, and Lily as their matriarchs. Hillary Clinton may sympathize with their cause, but she does not go so far as to publicly implore it either.

After the fall of Man, Alison hid in the womb of a female zebra to exchange men of the land that is flat like his feet so to avoid God's wrath. She claimed God raped her, but really was intoxicated by an apple Adam picked for her. In exchange for her guilt, men were traded from this land, (that which I was never there really,) to redeem her notion that she was not a lesbian, which is true. She might have loved another boy, but blamed God for her predicament. The zebra kicks from time to time to confirm she still exists and she will maintain her innocence until God forgives her.

Lily loved God in a way that she should inherit the gold of the Incan Empire in exchange of her betrayal of his subject, an Incan king. In the transition, she forgets about the pact and seduces a young boy whom she treats as a gigolo. The flower in the acquisition is not hers really.

Ilona offered her only son, a prince in Poland, so that she would prove, in this act, that she is stronger than a man. She pretended to love Hitler, but really seeks clemency so she would seek favor with Mt. Fuji and, thereafter, rule the ocean.

The combination of these three entities promotes the lesbian cause which is Venus Pools Inc. and rehabilitates their secular notions.

"Continued (the Great Sleep)"

From any corner of the globe, Benny the Fly hears his aboriginal brethren blow the fog horn and an airy submission to the sound puts the sheep asleep. They go to sleep with their eyes wide open and this sect is a remnant of all that exists from Mercury and their next to kin, Jason. He is all that is left of Mercury. This is like a photograph, but the sheep are real; they have bright red eyes and they glow like devils and Jason was not a real descendent of their home. Where it is now, is impossible to attain? He is rather adopted brethren similar to the way the Aboriginals think of Benny as kin. Sometimes the natural world repeats itself as though to reinforce their inadequacy; when the sheep sleep, there is this aura and its blinding light. This occurs in the hills of the backcountry of some desolate place in Ireland where there is nothingness as they sleep near waterfalls contending the notion that dairy and water are the same and the color green forever lost in the exchange. Venus Pools Inc. now might show its true colors. Rather than a mirage of women working at a car wash in cut-off jeans and pink shirts without the sleeves, there is a cesspool of women churning in their own feces and calling out as though to forebear their yearnings here. It is unable to meet like a grand rainbow crossing the sky from southern Africa and touching down in Myra's home across the sea as far as Australia or New Zealand. Unfortunately, this picture is rarely viewed and rather one such person is Jason, and he has sympathy for those who must listen to their constant callings, and he basically offers tapes to muffle the noise. He hands someone (in his sound proof barricade) a tape and Jerry replies with his hand on the tape, nothing as Jason cannot hear the words outside his vehicle. But, Jerry said something like "keep making tapes louder!" This translates as "thanks" for you caring enough to do such a mission that is white noise. Once you have heard the sirens, nothing will allow you to forget the callings and with "noise" Jason may be immune in the "Mercurian Reprisal." Anyway, Jason is able to escape by muffling the sounds and, as though reaching through the waterfall, his hand crosses out of the car to give Jerry the tape and no sound gets through. Zombies may hear the foreboding sounds of sheep and cross over lines as "men at work" and like trying to turn glass into water, there is otherwise no way to get to Mercury from here. Still, I will leave you with a picture. What secrets remain are not dispelled?

(continued) "mirage"

At the poolside (a suburb of Philadelphia) Lindsay basks in the sun wearing Ray Bans and it is a site like any other except Lindsay hardly does anything. He is slightly annoyed by the fly that keeps zipping around his face. David, a friend, is cool; not gay or anything like that. But, meanwhile, Lindsay is listening to a Phil Collins tape on a walkman and earphones and does not hear David's call inside the house. Lindsay thinks to use his cell phone, but the year is 1986 and cell phones have not yet been invented.

Adam and Eve Hotel Theater Productions Presents "Ridiculous Penny Loafer Prelude: Dressing Leonardo Da Vinci and (thoughts on the creation of the first running shoes)"

The sport comprises five players on each team and harkens the penny loafer on his left foot and a dismal portrayal of what is apparently a stubbed toe hidden? He did this to disguise the side with the inferior toe and thus creates a shoe for this fool. But, both feet maintain the secrecy of the ordeal. Hiding the embarrassment completely so as not to reveal that which is inferior, but rather places a shiny penny on the tongue of the shoe to remind him as such and not to have to worry as well. Everything else is underway and he thought a muzzle might be nice for Mr. Perfect at the center down below. Neither foot is invited to its opening fashion show, tailored in pink cotton. Funny, as it is, the left shoulder has a rash and consulting the toe (her name is Vera and is from South Africa) it is better to hire a body specialist to fit the garment over the shoulder. As his bellybutton is exposed, this implies the work is unfinished. Still, he wears a kilt so the lady friends won't get the wrong idea. Being at a gay bar, he does not want to seem rude either. Meanwhile, the first tailor's job is a body specialist and high-priced designer named Gucci Forakis, which is in fact a pun which seems totally stupid. What drives at the epicenter, but lower, is not important. But, to make sure it is legal, he says, "ask Sam?" the lawyer who is gay and for short he calls it "ass" and this is all very well. As long as one's loins do not explode with all the attention and for this it merit's a cup for it which is woman? Now, back to the game, he does not mean any insult to the other. God ponders which foot may jump the farthest? Instead of falling into a slump of depression, he disguises each foot with a penny and whichever foot might jump the farthest carries the reward and thus "penny loafer." The athlete down the street is Fred and he is also a gigolo as to say a lion statue in the park.

Neither foot really likes him anyway, but women seem to like him still. Therefore, each foot is always at a good distance away from him as he runs looking for a sign of life (there is none.) Still, he runs one foot and then the other, having both succeeded in comprising the first running shoes and God gives each shoe a penny. At the gay bar, Jerry Garcia is performing. Though, he has not heard of him, he thinks he might stay and listen for a while. Sitting next to him is a somewhat older, but attractive woman named Tina Turner. Anyway, they got to talking and the rest is history.

Lilith's Fair Alternate Ego: foie gras (the mice eat foie gras in lowly places) "A Picture of a Girl"

She stares at herself into "the pond" that will immerse her later like a hug from her father. The girl does not see a pretty reflection, but rather someone completely alienated from the world in which she lives. "Foie gras" which is French for ground goose liver, is an escape which invites a short loss of self-worth and then she dives into the water which hugs her stomach so that the life within her is repelled outward. It is a metaphor for the sickly way that will induce vomiting later that night? After she has sex with one or another male counterparts, her skin is somewhat alive and she thinks it is worth the toil.

This is not a personal imposition; it is French like French fries. A way of life, it permits one to endure the dirty fantasies of the male counterpart in return for sexual pleasure.

When she awakes the next morning, she goes to the mirror and looks at her face which she does not recognize. As she lights her cigarette, all she thinks is that girl, how pitiful. Rather than getting sick, another guilty pleasure, she stares out the window and suppose she will meet some other guy and the day passes like the last, guilty pleasure through the window of her life, the toilet. The water, whether in a pond or a toilet is her mother who will never let her forgive herself for the things over which she has no control.

So, she finds comfort in throwing up what is foie gras and there is peace for a short time. Foie gras might as well be dogfood to a dog as it is a way of life in which there is no substitute. And, though, rarely is the foie gras digested completely, she finds her peace in the ritual which proves her better than the gofers that others at the country club subsist upon while her father plays golf. Rather, she does not make the same mistake and feels alive at the intervals, to what injunction? She likes the taste of foie gras as it fills her stomach for a short time and it is then dispensed outward; this and other luxury products like cheese and toast? It becomes a disease of conscience and vindictive as well, as animals should allow such a bleak reality to occur?

She is her own master and the struggle makes her stronger over time. Though she loves her father, she knows this would be enough in a better world. Instead, her mind compels her to know why she feels the feelings she feels? She might subsist like this for long periods of time and, though better than the animals, she feels no pride in not begging when desperate. It is the antithesis of the mother/daughter relationship, as though a choice, only to become stronger over time in the derision that she does not fully understand anyway... "Foie gras in the morning, foie gras at night, foie gras on toast, foie gras anytime."

"Darien, Connecticut"

The boy, eight and a half years old, stands in the rain waiting. He wears a wool jacket, probably expensive and from Scotland as well. He wears bright yellow rubber boots that stand out like duck served out of season at the country club. He does not know why his dad does not pick him up at school, and is brought to the principal's office while Maria the Guatemalan maid crosses town on the bus. She does not speak English and, of course, does not drive either. She, of course, knows when the mom is having a bad day, which seems sort of regular. She, the mom, hides in the living room by the fire, sipping expensive cognac at four-thirty on a Tuesday afternoon, as though unaware that Morgan, her son, is not home yet. In fact, she almost forgets that the father is not picking the boy up and sends Maria at the last moment.

"Darling," Mrs. Davison calls to Morgan, "I am afraid that your father had to leave on business." And her father, who happens to be Morgan's father's boss, thought to take Morgan out to dinner that night. The light in the house seems dim as usual, but moreover because of the rainy overcast day. On the stairs going to Morgan's room on the third floor is a note saying, "Here are a pair of penny loafers, hope you like them love, Dad."

The next Saturday, Mrs. Davison takes Morgan to someone she calls "a child psychology counselor." Mrs. Davison is feeling much better by this time.

Across the wooden desk that looks mahogany and old, a man explains to Morgan in a somewhat serious, but gentle tone, (like Grandfather's voice) that his parents are getting a divorce. He asked if he understood this, which he sort of did? At least he knew it was something bad. But, he felt sobered; maybe is too sophisticated a word, but liked the person's office anyway, as it made him feel older. The mother wants the best help in discussing the matter, and she lights a cigarette in the office. It is a long thin brown cigarette that makes his mom's fingers seem long and bony. The doctor's name is Mr. Brown, but prefers to be called Frank or Dr. Brown as he prefers. Dr. Brown looks at Morgan and tells him he is a professional counselor and he could ask him any question he wants regarding the matter.

"Do you know what a divorce is, Morgan?" Frank asks. Morgan shrugs no, and Dr. Brown responds that this means that your parents are parting ways. He says, "you will see both your parents, but at different times." This seems confusing to Morgan, still he shrugged yes to the doctor that he understands.

Years pass and Morgan sits on the bottom bunk of his boarding school room listening to Bob Dylan "Mr. Tambourine Man" on his boom box. He thinks life is a breeze since he will be attending Harvard next year as Morgan is smart and proves to excel despite some early inconveniences, like his parents getting divorced. Furthermore, Morgan has acquired a sizeable music collection which includes the Grateful Dead, Jimi Hendrix, and of course his favorite, Bob Dylan, whom he fantasizes of being like. And he is well on his way as his guitar becomes a tool which propels him to high popularity among other students. You might hear Morgan talking to some other kid in the school hallway (after Spanish class) saying some gibberish about Fillmore East etc., etc. "You got to get this bootleg," etc. and Morgan seems to have fooled everyone. He turns out to be a dashing young man and still wears penny loafers like the ones his dad once gave him. (Little does Morgan know that his father also liked Bob Dylan back in the sixties.)

"Chickenhawk's Crucifixion"

Chickenhawk was in his room studying as usual and though not completely "un-rounded" so to speak, I give him credit for not wanting to leave his boarding school room at such a time. Actually, I am not un-rounded either, but had the ability to stare into the eyes of wolves that occupied the halls of Achincloss, the dorm we shared that freshman year. Furthermore, I knew any aggression may have been directed at me in some way too, but this

12

was my secret as well. It is sort of funny that we all were putting on a skit of a bashing? But, deep inside, some of the kids had a strange Freudian way of thinking that assumed Chickenhawk was not worthy to use the same toilet.

And, so I too participated and Freud was much later in our education anyway. The humor is that though we stared into each other's eyes, we never really looked at each other at such times. Like at a low chant, there, after study hall was over, everyone would begin a frenzied uproar and throw Chickenhawk, sometimes head first, into the trash bin. This was to be a lesson in male juvenile delinquency. I suppose Chickenhawk is in Chicago now as an architect in some big firm. He laughs that he was semi-unrelated to such spectacles of adolescence and the life he leads is better as not being a culprit in the prior ordeal. No one in our group of frenzied spoils of male youth would know it is a sin to save a beached whale, as though in God's eyes it is also the same sin, to kill it.

"The Winner is a Woman and the Anatomy of Freudian Juncture"

She sits in a wooden chair, the embrace feels like her father. Again and again, she combs her long blond hair as though gripping a spiny beast by its neck, asking some painful question, "am I fat?" In plain view, the TV. is visible through the mirror. I talk back, not satisfactory like payback for the nurturing she will endure for that of another? And she looks again at the TV. to confirm it is just a TV. and not her father? And she touches herself as though an impromptu "to speak" and now it is playback time; the TV. is a girl's best friend.

Furthermore, she will prepare a meal for "the dog" with which she shares the table (not past eight) but early enough to get some sleep and plan the next meal for tomorrow. She prepares each meal as though a feathered friend which reminds her that she will someday wake up and call her turmoil just a dream. She addresses the mirror as she always does, licking her right thumb with the flat vigilance of a pink and nearly red tongue. And she awakes from the dream, and goes downstairs where the dog waits for its dinner too.

But, first, the chicken is frozen in the freezer as she holds it now like a halfback does a football, and hands a beer to her husband, who waits in the living room during a commercial break of some football game. She feels like a commercial; though not to blame her father even as he too would rather watch a commercial than get off the couch to get a beer!

"Who is winning, honey?" she addresses the table and splay the slimy plastic. The chicken will fall out onto the counter near the microwave that has found a few remains and such of cockroaches. It is comforting since she would otherwise cook her father a delicious meal? On a Monday, so it will wait like a trip on a cruise ship, and she sets the table showing an unusual tenderness with the utensils especially the forks that align the plates perfectly? She is a real pro.

You might say this is a wake-up call for tomorrow's dinner, as each detail is in focus; the car, the windowless counter, the dead shells of cockroaches in the microwave, and then his footsteps. She carefully reviews what she will say to him without any hint of the previous night's dinner. Again and again, she becomes an actor in her own play. And the chicken is roasted a slight too much as the skin becomes a weapon left unnoticed by its perpetrator, the shower is a tad bit too hot, and next to the bed on her side, the alarm rings the next morning, a minute late at seven o' one.

And who would notice, as it is her play, in which she has the leading role? And the cockroaches are her loving fans that would gladly give up their lives to get a glimpse into what's cooking for dinner the next night.

The next day, she combs her hair like any other day. She rewards herself with a dark chocolate for execution of a father slash husband relationship. If Mom was still around, she too would indulge in the stratosphere she calls her meager existence. Unfortunately, she was not one of the lucky ones and dies in a way unbecoming of a saint (car crash) and swears this would never happen to herself. Why does this guy Christopher Lowell talk so funny? Doesn't he have a life? But she likes to watch, anyway, in a sort of stipulation that warrants some time wasted. The dog is a mere incarnation of what was yesterday's news. Her husband too would talk about sports as it is another Tuesday and he likes to read the sports section on Tuesdays. How pitiful, she dumps some more leftovers into the dog's bowl as if to imply the turning of the page into a new day and pours herself a glass of orange juice as well.

If only he knew what sacrifice eating a single chocolate truffle imposes on the female infrastructure, namely her body, he might comprehend why life toils take on the shape of a belated task. It is her job to weigh the pros and cons of every act that comes through the door. Although, she might wonder from time to time what it would be like to be him? But, she thinks this would be regressive too? Instead, she reads about some woman who cuts off her husband's penis. This might seem interesting at first, but she does not show any notice. She would not do the same as it makes a woman look weak, like she has to go that low. Seriously, it has happened before, in order to gain solvency, I guess, her duty as wife. And definitely too messy, and maybe the dog will get run over by a car? But, just the fact that such horrid thoughts could arise and do happen occasionally, proves everything I have written so far is plausible, if not trite. I guess the depressing nature of such thoughts drives a woman to such shows like Christopher Lowell, because a gay man on TV. is the next best thing to an act such as the one before, and definitely too messy!

Why does a woman even bother, and I address this as to say the woman is the winner in the end? It does not matter how beautiful she makes her hair seem with a comb, but rather the endurance she obtains with nasty thoughts that makes her stronger than the male counterpart. In fact, I think some women try to dress up because of a confidence that the other is weaker. In an odd way, their toil is a stepping stone to a world without any subjective inquiry. A woman sees another woman as equal always, and this makes them better, even though, the makeup, to a man, means otherwise. And the fork stabs the beast just another day closer to destiny; "I think with chicken, rice and peas." Really, who would possibly think all this indulgence could be free and she carries the weight of the chocolate to bed and let the devil conclude which is the stronger sex?

"Christopher Lowell, who do you think is the stronger sex?" And she combs her hair straight down and she knows what is already too obvious? "So, how do I get by, you should ask?" she replies, "the horse's balls point down." It is the sure fine way never to cross into the territory of the opposite sex and not knowing is gold and will be her saving grace in the end.

The vertebra was made in the form of a man. With this fact, man may stand forthright and it is assumed that the woman is his lesser and was made from one of his ribs. So I say with all the shit men put up with, heaven is just compensation for the mess he knows is not his. If you asked the animals, they would point their finger, if they could, at woman. Furthermore, women find this fact hard to digest, since the other sex feels somewhat betrayed by, in this case, a dog? She uses this to her advantage even if it is not completely true. So, if she jokes about what if he makes it to heaven, her laugh is real since she figures her reward is greater than the antithesis of life after death.

She pokes fun at heaven and supposes it is a reward for losers. The remaining issue is not woman's betrayal of man, but rather her embracing this relationship in order to prove to the father that a woman may be better than a man. Here lies a competition of sorts, and trifle over what socks to wear is taken more seriously by a woman in daily life than whether to take the dog out? Still, man is catching up in such precocious matters. More importantly, woman may invade space undetected as the dichotomy of this competition makes the advantaged male race extremely insecure. The point here is man might have God and all of creation on his side, however, over time there is greater incentive to overcome these obstacles by woman. By setting higher standards and goals, the woman excels, while the male always has to settle for mediocrity, which is another way of deflating any man's ego. She chooses how to play the game and, over time, this makes woman the winner. Contrary, her father is just a tactic to acknowledge that which she gratefully recedes, the tail that follows the dog (intended not to make sense).

The rest becomes history, a toil that merits the flowers that bloom in her garden and she will never know otherwise? Unless, and again I say emphatically "unless" she is willing to negate this temptation and consider being good in a sense, she is able to be an equal or partner. She might find a scenario so invigorating that she convinces herself that she too is a man. This would be true if a real woman might not conspire, but the dream is plausible anyway?

And at this point, God is not bothering to keep score anymore and the record he was playing for some time now is obsolete, as woman might become a super being and, if she chooses to, she excels like no other. Almost like that which inspires God to create the unimaginable and such a deal becomes tolerant to both sexes? No matter how guilty and ashamed the animals feel for presuming woman evil, it becomes the exact opposite and God is now on the side of woman and thus completes the cycle. The antidote for that which is bad is now super good and, therefore the human race becomes effactually quite interesting, if it is not for the dog. The dog, who now feels betrayed, then becomes the demon and it knows just by pure stigmatism who will win in the end.

Now, what is fair is annulled by the creator at this door for a more interesting cruelty in which God accepts whether he is a man or a woman. Some guy at a bar downtown makes a snide remark and it feels like the backside swatted like a common fly to a place more suitable for losers and women are carved into statues in every park, in contrast. In fact, now, instead of the male persona, it becomes an advantage effactually to be a woman and the efflorescence of man à disadvantage which is worth noting by any dog-loving degraded dude going downtown, if you know what I mean. Now that she has the advantage, a new word is formed namely "boss."

"Who is your boss?" and God throws the dog a bone as it laughs with a sort of arcane smile across its face. Meanwhile, it is fashionable to be that which is unreliably neutral. The chess game God is playing and planning his next move has all the pieces now and couples flock to Lincoln Center to see the symphony together.

So, what is the definition of "gay"? as she asks while blinking, thinking that things have been so much better lately. And, now you must decide which side you are on and "no sex" is not an issue. "She", the remaining piece on the table, is defunct of the pride needed to return "the princess" to Lepure and this is the question at hand that comes up later on. This is no longer a mystery, this is reality. She leads her soldiers awry just once as she is having a bad hair day and God at such times seems obsolete. God then looks at the dog, sort of funny and it is no longer laughing? It has just begun to get interesting he should think. Man or woman? God says neither to both and now calls himself "super cosmic utility man" and the rose petals drop off her bed like rain in London.

The Diagnostic Wall of Lepure

In dreaded fall of the mountain quake of the Lepure Wall is ridden by the Trojan's quest of the sanctity of golden purses embalmed in the hand of a half-blooded tear and a scalp-beaded sapphire feather. It is not the worth, half feather and half omnipotent fire, that bequest the curse upon her left knee? Otherwise, wanton cries of wolf between hidden scars of mustard seed upon her frowned shoulder are lined with purses of gold between her cheeks is tolerable? It is the dismantling of an old silver checkered cab left by some crane in a dump called New York City, traced by anthropoids to maintain the last traumatic quest for a silver grind left in her teeth? So, between the dove and the pigeon feathers she appears here to foster one silver picture, her father.

Skyscrapers of kind demise line the walls of city neighborhoods. I cannot return to this place, so distant in memory, so different as when a Coke bottle is set by its throat in the sand and so far away? Now, this place is lined by emerald pearls of spiders' green mustard and cold fosterings of its slimy quest along the forbidden path, up to "central seizure" the park? The doves have returned now to mate with the pigeons, forbearing the truth of winter's long cold edge over the autumn's color. Then, the witch, when turned dumb, coheres this, in a stomp stare of ash left by the broom of her cat's tail. Now, the quest is over and doves, in their innocent light, return to fly with pigeons in a city asleep to all bad things. The curse should become solvent in the wake of air; the snuffle: in the air gone with the wind of a prince's nose?

Yes, the city is asleep for a time, but more innocent than dead, it faces the end of a chivalrous quake with the return of the dove to the forbearing city.

Furthermore, what demented souls could foster a stick that penetrates the lost world of the dust left by seagulls in an attempt to ferment the loss in their own salty tears or understand the lowly changes in animal temperament?

Effected to this one isolated prince, a nerve line wild with dismay, ferments the rock basins attributed to great sluggers such as Babe Ruth. It stretches virulently free, in the air, that which an energy not unlike TV. was once here? To return the shrouds of only the bold, as if to wake from a dream and foster the silver in value of the prince's lost gold watch, necessary in exchange to return the half-Indian princess back home to Lepure. Maybe, the silver in a lost gold watch is a picture that will free her at some point in the future.

Not to mention the lowly pursuit, her soul endures at the site of only pageant bell bottoms have the discomfort to endure? Not even the ants remember such a spectacle of squander?

Rich in envy, the prince's soiled pocket is lined with a dust of red consequence. It is all that is left him, the pondering of gold lost near the swampy marsh, central to what was once there, a watch. Now, just the red saliva the green emits in the old swamped terrace, where once the veins of her blood might have fumbled down his fingers reaching for the watch, which is now gone. Cold and sad tears, I know, the seagulls dare to trek bygones of dove's feather in formidable pigeon saliva of what was once there? It is a delicacy, I was told by a head waiter with a knife frozen in the skull of a tree on dainty wafers and such. What is so revolting is the color green of the ivy jubilee should foreshadow? It is in locks of her hair that green should pass the desert of blackened rock shoulder on semi-deserted streets named after a voluptuous line of nine democratic mayors? No, not even the rhinestone pearls hidden in secretive gardens of upper westerly terrace should speak? She speaks from the east; they say, "Doe joe, ma, wa, ma, raven's squall." Furthermore, there are non-figurative gestures of imitation ice like cubes, should it stare through the glass at one? They are left at different high society gatherings, from time to time, in the throats of infidel entrepreneurial protégés; the black fly curse.

"Forever and ever," she said mildly, the good only left in it by the tasty bourbon in his northway apartment lined with an effectual fireplace and clean chimney sweep, a rare breed of compensation for just a lonely prince? Like a fountain of tiny mustard seeds, the half-moon curse and red tiding running through his pocket of un-caressed lineage should sleep for a while?

In this lineage happens a reprehensible virus of a mosquito that ripens only the purple mesh of orange sky and a black cat. Otherwise, the complacency of the city is quite forbidden and normal. A passerby walks mumbling the yellow curse of the southern yellow sky, "That is what is left," as though dictated without comprehension to compensate the long distance runner. No, just a curse fermented solid in the lashes of "the Cube of Hyperberbalee." She ferments its disease and never leaves not even a trace of liquid, just the light that should it refract through the glass hindrance?

"Fear not," the furry beast should ponder, "only I hold the key," said the prince "and only I should close its gate when teeth appear in its chivalry and dismay of one's offspring to the sight of day is not nightmares gone sour."

"Oh," said he and he bit down on his tongue. She tastes the day like orange juice does in a thirsty mouth... (The doves have left for too long and normalcy bequeath her space.)

Behind the wall of Lepure are a few cat hairs and that which wakes those still slightly less than sober. A headache like the city streets that shine in the daylight is as though any other day that might permit it.

"Why not become more sober?" they ask, as though a shadow as its perception rises in the dense brain area of the city. No one bothers you in this light and the sleep potent resonates for a passerby to penetrate? Actually, the sleep slowly raises its temperature and the cat notices this. The only peculiar thing is a lady walking across the street, which is like the peculiarity of its own self-consciousness and as though on the forepaws it stares down on every day. To cross the central seizure in the west is a diagonal line that which she walks. She wears white fluffy linen and the cat notices this now with an alert sobered interest that might be categorized as a violation of blatant aggravation. "Why walk to cotton like in my own path in spring, that I, I should only wander in winter?"

> *dead space, dead space follow me out: and*
> *wallow, wallow; a squirrel a dog and two birds*
> *she has, she has not she has, she has not*
> *wallow, wallow; a squirrel a dog and two birds.*
> *wallow, wallow, she's out. Damn the mice that squander the ground!*

The lady with the birdcage was doing her business mainly in an effort to play birdcalls in a jar for the night's swath. She prepares this juice every day so that her business is prepared before contemplation may swallow her. Between gypsy calls there is a tapestry pageantry of linoleum floors cleaned by the swath of someone else's pink slippers and the fat lady with a bird riding upon each of her shoulders and even more blooming in her cheeks, she sings from the east. To cross the park would be a test of forbidden love pageantry, while everyone else is at church, so to speak. The sun rises in the sky and the awakening of the floor laced in wax and dirt forms at the swarthy bottom of these pink slippers, but her cat does not seem to notice this, though. She is not unusual like any other person. The fat lady carries the two birds; one on each shoulder, blooming in her cheeks, as though walking to the store. Meanwhile, the pink lady in the west calls long distance to forbid contact with other as the cat sits in the corner too. Maybe, it is too obvious that the fat lady in the east and the fat lady in the west rob the soulless many. This is a perplexing challenge to the lady of Lepure?

Wakening to the dense light of the park, she carries such dignity as though birds on her shoulders so that the stroll, like a carousel, should raise the spirits of the New York Stock Exchange a tad. Now, not its potential, only that of a hornet's nest; it falls in the sky during the day's hour and rises in the night. Where taxicabs wander on paths, who have only been misrepresented by the weatherman's assertion of light? That which drives the senses of orange juice and ignores the graces that bring on the night between the two feathered wings of the dove. The pigeon rises into the gray like the turning pages of the New York Times in the wind. All that is left, really, is a rock that fell flat from the sky in an air empty of bygones and empty of light. The whale swims backward by the rocks.

The midday pulse alert is cankerous in an allergic fecundity in the office of his pocket lining. Still, no gold watch, just a reminder of it in the tremor of his hand offset only by the gibberish of the half-moon's red tide quest for the lady of Lepure. If it had been across the Atlantic, the sharks might float in a perfect circle, dead. However, the reminder is enough to continue the quest despite the odds of doom shadowed by a lonely image of himself. At this time, sharks might swim upside down. (But, no one would know given the secrecy is the only grace the tremor may concoct.) Meanwhile, the prince in his Northway apartment says to himself, "Simon says touch your nose," and woebegone he does just that.

Enter the three "jargons" (I made this word up, meaning idiot)

"What are these?" the faint prince concurs. "These are the gifts from the prince of Jubilee; one, two, and three," lit by the light of their arcane smiles.

They are three rare selcouth eggs that should one break, the path to Lepure should be closed. Each jargon stands upright to the older man in the daze; an egg in each of their modified hands, while the tremor in the hand of the faint prince rested into the light of day.

The gold watch musters a seed similar to the swatch of silver that shells its dismay out of its grasp. But that is old, and the day passes like the clouds and the cat waits in shadowed streets for the woman with cotton dress to return from the on-goings only familiar to it like the cabs racing along the park on the west side.

However, a gold watch is more valuable now that London's chime predict its increase of value as its mentor, silver find itself in a downright demand. This may be why the fat lady, crossing the park, brings her two birds as though on her shoulders or why the fat lady sings... And in day, this march, continues like cycles of a hubcap hanging onto a taxicab. For a lady it is a bit of a dive, especially if you should be from Lepure, to be consumed by a demand for silver in the middle of a gold rush, when that is all your background allows. It isn't the value of gold that increases the value of silver, but rather a sort of demented lazy approach towards precious metals that the chrome of bumpers of taxicabs might adhere to. In a city of glitter, she waits until the night appears and this allows the cat to retract its path in the path of the fat lady's upheaval across the park. The secrets of the metropolis know this exchange, especially of silver like the smack trade to drug dealers.

Where does one find a square chrome taxicab ring? The street talk is "pigeoned hubcap" of which dimensions and absorbency to light nil, might transcend a picture of her father sending the lady of Lepure home. Here on the lowly streets where she walks, the cat's tail, at dusk and into the night, tenses slightly. There is some value for such an object, a ring without gold glitter like a counterpart at a square dance. Without any memory of from where the overbearing metal value comes, like silver, the pigeons are void of seagulls and dove. Here, there is complete complacency like pigeons that flutter. The time it takes for angels to befall such a feat, really angels, "We do subsist on glitter, not unlike the stars." Meanwhile, a dark-skinned woman comes out of the shadows. This would not scare someone normally, if it were not for the darkening sky that even the pigeons should trek from the park; maybe of which is a lasso of metal chrome? No, she walked out of the dark like a silver rose with all the glitter cheap jewelry affords, even if some of its verisimilitude is real, particularly to the sky. Still, things divided at such a time. Real diamonds afford only danger even to a decimal of sound screeched pitch in the darkness this woman should forbid on her own street?

The silver rush occurred in a time where there would be no record of its occurrence, maybe out of convenience. Half high, half short; the reaper left a place off the map entirely. This had become a hive for lost pigeons, the lesser in the trolls of doves that once flew free like gangs throughout the earth.

Legend says that there is still a deserted freeway that enshrines the metropolis to the silver aspirations to which it once strived. As the fat lady fastens the reigns from her Easterly Terrace that night; these chrome creatures actively engage the perimeters of an island once given up by the Indians or tree-like entities. Selling itself for a few trinkets, it led to the flat terrace of bee's hive curse. The metropolis is surrounded by the water infringement and is now nearly dry of tears. So, as I speak, I feel the piercing of a hornet's sting, piercing, but dry of all impurities. Still, these chrome-driven vehicles cross its boundaries into the night like music without a soul. Chrome is the metal of mirrors or the pursuit to rise high above the water limits and merits some truth in the legend. Like a lost city of water-bound centers, the city fell into a sleep and the hornets naturally move around its nerve center. And, to see what water is left, "Say goodbye to Coney Island" the sign at the northern end whispers meaning in the wind that no one would understand anyway. (The line of the sky meeting the density of chrome and the night speaks of the lost prince with saddened frowned empty pockets.)

Crossed over Duncan Street and let me out on the corner the lady of Lepure announces to the driver as though decimals of sound, one hundred vibrations a minute. The sky broke the interchange of the day to day conundrum, what was otherwise a cursive in the eddy in the river below. Slowly, people fall into the sleep of dense mosquito sanctuaries, hidden from the shadows of the people of the concrete jungle within. The buildings rise in tall places in the sky, broken in a slogan of dental hygiene, but turbulent, looking through the hour glass of a mosquito's belly flight. Here, only man and its leggings sweep the floor of a platform that propels the energy of its sway from one place to another. But, really, they are just forks driving the dense ground below as her foot wakens in casual wear, stepping out of the cab while wearing a serape. Ground zero at the department store is just the leggings I suppose in time.

She enters the palace gate with a fertile energy. She is optimistic still. And, on the other hand, the prince of the northern sect faintly sits back on a rugged plaid twisted couch like the heart he hangs onto through his belly from long ago. She enters the front entrance like the strident confidence of her father she desperately wants to void herself from on her visit. Little does she know that the tremor of their once-forgotten and lonely prince's pulse, a point of lineage of dense no return at where he lives at the northern end of the island, and he fidgets for the silver in a lost gold watch? Through his "empty pockets," he holds the key to her return home. A demand for the gold lost, imposes a demand in silver and other precious metals as well, as though a football team without a safety. It is only a mosquito belch in a metropolis of millions.

The reason for the mystery lies in the ubiety of a cat's tail that forbears the curse of central seizure in an emerald instead of the ruby. When the interchange occurs, the half-moon's red tide will cease slimy mixtures in the blackened calluses of the city's streets. The faint prince lives like a hermit, an anomaly that might in her desperate plight, return the lady of Lepure home free of the curse. Her father is fixated by the emerald's red tide and half-moon scenario. So his existence is bequeathed by this occurrence. As she enters the door, the prince of lost dreams falls into the web of his own nightmare, a pulse like that of a mosquito is present and she passes a display of chocolate molds wrapped in gold-colored materials. She does not know how far she is from where the flight may lead?

The sun has a way of rejuvenating its peace in the light of day and emptying its waste in the verse of a blank page. If I lived on Mars I might see this small dark spot on the sun we call Earth, but instead foreshadow a poet's verse in dismay, hearing the chants from below; "so far away, so far away." This stolen light becomes owned by the night only after the passage to the main thruway is toasted by lit smiles on the streets. It predicts the autumn of the day rather than the summer, and all the toads in the streets ineffectual loss with their smiles? Still, it remains the smile lost between linen napkins; to sit down for the salmon feast with her unknown guest like the father she does not know either. When the keys of the polished piano strikes twelve, the parakeets in the fat ladies; private easterly terrace decorated with red corners to shade their eyes, turn into snakes? Then the white linen napkins in a fist under the table she harbors for a while, go a thud in the distance. Just kidding, it is tabula rasa, a blank page, and passageway to night's afternoon chime of smiles are bequest at the sight of the moon? Activity seems so alert at the time when the suction of the lesbo's locked embrace frees the cat from the moldings below, "Where in autumn does summer smile at fire?"

The street numbs itself to the pulse and panders to further ponder in a stretch of the sky lit by moonlight for the woman lost. In the disease of foreigner's tongue, the culture and fabric, and white woman's lace forbids the basins that such a parody should fall like a frown from the sky in the retrieval of the night for chocolate dreams in this silver array? Then, eyes to before the fall and the garbage trinkets lay awaiting in the streets?

A mixture of this concoction numbs the most feral of minds even in a lost city deserted by its only prince, who tiptoes the northern sky in his apartment with a syringe pointing like piercing spoils of milk. From across the way he goes out on a ledge as though able only in his mind to walk the wire destined to him, yielding light upon an offspring futile in his veins, he knows. Now, the halls to his empty window reminisce the garbage shells that light moonlit passages in the sky like shedding the shells of his next of kin, cockroaches. And he falls nearly ten stories below, the awning being the ninth.

Falling into a stare, even the drugs of the careless few cannot break this detriment as he looks down his spine deeper in himself than tears may reach? The fall catches him on a lurch and all he may produce is a slight sway of his arched back. Like waking from a fall, he already detests and, by day, he clasps his pocket once again; a loss in a city too big to hear such a tremor as if to say let bygones be bygones? His forehead resting on the metal bar, protected high in the night sky, is peaceful attribution for the next day or forever. At this time, the park opens enough to catch the rain, and cats swim with fish in secretive places that ride the senses of such bizarre occurrences. It, the cat, enters an air-conditioning unit and trips over the cord.

(Tangents)

-the electric release shadows a piercing image of what does not pardon it nor the doves that fly in the sky only to fall (in the back of a shaded window) - "What does a shoulder cost in its weight in gold in silver?" -(the TV. picture of a psychedelic orange juice electric cat) -the friend's hand meet like hands joining two dissimilar butts; away, away... -wars bought to buy peace... - flower children lower the temperature of the thermostat (cold and calloused retrieval of the dead) -the roads meet in the grind mesh and frame one strand of her dark hair. -witch's meal for dreaded tapestries in the sky, (what is left is two can trinkets thrown out the window.) -(Left behind in a cold sweat, the clasp of this glass raises even the most disconnected adult to a levy of common ground? Alone, not swallowed, but a curse raising into the sky, the hindrance of "the Cube of Hyperberbalee" before a sip may trace its tear? Wet and sloppy; a kiss to the two birds before lights out and she goes to sleep. Pigeons care not, but leave some trace anyway and the vision of the prince's bold hold pass midnight is a drowning of sleep past bedtime in Lepure. What is left is two can trinkets thrown out the window.)

The beginning of the wall with night sky and morning to boot; rise, rise, fall, rise, smile, fall and rise to the height to see pass the Diagnostic Wall of Lepure from where pigeons fly. Here, the degrading of gold is detested to determine the location of the silver this person may manifest through the eye of its camera; a lonely prince walking the wire of his Northway apartment with pockets soiled with red consequences. This is just a thought between two dissimilar entities standing next to one another. In a bar, who should drink like that which predicts its future for a lady standing in a colossal city pending defeat?

Through the narrow glass, a man with thick woven hair leaves it untouched at the bar for the night to show the black fly curse at the very least uncertain? Isolated in "the Cube of Hyperberbalee, she, the woman from Lepure is slightly rested in bed. Still, the walls ferment the green slime of the red tide and half-moon curse in his pocket. At such times, the curses will converge (as the jargons hold the three valuable eggs with their modified hands) and a photo is taken of her father. At such a point, the lady of Lepure will be free, like the silver found in a lost gold watch, like the blank page of a morning sun.

Dry spells quake the autumn heat with virtues of its fruit molested insect shells. The larvae confines is enough for the fat lady to test the boundaries of a hodge podge porridge (the best the city has to offer) not different than barley meal or grits made from corn? The recipe it delivers resonates as something imposing, but good. The woman speculatively not too large, spends facets of her time in savoir-faire creative pursuit. The black fly curse belongs to the pink lady in her upper westerly terrace with a cat and two birds blooming in the fat ladies cheeks in the east as well. Meanwhile, the beehive curse is reined in by her at her private easterly terrace and is across from Central Seizure. Accompanied with her parakeets with no pink slippers; she might well be worse than the witch in the west. The pigeons in the park look eloped at such times that she will feed them. They know still that the curse is mostly directed at man. Meanwhile, the worse is the curse directed at one sole prince in the northern sky, a curse of red consequences he might not be freed from and the soul of the city shutters in its wake. Anyway, the fat lady's fleet of yellow taxicabs swarm the city and is a paradigm for the tears of Indians from long ago. Though, less potent than "the Cube of Hyperberbalee," it maintains the weatherman's assertion of rain like no other city except for London maybe. Such a curse dispels the notion that configurations in the sky do not shed a tear from time to time, while the black fly remnants are just a menace they say?

Three jargons; if one of the eggs of formidable doom should break; a curse will be bestowed on her left knee and she will not escape the curse that which is her father. At such times (back and forth) the hornets cross central seizure while the pink lady's space is spoiled with cotton materials. The only luxury she maintains is in the form of soft pink slippers which, unruly, turn to that of a migraine in her sleep, but does not appear to deter her motions by day? The cat and the broom are left in the corner unnoticed. It alone may well feel sorry for the prince of the northern sect? Which is, consistently, seeming forward, fluid; yet not too erratic, anyone might bother to shamble questions to do with her busy work not? One might say this woman is a well-adjusted pink platinum lace in a blackened world diced with ivy walls? She spends her time nearly with an obsessive completeness unaware of her surroundings, yet functioning well just the same. Across the way, the fat lady sings to her parakeets which turn into snakes at night. She is a bit aged and in this time, the fat lady foreshadows none of the youthful qualities of the metropolis migrates below?

On the street, this would be like being a poster on the wall that evokes an eye too deep to see and consequently dispositions, "where does porridge smell so good?" (she unties her apron and turns to the window; "nothing" an illiterate spine of functioning well?) She is actively unknown to her surroundings and now the pink lady; "tidder tat," the foundations of stonewall are now converted to steel. "...and what is it in the chrome grind that pass in the streets in a still life where steel should surpass in its rise and fall; the quest for the silver like chrome in her teeth bequeath the, in the form of a picture?

At the break of noon, the red rock hidden somewhere, they say, becomes a turning point as the lady of Lepure finds her way through blackened stone, to meet the fenders of chrome in a day which turns in a flash to nowhere? An upward spiral of leggings in cotton dainty buffers to "central seizure," when otherwise, the workers dispel a notion of the sun in their spellbinding gray attire; worked through the cast, a headless class of workers and such?

The period of four and one half hours is like when the dove makes a pitch for the workday to subside and the clock either sinks or falls? Behind the wall of statuary fists wandering about like ants on a hot rock in summer; is the seagull's mist, lunch's call and also the call for the red rock to undertone the cast of day by the heat of the five o' clock bell?

Sinking bellbottoms through the passage of her mind makes for a feast. Though, like the black fly curse that might have manifested itself in the seventies, it is premature to act yet? An emerald cast covers her splintering epidermis of her forearm and sinks low "a thud" in a drum roll like Dunkin Donuts falling from the sky? This is a retrieval of praise for the hippies in the sixties maybe again, as though not the faint prince? But another person engages her out of sheer consequence and leads her slightly as she hands her a bag of pigeon meal? She throws nearly nothing to the birds, as though the curtains were meant to fall at this time? (lapse of time is marked by foraging pigeons on the city streets of which she stands alone.)

A few seconds pass while two elderly women cross by the synagogue in front of her, howbeit in black drab; and tensely their arms clasp one another and reach out, but no response; (in the time it takes to load film into a camera?)

The woman from Lepure passes the street corner where she stands like a fixture and stares into the dark embrace of the park for a moment without blinking. She is not scared. But, she cannot feel slightly different from the open sky that forgives from time to time, the green film that the red tide might produce. In the curse of what is left; a red tide and half moon flutters the senses of any person walking a street unsure of their destination? Along the dark seams of the park, she sensibly heads north in the shadow of its breath. It takes a lot of nerve, but along the park she stops to look down at the chrome film of a pigeoned hubcap, so to speak. It glitters in this sort of light. Nothing may diminish this light that produces a more tense greenish film of this object as cars vibrate the ground as they pass? The hubcap lying in a futile fall in a yoctosecond like most other persons in such circumstances? It is not the light of the day that causes the glitter on the rim, but rather the positioning of the cat's tail in the night.

Here, at the right moment, she will see her father just once and be free, as though holding a photograph that renders the moment simultaneously? She need not look at it, though? Reverberating fillings of an unwarranted relapse, the outlines of faces might impose such, staring at her in the night sky through her father's image in the trees possibly? At this time, a fender of a taxicab pulls up to the curb that she walks gracefully along. She assumes a magnetic response, similar to the way she is drawn to the chrome hubcap, she passes moments before? She fosters a slight sway away looking at a dark figure standing like a still picture or statue across the street. She sees only something sort of shaded in the street light and is not startled excessively?

(Enter the three jargons holding the eggs of formidable doom.) Here, stands a quieting pulse that begins to bequeath the greenish film hanging over the city at this time? The function is more defined and less edible now; just callous reminders of foreign lands? The city central sways with cultured lines, but does not detest the lines that separate them? In a rare breath of hope, the eggs offer a minimal share of mercy with a faint light, they rob the soulless many? Meanwhile, the lady of Lepure continues in a sleepwalking pace up the path along the park of westerly terrace? After dark, (as it is late) the soldiered terrain is populated with a vast array of diversity? However, to call them droids, now, is fair, since the curse that the plastic cube spiked with a black fly in which it symbolizes, has infused their souls down to the core; to the point where the outward appearances is the closest emotion to what is felt in the waking worker's inside? Soldiers of configurations in the sky not unlike Indians were here that tend in vast arrays along lines of a concrete jungle? As for its dwindling pursuit, like a candle that was out long ago, the wick and skeleton remains; old tarnished gray suits and makeup upon the stolid faces of women? One apparent characteristic of the design may be death? But in the glass of a blue soldier's eye, it is tested by the weather and the social infrastructure. There is an unusual glimmering in his eyes; quiet, contained, yet alive? This is a rare occurrence on the streets, but resonates throughout the workers at such a time? Holding though a dead baby in life, he clutches a slight breath quietly in its disease? She soon rests completely dazed with a clearance shopping the next day?

The cat jumps on a ledge outside the window, and embraces the cool air that maybe the next night will be better? When the lady of Lepure walks to the end of the park, she returns to the palace where she stays and eats alone, expectantly?

The next day, the southern yellow sky swallows the night unforgiving to the point where purple is drowned into the northern over passed sky with red and green, to produce a different yellow-hued orange sunlight? The air provides the circumstances that compose the wall? The fabric of flags of different backgrounds eventually spoiled the melting pot to bring out the best in the worse of people. The cat walking inside, hops on the window ledge at this time, with the light in full presence?

The ritual flashes a telepathic pulse to the pink lady to wake from her slumber where she begins and plans the day's spoil? It is a natural attribute to some women less noticed by most, a peaceful solitude that gives a pulse to a city's tempo between a sway of the red tide's green cast, and the moon's own, a disdain of itself with precipitated light? The worker's tempo trolls the grounds of the concrete jungle like the metal detectors that fasten on silver bits enough to drive the princess to Lepure home.

Meanwhile, the prince of lost dreams still reaches in his pocket of red consequences for the gold watch. A flash separates the worlds and allows them to meet? It is a sort of energy or shuffle which on the streets becomes a web, breathing air into the foot soldiers among the different sects?

Alone in his apartment, the prince is even more faint in the northern sky. Among the inhabitants below, their squalor is just a mirror reflection of the situation at hand? Barely clasping nothing, in his pocket, midnight passes; as the pulse in his wrist still defines the moment in an oblivious ration for blind inhabitants of a lonely person, with little reason to live?

"Half-Moon with Red Tide" (the anatomy of the tiger: the goldfish asks how it got in the bowl? Will is a red-headed woodpecker which eats his own seed that of a grand Redwood Tree)

How he sidetracked earth and landed on Mars, I do not know. But, all I know about Mercury, I learned from a friend. He who maintains the DNA transmission from a mother; "Christ, imagine that?" And all that is left of him here is salt from a tear of a red-headed woodpecker outside Paul's Transmission in Santa Monica, I think. I think Will was afraid of his reflection and all this time he was telling my story, until we meet briefly on our way to Scarborough Fair, I am told. He wanted to be free of his past and God offers him a clean slate in exchange of his tear.

"Rock and Roll," is all raccoons bellow after he left and he did not stay long. In a goldfish bowl, he relinquishes the tear of a grand redwood tree.

Outside of Dallas, Texas, our paths cross for a short time and someone asks, "How did you get in there?" and Will replies nothing as not to care.

The lawyer oversaw the transaction and said, "Write your name on the red dotted line."

And I then took my black pen and signed my name. Someone said they saw a naked guy with red hair run through the woods over there, but were we really ever there? It is true that Mercurians have big feet. Anyway, you may hear the sound of horses crossing the Great Plains as they pass Venus on their way to Mars. Their hoof prints lead there and they erased any trace that he was even here.

In a mirror, he says, "I can't see myself." But, I can feel the wind blow very hard.

"Life without the crucifix..."

I plundered the other side and inherited three crosses that denied the holocaust and thereafter would raise Jesus into heaven. I attend a church without regard to God's sacrifice, but still I believe just the same. It might not be a world without God, but instead it offers the grace of mercy one more time. For those who do not believe it is time to lose the grace and I think Jesus will return soon. For Christians who believe, it is an honorable life, and prayers are not imploded as in vain. I think the Jews who died in the holocaust will ascend into heaven and the blood would only infect those who deny Jesus. I am sorry, but two hundred years today seems like a long time to believe. Instead, God might serenade Africa so that the drum roll pierces the spoils of the dead. The fact that I did know Jesus on a cross, might denote that it did not happen.

God forgives those who pray for forgiveness. Otherwise, I believe anyway and that is enough. To those who do not believe might find God's grace less than bearable. He is not yours for the taking and it might be too late now. I attend a church where there is no crucifix and the mind-altering drugs are one way to see when those who deny him are not. I may be the Holy Ghost and the milk that spills over seems like a lesser crime. They absorb the blood of others and will remain somewhere else with a hope of a better future. God will forgive those who do not sin. I do not blame the Jews for this but, tactically frame my picture on the wall to open the door through which others can enter. Otherwise, I am not a Jew, but wish you well anyway.

"Somewhere else…"

The abrazo of Adam and Eve abridges their loss in a distant land, though. Their pending sin leaves as though following a black cat's tail. They will hide while a garden snake will address such a primal sin which does not belong to them either. Someone else said, "Don't cry over spilled milk," and she points to heroin as though better than heaven. Otherwise, the real serpent is not common like its predecessor a common green garden snake. It exists in the guise of "after the fall and before the rapture." It feels the skeleton of a rock like the wind too, her father. (An apple tree is replaced with a fig tree now.)

Eve tastes the absinthe as though mint to the devil, and their path crosses only once. Meanwhile, Adam absconds the apple from yesterday as proof of a primal order that belongs to my mother. She abscedes the notion of sin and adopts it as though hers as she has nothing else really. She would rather trade a primal sin for trinkets as something is better than nothing. When it was time to leave, God keeps the light on at the kitchen door. The gesture is subtle and he closes the door behind him as well. There is no fruit to reap from the tree at such times. The lovers enter a world which is not God…and they say it is better than the alternative. "To know…" is sometimes better than other. They live now in Nebraska and own a pig farm there. The address is left entirely off the map.

There may still be a garden in China where an abbeylubber sings a different tune now. Meanwhile, Jimi Hendrix's electric guitar is all the compensation I may find for a garden now forsaken. And good Christians will find, at a later date, a way back in the door. Meanwhile, God drinks his cherry, cherry wine.

All of creation might have been done in hindsight. It is not what God created, but rather what he recognizes to enter a door once closed? With this recognition, something exists which would not without God. An American flag may exist without God, but it "is" to say in retrospect when seen through God's eyes and such is creation. Maybe to deny God is to deny heaven too, I think. That which is "somewhere else," is to say without God. The alternative is better than sheer damnation. Now, all the pieces of the scrabble game he is playing will fall into place. To those who made it where "poetic champions compose," there is more, like the road kills of animals left on some deserted highway in Arizona.

"Israel"

I do not know what Israel is but I believe it is good anyway. If the Jews died like Jesus then a void remains which asks "who are you?" In the core of its infiltration, there is a diamond in the rough that asks why things like the holocaust did occur? The answer may be so that Jesus may rise into heaven with the many faces that infiltrate the phenomena. Diamonds seem to compose the ability to alter its light in common with rubies, emeralds, and sapphires. It may create 10,000 specimens like "Ziggy Stardust," in this light. This reflects the ground that God stands upon too. For the Jews who remain in Israel, the blood of sin will not spill over and this is good. They will not know God but rather the witch who creates these notions in this guise and she lives in England pondering the number five. Israel may be a devil frozen in the confine of a plastic ice cube should it stare through the glass at you? In this vein you will live forever, as long as the blood of others does not cross over to you. The memory of the faces that died in the holocaust live forever too. Will might have died on a cross too and represents the center inside on flat feet like God too. A bear remains somewhere else for those who must believe.

"The runners from Germany..."

I think it is appropriate that the Germans are forgiven for the death of Christ as God may be a culprit to respond to questions that have no answers. It represents the third dimension which is sort of a catch-22. At any given time, three Germans run messages from Earth as it rises into the heavens.

"The Jewish Phenomena"

Though I do not believe it true, the Jews actually died at the hand of a German autocrat that subscribed to a world without a God. Yes, maybe it is true, but I believe that those who remain are like Christians, if not the same. Maybe a lion; time after time after time, is putrid with hate and in a way, its metaphoric sacrifice brings deliverance into the tolerant world we live today. Jews, who I like to talk to occasionally are not what they appear to be. My grandfather was "an old-timer" Jew, in a sense. He led an immaculate life. And, though, not having any children of his own, he adopts and raises my mother and her younger sister, my Aunt Teri; (without much regard for himself). He liked talking to other Jews and think about old times. He never spent a minute talking about the holocaust (at least around me) as he appreciated life too much.

Though I am a Christian and was raised as such, I do not think I am any different than these old-timer Jews. However, we were taught not to put down other religions. And when a Jew informed me that since my mother is Jewish, I too am a Jew; I would respond that no, I am Christian, but the sentiment is taken kindly. The distinction between Jewish and Jews is somewhat complicated. I pity my grandmother who is really just a pointed little girl inside and less remains of her life exploiting the Jewish phenomena, even though she considers herself a Jew. In a sense, she is the kind of woman who knows the conveniences of following a faith of these interesting old-timers without defending the holocaust Jews as they are now gone. As she is really not a holocaust Jew per se (I make the distinction) but rather is born Jewish as without consequence and has lived a good life in this tradition.

We continue the faith of Judaism mainly out of love for my grandmother, who really misses the advantages she has obtained over the years in the Jewish faith. In a sense, she does not have anything else. If not Jewish, she might exploit, in an innocent way, another faith. She does not conspire! She just thinks she has had a wonderful life in this culture they call Judaism. She is like a girl stealing candy from the corner store.

Now, I must exclaim what a Jew really is as I do not know if I have ever met one really, (so, in a sense, I live in a world void of these people prior to the holocaust, I think). I do not mean to say I do not have any Jewish friends as I do. However, the Jews who died and will return one day, I know in the guise of the past or the future, but definitely not in the present, and for this I will never know them really. I think, if you put a mirror up to the Germans who supposedly killed the Jews, you would find a paradox. Maybe, a Jew is a dominating mother who would rather indulge in a life of vanity, or other, for that matter out of pure jealousy or maybe not? She is a Jew like Joan Crawford crying? Those who seek the stars beating down on the lives that live without such guidance counselors, find them immensely intolerable. Without going into much detail, as I do not know, but I suppose without this entity that infringes upon the masses; Jews and Christians are the same. The Jews came and they will come again, and some think that life is better void entirely of these individuals?

But, I know well, I would not kill them twice. I wish you well even still.

"Beginning" (Scenes from a dreary life)

"The Jews are trying to kill me?" I say to a friend in a low voice of disbelief as my thoughts are in disarray and my heart pounds faster to the point where it is convoluted inside like a train wreck. We were in Washington Square Park and I now know what Ilius wanted to say blotched in the refrain of a Simon and Garfunkel melody, "Me and Julio, Down by the Schoolyard." And in his dark hand, the likeness of oil on this Easter Sunday, he throws a jumble of different colored jellybeans and lets them go into the air. And at such a time, he returns to Mozambique without a farewell.

Leading a path of blood all the way to his burial site that the fangs of wolves emit in the form of a cross, he does not detest the past, but he laughs a bit at the onslaught. He was taut with a female zebra which was his spiritual mother in a sense; and it holds the key to the return of the brethren to a darker corner of Mozambique. Yet, Ilius is not my only friend with a dark complexion; I claim all as brethren too. We would kick the soccer ball which is gone with the site that the two worlds may join as one.

Another friend of the zebra, a gazelle is known to occasionally outwit a cheetah, which is a spectacle to see! Like the sun, it offers the blood of Ilius instead, as he walks back to Africa. And what a fine Easter it was, but the zebra bucked me as though him and there is mercy for Ilius as it is shameful to bleed from the fang of an animal outside of his native Africa. The procession included twenty-four elephants and if you include Simon, a whale, and many kids should follow. And the secret of animals foraging back and forth, there is one pregnant zebra and with one blow,, I woke from what seemed like a strange dream.

I bleed for Ilius so that no one may see his shame. So brethren of all colors, what sacrifice is true? I sat in a hotel room watching cartoons and ate a Mounds Chocolate Bar, a can of Pepsi, and a cherry Blow Pop. The door opens and closes to the "spirituals" song "all things are possible," but you would not know this unless you have been to Georgia. But, do not ask me for directions as I do not know how to get back to Africa. There is a mirror, I know in the west, and you will know yourself instead. That is the gift!

He knew I would find out sooner or later. Although, I feel his presence, I am now alone for the first time, "no shit," and the apple falls from the tree and a friend is just a friend and we will never look into one another's eyes again, I think. Who is behind this I try to ask Bill, as though Jamie, or even Will? And he looks back only slightly as to say the Jews? So, here, I am, only fifteen and suspicious to say the least. The way young kid's hormones will pop like popcorn inside you and a guard is formed that is more like an instinctual friend. Though, I was raised Christian, I would never suspect my mother who is Jewish, but not really as she is not acclimated as such.

"What does this mean?" I ask myself. "Are the Jews bad?" "Do Christians feel superior to Jews because of what many believe as the Jews being the culprit to the death of Christ?" But, such thoughts seem foolish and oversimplified as I know the god of my heart would never put me in danger. (The next day was much calmer and the storm seemed to pass) I never saw Ilius again and I suppose he returned to Africa. I hold him in great esteem, for he came from there and so far, just to warn me. And I consider him a true friend, though I do not think I will see him again. This is a forte to the danger I will inherit as long as I will live as a Christian. I will never know what it is truly like to be a Jew, enemy or not? I am here and not going anywhere soon. I suppose a forte is like climbing a tree and falling for the first time; in this case should I dare?

But, trouble could lurk as long as fear invades your own domain. I was determined to face this head on and this would lead me to a lack of trust in others. So, I will tell you a story as it is much better than the alternative "fear?" The apple that falls shall not land on the ground. Like a tiger lost at sea, "other" is in its element anyway. Will no longer acknowledges the lesbian cause and escapes the fate of a lesser man too, like Adam tempted as he embraces the fall of Man thereafter. The fruit may be only accessible to God at such times and he reaches in his palm ascending into heaven instead. He has a symbiotic relationship with his son too, though he does not recognize him either. There is a picture of a little boy's excrement by a tree and Satan is a vision of the apple lying there on the ground which may not be eaten. Eve smiles at white doves before the fall with long flowing brown hair and claims God raped her which is not true.

"Beginning"

The winter of my eleventh year, I sat in view of a window where the snow absorbed the sky and, seeing a bird there, I knew there was more to the story. Space frolicking in the snow drifts below preserved the world I thought I might someday explore. As a young boy, you know this is different from being a girl, of which two others, both older, share the same parents. And opening the door, it is more fun from a boy's point of view, I step into the snowy landscape. This is what a photograph is; it invites you somewhere else and the rocks you trip on are just reminders of this as you might step with clumsy boots into a pile of luscious freedom. The freedom to be young is not beyond me yet, and I hope it never will be? A bad kid is a bad kid though and he throws a rock at a bird and even all the love in the world will not unlock the sequence, but I did not! They are guilty of being the children of a black rose and will not tarnish the spectacle either.

So, now, I am a boy and enjoy what I have learned and suppose my sisters have discovered a snowy paradise or two, before. This is a fork in the ground as I will never be that which the other sex is in a girl, but it is fun to try to find common ground anyway. Whether like the other sex or not, the attempt to solicit differences will help most later on. But, the fork or shovel for that matter becomes a persona for that which divides and the past never happened, only delusion.

So I rather remain dumb in the present, but the rock that bad kid throws at a bird is a glass house broken for all time in the past and how may this be? Besides, I see wild horses and girls like wild horses. All I see are the footsteps the squirrels make in the fresh snow. Not knowing if this is past, present, or future is better than the alternative and everything else I blame on my sisters.

"Beginning Continued..."

Why take a picture at all? A photograph depicts that we were here once and for all? Anything that manifests itself as important enough to photograph is in itself a photograph. My grandfather, who was my mother's adopted father, gave me a gold watch after he passed and this, to me, is a photograph in itself. I think it is important to be careful how you spend your time, as eventually the present becomes the past and a past is without a future. Christ on the cross is a picture, reminding us that things do change eventually, and so be prepared!

Most things are not as tangible as a gold watch, so why photograph anything for that matter? Why take a picture at all? I ask my friends "Simon and Garfunkel" as they seem effervescent in my early teen years. The point is to outlive your opponent and assume only the good. A picture might do that. My grandfather, though not my blood, was a Jew and he knew all this before Annie Leibovitz was even popular. He exhibited a sense of individualism that was unique and rather did not dwell on things for whch there are no answer? I can't say that my grandfather Jack is still alive, but the watch is permanent, as knowing that he did exist here like a photograph. And in that sense he is still here. Rather than dwell on things for which he had no answer, he guided my sisters and me to embrace life fully, the good and the bad; and this makes people stronger over time. I guess this is one thing I relate most with Jews, "time?"

By the time I have a recollection of my grandfather Jack with white hair and a smile for Tuesdays, he would eventually lose (depending on how you look at it?) He had no children of his own; so he would leave the same person as when he entered this world. He had nothing to lose anyway. Maybe, you have an uncle or cousin like this, but I do not know whether this picture instilled in my head would last forever?

"Time" is funny word. It implies age, but this is not always the case. When, suddenly at one's own surprise, life plays tricks on you and the elder is a kid and you become something else. I may say "time" is a funny thing? But, it does not mean that since, I, at age thirty-two, still get carded for cigarettes, that this is who I am. It just means that one ages a certain way and only a fool would assume everything at face value? "Time" for most is a punishment, but for me it was not! The real punishment is having to show a picture of myself which is generically younger than myself to buy cigarettes. Getting carded for cigarettes at age thirty-two is not the worst thing that ever happened to me, though.

"Like water makes water...while a cow harbors her milk too etc."

Religion is a pencil that writes its own vision. Although it is not unnatural, it definitely unearths questions that appeal to any heretic, as it should. As assuming the word of God, even in a guise, is blasphemous in itself, it therefore preens further questions. In contrast to my religious belief, I am one who believes everything that happens, happens for a reason. This may or may not be acceptable to God, though?

Sort of like the notion that tobacco grows independent of all those who claim to harbor it, although it is, in my view, an entity in itself. Furthermore, the farmer is part of the machine that would rather impair its natural course in the wild. No one knows how tobacco grows really, and as a metaphorical vanguard of agriculture, this discrepancy leads to furthering my discussion in the topic. Sort of like tobacco growing in the wild is a premonition that manifests itself in the form of a black cat that loses its tail; it is just suppose to happen for whatever reason.

Tobacco is not grown by farmers. It grows on its own for whatever reason. Like religion, it grows out of its own recourse. There is no need for tobacco like religion and, therefore, like clergymen, subsists without any obscure voice demanding it. It is a means to an end without any beginning. Similarly, I might ask, does God have a sense of humor? If tobacco subsists on its own inclination, why does God have to do anything at all? I think religion is a nemesis of God's greater plan as it does invade his space for answers for where there are no answers. Actually, I think one may sin for eternity without being rebuked is preposterous. Such a demeanor evokes one's own agenda and not God's. There is no way to prove that tobacco does not grow entirely on its own and therefore there are no answers in the greater picture. When I said that everything happens for a reason, I meant just this. If there is a demand for a carrot, then one appears magically and things exponentially occurs this way in all aspects of life. In a sort of backward fashion, the Virgin Mary has a sort of affront toward human waste and it grows out of this perplexing dynamic. The waste, in a sense, produces surplus. Therefore, with the exception of creation, God does very little. More importantly, you might ask, why is there famine and disease? I answer this by evoking why a farmer must fertilize his soil by burning the field for its nutrients and similarly, this is God's way? But, the answer to all such questions is in knowing that when a farmer acts to such ends, he is rather God's tool and is not God. Maybe, the world is on auto-pilot, in a sense? To think that one may act outside of God's mission is disease itself for which I have no answer.

To think one may control God's will is a form of mental illness and, since God does really little, it is easy to see when something happens unnaturally. It is instantly apparent when something occurs outside the scope of God's will, it stands out like a sore thumb, but to God only. (And we may not assume a contest like arm wrestling with no way of winning. Therefore, there is a certain degree of respect, a presumption that only encourages one to try harder to reach the ends God desires, I think.) This brings me back to the analogy that everything happens for a reason. Even famine and disease like obesity; when not confined to any stigma might in fact be natural and such a presumption is just that, truth that manifests itself in the eyes of God only.

The following may be a little more difficult to digest as I learned this in the confine of a mental hospital where I was a patient, "cigarettes make cigarettes." The truth is in the pudding, one might say. In other words, to make a cigarette, there must be a certain degree of excess, which depends detrimentally on how one smokes it. Although there may be a dozen ways to smoke a cigarette, one process intrigues me most. As I learned in the confines of a mental hospital, to grow tobacco, one must give back to nature a certain degree of waste. This may include the cigarette butt, but ideally one must shed a minute amount of tobacco extract. Two things are important here. First, after what I call "the breathing the life out of the cigarette," one must dispose of it at the proper time. At which time; one, must ruffle the paper with your finger to let nature have back the remaining extract of tobacco. The second thing is to listen to God in the guise of intuition where one must dispose of the cigarette butt by putting it in the ashtray as appropriated. Or if it is symbolic of something, burying in the soil might work. I even went so far as consuming the butt when no other receptacle was sufficient, including one's own pocket, which I categorized as "the friend." Sometimes in life, it seems hard to find a friend, but you will find one sooner or later.

In reality, a cigarette; with its filter and paper holding it together is no different, in my opinion, than a pear, in the scheme of God's creation. To grow tobacco, tobacco being the prime example, one must smoke it. Similarly, to grow a carrot, one must eat one. There is no surplus without demand, and similarly, in one sense of tobacco previously mentioned, it may grow out of a certain degree of waste, like a carrot is to fat on the excess of a human being's body. It is part of the larger picture, as perhaps why capitalism in its vanity has succeeded in doing so well in the United States of America. Part of the process is knowing what I call "the chefs," which is the portion of the meal you may leave to waste "the chefs" entity in the meal. By contrast it is disease to lay waste to meat, I think. While waste of animal products is disease, its waste does not deter the production of domesticated, and all edible subjects, in the process.

The "chef" might be represented as a piece of lettuce, a carrot, some cheese, or even orange slice garnish on the side. No matter how well a chef prepares a meal, waste in the form of "the chefs", fat, or even other becomes part of the mechanism of greater production. Since to produce food one must lay it to waste, one would not eat another human being and, therefore, its entity is laid to waste. While in few examples you leave waste to "the chefs," those who prepares the meal. However, when you prepare a meal for yourself, this is usually "fast food" which is okay to consume in full. Like a cheeseburger at McDonalds, it is okay to leave a crumb from the bun as that is sufficient. (Though it is almost impossible to eat that which is still waste?) Part of the process of production is waste in all its forms. The previous conception is not law; and one might say laws are meant to be broken anyway. "Waste," on the other hand, is the food one leaves on the side or food one need not consume.

That which is in excess is sometimes called fat. As a result, it is part of the process of production. Similarly, one may say fat is not bad, as it is a means of further production, what is in excess. And further, one does not eat the element which is the chef in the meal! Waste is offensive and may be a means in which greater food is produced. The dismay one finds in the effort produces greater hunger, though one consumes and this fertilizes the soil and anoints water for its greater production.

Nevertheless, food is meant to be eaten and tobacco likes fire, to say the least, and this is enough in the larger picture. Also, waste through consumption increases the production of other foods like poultry? One may ask, which came first, the chicken or the egg? In respect to this writing, I think it was the chicken as it shed waste and therefore used production of corn it harbored for God in a sense. A better question is which came first, the vegetable or the hen?

However, this is a trick question, I think, as God came first and he lay the groundwork for food through the concept of waste. Still, the answer would be, if I could only prove it, the vegetable. The point is that we are mechanism of food that, through waste, produces greater food as a result. Like sin, the object is to maintain as little fat as possible or necessary? Similar to religion, greater sin is not the object. In this guise, evolution is fundamentally flawed. (Remember, everything happens for a reason.) God did not create us in the likeness of chimpanzees, but rather he made us in the likeness of himself. For those who remember otherwise, there might be no answer for this.

The problem here is that there is no way to know how much "fat" God wants us to absorb throughout this process. Therefore, for production reasons, religion is obsolete. However, I think religion helps many come to the truth in oneself. So, I do not deny it as an institution entirely? In fact, I attend Mass regularly and find it very enriching. You do not need to know about God's sacrifice to live a good life, though I think it helps. The answer is to love God as yourself. As a result, of its many forms, whether through Jesus or not, he will love you back! Christians may have the advantage here. Still, he loves all of his creation. Consequently, I claim that "disease" as part of the process is natural, but not desired. Therefore, I ask, "does God have a sense of humor?"

"May a carrot produce food through the object of waste?" "A cigarette makes a cigarette, and is as natural as a pear?" When I said that God does very little, I did not mean to say nothing. Actually, the cigarette was made as scrupulously as a pear, but as I said before, most things maintain themselves without altercations by God. A cigarette is God's creation, as it is my mandate that God created almost everything. Therefore, I ask again with things like famine and disease, does God have a sense of humor? Otherwise, tobacco might just like fire, which is an answer in a picture without answers. We are the food! Therefore, waste makes surplus, and tobacco grows naturally on its own. "Do not eat the chef!"

"Jews"

Like the wolves in the wild, Jews subsist on the death of other things and this denotes a flaw of practice. This is not to say Jews are opposed to Christians; but it would seem like a storybook without a beginning. I wonder, as a Christian, if Jews were consecrated right? But, I do recognize "the Ten Commandments" and the Jew's tireless effort to bring God's laws to others who believe. At such times, I may be an alternative point of view.

In another light, I do not dislike sinners. I dislike the propensity to sin! Here, I must give credit to Jews, though myself a Gentile, they do have a leg up in being truthful to the word of God, even beyond "The Ten Commandments," I think. I just think differently, as to the notion that the beginning is with "Christ," not Abraham and not chimpanzees. The beginning and its end is this enigma that answers itself in this way which is time and Jesus too. However, I told the Jews in the park that I do not believe I have been born yet, and this may be my saving grace in the end. Anyway, sinners do they not reward themselves for opposing God's word, which does not mean anything at all?

Though I am not a Jew, emphatically, I might have been born out of my own resource just like Jesus. Still, I believe Jesus died for our sins; but I guess I am cheating death in a way. In other words, I am a Christian who was baptized as such. The problem with religion is not that it is wrong or right, it is propensity of sin for one's own personal satisfaction through itself, a vice really. I went to church the other day and, after singing some psalms, the father, (and I am not Catholic technically, but rather Episcopalian though I think I am American/Italian, which I am not technically) he asks for money. Does this perpetuate sin or revoke it, I ask? I do not know really?

Similarly, I went to another church a few months ago, also Catholic, as I feel home here after my father converted to the faith some time ago. Anyway, the father rectified the loss of Jesus as though to be the fault of the Jews. And I know something about Jews that others do not. Tobacco may grow on its own, as for the demand of it compels it further, and I think that Jews subsist in a similar way. Still, I wait for the day when Jews and Christians worship together? So, I think the boy in "The Catcher in the Rye"—was his name Holden Caulfield? —would agree with me that hate for the Jews was not the message God intended! But, rather, just the mere sacrifice should be sufficient to evoke the awe that need not be the weather pane pointing up? I might fear the Jews a little like a lamb fears a wolf. Whether Jews had anything to do with Christ's death does not matter, just like religion is not necessary in order to speak the word of God. It is just that one needs not grow tobacco, it grows on its own, and money spent to buy the packaging of my cigarettes is similarly an insult to me as religion may be to God? Still, the ten commandments remain for those who believe, and those who speak the word of God may innately be blasphemous, as I am? It is just a question?

In summary, tobacco grows to be smoked and no one knows why? Why I should put twenty dollars in the basket at church service does not apply to such a principle that claims to speak the word of God? Maybe it is going a bit too far to point the finger at Jews, when Jews are not opposed to the word of a priest at all, and I know this to be true very well, but I will not tell why, as Hitler was killed cosmically and did not, in fact, commit suicide. The Jews did not kill Jesus, God killed Jesus! And I still do not like Jews. But, it is an inclination, like someone who does not like dogs out of pure perception and not anti-Semitic, should you ask? Otherwise, I think that the Jews have a right to subsist further, and I do not have any hatred toward them. I just do not like them as a concept, is it clear? Still, I go to church because I believe? The Jews may take the blame for the death of Jesus, but that is a whole other story. And food does grow out of its own resource, as do animals form from the first kill (whatever that means?). It may be waste that creates surplus. And the fact that this is an affront to the Virgin Mary is not an issue?

"Furthermore, does God have a sense of humor?"

Going to church is like fly fishing in the dark. But, who could ever dispel the notion that truth endears only those who seek? Yes, Jesus died on a cross for our sins. However, the wine tastes more like alcohol and we never tested the water before going in. I have my sanity to maintain and it could be that God is a trickster and the folly of allowing us to believe has a rebuke in time. Why not assume that heaven is now, whatever the past should placate in the mind of the masses, and is just a dream? Then we wake one morning, only to take the trash out like good Christians do, and not say another word. Yes, Jesus died on a cross for our sins, but light might blind too.

I know something about the Jews that would astound a man riding a subway train to Brooklyn and it is not heresy to know that the past is the past and the present something totally different. I think the Jews died on a cross too! But, they forgot that the sins of the world could bleed over. In the sunshine and to drink the blood could only devour their souls too? The Jews could only forbear the sickness for a while and now they cherish their sins in the past, where they are allowed to exist as someone else. When the bleeding of sin becomes their existence, they perish on a rocking chair and will not return from their plight. Yes, the Jews died on a cross too, but I cannot find them around anyway. The Jews will embark on a journey and that is all. I would not be so bold to give anyone the time of day, for a crime that is fictitious and reserved for those who are able to embrace it. But, you must believe, as do I. And when you walk the walk where all the pieces fall into place, rather believe the literal meaning behind the death of Christ as that is faith, mother!

Anyway, I told someone once that you must drink a little blood before you can sing with the angels. And, should your step be miscalculated, I told you so and you might be a Jew too? But, not I. I think that knowing anything is to know nothing. You may exist in sin and perish this way where the ball bounces and does it return to your hand the way you thought it would? God plays a joke on everyone or no one and I think that is enough said. Though I do not know the Jews, really, I think when one sees a child play out of God's realm, he might laugh as though the first time too. I do not think evil will conquer the righteous in any way, but hate is an illusion darker than the clouds that rained down on that day. So, humor might be a vice of God underestimated, and I will never know, just to be and that is all for now. Until I go down to the river to where it is okay to seek solace for the sins of yesterday, and only then will you find yourself true enough to carry on and the chuckle is just one way to envision the many faces Jesus will offer and that is where you may find God too.

"St. Stephen"

When I went to the church that day, I saw the clouds conform in a way that could only be called dangerous. I do not know how wine may be tasted and then after church it seems so sinful to have another glass to wash down dinner and that is St. Stephen!

"Milk bequeath thee the moon be thee thy departing! And, mint jelly thy in an electric shock, my heart..."

"Like Duck Served Off-Season at the Country Club..."

Native Americans might not be far off than duck served off-season at the country club. A reservation inducts its members from within, which otherwise would lack its cohesion. Though a nation in a nation, their denizens hunt for the same duck, which may or may not be in season? No matter how you cut the meat from the bones, there is a degree of assimilation, as well as differentiation too. Native Americans find the assimilation amusing as the reservation is not a choice, but rather an agenda in a club, that is not only a right, but a responsibility. A young boy born in a tribe does not choose to be a member of the club, so to speak. Still, the reservation represents a nation inside a nation and there is no choice here either. Native Americans must find this all amusing, as though duck served off-season at the country club. This odd metaphor may cross lines by signing a compromise in their outhouse that rather takes more than it gives. It seems to a young boy, that the toilet is a way of life, so he may be inducted without a beginning really, and his children may do the same.

In the past, the native people drank "Country Time Old Fashioned Lemonade," but it is packaged so that the labeling of the carton seems to be without merit, without meaning too. Similar to the carton that encompasses the lemonade, the natives live in a reservation inside another nation, and this is somewhat amusing. To be a member of the country club, one must apply, but the land is divided in fragments and this seems like a test of the spirit that one should own the land really? Is it a trick, and the knife that separates the umbilical cord from a son to a mother, now has a name which otherwise existed without the presumption thereafter. There was never a question that the land should be owned by anyone. Instead, those adopting the land as their own, eat the remaining flesh of the mother like duck served off-season at the country club.

Still, the way the food is prepared might be something entirely different. Duck eaten without a soul has no meaning. When someone at the club complains that the meat is too dry, I hear a laugh from an anonymous source as it is and always has been prepared this way. Kids will mock divinity and then paint a picture too. It is a spirit of life that will not allow the other to join the club so to speak. The mother provides that which is food, and that is all. The canvas absorbs black paint only, and hangs on the wall of the country club, as the light will not penetrate the venue at hand. The soul of the duck at the country club is lost in the process. Whether duck served off-season at the country club, or the packaging of lemonade, there is division and that which the children do not understand, they will never understand. They will be here for a while and the ones who remain may inhabit where poetic champions compose. The lemonade is separate from the carton and a nation inside a nation is the same. What is left of the mother may be consumed by a baby in full. Still, I am offered a full membership at the country club, and I hope this does not seem funny?

Country Time Old Fashioned Lemonade might be their invention, though membership to their club is assumed anyway. Duck may be served off-season at the country club, and this will not deter their spirit either. Children may hide in a destitute place and not know where their fate will lead. Native Americans still watch them as though Bart Simpson, and feel some responsibility as their mother is long gone. Beef jerky seems sort of expensive at the store, and someone has to pay the bills, anyway. The country club will not allow Eagle Claw, membership to their club, but they say he is on top of their list. Meanwhile, Ziggy Stardust divides them even more, as he takes off in a rocket ship and others wonder where this will lead to, really? Red ants on a hot rock is all that is left of his mother, and he eats beef jerky instead. This might reflect their existence here as well.

Dark Star in Nine Parts
who are you? Two: death
(Lindsay Stroud)

A waiting place for the unrecognizable,
where one's profile in a mirror exposes both
sides of the dove that cries in its longing;
unfolded like a pressed white shirt in
early morning light.

Part Two: The Censorship of McCoy (And Four Short Skits:)

One: Conversations with the Ghost of a Black Marilyn Monroe (the derogatory word "Black" is used prior to my awareness of the cause and is a timely response in respect to this book.)

"Do not feed that dog any chocolate!" she says.

"Enough is enough, I know what to feed a dog, dog food! And I feed him lamb, if you want to know," I retaliate.

"Dear Mr. President; you beat down on him like the sun, every day; all he needs is a hug? Goochy, goo, nothing! Give that dog to me and I will show him who is boss," she barks back.

"If only I could get him out of the sun as I am afraid he will dehydrate. Here is some water. Some dog at the motel tried to take advantage of him. Besides, it is the witch's dog and I am just watching him for her." I ponder the situation at hand.

"And you let him run around without a leash?" she snaps.

"No, the dog ran out and I could not catch him in time," I shrug as though embarrassed.

"Oh, one of 'those' motels? I would not allow my own dog in one of 'those' motels," she says deploring it as though at this time my skin feels molested in a way.

"...Anyway, the people in the room downstairs, with the door wide open, fed him Chef Boy R Dee and I only feed him dog food and occasionally a bone, so it was too late and I tried to tell them not to feed him that junk," I state for the record.

"Oh, just lamb meal, like the doctor ordered. Put some black eye peas in with that stuff, it is much healthier." She twitches in remorse.

"Yea, I know what that does... Why are you so interested in him anyway?" The table is now turned and I interject.

"Just, I never had a dog of my own and he being so cute, I was wondering if you would give him to me?" she asks most objectively.

"Absolutely not, this is my dog, and even if he wasn't, he is my responsibility and such, I will take care of him..." I snap back.

"Who raised you and such to take a dog into a city like Los Angeles and let him roam around without a leash? He might get run over." She concedes the notion.

"You don't understand. This dog makes his own decisions and, besides, too much attention would be caustic to his instinctual prowess," I say in defense.

"Just because it roams around like a wild dog, does not make it independent; you must train it so it won't run off and be bad and such," she states without remorse.

"This dog is different. It talks to me like a person does," I plead.

"I bet it has a bad mouth and saying black people are like this or that..." she superimposes the notion.

"Are you saying that my dog is a racist?" I am perplexed.

"No, I am just saying that if it could talk, it probably would not say too much nice about black people; I can tell between a white people's dog and a black people's dog and there is no question, that it is a white people's dog," she infers most congenially in me.

"Then why do you want him?" I hesitate to ask.

"I thought I could teach it some sense before it is too late." She pauses and then implodes.

"Too late. I do not understand?" I remark.

"Too late for the end of the world... the reverend in church the other day said the end is coming and I believe it to be true," she reinstates the prophecy.

"This dog is not going anywhere, believe me, and if it was a racist, he would be subtle and would not say anything rude outright," I state as though it were obvious.

"Subtle, is that like saying, slave master or whipping chain?" she says.

"No, it just means he might not like you or me, for that matter. It does not make him a racist and suppose he was, it would not be like anything you say," I say embarrassed.

"Why can't he do any tricks?" she asks on a platform like a kid.

"He is not a clown in a circus and that is why I do not trust you. You would not know how to treat a dog, tricks, right?" I administer by discontent.

"Can it swim? Because I am going to swim back to Africa if you do not stop insulting me the way you do," she says, as though amazed.

"No, it can't swim and, in general, he does not like water, there!" I state the obvious.

"You are a fool to think that dog is your friend; I will say, you do not know a thing about animals..." she eclipse my expression as though a warning too.

Two: Leonardo da Vinci in Modern Day

If Leonardo da Vinci were here today, he might be somewhat of a street artist. I think this because his work seems so natural in form; a lot of what is painted on walls of big city streets would serve as an inspiration. However, the stages of this development would take time and even street artists have to survive, one way or another. I see a young Leonardo da Vinci driving a taxi cab in New York City and say this from personal experience.

The vehicle is like a horse at first, compact somewhat, and fast. Mike, the dispatcher, is an admirer of his work and tells him to feel the sheer adrenaline the contraption emits. Purely, instinctual, the cabs race like horses up the avenues. On First Avenue, Leonardo will eyeball another driver waiting at the light and it is time to feel the wind blow through your hair, dark black emissions of sentimental longings that manifest themselves in raw freedom like Indians. The cars are alive, it's true, though you would not know this unless you were artists yourself, spilling the paint in harsh splats like that is sort of spellbinding. Indians know you are here once and only once, but the horses return to immortalize the moments from long ago. And power here is not a problem, as you will feel part of a web that is alive here, wherever you go. Somewhere later Leonardo calls the dispatcher as the taxi cab broke down near Tenth Avenue and needs a tow truck? Mike responds, "What is the problem?" which is another way of saying, "You killed the horse!" Mike thinks like that and is truly religious about the business in general.

The next vehicle would have a different personality and feel. Leonardo would have to start over again like painting swerves on the pavement as though a paintbrush to an artist as he feels the canvas and, in this case, the city streets. Leonardo will eventually leave the horses behind and may have a fare to Brooklyn, which is a strange place at first. The rain begins to pour outside and the city lights around Times Square are almost like a water color painting, but harsher and with more contrast.

Feeling the pavement, he drives cautiously and will avoid oil streaks and move like a hungry shark instead. The sharks instinctually work the streets aware of one another. There is a woman with thick mascara dripping from her eyes and the plaster of a smile on her face is a warning like the danger which possesses all women that merits some respect. You probably did not know that the *Mona Lisa* was inspired by a tiger shark, which wholly, like a woman was like Tina Turner, the mistress to the sun. Like "before the stars and after the dinosaurs," she returns to remind us of the death of her lover, the sun and he was here only once.

But, a ghost remains in the sea, a reminder that love existed here once before and the dinosaurs should pass to extinction in the form of simply bad hygiene, she detests to the pope in a plea. "Polish Peace," the dolphins laugh at the sharks in their plight. She is a tiger shark and will eventually eat her lover as there is no other thing she can do. Eventually, sharks will die out too. One wrong turn and Leonardo dents the fender of another. He calls Mike once again and he replies to Leonardo, "Smooth and watch out for oil streaks and sharks are graceful creatures." Yellow cab drivers inherently do not like African/Americans and heralds the new race as though Lenny Kravitz going downtown to somewhere like Tribeca.

The next day, Mike dispatches Leonardo one of the new cabs, which is shining and the rain has stopped by now. It is time to feel the nerve engine of the artist as the bees fly down Fifth Avenue, swaying dangerously in and out looking for fares on both sides of the street. He looks for his lost grandfather who is not me. Dignified in the sunshine imprint in the window shield glare, this man stands alone with his hand up, hailing the cab, and wears a beige raincoat he purchased on a trip to London. A few teardrops remain on the window from the previous vision, but Mike's head is turned as the word "dragon" is like the insult to him as though "madam" may be to a whore? The black boys smile now, as though in pinstripes at a Yankee's game is tacky; they know their fate is sheer luck. Occasionally, the dragonfly will appear, which in a brothel of yellow paint is a short flight of dignity. The respect of the other takes on the sensibility to trust one's instincts and, in the heat of the sun, the bees fly away and the engine overheats. Mike exclaims to put more water in the radiator.

So, why would a painter need all this experience, as Leonardo discovers the soul that was missing before? (And now the dimensions seem normal, and the anatomy subjective, and the composition precise.)

So, now Mike gives Leonardo a choice; either you do one painting and only one painting (there is a white wall at the garage) or lose everything we taught you and go back in time when you lived and continue the works that meet your fancy then? The point Mike is trying to make is that you live once and, therefore, the soul of the artist should manifest itself in the artist, once as well. This seems sort of romantic to me, but I think Leonardo decides to write his name in spray paint on the city wall. He keeps the *Mona Lisa* in his co-op in the West Village, though.

Three: Robert Mapplethorpe Goes to France

Dear Robert Mapplethorpe and fellow photographer:

Though I am not gay, I want you to know that after being introduced to your work sometime around the time of your death, I backed you once and now twice. The first time, I wrote an article at my college that explained the need of the artist to express truly to what he or she wants in their work. Though, a photographer at the time, I leaned toward photojournalism and did not consider myself an artist yet. I truly meant, the bad and the good and I felt your work is an expression that is worthy of your authenticity.

Somewhere between the cockroach shells and the devil paraphernalia, I set down your biography. Knowing that the ghosts of your pictures have left in the form that was once there and I do not have any explanation as such? Though, your childhood seemed somewhat normal, I do not understand what I knew was to come, which may be consummated in your death and for this I am sorry. So, I board an airplane to Paris and might spend some more time with you and void myself of any fear reminiscent in your photos? Yes, I said somewhere between the cockroach shells and devil paraphernalia, I lose you? The cockroach shells being the city landscape and the devil paraphernalia being that which does not allow such to breath, as opposed to natural intercourse, it is a perverse landscape? I think it is right, as a fellow photographer, to dismiss the other and take a walk with you in the park, (in France) like a metaphor for your earlier childhood. And, so, your parents won't worry that you are coming home late for dinner?

So, we walk through the park or along the river for that matter? You only see the bad and I only see the good? We are brothers, I feel, but are separated this way ironically. In the distance, the Eiffel Tower resonates with me like a giant erection and you reply, "No, actually, it looks more like an industrial monument or as though before the father at communion." There is a giant cockroach on the dirt path and I imply it is a dirty creature and, in response, you say something about how cockroaches in New York were your friends,

"They would occupy my apartment like a dog would as a pet, comforting and endearing to say the least." The statue we pass is definitely someone I have never heard of, a nobody. You reply, "No, I recognize the name, although Americans always suppose that." How about that old lady over there, doesn't she know it is a little out of place to be wearing Sunday's best on a Tuesday afternoon? I mock her. Mapplethorpe replies, "I am wearing a dog collar around my neck, and I know what it feels like to be out of place. Anyway, she is probably just looking for a mate?"

And I reply, "Gross," and Robert does not mean to be rude, but responds that I should not think of sex as gross.

He says, "It is natural and whatever sex this person relates to, it is no different than any other sex, that I know, that I know..."

So, I ask you, "What makes you attracted to your own sex?"

Robert responds, "The same thing that allows you to talk to me now." He continues, "I know you think it gross, but some of us live a few degrees more rowdy than what you are use to? If my work resonates nothing to everyone, I would be surprised and I pity those who are offended in the process. Dogs are fun; why don't you get one and stop wasting my time..."

"Mom, I am home and sorry I am late..." Spoken from a tintinnabulate, and the church bell rings twice.

Four: "Inverted Ham Sandwich." A conversation between Winston Churchill and Albert Einstein

Churchill: "That which divides will find a means to an end in hindsight and we were lions then, no one knew, on their terms, the machinations that would come thereafter...? Everyone died in a flash and you and I escaped that judgment. We were lions in flight and even Hitler could not face up to the reality; saviors of the world, right. We claimed the world and that is the difference we need not justify or defend now?"

Einstein: "So, what if we are friends and the world came to an end, who could possibly dream up such an idiocy? Certainly, I wanted to prove that physics is a science that we may learn from, but never is it our savior? Actually, I subscribe to the view that we are destined in time to the revelation that even an atomic bomb may not dwindle or even impair the human spirit? God did not plan the end of the world? Rather, he resurrected the world as one and the timely friendship of say England and the U.S. around July, 1944, is a testament that what was to come, could not be forecasted or even expected?

Instead, it is loathed as the bombings in Japan did not happen, a flagrant lie as we are still here? And, if God does plan the end of the world; this certainly would be a warning of what cannot happen. Whatever time should pass as a consequence shall be regained later. And this is what killing will hide in wake of war or even atomic explosions; it is a simple paradox to everything I have expelled in science: we are not friends or enemies, we are not lions in flight, we are that which God recognizes solely and that makes us special! The end of the world will not occur without an equal burst of life and therefore there is nothing to worry about and hide this truth in wake of Hiroshima and Nagasaki? What fools! We are not our own saviors and this is dismissed with some theory too, though I think Newton was right in some ways?"

Churchill: "So, what if we all are a protégé of life and in this greater plan, why is it that we toy at all with these questions rather than dream a better dream? It is possible to create your own destiny. And, you might say the Americans were fools to drop the bomb at all? I am here and you are there and that is the difference? I will not budge from the premise that life absolves everything I do thereafter? And, now, I may prove that I need not worry as the world as we knew it came to an end in the early fifties, or at such a point, began? Therefore, I need not justify my existence? God knew this from the start, and even an atom divided should not tarnish this spectacle and proves your theory wrong." (Einstein makes a gesture to say I don't disagree with you completely?)

The Censorship of McCoy

The television is left on, eleven past eleven, in the evening of the twenty-sixth of October in a downtown hostel in Detroit. Here, a person is alone watching in a naked white undershirt and baggy pants. In this particular room, the person is a regular denizen of the confines where he is paying a weekly fee for the covert space. Like the interior window which looks out on a cramped brick outlet, he is sheltered at this height from much of the light and sound of what otherwise would be just another night in downtown Detroit. Furthermore, or just another night immersed in his own body odor which is shed without any modesty, from armpits to the flesh that flanks out his stomach and manifests even more in his behind. He sits in a comfortable seat, ten feet from the TV. box, which flutters with a slight degree of static and is obviously left on. Despite the odor of the faint image, the air still allows for this one person the candle-like light bulbs which foster a light not ideal for any educated individual.

The room has a cozy disposition to the pensive disorder of the circumstances. What makes this particular incident of psychosis creditable of American toil is its value to foreign markets, which is uncertain, but holds the breath of such a picture with tongues sticking to the television? These markets are competitive inhibitions similar to a quiet hysteria marshaled by the exposure of the Kennedy assassination on television. What makes this person's interior living circumstances a marketable capital for markets abroad? Why is it in this frozen image of such squalor and uncertain credentials, a primary commodity here? Most speculative predecessors of a selling of an icon in American culture might protest!

If it were just for a controlled export of a commodity in American culture, Disney World might be one of the highest-selling mementos of the American people. But, this is in the fangs of dogs much more fierce than the poodles that protect the images of these icons and there is no way of conceivably altering this demand, which only causes the well-wishers of the land to become disposed in a slight tremble at its power. Here sits an overweight person in the privacy of a room, completely isolated from the adversaries' libel on the American way of life. Yet, if it were France or even England, very close cultural links, this wall may not protect the kinetic draw that shall swallow the image through the wake of the television without a word in defense. This person sits in a repressed city where large areas of the downtown metropolis is deserted and clearly at a loss of capital for cleanup and development, yet the T.V. remains on like a zap pool market in a telepact vacuum to what is foreseen only in this writing as back to the future.

"What is on television dear?" says the ghost that every soldier of lost American glory is allocated across the land. It is a staple in the chest cavity and stuck in the gut of every American male, no matter how seedy. The person sitting in his love chair embraces the whole of yesterday's breakfast, composed of metal scraps of last year's war and to speak of his ghostly white legs with a rash bearing something like eggs, bacon, toast with butter etc.

There is something revealing, to speak of, under his sincere breath of this American way that lifts this person to a number representing the masses. Despite the unattractiveness of the individual as a person of merit, the American coalition for equal rights of beef products should support fully as though a fine piece of American art at an auction? This rash exposed is as though a casualty of war meriting the honor of a dignified person in the global reaches to befall with a slight degree of reversed attraction of seedy markets abroad. The vidiot responds to the stiction in a voice from the room he sits alone, "tiger swells and old Hawaii Five O telepathy."

In another room nearby, a woman, in her naked last breath, sits nearly rigor mortis in a freezing confine of the ledge that speaks to pigeons and such. On a bed she is dead, wrapped in white linen and trumpeted by the wooden bed that should isolate a sin in the four corners of its outreach. A shiver would numb even a mortician's spine. The naïveté mystifies those who watch and then sinks in the television as though the foreign demand for meat products includes human subjects of this morbid infatuation.

In such circumstances that should befall the American public in such large proportions speaks in his own words, the father saying, "Should you follow my path as I, you may reach a quality of life that surpass the standards of our ancestry and void yourself of the poverty and disease that an Irish historian asserts in distaste of the plight that once attacked our heritage."

The children of eight offspring sit respectably below the mother, and are given to the television a small army of believers. Believers in the telecast for abandoned patrons of foreign lands cut off from the blood thirst. But they are highly visible to the open scab of a television set they foster in their mere numbers of eyes willing to absorb the dream of such a father, an anybody, should administer as though a religious order to his own family? Should trifles minus the capital relapse of alcoholism be a secular commodity through a dysfunctional, affluent, and righteous riddled landscape of American culture, be tasteful to foreign lands like sherbet or goldbrick on ice cream? "Let it be," the English profess, opposed to the wolves shedding a dream in their bloodthirsty fangs guarded by the feelings of its dead martyrs, left cold and inaccessible thereafter in their wake.

The energy of the beeswax wallpaper make over of some ghostly Irish Catholic family that once professed such dreams of qualities of life shunned to be wasteful abroad. Still, it haunts this room, its manifesto on the faded walls. The wallpaper sticks in this very room or a room just like it, while retired anonymous individuals occupying the space sit representing almost insidiously what is frightful to the American people. "What's on TV?" a woman asks again, replying only from the belly bulging out of a cotton white undershirt, "Tigers, tigers are on TV!"

Most exponential in nature, these predators stalk the electric interiors of this television like any other room in almost any place at any given time in America. It asks like, "What's for dinner?" spoken in Japanese for a change. The circumstances show the authoritative pull of one Catholic family's liberal vigil that should speak in diffracted tongues of light in a forbidden world by the predecessor's liberal qualities it might yield.

Slowly, the quest of good and well-wishing individuals from abroad begin to manifest factions of gold to warn the American public of their sympathetic disposition and toleration of such lofty and unpredictable lifestyles that might be foreseen in the world value system. And, slowly, like the eight children that absorb their father's imposed views should believe enough that their family does not blink once? They pursue his dream here in America despite warnings which slowly become apparent to be a male-dominated reprisal of old lost worlds which tighten the cold uncertainties they might begin to feel?

Like the fading of wallpaper it begins to experience this through the mediated air of a back-lit room in downtown Detroit. There is no reason for the occurrence, just a lasso of forbidden love for a dream that fosters only believing imaginations of what otherwise would be unacceptable for an exchange of this one father's strife? Without a reason to circumspect this scenario, the lines that connect their beliefs begin to strangle and cut from them the air necessary to breath in such a fantasized world. What allows this person to be recognized as an American patron no matter the reasoning which leads to his strife and further plight speak only of "Tigers are on TV, dear," again and again and never be heard beyond the walls that foster its breath and sounds like a sheer yell in foreign lands?

And this cannot be easily understood even by America's own patriots, who should meet the curse of the land eloquently in their hearts? It becomes quiet suddenly, listening to the verdict that should remain pending and up in the air, leading to what might be a most verbally unspoken and horribly irretrievable faction, "the Censorship of McCoy" is like the man now falling asleep again in his head, "tiger," "tigers," "tigers?" No one or anybody, for that matter, should detest this openly, not even himself representing all of the American public in his sleep; by the sight of this box still flickering into the hours of the night? With its screen facing the delegate or draftee of the hidden disease of cultural affiliates throughout the land, like a video camera turned on directly facing the person in slumber; the film is rolling on for this person too preoccupied by his own sleep to even notice?

In this sleep, the tigers wander the electric cable and may travel far and wide the land and fester in the subconscious of the dairy products, lodged in cavities of the nation's spoil, to live without fear and succumb to its energy? Nerve-flashing wild telepathy in television, its eye and rhythm caress its prey in this small box of a victim unaware practically of the power that this digital display may impose? How much for this small box of wonders? Maybe no more than a hundred dollars at the time, after the craze of television had previously settled into the persona of the American trade of its own culture and further soul? Who should know where the wires should cross unattached, hanging out there in space like an electric cat in heat; enjoying the warm sensation the magic of the box should lead that is two loose wires? Manufactured to have some real elements charged through its circuit breakers and ending up somewhere, nowhere; just two loose wires unaffected and admiring itself in a dark current wake of a pool in the sky? Should these wires meet, no; they should reserve this paradox in its own suffering or fertile desire of it thereafter? It hides the program that should tell where tigers should roam?

Consequently, the human element of which the dumb box conceals entirely, is unlike this person participating in the event who is too unaware to consider itself the prey in this scenario? He sits in a lonely hotel room in downtown Detroit, asleep in a bed of fire now that flickers messages that never for a moment make this person think twice of the threat the instrument with electric wiring has? This is a wake-up call from abroad, a wired instrument so quiet in its stalking that this one soldier should sleep through the best part, feeding time? And when he wakes up in the morning, he slowly stands up on two feet and lazily walks somnolent to the set to turn it off and he does not know a single thing about anything that happens in the previous twelve hours? This is the start of the day and, on his walk, he brings an array of tigers to get some fresh air or maybe to plan their next attack, where no one should know where it might lead?

In the modern age, the giant Times Square TV monitor (you should think) is wired to other screens through electric telepathy of tigers in person's sleep, but is actually energized with its own design that hides the loose ends of its disposition tight within the massive display? Somewhere in its fantastic design, (though no one knows it), there are two loose ends where tigers roam. Still, the people about Times Square in this modern age continue to stare up, day after day, unaware as though quietly praying to a magical being. Its radiance prompts in beaten reflections of the light flickering in the radiated air there about its face? No one may make out this face. Still, unexpected victims continue to look up slightly interested, slightly curious; one person in the metropolitan oasis blinks?

Who is this person staring down from the mammoth screen? What does the person look like and with such a question engages the Times Square in the wake of its stare? But even in the nineties, such religion-laced and imaginary questions still fester and relate to the society at whole. What does this person, which is able to captivate the mob of persons below, look like if it had a face, if it had some sort of human like features? Could this face absolve itself entirely of the meanness we fear in a higher power that often characterizes monsters that wander our mind in our sleep? Maybe the person stares down at us, steadfast and constant, and no one knows it? Still, the obsession absorbs this public in the wake of the day hours and does not seem to discriminate against those so taken in that these individuals might be considered sleeping upright while awake?

Considering such circumstances, an individual might feel apt to protect these vulnerable souls, that the danger of such questions might bear in a world often less understanding and more cold than this image that those who should seek might produce? The digital god transfers from a Sony product to the control of NBC, an American Network which wraps the public spectators in loose lines of their own uncertainty, now staring up at Tom Brokaw's face, a little more familiar?

But it is still slightly cold in their heads, not free from the questions of God and such that continue to haunt so many minds despite the change? Maybe you would have to be raised in this Irish Catholic family to know the fear of abject poverty and potato famines that might transfer the breeding ground of such undulated questions in the fear of their father's eyes and in their own?

Now, on an American playing field, we look closer at ourselves, like the pulse of Kennedy's life impressed on the American public thirty years earlier? Now, those intelligent and daring enough to ponder this controversial aspect of modern American life through the huge Times Square TV. monitor electrifies us high above? The public, and the many American factions it represents, hang on to their throats and they face it and look up at it as it comes to view?

Now, the Censorship of McCoy and unknown groups of individuals who decide to partake of a quest to understand the nature of this beast, are an electric novelty that simply wires America in a single living room, telecasting news and entertainment faster than world markets may compete? It now may appear as a virus which invades homes across the land, producing a long range conservatism which, for the first time in history, shows the vulnerability of the American people? It is only tempted by foreign markets abroad and begins to have an appealing appearance no matter how scary it is for those who remember back further than schools are willing to teach?

This is a scary time in American history and the Censorship of McCoy is a primary concern electrifying the good Christians across the land? Dealing with questions from the past such as the following, there is now a quiet air that processes the American people as a whole? What good may possibly come from the election of a liberal president in times of a pending war? How can one support raising children in a state like Mississippi when capital funds tend to warp the balance of income for such states as opposed to states with industrial development and strong independent finance securities? Why are people who are against war, supportive of buildup despite continuing efforts of many individuals who undercut war efforts with such emotional strife? Why can a dog remain in good care at home and its best friend, man, fight a war abroad only to return in a body bag? What cost may presidential political playing chip at entrusted values from abroad in such an extensive manner? In good times and bad, why not share our toys when Mom is at home, and when Dad is at home, watch TV like a family?

In this climate, when television begins to take a toll on the behavior patterns of American families, the TV box not only speaks of the wrongs that were being committed, but also acts as a neutral entity in the living rooms that often become decisive promoters of family consciousness of goodness? Actually, the television begins to undercut values in good and bad times? And as though in easily joined households there is a new person in the house who might look good on some old metal table which is hardly ever used prior anyway; a new friend full of wonder and magic? A visual display, but how well do families really know their television set or new friend?

The question is still ignored today, it might sort of elapse in meaning given its continual strength that television has gained year to year? But, rather, what part of one's ability to grow with technology and mental skills may the object absorb without a single compromise spoken?

Today, the question is more like how much can we trade trust in return for electrical equipment and not education? The ordeal merits only a reevaluation of the culture that promotes the expensive toy to the pros and cons not? One might say, television is still as mystical and misrepresented as when the box introduced itself in the homes of so many without speaking of cultural clash, without speaking of ethnic strife, without speaking of turbulent seas abroad? The television remains on for reasons not understood by most? Yet, acting as a shield through wars and political coughs and gestures of something such as Marilyn Monroe's faint hand, "Why ask why, not?" and you are here even in times of peace? "The question please..." someone announces. This lug of human spirit repels his dinner on the clean target of his own undershirt in a seedy hotel room. Half asleep, he has the TV on still, and this question is to be (after all this time) and what promotes this fantasized re-enactment of a most cultural hysteria, "the Censorship of McCoy?" Have you heard of it, probably not, and the question please, "Why ask why, not?"

It is sort of a deranged pretense of a cultural climate that does not understand why it asks why, not? It is difficult to understand, given the flickering lights from the large screen or speaking in screams from above Times Square with no sound?

Suddenly, the cable wave begins to chant this question again and again, and the scene changes from what would normally be the sunsets of *Baywatch* on TV to this small room pitched in downtown Detroit like an outhouse for a disturbed soul, probably of Irish Catholic descent, probably a little bit red with alcohol intake over the years, and probably half-dead? Quickly, the camera prompter zooms in on the speculation like pigeons in a path of dry bread crumbs in the park?

This is real television; a nun's half-breath assures it at the very site of this somewhat morbid picture? How many *Baywatch* beauties all of a sudden become alienated by the sight of a drunk person staring into a television as though dead, while the defunct television must be a metaphor for the health of this disgusting portrayal of human defeat? It echoes, "He is probably near death." Maybe he is sleeping, but he does not even know he is on television and at this point the void of sound in the huge screen hanging over Times Square increases from being a mere yell to a scream, and volume need not be turned on to hear it?

Beavis and Butthead appear suddenly on the screen as sensory objects of the joke? Maybe a cover-up foreshadows the character as one laughs and, meanwhile, as the other characters bounce around the screen desperately in their strife trying to block the screen from viewers eyes and Bart Simpson appears flying a small plane across the screen with tape hanging behind it saying, "This is just a joke?" He is also part of the censorship vehicles that, as a matter of unfathomed hysteria, tries to mislead what on the screen seems too late to avoid like "the indicted" former president Richard Nixon, pending the Watergate findings? Beavis and Butthead try to block further the uncensored material like heroes of the evil dictatorship and electric hierarchy which, ironically, seems to be an inverted soul? As on the other side, wanting only to block out what is hiding behind them in an animal heated like trance, eyes staring wide open back at the audience? This is real TV, one might say for a change. (it is said viewing the material from abroad) some people are laughing while viewing the material before them as comedy? But, something to do with the lack of volume makes it clear this is one of those unavoidable accidents, a time when a person finds oneself in worlds of lost or gained innocence, should the pun matter, not really, maybe tigers are on TV?

"How do you like your sushi?"

"No, we are from Nebraska and never eat sushi there, but anyway did you hear about the end of TV?"

"Ah, ha," the waitress spoke in her tight traditional dress, "no, all I heard was that it is going to rain today."

There is not much communication, but these kids are on a mission and want to know.

"Want to know what?" A subliminal voice intercedes, and the question responds to these gestures and slowly fades to the sound of tigers. "Tigers," repeated again and again in some unknown person's wake.

(Scenes change to an office where a young lawyer in Ohio is reviewing files dealing with the incident which speaks of a review of censorship regulations throughout America.)

In an Ohio law office, he shuffles through the files in a cabinet marked "the Censorship of McCoy." The name McCoy is given to this hearing as the name of the young entrepreneur/writer who happened to be mainly interested in questions of censorship in America. It should compose this hypothetical trial to find it in hot markets of red tape and feared a consequence of menacing foreign investors from abroad? Among the panel include three young lawyers from California, a Japanese businessman, a Malaysian furniture builder and exporter, and a representative of the Vatican in Rome. In this array of random delegates of a curious configuration, they press a small law office in Ohio to reevaluate the records dealing with issues that accumulate in this one filling cabinet. And the paperwork with pensive eyes through the circular spectacles he adjourns on his nose that which is to be of merit in this secretive imposition?

What could these foreign and domestic entities care about what is stored, the old-fashioned way, in a small law office? Dealing with the censorship of the day, it should be retrieved under the category entitled, "the Censorship of McCoy." These unknown files might, on a world scope, have the significance to the public of that of a bumper sticker saying, "Nixon Sucks," on a Ryder Truck in the nineties? Still, this small group of individuals want to assemble in a small law office, possibly for different reasons and motives? Just the same, they pay this lawyer's time, a standard fee to have access to these files. It is determined that a ratio of censored television programming in America gives certain foreign markets a leverage in the global economy, while giving credit to the United States. Maintaining their values, in a sort of vacuum of a hierarchal landscape of firescapes and lamp shades, gives a designated American public a credit line and misleads the very values through censorship of porn markets in foreign lands? It moves at a pace slightly faster than that of the American economy. It speaks a certain language similar to censorship so not to have Mickey Mouse ever seen with his pants down, so to speak? For this security, America must abide by foreign demands, including being an indentured servant to the break of this old story? Or even unspoken to the point of the unprecedented analogy in world markets, the waking of innocents in America, "What a good story to foreign and domestic entities," and they gather here to review this case?

"So, what happened here?" the Japanese investor and CEO to a small telecommunications company offered in Asian countries asks as he is restrained with grave reserve? But, he appears a sound person with sound sensibilities anyway.

Next, the Malaysian exporter of custom-made furniture is seemingly "curious," in his sort of Hawaii-style lose shirt, and asks, "What kind of cultural icons are present today with value and is still permissible to the public eye?" Not having to do really with his exporting company, it is saleable somehow in Malaysian-based companies? Purely out of intrigue he says that it seems like a flamboyant culture here. And opposed to his semi-liberal, stable, and small economy in Malaysia one must ask why this occurs?

The three Californian lawyers are all private firms that handle mainly Far Eastern and Japanese investors and are swamped by a quiet leak that brings them to Ohio representing these investors ironically?

Finally, the representative from the Vatican in Rome is conducting a study on censorship material that should occur in the late eighties in America which, by the appearance of the priest is somewhat apt toward traditional Catholic values that should follow the vein of the church exactly? The files listed as "the Censorship of McCoy" have little significance on the business transactions prior to or while the meeting occurs and, for different reasons, they are to assemble in this well lit office/conference room in Ohio? It seems barely relevant to the world with exception to the individuals involved?

John Fly, the young lawyer, fumbles with the two boxes of material reviewed in which he will offer a short symposium for the individuals at a quarter past the hour. He passes the individuals waiting in the hall and asks whether someone would like some water before the meeting takes place? Inside the conference room is an oval table seating up to twelve, and large windows looking out at the small town's cityscape and the buildings across the way. The view is not the best, but provides sufficient light to conduct the meeting.

In the scope of the day, the files are read and much of the material screened. From one document to the next, these individuals menace at what becomes more of interest and less of a consensus of moral standards which review that television, the primary media circuit of interest here "how does it communicate to the American public?" After reviewing this, the representative of the Vatican speaks with the Japanese businessman and asks, "What significance does material have to you or why are you concerned?"

He replies, "The same reason you promote censorship in America. No matter how hard you fight for censorship, the material ends up somewhere, whether it's porn or scandals, and we figure this to be the reason why the material is misrepresented so much in foreign markets? We cannot stop the material that America tries to cover up and eliminate from eye's harm. It just ends up on some other's plate on some other dinner table? The thing is that you may be from a distant land and never have traveled to the United States and still know more about America than America knows about itself?"

The priest quickly snaps, "Absolutely not," and becomes aware of his sudden fall, taking the devil's advocate position in reverse and he becomes controlling and domineering in his veins. "No, I suppose it is just the merit of the material that the higher powers are willing to broadcast to the public?"

The Malaysian importer breaks into the conversation, "But, do you really know who is making these decisions?"

"I suppose it is carnal knowledge," someone adds, not the priest?

So the Malaysian exporter continues, "The demands from the world market is beginning to be dominated by demands in America and I must say, I do not know how all this happens when really we were building for middle to upper class persons in my own country at first? Then the demand is simply curious, when we live so far away? Ask the lawyers from California and you will see that over the past ten years, how the demand for Malaysian furniture, a small market, has increased and we, a peaceful nation, find it has to do with America's infrastructure? The credit lines that close your factories opens ours. It really is a curious question."

The conversation continues in this boring vein, but still unravels the mystery of the Censorship of McCoy. After the meeting, John Fly feels he has accomplished something by meticulously gathering these individuals to come to this law office and still leave without knowing a thing about what the Censorship of McCoy really is? Out of fairness, the lawyer decides to answer questions and speak individually to each of the faction's inquiry, first the

Malaysian exporter (and explain to a certain degree what the Censorship of McCoy really is!). He assures everyone to meet individually at some point.

John Fly continues, "The material, all legal drafts of different court cases that have professed basic censorship, eventually landed in only a small town district now called McCoy, with all the input of work driving at county, state and national lines and all that it may muster?"

After the death of a young entrepreneur/writer, the area where most of the work is compiled becomes the county of McCoy, named for this person, a concerned resident of the area who kills himself, shooting one small bullet straight through his head? The corpse is wrapped and is given a burial in this town that he lived all his life. Written with a red pen are the words that all should appease the sins of yesterday and rest in peace. The suicide is very coveted in the area and McCoy is considered a sort of heroic soldier of American patriotism by all those who know him in the region. It is not until the issue of censorship in America comes to the forefront to a congressman from the area that the material becomes relevant to reevaluate?

The law office is the last one to work on the case and it is years since the suicide, so the congressman allows the opening of these files. They are not considered national security anyway. The person is a bachelor with few relatives. In what is now McCoy, a young lady who knew him, worked in a clothing store here, and copied the articles he wrote then. He wrote an article about how censorship has the reverse effect, by destroying the social fabric of the country over time? He was overtly against this and worked on a court hearing himself so to warn others of its dangers? Being a conservative area, it was coveted at first. He seemed like a social phantom, planning his next move.

However, the lady, Miss Rose Ferguson believed in John McCoy and copied his work in case he is indicted or something and covertly maintained his articles after the suicide? She too believed strongly that censorship would compromise the social fabric of the country and the articles he wrote were not fully revealed until after the suicide? He said censorship would compromise and deteriorate the infrastructure of the country illogically, like a rotten apple hanging to a tree?

(In the dangling façade of the pine floor, the stage was set aside; a river and a mountain stood blankly in the silhouetted black sky, in which the night rest with an eye of the raven's call? Yet, no evil could penetrate the turmoil that beckoned in the sky? A wanderer may have walked into the woods and felt the vacuum that crystallized the night, but made it feel even more distant though? Still, what could negate his feet that stood soundly on the ground? It did not perplex him and he walked to the stage where the women were preparing the set. A woman in traditional Japanese clothes then appeared and brought a large dish with hot water. This was the place in which he soaked his feet before going to the private space where he could dress for the performance. Anyway, it was traditional and who would ask otherwise? One day it rained and when he went on stage, he slipped to the ground which is where he lay in full dress and a nearby person, a young girl, saw this and laughed.)

The theater is normally a mimic of these distant perceptions into the night? This leads to Times Square that, with the cleanup efforts, resembles the dream McCoy may have strived. Though, no one blamed it, such squalor on censorship as it has a reverse effect most often, and the cleanup, a gesture that the fight will continue one way or another, but good. Actually, the cleanup and transfer of power like that which is festering with porn shops to Disney's reprisal with new boutiques and such seems far from the cry? McCoy may have wished in his last breath that Censorship be reprimanded as the culprit here? Though, he thought it would end up somewhere else anyway, so why fight? The smile in the exotic theater remains on the frowns of those still isolated in the town of McCoy; and the porn shops that remain on the fringes of Times Square after the siege occurring under Disney's retrieval of the empty barons of a wasteland are hardly visible? Leading to the final act, it takes place at the home of its most identifiable icon, the Statue of Liberty.

Here, in this made-up, grandiose capitol, a rape occurred, in a gesture of uncertain intention and denoted meaning controversially unclear, a rape of a nun? At this point, interpretation is primary in importance and further the wording becomes detrimental in characterizing the words thereafter? The actual meaning is indecisive and, most likely, the purpose of the few dealing with such a sensitive issue? The Catholic Church, at the time, might find it to be difficult to understand, and thereby clutching the turmoil by the throat, attempts to discreetly cover up the occurrence with its own lack of willingness to understand such an atrocity?

That is all that is known is true, but the occurrence, which in some areas is heard about in its early stages, symbolizes the fear that undercut the media industry in the time of "the Censorship of McCoy," and his further indictment of it with his suicide?

This devoured the area of Ohio similar to the ways the interiors of the Vatican may have experienced it through a leak at the same time? Consequently, the Catholic Church finds the sensitivity and questionable exposure of the matter horribly kept quiet? As a matter of ethics, such a period of chaotic secrecy begins, in the early fifties, to shape the county now named after the entrepreneur and writer, John McCoy? Among those who still live here, they give its name as listed in the file in the law office, "the Censorship of McCoy?" Having studied the Catholic Church, he thought it may have something to hide after such an isolated incident, like the way the word "rape" instantly becomes a fired rock and too hot to handle in the Catholic Church, but the sentiment remains?

...so we return to mourn the incident by recognizing the views well kept, which reflects our disposition and guilt is not being able to reflect on such a thing. In hindsight, the nun petitioned something, maybe that the incident which may or may not have been leaked at the time, to be closed? Meanwhile, to find some other occurrence, the church should not focus on the detrimental effect of the occurrence among other reasons; a third disposition, "our ties come here!" recited the priest, "to the suicide of a small unknown place?" So, now, after all this time, like a tree that trumpets it trunk, we have returned to see the accordance of what simultaneously becomes of interest to the Catholic Church, the wishes of the discontent? While you continue to mourn the death of this vocal individual, similarly others might mourn the incident too? The reverberation may still be heard today, "Why ask why, not?" And now we all know?

Episode of Seinfeld in Japanese. "Jesus comes to NYC " (The year is 2200)

Sean escapes Japan's fate. The culture becomes excessively closed to those on the outside and recognize The Beatles, including George, Paul, and Ringo as the apostles of John Lennon who might be that which remains of their brethren they see as Christ. Sean is John Lennon's son who is re-born in Korea too, that is if you believe in reincarnation? Actually, he is all that is left of Jesus to the esoteric few who believe in Christ from a Japanese point of view. Otherwise, the country becomes very closed and Seinfeld may outlive their transformation and is still very popular there. Actually, Larry David may have sold the rights to the show after closing the set that lives on somewhere else. Meanwhile, the brats of doom are reminders of how the Virgin Mary claims her own thereafter and the dynamic may be even more complicated too. Sean becomes an actor in a play that composes their witness to a cause that recedes and embarks on a mission that is which is like the ocean. It seems regressive to follow John Lennon's past, and his son who died and was reborn in Korea, is later traced to the very trivial point of reference, like a hair from the very gone Jesus Christ.

The dynamic is hardly anything to take too seriously, but the show is of an actor of this Korean protégé, who is supposed to represent Jesus returning to NYC as an actor in his play of who is not Japanese. The lead actor like Seinfeld is a Korean named Sean Yoo.

*

There are three entities I am not. They include my mother's father, Stalin, and the person who dropped the bomb. My mother's father plays George, Stalin plays Kramer, and the person who dropped the bomb plays Elaine, (reference the year was 2200.) Sean Yoo plays Jerry.

*

-Kramer: "Why do you not want to share your domestic servant goddess?"

-Jerry: "My geisha?"

-Kramer: "But, I just want to ponder the sexual nuances of forbidden love."

-Jerry: "She is not that kind of Geisha; imagine a world without sex?"

-George: "Yes, I know…"

-Kramer: "Imagine frozen sushi for dogs, I will call it Sushi-chow?"

-Elaine: "All I can say is that there are eighty-one ways to leave a lover and I am leaving through the same door that I came in."

-Kramer: "No sex?"

-Jerry: "The dogs will question why they are howling in the night sky…"

-Kramer: "No, Imelda Marcos too?"

-George: "I wish I had a dog too."

-Kramer: "I know, we can use the geisha as a foot rest when we watch TV."

-Jerry: "No, way!"

-Kramer: "Why not?"

-Jerry: "Because she is my geisha!"

-Kramer: "There are no orgasms either?"

-Elaine: "That would be a weird sort of club?"

-Jerry: "Which tie do you like more? I want it to look good with my geisha's attire, I think she wears mostly white…"

-George: "I think the red tie goes well."

-Kramer: "I still do not know why you will not share your geisha?"

-Elaine: "Because she is Jerry's geisha!"

-George: "I do not know why we can't put peanut butter on our sushi?"

-Elaine: "And then rice cakes may replace bread at communion?"

-Jerry: "No, that won't work, I think?"

-Kramer: "No sex and no orgasms…"

-George: "That sounds like heaven…just kidding…"

-Elaine: "Right?"

*

George, Kramer, Elaine, Jerry, and Larry David all hold hands and pray for a better world. Jerry adds, "May the force be with you…" or what would "Superman," say in this vein?

-Jerry "I do not know really?" (Jesus Christ is exonerated in the process.)

"The Inner Trinity is Bob Marley, Michael Jackson, and Queen Latifah"

Japan's door is closed forever for the sake of the bombings which tally mushrooms picked in foreign lands, and their loss is considered a suicide. Still, they subsist anyway and the door is closed. Death is just a nuance of their attire and a dog that commits suicide is lost in the process. A dog's ego is split out of time too. Like the inner trinity he represents, Mt. Fuji stands on the outside of this scope for the time being, I think? That which you do not see will not hurt you either.

"Love"

The day is dark and shines on the petals of a prom night carnation that smells of burnt rubber on the wheels of a semi-truck. Out there in space it is easy to get lost. Though, a dog wants to come inside out of the rain. He professes that love is the answer. Someone soaks in a Jacuzzi in moonlit passages in the sky. The stars are shining profusely down upon them, which might free the kids of a dark flower's configuration. Meanwhile, it seems so outdated at the time, though black, it appears much darker in this light. This is where the carnation's harvest shuns those who will follow a different path, and love fills the void where children are returned to a different land, as well.

Night becomes day in one motion, so that the best is saved for a different cosmic configuration and they will be joined again when the moon rises in the southern sky.

So far away, this is just a procedure, though. The sun rises on the back of the bleachers and the kids drink warm Budweisers in cans, but so far away. They ponder the day rather than night and wait patiently for the curtains to drop, a procedure before the night sky will elope the day and such ponderings. The sun may not penetrate the dark flower configured in a dynamic of what is China and reflects a better life in the future should their eyes meet.

Meanwhile, the kids take a field trip from somewhere outside of New Orleans on a ferry to Avery Island, so that the wind blows and cries that you are coming home now. Love at such times is color blind. The only rain that falls now is a memory and this is better than not knowing. This is a gift too. The children far away work in sweat shops and participate in a sacrifice that will transcend their realm in darkness. And light may be a gift as well as a vantage point that yearns to meet on another day should he remain in America? Otherwise, in Africa, day turns into night and night turns into day. Let's get together later?

Obama's Father

Obama's father is "When the Soul Calls," to go within and the "Mah," which is Persian for the "moon," sheds its poisons in the ocean below. Why does Eve hide in the womb of a zebra, is now the fashion of darkness for a while? It is debated and the sun rises like any other day. Maybe the death of Nelson Mandela's fifth youngest granddaughter in a car crash is a sign that God will be born in another soon? My experience of coming to a mental hospital proves I am the last one here, and I will stay for a while. Sort of like Obama's father, but our path like God, parts in the wind that crosses the saddle of a cowboy's butt, and I stay for a while. We will part to meet again when the sun will rise, I think. Darkness envelopes the sky. Night and day meet somewhere in the middle where there is the GOP debate, why not have both? The sun may be cruel. Still, I sit and wait for the show to begin. The dolphins crest the waves around the coast of Madagascar, and Jimi sings that the wind cries Mary.

Dark Star in Nine Parts
Who are you? Three: Jesus
(Brian Wilson)

Not to detain anyone of bad demeanor,
actually it is a wakeup call for those of good nature
and princes of the like. Like Africa/Six and
America/Seven, it is a fertile planet with
All the blue in the world and hope for a
Tomorrow for those who seek redemption before
three a.m. the next morning.

Part Three: Placebo Bar

Ziggy Stardust (the year was 1945)

Ziggy stood anonymous, in front of the Enola Gay on that day. Like the religious prophet Moses, the sky divided in an air of what could only be called an earthquake. It is a timely response, "as the lights are left on at the kitchen door." The rooster that crowed could be heard from as far away as Oklahoma. Persons such as Woody Guthrie are present and the fire burns with an aroma of that where the park rangers stand in Redwood National Park. It might smell like a perfume to Ziggy, a perfect specimen in his own right. The thunder sounds in the distance and signifies a moment in time which leaves America unified in his wake, "through the slipstream."

A mirror reflection of the Pacific with dolphins smiling at magenta skies could be seen. America is conceived in the period from 1945 to 1952 in its wake. It denotes cracked almond shells and turquoise scuba ware, where the shell of an androgynous man was once there.

Back at the campground, a rocket ship preps for a return to Mars, his mother in a sense. The red ants crawl on his skin that cheered to its pink aspiration in the shade of a pale white ghost invigorating a soul lost. He leaves behind a baloney sandwich (half eaten), some fig newtons, and a finished can of Coke. He laughs in a loud sort of fake manner as the ants crawl on his leg to say farewell. Blatant attribution to his reality, he then smokes a Marlboro, his favorite brand.

He says, "Farewell to England," and coined the term, "love ya!" which I inherited. There is no reason to remain here as cosmically the time elapses until the real party in 1952 (though he really likes the design of a Marlboro man on a highway sign in the desert.) It sort of reminds him of himself, a loner, but austerely fashionable.

The Indians are too far away in space to remember. Ziggy sits at the bonfire, listening to everyone singing "This Land is Your Land" and adds a background hymn as though the national anthem too. I walk through the tent pitched in some backwoodsy theater, a legacy like the national park system Ziggy aspired to. He left his bed made neatly, even in these circumstances. Like his friends who coined the phrase such as "ants on a hot rock," Ziggy was truly religious despite what "marshmallows" in his parting would say otherwise.

The plane zaps nearly straight in the sky, and we all watch, as though its aftermath in a Nasa mishap in the 1980s. (The Marlboro Man wears black denim at such a time.) Like "From here to eternity..." but he claims he should be remembered as more fashionable than the guy on the beach, though.

He said, "The clouds then rise before your feet?" His adopted parents from Kansas leave him a brown bag with a few Pepsis and the best beef jerky around. And written on it says, "We love you!" There is a banana in the bag as well.

Ziggy did not wave goodbye and stared only forward to which his journey may lead. He said he would return someday for his guitar, though that was a lie. The plane shattered into bits as it left the earth's atmosphere and its debris fell to earth like dust. He smiles with true courage and in a flash, his remains decompose as such. Indians in space dare to cross the boundaries of a thousand points of light and he is home.

Into the Heart of Darkness:

George Faulkner lives on Jelicho Mountain, Tennessee, with his wife, three kids and an assortment of ten pitbulls. To understand the darkness that could foreshadow a person, "squatting" on land in the most natural sense of the word, one must return to his childhood. His parents raised him so he would be self-reliant, yet the door in the shed where he spent most of his time was closed. Sometimes, he would stay in there for hours into the night. He played with explosives and thought he might kill some dumb raccoon with the contraptions he fostered. What made George Faulkner different from other kids was his patronage in which he embalmed a desire to serve his country. Even as a young lad, George was mesmerized by his older uncles, who would share stories from World War Two, around a campfire. It seemed only natural that he would volunteer, what he thought was his duty, in Vietnam. He served three tours in a distant cauldron he would find out later. Unlike many of the other soldiers, George is schizophrenic. He may only relay in his mind, one set of circumstances at a time, without going crazy. He might later name his tours of duty after each of his three children which in order of age consist of Chris, Susan, and Charlie.

The elements at hand are "fire," "rock," and "ice." The component that was missing in his early years is death. No one may understand the former three without also including the element of death. In Vietnam, there was plenty of it, and I do not mean the kind of death of exploding a furry little rabbit, but the kind of death that allows one to believe you are the object of your own destiny. Once the line is crossed, there is no return I am told.

While fire is bearable, it is the lack of it that drives a man insane? Chris is a proponent that, like the color red, fire adheres to it. George imagined that after returning from Vietnam, he would be able to venture from the past and bring with him the fire in which his passions desired. Fortunately for George, it is a simple plan, "never look back." However, soon the ghosts return and nothing, but fire embraces him. It is a bearable situation. The color red is that of vindication. The return of those in body bags is the price that such a relapse embodies. If they died, so did we; that justifies the notion that they are wrong anyway. Red embodies pity. Each name is carved in stone at the monument in Washington, D.C.

The concept of death is not developed in the young mind of George Faulkner. Most children think of death as the end. However, once introduced to it firsthand like the color white, representing rock, it becomes a tricky matter. Those who died at his hands were alive in his memory. However, he is dying to also gain life thereafter. Instead of dying to live, he then becomes a slave to the tombstone, living to die, so to speak, and white dainty flowers are grown near its final resting spot. The color white is a loss of innocence.

"What flowers grow for me?" he might ask. "Who is this stranger on my lap?" Certainly, it is my own creation, "I am God, I am God..." This is Susan!

The color blue embodies his younger son Charlie, which is ice. His youngest son is the color of a dare. To think that he should beat the odds and return from a dismal war, but should he invite the enemy to his own dinner table? George does not know how this happened, but relays the notion of forgiveness and that those on both teams are basically the same. Death is becoming at one end, but not desired on the other end. The notion is taken to bed with him, as though not knowing as, in his sleep, he fights with his wife for the covers.

George holds a picture of himself as a boy by an apple tree at the side of the road. "Am I the same person as the one in the picture? George is horrified and does not look at the picture again. It is a schizophrenic relapse of his one-time innocence in this picture in time. He might be a bear at the time who forsakes the past.

(Paint a picture with these three colors: red, white and blue, on black construction paper and you will see the heart of darkness too or at least the loss of innocence to say the least.)

Art Garfunkel as my imaginary roommate: "The Sound of Silence," I was there...

When they sing, "split the night," the words cut through my inner core. Something in my deepest semblance understands this. While on the one hand, it mocks a regal journey that elopes to Earth from darkness. On the other hand, it dispels the notion that I am a Jew, that I am different.

While visiting another mental hospital (though I am not crazy really) I conspired to think Art Garfunkel was my roommate and slept on the bed next to mine. I do not understand the song "Cecilia," but gain respect for the tune as they try to undress concepts of creation through song and I think of unicorns in the sky. I truly understand the notion that all of creation is manifested through a mishap. God does not have to do anything like assemble models of artificial limbs on toy human beings. He creates us in his own likeness. He is our creator and therefore denotes a respect that may conjure any responsibility for mishaps thereafter. While God is the creator, I am inclined to think our existence is tallied from a series of mistakes, possibly? This makes it easier for God to refrain from any blame when his "customers," are unsatisfied.

So, Art Garfunkel, thanks for your assessment and may God bless you, not to mention being my roommate in a difficult time. Meanwhile, we are, strangely, both jacking off, which invigorates any notion that I am no different from any other kid on the block. I know the darkness in the past and I shall return to this someday, I think, but not really. Art wakes up in the night and sort of verbalizes, (half-asleep) "the green blobs from Astoria, Mom!" I am not his mom, but I say goodnight anyway.\

Up Shit's Creek (Sheryl Crow and Fish)

When Sheryl Crow performs in concert, there is some dog, somewhere howling into the sky. This story is not about Sheryl Crow really; it embodies three components which are the Oriental lady behind the counter at Jack in the Box, a fish sandwich, and the moon. How all these entities might be at the same place at any given time is what makes the dogs howl at night, not Sheryl Crow, I am sorry to say.

One must be a real lunatic to walk into a Jack in the Box, barefoot and order a fish sandwich from an Oriental lady on an afternoon before a full moon? All I may say in my defense is that there is something compelling about the moon. She handed me the fish sandwich as though it were her own body. And, to make a long story short, I was not able to finish the sandwich, and gagged on part of it.

The question I conjure up is do dogs dig Sheryl Crow? Should Sheryl Crow be at some other restaurant and order fish (the white stuff) and also gag is proof that the moon is also as crazy as we are. Why should you try to eat "the chef" which is inedible.

And the moon is alive at such a juncture, but does not carry its babies for nine months in her womb; rather they swim free in the ocean. What evokes the moon to play a part in her own parody is the semblance of a sort of beauty pageant where she always wins, even though I describe this woman's butt as mediocre in form. The time it takes for dice to roll in a game of parcheesi is the time it takes for this woman to elope with werewolves and such.

Sheryl Crow drives in a Mercedes Benz to visit an aunt and no one knows why the dogs howl at the moon when she is in town. Could it be that she has a nicer butt than, say, Imelda Marcos, and the dogs notice such things and dogs rebuke the preponderance that the moon would say otherwise? Otherwise, the moon; she does not know how to get down from there, but clearly dogs resent her for her vanity.

Sheryl is tired during her drive from Toledo all the way to Albuquerque. So, she stops at a roadside saloon and picks up a guy named Jake, whom she whistles away as namesake in her bag and carries him off to her hotel room. Now, I know what Jim Morrison meant when he said there was a killer on the road. Sheryl Crow does not actually kill her victims, but think of them as fish and lets them go after she catches them. Simply, the notion that she is strong enough to pick up any man she chooses is means for sheer respect and thus she requests from her lovers that they pay for breakfast the next morning. She just likes it that way.

The preponderance of who the moon may be should it manifest itself in a single body and soul does not conjure memories of hitchhiking? Only that she might be mediocre and random is all I can figure; sometimes even yellow?

Sexual preferences are not an issue, just that dogs do bark at the moon, which makes you wonder why?

The Electric Mushroom Gatorade Cat with Brian Wilson (not of the Beach Boys) Remnants of a good trip!

A trip is a journey you may or may not walk back from? Why does the goldfish smell so bad? "Potatoes grow in so many shapes and sizes," I tell a friend. He laughs then I say the man in the Hawaiian Punch ads looks so constipated and ask, if I drink this then will I be constipated too? The average Australian is better at tennis than the average American. I think mushrooms are fattening? Men who play too much golf are nematodes who dream of rendezvous with their wives' fathers. My mother bore a cow on a hill. The man driving the limousine asks how this is possible and I say I do not know?

Gatorade is the best drink ever made. The bears dance forevermore into the ocean… Water tastes like fish urine to me and the bartender fixes me a gin and tonic instead. He smiles in a still life and this is how I like it. I go to the bathroom in the back and through the fishbowl of the toilet a bear smiles back at me, but it is alive really.

God screws a bear too and this may be seen as self-defense. Next time you go swimming naked, think about how a bear feels like when human beings invade its space?

I return to Musgrove Plantation and the raccoon is a reminder that I am wakening from a former trip, but this is not always a bad thing either? I tell a friend that every leaf that falls has a story too. I tell the artist as though Leonardo da Vinci that I might help you get to where you want to be, that I have soul?

Shepard Fairey just smiles… A pigeon poops on my head and this may be a sign that God is watching too. I am in the garden now and my tail watches from a tree like too far gone to retrieve that which is a bone to a dog I think.

Bears occasionally cross over God's realm and the truth may kill too. I ask if he wants my ATM card and I am now homeless too. M&M's melt in the kid's mouth and the fire absorbs those now not willing to participate. Meanwhile, each child inherits their two cents and buys notions like the reincarnation of the David. The dream may be real at such a time. They accept a horse as a gift instead. The airplane flies from South Africa to Australia and drops Skittles on the kids below.

The color black reminds me of a dying sun and God is in his element now too. Meanwhile, the devil buys the color green and I am not for sale. The wolves make obscene cries to the moon as though it is Imelda Marcos's butt. The gesture will not separate those in South Africa anymore.

The devil is now fired and Barack Obama does not care that someone is not listening in the back when making a speech to farmers in Ohio. Have you ever let a girl win at ping pong just to get her to sleep with you? The art represents an untouchable entity and waits for the end of time to be born again. I got an A-plus in second grade for drawing a picture of an alligator with flaming genitalia disproportionately larger and may be said to be rendered in truth to its anatomy. My mom told me to watch out for nuts. Purple is the color of popsicles on Pluto which may or may not be a drug too? The urns were left behind in NYC to buy time in that which is heaven. Bad witches never smile back at me and rather compensate their demeanor as an extension of the devil. I am not the fool who makes a deal at such a juncture. Mike Tyson just says that civilization is beyond the computer chip that designates Mother Nature's truth, as though there are no secrets kept anymore?

The hippie's Volkswagen bus has a Jesus fish and reminds me of my father. My dog dropped two bombs on Japan but does not die in the process. So far away, and the lion on the African plain is bothered by the bee that keeps flying about its nose. When he turns the light out at the kitchen door, the kids are still smiling in the dark. I do not know why the moon seems so bright too?

The trash dump we call Earth is rich in history too. The horses still remember a time when the Earth was flat and Hitler is on some deserted island that his kids abide in him and things will remain like this. Children do not grow up, everything else just gets smaller. There is light in darkness and we never met and please close the door behind you. Fire has no history and the past is not the present either.

Why ask why not? I ate a berry from a tree as though my blood too and it will live on forever. Her flower should not be picked as the Earth transcends into darkness. I kept a bag of gummy bears, which I will eat later too. Kentucky Fried Chicken is hell and the Colonel Sanders "the devil," in this scenario? Every time I look in the mirror, I get the weirdest feeling that I am looking at a complete stranger? "Darn, I locked the keys in the car again!" As far as I know, I have never done hallucinatory drugs, but this is what a good trip might feel like?

The Women of Barbados

To refrain from what actually happened, I was stuck on some island, three or four miles out from the eastern part of Africa, which might be Kenya in modern day. At this time, I think I was blacker than the night sky and though I am making up this story, it is in hindsight, true, like a fable is true. There are two dark-skinned beauties on the island with me and I think the scope that leads to this scenario is no different than a game of backgammon. The object here, though, is to impregnate one of the women without the other getting jealous. The problem that arose is that if both women were impregnated, there is a possibility that incest would occur at a later time. This might lead to the rise of disease. As both women are young, in their early twenties, it is possible to perpetuate our future with a combination of this scenario, but more likely than not, it is futile anyway. We live in a microcosm and, in hoping to join the greater population of nearby Africa, it is our only hope. As none of us swim well, we think it is hopeful that, by some other means such as a raft, we might at a later date rejoin the semblance, in Africa but ships have not yet been invented.

To me, the women of Barbados are a replay of what has already happened in the past or may be in God's eyes a notion to see the rendering of what is to come. The fact that I may remember the time or at least conjure up a story so farfetched is testament that the story does have some basis. Bob Marley, of course, had not yet been born, but reggae must have its roots in ridiculous situations and the humor has not yet been discovered.

If Africa is the cradle of civilization, then God must have foreseen that, like an island, the concept of incest is not impossible. Why must a man trifle over the possibility of subjecting his loins to disgrace? I must admit, the thought of always falling into a trap of incest is enough of a reason to want to leave.

It is better now, however I did not make it to America then and was never in Africa really either, and was probably lost at sea to escape to some tropical island or something? Every move on the playing board is seen as though in reverse in a larger picture somewhere else. It is a natural phenomenon to want to breed subjects well, so the propensity toward life is greater still. It is as if the people on the continent of Africa are in a cloud of dust. The devil's craft of reversing a situation is in God's hands too, so to speak. So, where in the bible does it say slavery was invented by the white man? The song of freedom that Bob Marley sings about is not obtained on African soil, but the lack of it thereafter is what makes it accessible. Anyway, the three pawns on this island, out to sea, are never rescued, nor do we know how we got there. This puts an air of uncertainty into the game, so that those yet indisposed would try harder to fulfill God's greater plan. I do not know why God does not inform the ladies working at the Holiday Inn in Barbados that they are done with their work and let go in a way. One woman's toil is another woman's relief, and I think they moved to Cleveland and live with their nephew there. You may exist without procreating and this is freedom. In time, God will free Africa and you may return as though you never left?

Apple Tree on Uranus

Uranus is an interesting planet to me. It is what I call the planet of the birds and resonates a longing to arrive at God's door. In looking forward, it rectifies something so lodged in our past that it may only be rendered in respect to what is to come. I do not think God wanted Adam and Eve to leave the Garden of Eden so that there was no window to re-enter at some later date. Actually, I think the whole scenario is a farce in which, when looked at in reverse, is to say "the right way," it is to see the way God sees it and this is quite a beautiful spectacle. At present, the Earth as we call it is a sifter to determine those attractive enough to regain order on the planet Uranus in which God predisposes at a later date.

At such a time, the color purple from Pluto and remnants that yellow foreshadow on Earth will be joined in a colossal fruit of "the poetic champions." To say we may all be in the core of an apple might not be far from the mark. Wild horses will be rendered necessary once again and their tactile journey made useful. It is the missing component to think that God does not love horses too? But, for now, they must feel lost, roaming out there in space. Like "today's old, new novelties" horses may be rectified some day, somewhere else? To admire a horse now is fitting, as they inhabit the tenth dimension, and though very real, really only relay in space in one's imagination. To ride a horse really is as rare as to say you have eaten apple pie on Uranus, whatever that means.

In some cosmic mutation, it looks like hard work, carrying baggage to and fro, but I think it is fitting that the horse feels as if it is riding you. Galloping in its sleep, it does not know whether it is touching the ground. Ironically, the earth follows the horse and therefore it stands out there in space. What an absurd juncture. (It will carry you to what it calls home, but you must walk back on your own.) The apple is a prize to the horses among the many sects, fleeting in my imagination. Such horses are smaller than an ant. Yet, in comparison to me, they must be very large; and they roam free.

The Doctor Rings Thrice:

As relevant to the main story in this chapter, Placebo Bar, apples are hard to come by. However, their by-products which doctors implore as edible such as impurities, insecticides and even worms are obtainable. You do not think God would give his best apples to anyone who might scrape up a few pennies to purchase one? Like horses, apples on earth are mirages of what is almost unobtainable, but maintains the curiosity to seek? But, they are really hard to come by. Eve thought she would trick man (Adam) into picking an apple (of primal sin) for her so she might eat it, but rather obtains an existence that reminisces only man and not the God she sought really. Still, suppose you had the best soil around and plant an apple tree, the apple is as obtainable as the person who seeks it. When one reaches to pick one it instantly spoils in the hand that one should determine as unobtainable. If it should fall, worms instantly form at its surface and is penetrated in a bowl of waste. To pick an apple one must basically be an apple, as there is no one in such an act, and I know it sounds funny? It is like a security system to prevent anyone from what is in God's eyes, a perfect fruit, and therefore deters the quest? The lesson learned here is that man, no matter how you look at it, is not God! Therefore, Eve did not eat the fruit, I think, and Adam is innocent.

Wild Horses

Though not the tenth dimension yet, horses relay in one's imagination somewhere around here. What other discoveries may one find from their experience on the planet we call Earth? To the horses of the plains, it is a story about a place that was actually flat. It is hard to believe that wild horses trek on such a domain. But, as my previous theory invites the innocent bystanders if not enthusiasts; the horse does not stick to the Earth, but rather in reverse, the Earth sticks to the horse.

Similarly, riding a horse may be as tricky as picking an apple. However, the previous infers to cause a phenomenon of a flat domain always. Why do you think many of the Indians died out once their horses, though not native, but home in a sense, once they were discovered? Once Columbus discovered America, the world was no longer flat!

The Brats of Doom

The brats of doom always live where there are horses. They live outside the confines of Pluto, though are at home on planet Earth. Like the snake woman's torso as she walks, it is possible to see one, but they will usually play in the distance to the point where they are virtually invisible to the naked eye. They claim to be a mixed breed, composed of half-sky and half-Indian, in a sense. As the sky subsides to rain, they will appear here as Indians who subside here in this light, I think?

Though they are composed in a plethora of color, white is the norm. No one knows what they are thinking either. They need not put on a show, as no one is watching except for God maybe, and consequently, they behave like perfect specimens even though they are only part related to the sky.

The interesting thing about brats is that they are rather resilient to the notion that they are in some way or other related to the very Virgin Mary; go figure? Somewhere in history, their blood line intercedes if not in a spiritual sense only? Most brats are all looks and little substance. They are models of what the sky has created and thereby loved by the father only. Ironically, they cannot blame the Virgin Mary for their plight and rather direct their aggressions at their "birth mother," instead.

Otherwise, a metaphor for Mary, the Jews are targets of much grief and hatred. In an odd way, my dad, a brat of doom also, resembles to me the criteria of that which is a Jew. Without speaking a word, it is sort of like being Mother Mary, except you are a boy, and have urges like most boys do. His ability to behave well makes him a modern man with caveman instincts. One or the other is good and the other not. Anyway, he is a man and escapes the plight of other brats as long as he keeps a secret, that which the Jews confided in him?

Brats consider this kind of love and tolerate only so much without causing tantrums for which they want to know who their mother really is?

And the father calms them and replies, "I really do not know?" My dad has umbratile motherly qualities, while as a man, fatherly stature as well. I call it "the African Jew Phenomenon." He never left Africa, yet his people are other brats, who are putting on a show, for his footstep in Africa he took for me. Jews perpetuate the cause of the brats of doom further. Meanwhile, the

Virgin Mary has no children of her own really. I think it is presupposed to say the Jews perpetuate the cause as though God is raped and the evidence thereafter killed, but no one knows for sure, really?

He is my father, but is different from other brats as he entered a lake once and never left really. How could this be? A silver fish gave its life for the foot it photographed under the water among alligators in this lighting as he tried to exit. And legend says he still remains, but he has the instincts of an alligator and may appear anywhere without much notice as such. Meanwhile, the other brats are putting on a show. Despite their plight, I think they are still mostly instinctual. They like each other a lot, just not outsiders.

If I was alone in the dark in Indian Country, they would probably scalp me and leave my remains for vultures to digest. They want you to believe they are Indians too, but never wander away from the wilds in which they abide as their father? Other children are combinations of toil, sacrifice, misguided love, and promiscuous behavior. Brats do not relate to their burdens and, without such guidance counselors, are sort of lost forever? Children must be touched by something real; the rest pretend to be pirates in storybooks and such. I think that it is true that such places exist. Children remain in this world too but they will not cross the path of a dog named Nemo, either.

Nemo the Dog

One thing brats cannot fathom is being separated from their pack, and such is the case for Nemo the dog. Even in the fantasy world, and it is a real imagination world, the word Nemo is taboo among them. He went out to where the brats call the outer fringes; a place no one will dare go as no one has ever returned to tell about it. Somehow, Nemo embodies all the fears that brats have dealing with getting lost. All each has as a brat, is each other and, one day Nemo disappeared and such is his story. He is a black-and-white sheep-herding mongrel. Yet, most dogs always return to their masters, Nemo had no master, which is why brats usually fear places outside which are totally undocumented, and remain inside a lot? Brats fear getting lost forever and therefore bond well with each other as a deterrent from anything like this happening to themselves.

Nemo's story goes like this. Being black and white, he eventually became crazy as he did not know which was the better color. Therefore, he had no sense of direction. One day an Indian came into town, a Navaho man named

Fred Harvey; and Nemo thought he saw a ghost, and followed him out and he was never seen again.

Spanish Harlem Mona Lisa

She is a pretty girl, walking down Madison Avenue, past Ninety-Second Street and looks like she belongs? She would rather not say that she lives farther uptown, which is not so far away. Still, it is decisive to her. She is rather use to her job as a nanny and leaves a faint scent such as perfume as if to say to any person enticed to approach, not to bother as though a fire that should not be touched either.

This is fine with me as I passed, but I thought twice, which seemed strange as I kept walking. What did she know that I did not? The warning was bold like shaking the hand of a doorman along Fifth Avenue; I need not think twice, but the pause bewildered me. I do not think now that she ever considered herself from the upper reaches where she lives and though my mom once had a "nice apartment" nearby on Park Avenue, I still did not consider myself as a part of this world.

Instead, I lived between Second and First avenues, which was sort of a semi well-off and even, eclectic neighborhood. It was no different than any other part of Manhattan, south of Ninety-Sixth Street though? Sometimes I would go to the Metropolitan or the Guggenheim, and I felt not entirely out of place and, besides, my mom was always with me. Still, at nineteen, I am mostly on my own and this felt good. I wanted to ask her if she had a mother that she loves dearly? Sensibly, this was not a good start anyway, and I thought as far as the world she created for herself, well, "she could keep it!"

Lucky Thirteen

Lucky Thirteen is a card game Indians play. It is a simple game, but the stakes may seem severe. The dealer is the person who picks the highest card to begin the game and then the cards are reshuffled. All one does is deal five cards to three players (including the dealer) counter clockwise. From the dealer who begins the game, he or she must add cards equaling thirteen to begin a pile at center and must draw cards otherwise. Then the person to the right must put down a combination that amounts to thirteen; face cards being ten and aces may be eleven or one. Also, jokers are valued at thirteen, which allows one to skip a turn in a sense. (Jokers are not necessarily a good thing), but allows the player to not have to pick cards from the deck to come up with what is thirteen in a hand. One must place cards equaling thirteen in the pile when it is their turn. If they do not have cards equaling thirteen the player must draw cards until they have such. Then it is the next person to the right's turn. The person with the least amount of cards when the deck is finished wins.

The game plays out like this. The one with the least amount of cards is able to dare the one with the most cards standing, any dare that he or she wishes and if not able to meet the dare, the middle person must pull a hair from his or her head. If there is a tie, the losers or winners reshuffle to play for the honor or disgrace, either or. You may keep score if you want to play instead of for dares, etc. This game reminds me that I am not an Indian really. But, I made up the game so you can play anyway.

14 Outlaws

The Wild West was won by a semblance of fourteen outlaws that gave punitively to the term straight faced. They were the remainders from a sea of sharp shooters who would judge mankind like a hand of poker that is passed down indiscriminately in a sea of benevolence. It is funny that these individuals were degraded to mock an epiphany of cows and such, and would compose the human race. Their complexion at sun down, denoted characteristics of stolidity and euphemism. They all gave their lives at the hand of the gun, but left behind remnants of the embattled west. Fornicating with whores and barmaids, they would stop at every town; their guns enjoyed the company of for just one night.

It is argued that every complexion in the human race denotes some aspect of these fourteen men. If Abraham is the king, these men represent the knights in shining armor. Also, they are the remains of brethren to man who may foster in the end, a long traumatic quest. They do not know that they are brothers, but are equal in being the remains of a mission to populate the world which, at the word of the father, die thereafter in a long, enduring fight. Hollywood has these faces plastered on every screen in America and the infidels live in eternity as scapegoats for such plays.

Etceteras

After World War Two, when birth control may have been first instituted, it seems to me that the Japanese are the epitome of protraction to natural intercourse to anywhere on the map? It is not that sex is greater at any one place on earth, but the style of promiscuous behavior that perpetuates sex seems more accessible to the Japanese in their way of life? Just looking at a modern Japanese woman shopping in Soho, I may determine that this woman has had a lot of sex? The dark sensual nuances adhere to sexual behavior moreover than average Americans. It may be noted with the exceptions of Icelanders , who seems to me equally sexually active, that Japan is the orgasmic capitol of the world.

On this island oasis, one need only say the word "etcetera" to determine the amount of sleeping partners one woman has embodied. Rather than petting the horse, they must infer the animalistic instincts that should abide that foreplay is just a waste of time. Also, such things as dildos may not be uncommon to this scope. There is a stipulation that the harder the sex the better. Sexual activity may be three times greater than in other parts of the world, which is a leap from normal promiscuous behavior? I think if I was to be with a Japanese girl, we would probably do it three times in one night which makes cats seem like idolatry without a propensity toward sex? Sex should not be mistaken as beauty.

In fact, there are many women of different races that I would consider more beautiful than the average Japanese woman. Rather, it is the injunction that disposes beauty as secondary? Therefore, beauty is fornicated at a slower rate in Japan than other places. Sex is a healthy way of releasing tension that should not be there otherwise. Japan is such a place that encourages this fruit on a daily basis to say the least. On most places on the globe, sex is a part of life. In Japan, I think it is justly, a way of life. Other women may have as much sex as the Japanese, but the propensity for good sex, is greater, I think, in Japan? I think *The Rocky Horror Picture Show* should be re-created in Japanese?

The Chalice of the Microbe Cadillac

Somewhere in the outer boroughs of New York City, there is a guy driving an old Cadillac who steers about most notably, infiltrated with microbes, which the word itself sounds like placebo, but is actually just the opposite. He is a gypsy cab and though not legal, he shepherds the yellow cab in the outer boroughs with the stealth of a leopard or black panther. Though I would not compare them to lions, as a lion is regal and noble, he works on a terrain that is foreign, not unlike Africa, I think. This may be translated as such as a wild dog chasing an impala; though the stealth that such work requires is usually not so messy?

A gypsy cab is someone who illegally competes for fares with the legal alternative of yellow cabs in Manhattan, south of Ninety-Sixth Street and car services outside this area, which are three times greater in number. In other words, gypsy cabs are not recognized by the Taxi and Limousine Commission. In general, gypsy cabs have a certain décor, especially functioning a personal libido. Such decorations seem tamer in yellow cabs and car services, though less grungy as well.

When you enter at one point, like the rainforest; it is not certain that you will leave exactly at your destination. Characteristically, if you are lucky enough to get a driver as such: a destitute Latino man in his early fifties whose girlfriend will not allow him back into the apartment (which is in her name) until he scrapes up some dough, this is good. Also, if you mention "Calcutta," and the driver responds you are also probably in good hands. So what is the chalice of the microbe Cadillac? It is something said to be handed down over the years by pirates and such, to be a replica of that which Jesus Christ drank from at the Last Supper. I do not mean to sound intimidated, but this is a serious business, and those who believe here must part with the unbelievers. No one asked during my stint as a yellow cab driver, but I wonder how much a fare would cost to go to the Amazon rainforest? Some gypsy cabs might not be far from this indoctrination, but I wonder how much it would cost anyway?

In the rainforest, there is a hole in which sharks form a perfect circle. The savages one sees in *National Geographic*, (actually they are people like you and me), are accustomed to the rain falling upward. Such a world cannot be penetrated easily, like taking a photograph, it just fuels the mystery in which the key cannot be found. Fidel Castro might do well in this environment, as he seems fatherly? But, over time, he would probably find himself as food, like a wild pig. They do not penetrate each other's souls; they exist there at the mercy of nature, which probably puts a "spoil" on the game, if you want to call it that. The outside only appears as ghosts to them and they know who is the guest if they should come upon some freak who thinks he is an Indian? It is easy to be mistaken for a wild pig! Still, I think like the Indians that are now gone, they are gone for good, however, they are not, if this makes sense.

Again, I think they are the other, they are here and we are there, but that does not mean we are any different anymore.

Next time your girlfriend tells you to find the door; you might gain some respect for her as the door in speculation is like the rainforest and it may not be re-entered. The history books do not tell this story; once you drink from the chalice, you may never go back!

Holy Cow

Animals do not sin like mortal beings, but rather intrinsically maintain a primal disposition toward it the way God sees them as subordinate to mankind. Animals are all guilty of one sin, though, and they know this sin through God. But, in respect to homo sapiens, they do not cross over the line and, therefore, may only be categorized as "different," in respect to our brethren. God would rather not consider them as part of the race, he calls heaven and invents a sin for each creature, to offset them from the greater population. Otherwise, animals harness this one sin in a useful manner in aiding to procreate their kind. There are exceptions, however.

Somewhere in China, there is a cow that is like other cows, but special. Its name is Betsy and it has never been touched by human existence and eventually it dies like its dereliction, of old age. Where it was laid to rest, no one will touch it as it is holy. Only maggots eat every morsel of its flesh and leave its bones which stray dogs would gladly accept as payment for their good deeds. Now, it is free to jump over the moon, so to speak. Betsy sets a good example to other animals, especially lions, tigers and bears, which maintain an unusual sensory of its pre-ordained existence. Here, the road divides in a fork for other creatures who strive to do the same.

Whether good or bad, the animals may not otherwise admire the spectacle of her jumping over the moon, which occurs like clockwork every month. But, no one has actually seen it, except dogs, who remain on the fringes of domestic life. They will tend to beg for mercy, and howl to the cow as a spectacle, which is much like praying.

Sinful Ways

So you might argue that there is nothing wrong with eating meat products and it is completely normal. This is true if you are willing to risk the stark leprosy which is inherent to original sin. Animals only sin once and would rather go to hell than be caught out of nature's domain twice. Domesticated animals such as cows, pigs and chickens are rather scapegoats and, when you eat an animal, which is for me taboo, as I am a vegetarian, the price you pay is inherent as the original sin. This will free it of blame as you have, in the long line of sin, eaten the evidence so to speak.

To animals which I would argue adhere to natural tendencies, it is not their weakness, in the end? Those tribes in Africa who take a chance by eating a lion are rather in luck as they, over time, make this a way of life and for that kind of respect in rituals etc., it is mutually respected by the animals? They who respect the animals becomes stronger and rather give themselves to the animals and the animals respond favorably. These peculiar dances are not a joke and may be seen in different degrees in many cultures including North American Indians. Like one might ask for the salt and receive the pepper too; it is a sort of ritual. Animals might seem stupid when one does not finish the food on one's plate, but Mother Nature is not.

I mentioned earlier in this book about how waste sort of perpetuates surplus, and all I may exclaim is this is really a catch twenty-two. The germs which frequent the air are passed by the ghost of the animal that you disrespect. I guess a little waste is not detrimental to your health? I doubt you respect the animal you would leave to waste in the trashcan, and it is relative to original sin and the open scab it invites is disease in the air. One alternative is to become a vegetarian like me. There is one exception to not eating leftovers and such!

If you order out beef and snow peas for example, from a Chinese restaurant, such waste will not contaminate your air. It is considered okay not to finish all you eat and it plays into the rule about waste and in this case "the chef" does not expect you to finish, "there!" Like the saying, "Don't cry over spilt milk," it is a ritual that abides the waste. Do not worry about not finishing everything as this is the final ritual and parasites need not bother with it? (This is about all I know, I am afraid, and listen to your parents!) – While I am no longer a vegetarian, it might be presumptuous to call this section moot?

Chicken Rodeo

In the ring stand two very fat women who begin to fight like sumo wrestlers. Their fatty frames carry more than one dinner at Kentucky Fried

Chicken and rather than feeding Christians to lions, this is the next best thing; a spectacle sponsored by Toshiba which draws crowds from all around Knoxville, Tennessee. The motion of their feet siphons their plunges at one another and chicken fat as though live chickens ride the women like cellulite pride day; I suppose chicken must taste a lot like lion.

Meanwhile, a lion in Africa is quite pleased today though slightly annoyed by a bumble bee that keeps flying at his nose. Otherwise, he sprawls, meanwhile, upon his living room, the African plain. Only in America would so many spectators come from all around and the British agree, "It is all in good fun." Somewhere, someone is eating chicken and is a vestibule to the sport that fuels a weird rage at the arena and the women protest, "Can't you see my beauty now?" Even a French butler in Beverly Hills is not without the vanity that chickens displays upon his shoulder riding down Bundy Drive in his Camaro? (The world is like this sometimes.)

Sheriff Pig

Somewhere in southern Arkansas there are two brothers who are of African American heritage, but that is not important. And in this remote country side, they have a pig farm that has been in their family for sometime, and passed down from generations to Pete and Ramsey. It is agreed by the brothers that these three pigs, which bear the same bloodline are the meanest, ugliest, and fattest they have ever seen. Furthermore, they thought to make a contest of it so that the two prettier pigs would be called "bacon," and slaughtered and the remaining pig brother who showed to be uglier and fatter would be spared and receive the title, "Sheriff Pig."

The pigs talked to one another as they do in the slough and agreed they would be like perfect gentlemen about the ordeal and all try to lose amiably, so that one of its brothers would be spared the slaughterhouse. Two of the brothers were killed and only one remains today. "Sheriff Pig," watches the two brothers Pete and Ramsey working about in overalls and suspects the obvious – they being also sort of fat – and "Sheriff Pig," stares, in the distaste, at their backsides. Pigs are raised like that.

The Alternative Lifestyle

I picked up a young Japanese person at Fifty-Seventh Street and could tell he was of a nice composure and he resonated as someone who loves American culture, and I could tell he was a friendly person as well. As he entered the cab while I was heading east, in the middle of the street, he said he wanted to go to JFK Airport. He seemed in a rush, though he did not carry any luggage and at most a small duffle bag. It was one of those days that I would become a man. The energy was behind me, now, and what was going to happen thereafter, my age maybe nineteen, would not protect me anyhow? The energy now increased around my backside and I entered the street on Ninety-Sixth leading to FDR Drive. I do not remember a thing except a giant explosion in my rear that instantly made me pass out while waiting in traffic. It was not a physical experience in a way, but I suspected the passenger knew what just happened as I was defenseless to it? The traffic cop was talking to me like I was still in a trance. Meanwhile, the person in the back who I will call Fred, shakes my shoulder to help me come to. I did not enjoy the experience at all, but thought or hoped it would never happen again. I told the young person in the back to catch another cab as I was not up for the drive.

Libra is the sign most notable for that which manifests as Mt. Fuji in the distant, but still not that far away of a place. Once there was a man who was scared of the sun, and he decided he would hide in the ocean at any cost. Years had passed since the bombing at Hiroshima and Nagasaki, and he came to and dispelled the notion that finally the sun could no longer cause him any harm? Japanese survive on the fruit of his excursion, namely food from the sea. Though there are orange groves in Japan, it is not preferred unlike seafood, which is a way of life. It is the alternative lifestyle, and if eaten the right way, it does not harm one like the poison the moon emits to this stark landscape. The bookends, Ayumi and Makikho, returned into the sea as to a formidable exchange for the return of their native son that is now a hero.

In a sense, his people escape from what could have ended his civilization, and rather he promotes this alternative lifestyle now. Once the world was much divided, but now there is no worry to marry whoever as long as there is love! There is a distant archipelago, but dark as a raven's eye and even Stew, the horse, could not find the sky. You shall not cross this line, though and I hope I will never either...(a forbidden fruit manifests itself from my behind) and a righteous man claims this to be the end as though saying in his sleep, "Never again, never again..." Satan is sacrificed to the ocean and such which is better than the devil's ordeal, I think. The devil is naked and broke and their redemption may not be paid for with money made by man either. The lion sits on the African plain in which my father once stood. The children who return here pay for their existence in memories rather money made by man. Africa is not for sale and frees my soul in exchange of bread for wine. Money seems worthless at such times.

`Placebo Bar`

"The analogy of the 'soup' apocalypse (this story has no scientific basis)"

"The first to go are the banks." The Department of Health is hesitant to dismiss any information at present, but there are rumors that a black hole is forming on the surface of the sun and it is causing minute hindrances of sunlight reaching planet Earth.

Well, "how minute?" the mayor of Sunnyville, Wisconsin asks as though it is inconsequential?

Actually, we have certain sensors for scientific purposes and it may just be specs of dust that are harnessing a dark cast to certain parts of the globe. There are minimal food shortages in production on a line that affect mostly equatorial regions in a perfect parabola relative to the sun and the earth's evolution.

"What this means," a former employee of the State Department on the phone from Arlington, Virginia states, "There may be signs of impurities growing like fungus on the sun and depleting relative sunlight so that areas that are most directly absorbed in the heat of sunlight have a marginal degrees of depleted food production."

The phenomenon will grow like the contours of an atomic bomb and eventually form a dark star on our present sun, blocking sunlight from plants so that we may have to change our methods of producing food. Chances are it is like the size of an ant to an elephant, but eventually its impact may be severe. It is not the sunlight that is an issue; this star or dark entity, so to speak, could mix with the gases on the sun, changing the dynamic and making it somewhat vulnerable, to say the least. It would probably take 50,000 years for it to have any serious consequence. However, we will not know how it will affect us until this dark component grows to its maximum size, which could take anywhere from fifty to a hundred years.

What you are saying is that we have to find another way to absorb rays which may or may not come from the sun. It is possible that chemicals from a sort of fallout, a dust storm, though not anything as horrendous as a nuclear winter, could have an aftermath and reach Earth in just a few years. If the clouds of darkness have reached the sun, then the Earth is not immune to similar circumstances repeating itself here.

It is not surprising that on Iceland there is a method of harnessing bad sunlight and transforming it into a radiation that grows certain entities well and not surprisingly grapes used in wine are very agreeable to this methodology. In other words, growing a watermelon in this system causes a slight meltdown in its deliverance, while grapes have less demand for the same sunlight. Therefore, it is plausible that categorically, dark foods which include grapes, prunes and nuts, are well adjusted due to the transfer of energy in its predisposition. Solanaceous foods such as tomatoes, peppers and eggplant grow adequately, while corn, surprisingly, has a poor response and it is considered that a mutation may occur in the process, which would render these food groups as inadequate or even poisonously redundant.

A John Z. Sanders (no relation to the other) in Berea, Kentucky, made a breakthrough, after one of his pigs died in an early injunction. Mr. Sanders had been feeding it vegetables which had contracted some strain of the virus plaguing the sun. He discovered, out of sheer poverty, that by eating the carcass, he is able to use the dust and, by doing so, it serves like a sponge to hinder the adverse effects of hunger. It becomes somewhat of a buffer that, when mixed with alcohol, may maintain life in this brave new world in a form of benevolent zoonosis. The problem is that while alcohol feeds its fire and prevents things such as hunger, rather alcohol must be taken with the dust so that a chemical reaction occurs In other words, there is no way to determine the timing of the phenomenon. But, this is top secret at the present time, since any of this information would cause a catastrophic panic.

While the few individuals aware of the goings on go to supermarkets to purchase exuberant quantities of soups and canned vegetables or the like, they are not informed of the larger picture. Without the virus, its congeniality uncertain, the food is actually superfluous. Even healthy stocks are rather ill-equipped to reverse the phenomenon (rather than avoiding the strain or impurity, one must ingest it and then, and only then, does food and alcohol seem useful.)

Otherwise, there is a calming in the air where few individuals are aware of a dust that may have an effect on food production which will tarnish life thereafter? One must invent a way to adhere the virus, similar to what is posing a menace to sunlight reaching Earth and cause a timely chemical reaction so that the survival of mankind may continue onward. Otherwise, food is virtually superfluous of that which a virus; which may be subject to us like the scope of that which is a placebo bar and perpetuates a lifestyle that is soon to be drastically altered. Still, no one knows, and this makes it even more interesting when viewed on a microcosm proportion and scale. Humankind is dependent on this viral substance as a result of a depletion of food production, and food is like a placebo, but without the virus, food seems only like a temporary fix into the future.

Placebo Bar, Placebo Bar

The lapidary spell drinking through the lips of the solicitor's expression, solid upon the glass that the endnotes of ripened fruit of dark leprosy? With caustic anticipation of runt fetid prostates, it mixes together in an arsenic bath of the protoplasm of the dispelled forest which sticks to it inherently? Feign markers with a salutary appetite to who is drowned in its own sobriety? There rests a fedora on old boards, polished and clean, and an open door to complete a resume of lint and loose threads; it glows on the table with a match and green thumb to raise even the portrait, retracing a link once to the very dead president, Abraham Lincoln?

What may be spoken so eloquently then, a reminder for the damned souls of waken yesterdays and skies that turn yellow in its light? Further, broken sedatives of moist retrieval of the very tenderloin of the eternal reprise of the language English and spoken tongue, "How much for a beer?" one might ask. Then "no!", hanging by a cape like a seltzer in a dandelion pool, its neck tolerable to the haggard look embalmed in the truth? Speak so much of forgotten promises or careless frill endearing ghosts in crevices and achy corners of wooden trellis and beer refrains? Piece by piece, a puzzle qualifies to a most certain red sky and casing? Temptations, to continue its pursuit into the evening which touches ground, the flickering of a sad candle absorbed and extinguished in a wax parade too deep for bygones or even tears?

The person, drudged by a cape and clairvoyance of the distinct fedora still sitting on the table which promises money; now standing like a phantom bequeathed by the standard it demands? How much for this image diverged by a golden amber pierced identity lying awake, wide open to this careless picture show? One bill, second only to the pointer finger that presses against his wallet's leather interior for more money? Why take a cab and sit and ponder inside the snug confines of a coat with a let out tattered back to talk on the telephone and return in a flash? What does this caped figure leave to be; a brandy, a scotch on the rocks, tidder tat and a few nickels? Left to speak not of generosity or even good fortune spelled backward, fine ; and push the step in footstep tracks that maybe a bear once left in the snow? No remorse and just kidding as one who does not recognize the church that pays the bills in a belated stand of golden hair or enough of grotesque no-nonsense disposal of its very shameful sham of discontent misfortune? Slowly, it rises to the occasion leaving only the door behind him?

The grateful dead accosts me and asks me what I am drinking and on a flat plane I continue that coffee, "What?" with the same consistency of different beverages, "What is in the coffee, he asks?" Dismal containment "not," that I should know anything that is put in the coffee, as though someone should know anyway, and I put down my coffee on the pay phone without replying pressing the numbers for a ride sequentially; a deer slightly abandoned by the bullet it forfeits and jump in before the dusk hot lights should steam my reprisal? Left behind in this faltering cup, the cream cleft and the coffee waiting below for the night immerse within its bed sulking by only the extent the hallow lost incision should plunder? In this modest refine, the steamed milk should be the moon and the coffee the ground; while everything in between unknown? In this delicate syntax, one mourns the cry of the most holy of ghosts lost in the bounds a tailgate should leave like an absentee ballot and otherwise the child is unknown?

What boat should ride the turbid sea or an ocean so turquoise, yet so bored? There sit the spoiled substance resting gratefully in its fedora on a grand junction bin and smiling at the moon? Should someone find you here its unlikely. The morning should pass this one time, into day at the mercy of the poet's pen and the retrieval of its cursive explanation point? Why sit here like a deer in the light of day, when a barrel points its trigger down your throat by night, the poet must confess? Actually, without a delay to siphon a thankless sea bath in an armpit device with a turban? High noon and the quack of ducks in the distance, it is dismayed to the prophet who has such distaste for such materials?

In a vinaigrette sauce-colored Haitian tie, the bartender arrives for duty of a blasphemous agenda? Where, he who should point the finger, a professor; meets a mildly gone poet with an eddy smile for such vast ocean lost trinkets?

Meanwhile, a person in black denim and open shirt to express the shedding of the light where the sun lays a faint sign upon the proponent's neck? This is a wild display which sits casually in someone's apartment unfathomed by a secular wind which leaves a discourse for such array. Here, in the apartment, one waits until the night should riddle a path to meet the darker tendencies of bewilderment? As a time to meet the strata of detachment familiar in the breath and alone by all other standards?

What do a professor with sullen eyes and a poet, hardly a dribble, share in common? At this point, when the configurations in the sky should meet and a short engaging handshake concludes? The bartender reserves a Fuzzy Navel and begins the contest with mirrored gin and tonics? One should leave decorously, the other refined; and neither a trifle, arduously muddled mutter a Dutch under one Aryan reply? In logic, the professor might engage the conversation to begin with, but rather lies back lackadaisical, while the poet considers the sequence and lifts a glass to his lip to sip what is becoming, a faint pulp of lime twist?

There is no conversation, but rather the professor digs within himself to test the waters of surely the more mature of the two drinks? This general age differentiation gleams a light blush on the older person's complexion, showing a slight embarrassment of the sojourner's delay in speech? The two might lock heads, but rather attempt a more relaxed approach as though the conversation had already begun and where to finish? Actually, he implores like a skip on a record, that his drink, a bit strong and how it tastes to the liking of the professor?

The professor invites a startled inquiry and replies though not to notice? Furthermore, the professor responds that the percussion of instruments in a symphony, does not dispel the notes unless the alcohol rises in a glass to a certain degree? By this hour, nearing dusk, the cordial conversation is annexed by a tone less inviting and sips another drink from the glass? The professor with stained eyebrows and heavy too, would rather avoid a topic less congenial to the tray that serves the drink and forfeit's a muster as they both drink?

At this hour, the air and particles in it fly about the glasses standing upright in their sleep and subject to anything it might be befallen to? This does not arouse an archaic cry, nor one should notice the archipelago the bar sustains along its shiny wood polish? As the two individuals finalize the meeting with a farewell handshake; one leaves to the outside and the other to the restroom and otherwise everything else is left unsubstantiated and incomplete? What has not been raised in the glass to should not be spoken thereafter? The professor leaves in a shiny yellow taxicab, while the poet is left wandering the street to arrive to meet a slightly unexpected other? The poet arrives at his apartment 4c and confronts his female roommate. She has been away for about a week on vacation and startles him slightly not to mention the lurch of her attire being that of all black. He notices the gold crucifix she wears and they skip down the street together to meet another friend. It may have been that she was waiting a while as he had not been back to the apartment since the night before, though maintained little notice of any change. Their quest to find the bar would not be difficult in the microcosm of the intended reprisal of emotions that the third person might share?

Here, on the corner, they enter a dive without consequence and Charlie is entering from the rear. Meanwhile, while the two enter the coffee house/bar, they suppose Charlie might be finished with his shift around this time? It does not matter to the two; together they seem that of a couple roaming the city streets maybe for a quick beer or other fanciful drinks? However, a certain conforming stiffness separates them this night and the two roommates sit sort of drained of energy and anxious as though waiting for a camel to arrive with the water on a desert excursion?

With faithful beers of somewhat frail cheer between the two impatient individuals, Charlie waves his hand at first notice of the two. Slightly rubbing the water in a redundant manner from his hands onto his pants without regard, he might have done prior as to avoid contact? Simultaneously, the two reserve any notice as though even to care? The light seems a bit low and this might be the reason for their lack of reply and Charlie engages both with a hug. He brings the patrons and acquaintances a round of Long Island Ice Teas.

Fixing them at the bar himself, he reserves the third, a glass of water for himself. Again, he wipes his wet hand from the glass on the apron that now only hangs from his neck loosely and, by doing so, signals his final completion of the shift. The two look at Charlie, surprised at his choice of drink, just water, while inviting them with more fanciful drinks. Sort of out of coincidence, but sort of accidentally, Charlie notices the two staring down at his glass of water and wonders maybe something is wrong? He pulls his chair up to the table in mid-smile and looks in the drink, wondering if something could have fallen into the glass like a fly or a bit of dust from the air? Curiously, the expressions have not changed?

Relieved, his male counterpart and poet thanks him for the drinks and ends the uncomfortable silence. To continue, Charlie, looking away, asks Sherry by name how her vacation was and notices her slight tan around the neck as though this must be a sign of a good time?

She responds having had a relaxing time, when Charlie intercedes, "Where?"

"Oh, Key Largo," she replies. What is it about the incident that Will, the poet ponders in his mind of the meeting with the professor earlier that evening? Sort of like a reflex, his hand rests on the drink he is nursing and slightly detached, jerks it away. He wonders something not quite clear then and gets up and walks to the restroom in the back and, in one motion, wipes his damp hand on his pants similar to how Charlie had also.

Meanwhile, Charlie and Sherry converse as she tells Charlie about her new boyfriend she met who drives a motorcycle. Feeling a bit wild, Sherry continues, " let's go to a club down in the village?" Responding as though, "let's go," but to finish their drinks first, and Charlie takes a brief moment to stare down in his glass of water and tightly embraces his torso.

A few loose objects are carried in the air rambling about in their wake as though to pass by.

The three, Sherry, Charlie and Will, ride a raged taxi downtown as though its tires are made out of basketballs and that which passes is not very important in the light of the excitement of the moment. While, contrary, a couple engages one another in their apartment, where in complete privacy, no one would notice this temulency anyway. The lights flicker in the veins of corpses wrapped about each other, unearthing the passion liaison to them. Pushing the posts, they expel the notion of cool air-conditioned accommodations in the privacy of one's own home. Further, pigeons make profane gestures in their living room so as to intercede the warmth that rises through the vents in the ground? Pensive behavior, but coiled perpendicular to the coitus that inflames their space? A Trivial Pursuit question asking in a cab riding like the "D" train downtown in rabid motions that secularize their conquest?

Raven posture and rat infatuation conspired through the night to where the ride downtown should lead? At "the Hole," the three are moving to a beat pounding through rhythms at the heart and draining beer of the sap that all is left? Dancing beer bottles and posed thrills of absurd gestures conjoined in the air while the couple rages in quiet ecstasy to a ferocious beat at home? The night falls through the sky to the early morning hours and somewhere in the outreaches of the concave imposition, a bartender is drying the glasses that the previous night should produce?

He stacks the glasses upside down in sequential motions along the two panels on the wall. The door opens from outside "the Placebo Bar," where a sparse nature echoes a faint ring in one of the glasses like a musical instrument? It festers some germ (that is harmless) that only a small goldfish might notice? And, outside, the storm moves through the sky, protecting people in different directions through the fisheye lens that absorbs such quakes in a distant cauldron? Maybe a recipe for the despaired that those in its language hamper this sort of mercy that its bewildered fruit may tempt to unforeseen and timely passers by? Heartfelt sways in the heat, conjunctive in slight streaks along the glass, a recipe for the disheartened few at the portrayal of what is caught all around the city like a speck to wake not many it captures without consequence?

In a distant place, a group of young children sit in a circle in a science class, staring at pictures of different bacteria and one-celled amoebas which are further trapped in jars? And in the distant imagination, the confines of what is nothing, but an immaculate room fostering the curiosity of children about how such a little thing might be seen speculatively? The small-fingered children, clean and pure, pass the jars around in a circle; the teacher imploring the ripeness of such things is the only mercy we know? The ripe little fruitful children stare up from the circle innocently, not understanding a word that is said?

The bartender arrives at five o' clock the next day (as usual) and things continue on this uncertain path as though unaware of what is to come.

"Undressing the non-androgynous xenodochial man" (in thirty-two parts)

One: "Idiot"

Love lost is where ground zero should stand forever. I am squandered in the process for a sake of three lions, who may be sacrificed in three squares like the pyramids they represent. In two thousand year intervals, the three lions represent the same as a perfect sun. And the skeptic does not know the time of day on a Tuesday morning. I may be a metaphor for an apple torn from a tree or a rutabaga and all of the baggage carried by the believers of Christ in the process.

On a Sunday afternoon, I am at a Jets game when the dynamics compose so that I am on the outside looking in. The seats are better than the alternative and the waterboy leads a procession to the medley "When the Saints go Marching in." Those leaving for good cannot see what is behind them. Those who would comply with the light of the day will not see anything, anyway, though.

The apple torn is like a football, a perfect entity but warped so that one may see all its imperfections as well. Actually, it is in this form, but may represent a circle like a brain diagnosed with a mental illness. Actually, I tell a friend that he has a "bird brain," and the pigeons in the park make the decisions so that he may not be blamed for atrocities like 9/11. The I.Q. is 136 and eight 17s is a formula for a perfect spheroid of wetware, I think. Lenny Babboo does not know this at the time, but squares "three" which is the same conception as though an eternal plain, and the children follow the land procession of the Energizer's pink bunny that leads them into the sea as well.

Two: "The Black Bird Curse"

I smoked for more than twenty years and the curse of the Black Bird is bestowed on my lungs. It lifts you up in a spirit that is there and remains to fly but not to touch down either. The lungs are now black and the Diet Coke I absorb is only a passing cleansing. It will eventually kill the protruding thoughts that are less than a bald eagle that scoops down to catch a mouse. I float instead like a hot air balloon and land somewhere else where my father will take the first step for me. I am able to fly to somewhere else, but was I really ever there? The left lung is Monique and the right lung is Katie, and represent Indian witches, and sing from afar a Beatles medley; to take the time for God to judge those who remain. The number 883 is the formula for their escape which may be good or bad, as I do not know. The souls that are not redeemed are asked to leave through the door in the back, I think.

Three: "The Golden Apple"

I may have been born in the dark, but I will not betray my past. However, someone picking the apple is someone else's crime, and I am now a Jets fan as previously I rooted for the Washington Redskins. I may have escaped judgment having been conceived from three points in time, but born not yet that which is in death. An atom is very small, but I am able to immaculately absorb the mushroom without picking a single apple, though it has no tomorrow and conceived out of my own disposition, whether the step is my dad, and my tail severed is my mom. Maybe God for a while denies others the right to this fruit. Eve is not without temptation and her sin still remains today at the price of the sweat of many dark entities in a foreign land. They are now bookends of a book that will eventually claim their innocence in the end. If the apple will not land, God reaches for it and claims a right to it so that it does not fall either. An apple from this tree will intercede the void and become his heart immaculately. In exchange, my dad uses his sperm. A gorilla screws a bear, and this in hindsight is considered self-defense.

Four: "Moon Mark"

(It is not that I do not like the moon, rather I just do not understand its light.) Even if Imelda Marcos has a less than average butt, dogs still bark at it into the night to diagnose that something is in fact there. If the ten commandments are on stone tablets to lay down the law for the Jews, my mark on the center of my forehead down below is a reminder to me that there may be only one God. I guess our exploration of it denotes that there should be respect for it too. Like respect for one's mother, there may only be one too. There may be thirteen suns, but only one moon. The bookends evoke a curiosity that there may be a story here too. The face of Jesus is many and goes on and on, like the children who will play and play. (I will try not to order a virgin coconut daiquiri at night in Nassau while playing roulette at the casino?) Vanna at such times will not take her clothes off either.

Five: "Adam's Apple: (Martian Model in Pink)"

Davis Bowie is a superman who composes melodies "Hunky Dory," of my child's earliest soul. She is a model of such an androgynous male that may not be anything other than a male trapped in a world that he envisions his mother here as art. Otherwise, I conceive color samples with pink undertones which may only be seen in a woman's world. From this point of reference, she is my Adam's apple. David Bowie, at such times, buys her right as though Andy Warhol, who paints a picture of her shame which may be misunderstood anyway. She was never here and, therefore, may not be accused of any crime either. David Bowie and Andy Warhol throw a baseball in the park which diagnoses a whale in the ocean as not crazy but is proof still, that he once was here too. Otherwise, they will ride mopeds in Italy to spread the word further. My Adam's apple is mine and not yours!

Six: "Strawberry Fields Forever"

Strands of her hair are like the DNA of cockroaches that join hands as though dancing bears in a paper cut out on and on. It is not without remorse too? What may be the blood of another is not her responsibility. She is just the testament that no is her response. I will bleed for her just once and it denotes a loss that will not be regained later She will survive the fall of man and the animosity she feels is real. At the doctor's office, the nurse pricks my finger like a thorn from a rose bush. She tastes the harvest like wine, like her own. The dancing bears continue exponentially so that it may symbolize the spoils of the ocean and not other. Her blood is shed in reality and a shark is sacrificed to hide the evidence. Without a stroke of guilt, the grandfather's clock will not claim the disposition and bears continue dancing in this vein. She reaches to put her right hand through her hair, strawberry fields forever?

Seven: "My Dad's Baseballs"

My dad gave me his baseball collection that had the signatures of the New York Yankees from 1950 and 1951. He had the balls to decide to be his own man, and I redeem his courage and nearly sell his soul to the devil. (I would not be forgiven for the act, had I gone through with it.) He did not want to die in God's world, and instead buys a cloud with a view of Yankee Stadium as well. He was affected by a gallbladder sickness and his infected area swells two- to threefold. He is a model like a statue of a lion in the park and represents that he may be so bold to create his own world, and God may forgive him in the end. He sits in the Forbidden City in China, and leaves behind a salty dragon sculpture in Central Park, to make the exchange real.

A righteous man may be rewarded as such and bubbles float out of the ocean where seahorses ride the wake of his courage, not to care either. I guess it is possible to be something in the eyes of God, and I am neither. I think lion tastes a lot like chicken?

Eight: "Circumcision"

The skin is cut slightly so that it evokes a memory of my mother. (From here we part like a tail of a "Little Black Cat.") It conveys memories of paradise and for those who escape the fate, they form a circle in the rainforest of Brazil. They mock lesser divinities in a ritual, and his remains are burnt in a fire from within. We were once one entity, and now just a dream that we will never be re-joined again. In the time an umbilical cord is cut like in the same time that it takes a Japanese tourist in NYC to put film in his camera, the sharks form a circle to die in a perfect dimension of twenty-four entities are here too. Satan and a female tiger shark named Lily remain in the ocean. Lily eats her lover and Satan might not escape the fate. In exchange, God may leave while at the same time, Mt. Fuji leaves an exodus of his brethren out of the ocean, just like Moses had done somewhere else. Good cheer fills a bar in Boston at such times.

Nine: "Virgin STD Warts"

As a virgin, I still have these warts on my scrotum and these symbolize a gift from another. At such times, I may represent the third dimension and the light that shines upon it is a lie. Two Swedish sisters are left untouched from within, and we will overcome a diagnosis of the death of Christ, thereafter. We are innocent of all charges and I say this emphatically. Somewhere, in the interchange of bread for wine, I somehow maintain these warts as without the penetration it will diagnose the condition as not real? Jesus Christ exists somehow, and the gift it administers here as a virgin is her gift, a group of warts to say never again, I think. This may be a rock thrown at the moon as a witness of all of God's creation. I may be a virgin at such times. The night will not allow the light to be witness to the act done prior. It may not be a miracle, it is just not me? The goldfish does not know how it got in the bowl!

Ten: "Right Leg" (Found in Vietnam)

Phil Dickinson lost his leg in Vietnam, but his sacrifice is not in vain. He replaces my leg as though he is rewarded thereafter his full use of a body unhindered. I have two legs, but his sacrifice gives him a right to my right leg, and I may have lost a limb in Vietnam as I walk for him now. He is my photography teacher in boarding school and, like a tripod used in photography, there is an extra leg, and for this he regains what seems so lost in Vietnam. This is a miracle that one may ponder.

Eleven: "Left Inner Foot" (Mozel)

Mozel has a slight deformity where his left inner foot that sort of bends outward is as natural as the manifestation that praises the creation by God in everyone is unique. Mozel is African/American, but was born after slavery. Still, he worked inside now that he was not needed on the outside of the property in Georgia. We loved Mozel, who was a servant for many years, and my sisters thought the perfection which was Mozel was sort of cute too.

Twelve: "The Friendly Stars" (Like earth caught in my fingernails of my left hand)

I am in a very dark place; still the light of the singers manages to add some light in this most dismal of places. I am in my motel outside L.A. and I am not myself and walking on the streets while barefoot. It is not proper to call people dirt, but in this precarious situation they find me here and something is better than nothing. They close with the African/American spiritual and sing "All thing are possible…" and they are with me here. All I can say is thank you. In death, they say there is light down the end of a tunnel and they are exactly that. The reverend responds that they enjoyed us too, and that is more than a gift!

Thirteen: "Freedom at the Dermatology Office"

Three moles are removed from my back, (representing three points in time) and one mole I will be so vain as to diagnose as the North Star from my belly. With this manifestation, I think the Milky Way Galaxy and the Andromeda Galaxy, will someday join as one. The three moles on my back represents the trinity to me. On the other hand, the mole on my belly is just a reminder that even after death, there is more to the picture, if you will allow me this?

Fourteen: "Stomach"

The stomach is a muscle which may ponder Joseph. There may be an entity which is Satan deep in the ocean; it is okay as the sun will rise again.

Like a mint is to a devil, the stomach is the most dangerous vice of the human body's form. Eventually, it will consume you through the belly button that once attached you to your mother. All you can do is hope this will lead to a better place? A prayer is the best way to join you with your soul after you die. With this prayer you may let go as well. The children find this all very funny, and Santa Clause may now be way too far gone, anyway.

Fifteen: "Right Hand: Five Gay Indians"

It does not matter who you are? The significance is that you were once here. I may shake hands with a Beefeater near Buckingham Palace and exchange stories of the Queen as though who do you think I am? The witch to God lives nearby and the cooks prepare venison, while I am a vegetarian, sorry. The Germans in World War Two thought they could create a god in their own image. (They came close yet are so far away; nice try and they will be at the mercy of others too.) The heart of another joins with a southern boy and they cook jambalaya instead. The runners from Germany (as there are three) prove that there is a God, anyway. Rather, he made us in his image, I think.

Sixteen: "The Left Hand is Death" (not to be touched)

There is a curse bestowed on his left knee and similarly it forbids that his left hand be touched. A bald eagle may not penetrate the sky. I am less than death and will not penetrate its realm either.

Seventeen: "Nipples of a man..." (two Chinese Witches)

The nipples of a man do not usually provide nourishment, and are rather a display of fortitude instead. A serpent floats above his head and, to this end, provides some protection. In my cases, they are sisters and leave me blind in some ways. But, in darkness, there is light as well? The Chinese Witches are like pigeons pecking on the head of Indian women, and are the eyes of which God does not see either? The abortion of a child is a phenomenon that may not solve a problem in the end?

Eighteen: "Heart #3 joined with heart #5"

Somehow the devil seems superfluous and futile to the cause of Kurt Cobain's death which may join with another in the end? The devil is a square that may not escape a fire that consumes a way of life, and this is not it. When Jesus and God join hands, the devil is propelled outward and may not enter here. God seems a bit vulnerable and may go through a cycle and never go in either. My heart is not the heart of God's creation, but I try to envision heaven even still? A southern boy may live on and runs a bike shop in a distant place as far as Portland, Oregon, but it is a choice too? God would not force a future even to a fool who would deny it?

Nineteen: "The Calla Lily Incident (the flower picked inverted from mushroom)"

Nature repeats itself and such is the case of one beautiful calla lily. I think it is not their fault, and they settle for the lesser crime of suicide in hindsight and are not blamed as such either. The real estate in Africa may be worth more and otherwise the Jews are a calculated mistake where a woman loves a boy who is not God and denies the holocaust as well. For this reason, sharks and dolphins do not mix, and such a scenario is cursed as to assume anything other? Indians were born from the picking of mushrooms and die later at the hands of Stalin, to free the accomplice in a crime which is not theirs anyway. Mimi forgives the one who would assume otherwise, and may be in her own element, and weaves silk in a sweat shop in China. She does not curse anyone in the process, I think. She represents a dimension where I live as well, but we are more friends than lovers. My eyelashes are the fans that dry her tears. There is nature too; butterflies float, birds sing, and while ants toil with other matters too. She leaves behind Vera, from South Africa and she is my right big toe.

Twenty: "In the beginning..."

Three blue devils worked on the sky. Two of the blue devils were infected by the sun, and became my eyes, and the one that remained pure became God's eyes and he sees through us. There may be at least three ways to see. Hazel blankets the sky and may see rain falling in the guise of the past.

Renata's eyes see only blue skies. Meanwhile, I may see both cruelty and generosity as the sun of the past may be both. The sun may be awake or asleep too, though I am not Renata and prefer to invade a space of a horse named Empty Blue. Mimi occasionally finds inspiration in her pursuit and we may be an alternative point of reference. Creation to God may be not what there is, but what there is not, and this falls under the category of darkness to the average Joe. I do not think it is impossible that he creates from this point of view and you may dream a better dream, and this is God?

Twenty-One: "Mike's Tongue"

I am an accomplice to a crime as to be diagnosed as innocent in the end. Mike is a lizard and sleeps under a Kleenex under a sort of a gondola, which protects him from the sun. There are nearby yellow flowers and tiny cactus too. There is a (Blue Eagle Summit) car of which I am a denizen. It rests in the parking lot of the motel in Malibu. The flower invites me closer and so close, and my tongue reaches farther, like a bee sucking nectar from within too, and all in one motion. Meanwhile, Mike is drinking an orange Fanta which is easier to obtain than the other.

Twenty-two: "Simon Says..."

I know Simon is real as we will meet twice. The first time, I stare through a bullet-proof partition at the taxi garage's dispatcher's desk. At such a time I see the contours of his face in void of a circle where the center lies. Thereafter, a whale says farewell and he drives a fancy Mercedes-Benz and with the splash of his tailfin. I do not think we will meet again. I drove one of his yellow cabs and waved farewell from the light at Sixth Avenue near Bleeker Street. I thought Lena (Simon's wife) and Paulena (Simon's sister) were equal in looks. I recommend you do not get lost in the mirage which is the Pacific Ocean. I sit in one motion on the couch of Dr. Emory's office, and fear you will do the same?

Twenty-three: *"Ferocious has nine lives..." but not really?*

I demand three things before setting him free. It may seem unusual that a dog like a cat has nine lives, but in our parting we still remain one. I am not ashamed that he is the eyes from which is *"Southpark,"* but he sees from within like the ocean that the waves crash, and then drain back into its infrastructure. He will earn his right to be free eventually. I told him to address the nine steps that lead to the reality he inherits. I also told him to understand how the wind blows. Also, I told him to recognize how even an atomic explosion does not alter the human spirit, and therefore with this acknowledgement, he must smile. He is not loss forever, I think.

Twenty-four: *"Ilius and my afro..."*

The negative of the apple picked is an afro which is the exact opposite of my hair. The photograph's negative exonerates those of this dark land of crimes, connecting to the apple picked for someone else entirely. This makes my experience in vain if not for one picture of God a long time ago. I trade it for a picture of a cheetah, and the exchange is made so that gold becomes obsolete too.

Twenty-five: *"Obama (I got your back)"*

Obama's father is a reminder to me that I do exist. I am here for a while then will leave too. If the past has no future, then what is the present? We are playing basketball and I say, "I got your back..." This only happens in America.

Twenty-six: *"Mick's Lips"*

I will not claim a right to the lips of a star and ponder a girl who wears the Rolling Stones logo on her T-shirt. She is attractive and may have been kissing him instead.

Twenty-seven: *"God's teeth and the ghosts of Stonehenge"*

It is not ivory or ebony, but Stonehenge is a sentiment which represents his teeth. There is an altar where virgins are sacrificed to convey what is a gazelle to a lion. The gods forsake beauty in this time, and the crimes of old, wrinkled witches become the law in places too far to reach, and too innocent to accuse anyone of any crime. Christianity will come later. The ghosts are haunting such sites and will be judged later. Otherwise, the Catholic Church forbids anyone from entering the circle. Vietnam will take many more lives, so the sacrifice becomes too great and religion is now obsolete.

Twenty-eight: *"Nobody's Nose"*

My dog had a nose of which I do not. I smell the pine wood panels in a house where termites smell mildew of curtains of green prints of palm trees. The bear smells the forest who claims a right to the river? It is not mine to claim, like The Who playing at Royal Albert Hall, when snorting coke backstage, it is nobody's business too.

Twenty-nine: *"The music never stops..."*

One ear hears only Jimi Hendrix (the left) and the other ear hears only Led Zeppelin (the right) and in the middle it sounds just like noise. The drum may sound so the sound has a soul as well without being menaced by subliminal messages that mean nothing anyway. Here, hip hop has a soul which is rap.

Thirty: *"The bones remain for those who seek..."*

I did not seek knowledge from the outside, but gained a silly disposition of what is on the inside as well. There may be three lesbians in time who diagnose that I was here for a while. I am a ghost and my bones remain for those who seek more.

Thirty-one: "Kidneys: An alcoholic named Fred..."

For those who seek the ocean, the bar is open for a while and the fish say cheers to an alcoholic named Fred as it is my kidneys too. An octopus is Will's mom who transcends the realm of a deep ocean, dark and murky. A young man on board the *Titanic* drank the ocean and drowned in it. He now lives there most sentimentally. I name my kidneys for someone who exists somewhere else. There is only one picture of him as he raises a glass with top hat on in the introduction to *Cheers*, the TV sitcom. A desert in the ocean does exist too, but is hidden from view here while an octopus will not release her tentacles from him as she thinks it is her son.

Thirty-two: "Hugh Heffner: chin"

Pink bunnies play volleyball on the lawn of the Playboy Mansion and, on the outside, there is plenty of brandy here as well. He lives an unusual life and his chin is his best attribute through the piercing spoils of a syringe, and pierces my chin as well. Outside of H and H Bagels a boy tries to crash the party, but the heroin provides only dreams in what otherwise is a nightmare. It pierces my chin for all of the women for whom I will bleed. I do not know his name, but think he may dream a better dream if he wants to? He sits in a dilapidated building on the Lower East Side and flips through the September issue instead.

Dark Star in Nine Parts
who are you? Four: Devil
(Will Blunt)

...the red planet is not his; however,
"too far" is forgivable for those that stand
On ground that is flat like his. No animals
To speak of, but amongst the sevens where dolphins
Play, it may only be redeemed with fire!

Part Four: The Illiterate Symposium

Prelude: "Satan's End"

A boy stands naked, alone in a field. A picture taken of his excrement that would lead him down a dark wonted path. He is a slave to the notion that Satan relogated would exist further. Who blinked first is the question at hand as God is busy at the time tending to the animals. And, in the shaded fortitude of his loins, she accesses the damage of the apple besieged from a branch, maybe a metaphor at best for her entire existence? A Mona Lisa smile eclipsed the scene in a grimace that hid in Eve's long flowing hair. But, before the fashion of the day had ended, someone would have at least one alibi, maybe two? A ghostly leaf is saved by the lizard that blinked in the time it takes for Eve to seek a covert game where she forbids her shady association to a coif piece of land.

Meanwhile, Adam holds the apple for her, a relict, and the photo adhered by the blink of a lizard's eye would reconcile and reconfigure the scene to that of one cat's black tail? And the participants left the crime scene so that God would not bond them in a riddance for those who are foreshadowed and know the outcome anyway?

A child holds a disposable Kodak camera, facing her to snap a shot of her smile with teeth out of place, like in the time it takes for God to slap a mosquito from his neck? Out of time, he is insanely jealous of the froth that builds in the mouth of a lizard close by, and someone heard someone laugh? Before light, there may have been darkness? But, for the photo set, a new entourage was formed out of chaos as Adam and Eve were long gone down a path not to return any time soon?

In time, Einstein drew a square that vainly reify a picture of himself, but for time, she was gone and a square remained for all?

"Revenge" Satan's End continued:

For the sake that Mike, formerly Michael, should judge me, it seems, at first, like an oxymoron? But the way the sun still shines despite global warming may be a reiki contingent for that anything is possible? His smile is the least attribute of his personality to which I make a sacrament to my spiritual mother, Mimi. But, he moves in a space long gone like the waves that crash from the ocean into the rocks in Malibu. Yet, he still has an androgynous quality that is attractive. It is not in time, I think, like the kids who play with his rocks in a brook somewhere inland; they should know better? Mike never woke up from his dream of dinosaurs and, therefore, is obsolete like the sun to this veranda nestled at a resort somewhere obscure like Mexico. He is not a participant and may play in the shade from the sun and not worry of a vindictive God despite the fact that kids still play with his rocks and time passes over like clouds with no imposition to him? Though there may be a parallel universe, for Mike there is only one God and for him, that is enough that dandelions grow by the freeway where he perches by spiny cactus? It is an imposition that is not good or bad? Time does pass, but Mike would not know it. God just does not consider him a refuge to the future? It may be a relief to Mike as he was not playing anyway! He is slightly bothered by the fly in his pina colada, as he waits for the bartender to bring him his bill.

The first fashion statement may have been Adam gleaming at white doves in sunlight before the fall? He stood naked, by an apple tree, alone. However, it was not he who saw Eve's smile first and the branch became a two-door coupe where they could hide and something bad happened that night, despite one proponent's jealousy? Someone lost her virginity that night through a vestibule of two lovers and she would never have to be alone thereafter? If it was a crime at all, more like an emotion. Otherwise, the serpent released herself from the tree, she slithered and the "primal sin" she claimed and adored was not hers?

Really, and this manifested itself like flies around a dead carcass of a rotting cow? She had the time to realize she had not tasted blood and this would become her fortress of solitude forever and ever? Jealousy became her vice, which most would consider a luxury? She had the money to travel and spend her time as she pleased? But, exiting the stage were Adam and Eve, and she felt a strange coolness as they passed? She may have had a bizarre fixation with the callus forming out of blisters on the two lover's feet, walking the path that others might feel at a loss? But, the exterior posterity grew and she was not even aware as the love match transgressed apart like the wearing of her leather bag in time, shopping at posh boutiques outside of Washington, D.C.? The fire was burning outside and she did not know how she started it or even how to put it out?

"Will" (keeper of the flame) Satan's End Continued:

Gorillas swim in the deepest parts of the ocean floor. He is not hiding there, but rather exists there, like on land. Meanwhile, the currents have a way of wearing down a female tiger shark named Lily who transformed from her home prior in a garden where she tempted a worker to pick a flower, (not hers) in a place jaded with past remembrances of purity, a white calla lily that she guarded while alone?

But, slightly curious as she remained a virgin in times when sinners flaunted their flock and followed Mt. Fuji into the ocean? She was the counterpart to lesser sins in the primal order. It may be a metaphor for Adam and Eve except she is alone and the foul waste of fish heads trapped in a red tide laced with bits of jellyfish is much worse than jargons of little boy's pablulum disguised in dandelions picked to express affection to a little girl and that which accumulates in the tides of what is today Japan?

It is the only door open to edible seagull waste on beaches "so far away" separated again and again in the lyrics of David Bowie. Lily was the girl who took a picture of herself with a disposable Kodak camera in the security of Einstein's drawing of a square which is now New York City?Should you cross the devil's path between the moon and New York City, you will become part of the play that I refer to as Adam and Eve Hotel Theater Productions. Crimes against the sun are foretold here like the Gay Quarter Show which is Mike's brother Simon. This exonerates me from responsibility as I am in God's light. Mike represents the thirteenth sun and the ocean will divide further and will not cause harm on other. Rocky Raccoon will lead me into the light and I see the sun of yesterday like that. I am the dark star that inherits the deficiencies the sun possesses.

And, as Lily's tear does not separate from where she is a denizen, and consequently becomes a magnet for the moon to penetrate her fortress in the ocean? As the song goes, she does not live with any of the graces most take for granted in New York City, and the moon befalls her lover in the distance?

Rather, Mt Fuji said she looked like an old corn husk with teeth out of place that detached from her jaws over time with the ocean's relentless currents? Mt. Fuji was the gardener and he led his flock from the ocean sometime after, as they fear the sun? And after the lizard blinked, it spread from cries of the whale and dolphins that it was now safe to return to the land? The brethren of one special gorilla live with orange-colored rotting eyes on land and the mulch forming with the addition of defecated waste saves suns from far away that die and are reborn in this form?

However, one gorilla had a love affair with a bear and left out of disgust with the imposition deep away in black waters that crash into rocks nestled on Malibu beaches? This is one of the few places in which one may hear the heart of the ocean beat which detests that God is not only strong, but also vulnerable?

Meanwhile, twenty-four Indians form a circle in the remotest parts of the rainforest and start a fire there that they cannot put out? The ritual was formed after their loss of an Indian princess who will never return home, and she is now reincarnated as a tiger shark in the ocean? Her half-sister wears a thick layer of mascara as she sits in a park along the Harlem River Drive where she stares into the East River drinking a rootbeer with a straw? When an Inca king was killed in an inquisition, Lily forsook his passing with love for another boy and was punished to remain in the ocean forevermore, a crime which she denies? It is a world where man is parched with only reflections of himself and does not claim the graces that God offers? Meanwhile, the trinity for woman is represented by a cow, a green garden snake, and a spider. Mt. Fuji will pick someone else's flower. She may be my spiritual mother too. She does not claim the green garden snake as her daughter though. Lily will remain in the ocean as a female tiger shark. Satan remains there as well, but finds their relationship to be a punishment.

To avoid a similar fate, Eve dines at Chez William and the meals are prepared without regard to appetite, but rather creationism? First, she mangles a chicken bone with her teeth and miraculously the meat forms on its contours when a waiter takes it away? She can eat and eat and never finishes what she starts. All of time bites at her mouth and she never knows what it is that she eats? But, eventually, she is full and Will or William blows out the candles on the tables of the bistro and leaves the dirty plates in the sink to be cleaned oddly the next morning? You see, Will does not believe in Darwin's evolution, but does every task for the reason that manifests itself the next day in his kitchen? He calls this "food." William serves Eve "food" and she never asks what it is, which children should never do as he says this is rude? The "creationism" menu defies titles and such which harnesses the circle forming in the rainforest and the restaurant closes at midnight and it is routinely done so like clockwork, (every day of the week)!

In the taxi cab ring of fire, there is waste in which they burn? Ten thousand maniacs, turning and weaving the streets that subsist on a greener form of currency and tells a story in its mist? Raspberry ice cream is Will's favorite, I think, and factories never close, weaving the clothes we wear? If we were not so fortunate, no, really I think fashion is a blessing, yet some deny it? One might ask how a machine may put together a shirt so quickly? His wife watches as he methodically puts on his hemp suit in the morning before going to work? I think Will would rather wear no clothes at all and he calls this fashion?

Satan's End Continued: "The Fire Burns on the Beaches of Nantucket" and (Half-Moon with Red Tide)

Before Lily, there was a red-headed woodpecker named Will, whose fire burns within the guise of time and within him, and transgresses in a linear form in this anecdote. His rage is kept by the ingestion of a seagull's poop in Nantucket and though compatible to God's contorted thunder, his rage is still less understood? Darwin claims that man formed from a mutation from primitive versions of our nearest ancestors our DNA in chimpanzees? Will denies this transgression. Gorillas nestle in misty habitats in the African rainforest and though they are animals, they live a peaceful existence for the most part? This proves that when a sun afar dies, it is given a grace to exist thereafter in this form? Somehow, a gorilla that subsisted here was not technically considered an animal, and retreated to the ocean floor? Similarly to this faux pas that encircles God in the ocean, Hitler did not commit suicide, but rather was cosmically killed in respect to this book?

People ask if it is possible that Jesus married Mary Magdalene and had children? I think this is a myth? But, in hindsight, "the Brats of Doom" do subsist. When the continents divided, the fornication of divinity and a bear may have symbolically formed that which is family, but was not Christ's brethren really? It was God whose lightning claimed blood of another and this may have been part of the greater plan of his legacy? Someone saw, in the beginning, before Adam and Eve, an episode between this gorilla and a bear? But who dare accuse anyone of rape? This would be foolish? Yet, "the brats of doom" may be his and spoiled by the bear in which became isolated in a foreign land, never to return to the site in Africa? Still, God in the form of a gorilla, retreated to the ocean to reflect? Is this a lie?

Are dreams real? There are a handful of brats that remain and are the result of a tirade that separates the rainbow in a malaise that hides their existence? Nathan and Alexander are brats. However, first the story of "Half Moon with Red Tide." Man may not penetrate the fortress of that which is God? The mirage of Satan does appear and gives spectators a sensibility that there is something beyond the rainbow? Deep in the rainforest, they burn their remains and nothing is left of the spectacle except ash? Similarly, the "Brats of Doom" sit around in a circle, staring into the fire, which may be a mirage too? Some comfort is kept here, but they do not know what it is really? In the end, there is Simon. But, first, there is Will, and he does not know the passive aggression that whales possess in the ocean that sweeps up on the beaches of Nantucket, safety at hand?

Where the "Brats of Doom" subsist and children play, there are no adults and Satan remains as a guardian as there is no other who may be around at such times? He has a leather bag that he bought in his native land in Africa, and walks on the boardwalk of Venice Beach, but may be seen and appear almost anywhere? Will's rage is beyond Satan and this is his story.

When the seas parted for Moses it may have been a metaphor for the division of heaven and hell, long ago? It may have been a parting for sinners and saints as well? Yet, this is still undetermined until Jesus returns to judge the living and the dead? There is proof of the tenuous matters that Christ's rage is one with God, but not for ever more? The students at the Mayfair swallow goldfish that share a bloodline of that which is food to God, and he keeps in touch while I was away at boarding school? Sometimes the order of things is in reverse?

When Simon blew water from his spout as a whale and the dolphins spread this message as a sign for Mt. Fuji and entourage to return to land, a small pool of fresh water maintained the remains of Will in the form of a goldfish which his heat intensity is greater than the hate in the gorilla's orange eyes? But, first there is a red-headed woodpecker. He consumes his own seed which is a redwood tree in Northern California?

The Indians of North and South America were at a loss, and the cumulative result is the death of many men at the hands of Stalin? One may argue this may have been a metaphor for the rape of his daughter or it may have been a metaphor for the rape of his motherland Russia? Simon witnessed the killing of the czar and his family and Will now calls the pond his home among the goldfish where he may be the negative space and his rage implores young school students to swallow them at the springtime fair? His brethren are trapped in a still life of a woodpecker falling from grace? Someday, the children of America who seek the trip, will be at the mercy of Simon, a whale and twenty-four elephants who may lead the children who seek it to find amnesty in Africa?

As the tides swallow the shores of the beaches around the world, the arc, in a sense, will arrive in a smaller, but more buff Africa, which they will adopt as their home? Meanwhile, Satan still walks outside of his homeland of Africa and might never return? There is a parade that Simon, on a float decorated like a giant whale, harnesses the power of twenty-four elephants and prepares for a journey someday in the future. The kids sitting around a campfire on the beach of Nantucket are a metaphor for edible seagull crap and the burning of God's waste as Satan, an effigy deep in the rainforests of Brazil?

Satan walks down the boardwalk in L.A. He carries with him a diet pepsi and a twenty-four-carat gold pen and a bag in which he carries his cassette player. There is also a random selection of tapes such as Cat Stevens's *Tea for the Tillerman* and Simon and Garfunkel's *Greatest Hits*? He likes watching air shows, but rarely leaves Venice Beach which he calls home? Also, he wears a black suit with red pinstripes. He wonders why the Indians in the rainforest burn their remains? He may appear almost anywhere as a sort of mirage except for his homeland in Africa in which, like Adam and Eve and the Garden of Eden, he is vanquished? The "brats of doom" remain out of this scope as well.

Satan's End

Satan's End is four plus four equals eight, just in reverse four minus four equals zero. Like the lamb who takes away the sins of the world, devils disappear in the playground, leaving ground zero where Satan is no more and morning dew dries in the midday heat on the dandelions that remain? Here, the musk in the referee's cologne repels flies as kids play at a little league baseball game. Something awful smelling remains ten yards from a small spring and confers that something once was here. I suppose I felt sorry for him in some way as he was an angel, I am told?

But, who knew the night could be so cruel? Before I could compose such a mathematical equation, it was time to feed God and he is our baby. Still, I would not go so far to patronize he who gives so much. I suppose the game ended with one more pack of Marlboro Lights 100s and I left the light on in case someone else might venture to his doorstep one dreary night? I don't think he really cares that you are proud of your sins, but rather if you wait just a second before falling into such a notion, you might find that everything happens for a reason?

However, some do not get that far. I suppose I have come to the conclusion that God is rather vindictive toward those who show disloyalty? As you should know, in life, it is not for "you", per se, but somewhere in the outreaches of your imagination, it is just for God and that is all. If you should not come to such a conclusion, life might get the better half of you? I guess worse than what convoluted messages your friends impose about life after death is just not there and I guess this makes one's life completely in vain, which is not something you could put on your resume?

I do not mean to say I would stand in judgment of you? But, I know that there is a certain loneliness that comes with the revelation that the mathematical equation diagnosing your life as nil, should sting only once and I suppose that is where those who "do not", go to, so to speak?

Four and four is eight and divided perfectly by "two" (representing death) or by subtracting four from four is zero, the same as life in death. Satan remains in the ocean for whatever reason. I know Jesus teaches that in life, there are ways of making a difference, which is true. However, at this time, I come to the revelation that Satan was just a dream and I have not been born yet! But, I am still here and oddly hailing a cab in the rain at such a time. I know better than you how an angel may be damned as there are those who do good too and for them rain is not some sort of excuse for waking up late on a Saturday morning?

There is here an unbearable attraction that will repel any notions you had previously about hell? A game might be sort of going too far, as you should fight silly mocks of divinity and God is a serious matter? However, the devil speaks in a double tongue too? The assumption is that "I" is a word and that the inconceivable notion that one may be "anything" in relation to God? However, don't worry too much as even the damned find this is a place where you may meet the intangible upside down like a rag in a janitor's closet.

Now is the time to come to terms with the nature of your sin and comply with whatever it is that could ever be eating at your time? The lesson learned here is twofold, later, like two quarters dangling in his pocket and do not reach for it as it is really not yours? And the dollar that blows out of the vendor's hand in Times Square as you reach for the New York Times is still out there blowing somewhere in the wind? And the anger I felt, let it be a lesson to you of what might dry the tear you thought you might render and feel good for a while, "it only happens one time a year!" The mole on the face of the Chinese woman turns out to be a good thing... Still, act as though you are loved, as you are!

Two Short Poems Written Just Prior to the Death of Bin Laden

"Money Unlimited"

It is a farce to think money is unlimited.
Let's learn from the poor and subsist in an altered state.
The tire is burned in the park,
Providing carbon emissions, "no!"
Live, breathe, subsist, and be poor in spirit in the end.

"Emergency State"

The president may make an order to provide only essentials for ten years yes!
The trains provide the grains and kids grow cannabis in the park.
Maybe school may be taught at home too?
An emergency state is our future and the Chinese will respect us then.

Written on 5/2/11 12:12 in the morning

To those who condemned Osama Bin Laden with his death, we are entering a dangerous world. To those who genuinely mourn our loss on 9/11, the death of him may be solace for a wrong that we share. However, those who randomly detest the act with hate, free the murderer with something that obscurely justifies the act in the past, and this is not going to make America safer in the future. I do not believe to kill anyone for whatever reason. His death represents the freeing of the disease that people like Bin Laden are ailing from. Others not yet falling in line with his agenda will find this act might fuel the fire? I pray for closure. I fear there are others who will follow a path that is detested by many, but we are not completely innocent any more either.

How many deaths will it take before we are absolved from this matter? The spirit of Bin Laden in his death is now free so that others may follow such a path, and we will be judged by God as well. Is hate the answer? Though I do not consider killing is the right decision no matter what, 9/11 conjures up in my soul so that I consider the killing of Osama Bin Laden may only be considered self-defense. I am sorry I was unable to prevent his acts, sorry! This negates my later defense of what I consider as unavoidable. The pain caused by his acts is unforgiveable. Bad things happen sometimes. We may now move forward and my conscience is resolved to the point that I really don't know how this happened? It is scary to think that there are others who would do this.

The death of Bin Laden makes the world a very dangerous place as a result. Should we kill many thousands of innocent Iraqis for Bush's mission for a false presumption that they had weapons of mass destruction? All I can say is that he is human, but wrong. No matter how much pain the families who lost ones in 9/11 are caused, we live in a very dangerous time. There will be others. I wish we could put this behind us and in some way believe as our innocence was once was, and believe that most of us are good again?

Fighting is not the answer; this is the way! We are a brave people. My mom must have known something about human nature before the occurrence and, though I still believe that things happen for a reason, you may find it sobering that I am now more aware and I will try not to forget the sacrifice and loss still, forever! I thought I could prevent something like this from happening, I guess I was wrong. At least it is over; I may say that in deep remorse. The urns are now gone…

The children have their two cents, and M and M's

I leave behind the children in trust, a horse, but more than that, a child inherits their two cents and M and M's will go far too. God really does not care and though small, something is better than nothing. Signed in verbatim Siaom L.B.C. Strawberry. Yes, I think…

"Jesus" Spelled Backward

The bitter snake deplores that Christ died on a cross for our sins. It is not whether this happened or not; rather a selfless act seems to merit faith and is what God intended. Somehow the serpent sheds its skin and would rather not believe. In this exchange, it may be before the fall and after the rapture and she might represent a sacrifice which frees her from the spell. The question I pose rather is that Christians and Jews join hands and religion will then be obsolete? A girl fidgets with a Gameboy at church while black seems the fashion of the day at a synagogue where a girl in the back ignores what is said and eats gummy bears in the wake of the rabbi's quest.

Little does either girl know that they hold the keys to a quagmire that should they hold hands, they would free the conquest from what God considers his mission. But, neither seems to notice. I will forgive you for assuming the word of God moot. On the one hand, the girl at church would rather assume that she is right and in the wake, the Jews are left behind to promote the cause for free? Meanwhile, a Jewish girl thinks it is a farce as Jesus is a Jew and therefore renders her right as though God's people are the Jews too. Does he not invite others to his dinner table? Both may be wrong too.

The Jew and Christian represent universes and the wormhole that connects them collides out there in space. Jews may not believe at such times and Christians must pay the bills too. Assuming God is a Jew is presumptive and Jesus died on the cross for Jews as well. In time, the two entities will collide. The Jewish girl thinks to outwit the other by the rapture of God that she claims like the death of some unknown entity and the evidence is killed accordingly. The Christian girl would rather not care. God's words are immense and so are the two girls' egos.

After the fact, the Jewish girl believes and other invites notions that she may represent God really and the sin resounds as she is not God in this scenario. The dissent allows for one girl to claim Jesus too late and the other is so bold to judge the other as though God merits such a preponderance. They are both losers in the end.

Though I am not a Jew, I will not deny a Jew's right to be a Christian as well. If I stand in judgment of other, I must plead insanity and the two entities should unite as one. I still believe in something anyway. The Jewish girl is bitter and the Christian girl arrogant, and God says to both to leave through the door in the back. I do not know if there is any redemption merited in their future either? The serpent will escape their fate and ignores their plight while reading a book in the shade of a tree where such silly contests merit no significance in the lightness of day or the darkness of night. The tortoise and hare race to the finish line while her skin is shed to separate them further still.

God does not care who the winner is, as both are not invited to a contest that divides them in an air so vehemently.

The door is closed behind them as they go backward in time. This may not redeem them in the end either! My grandfather's gold watch remains for those who believe. The two girls are no longer rendered the time and must acquiesce the past and future where there is no time relayed in the present. The future is as much a curse to one as the past may be to the other. It may be too late as Rodney King pleads for us all to get along. The future may relay as hell and the past does not shed the time of day. I am inclined to believe and do not claim to be a Jew really. My mom still ignores the contest and would rather read a book in the shade of a tree somewhere far away, and this may be heaven too. I retrieve my gold watch from the repair shop. Meanwhile, Manhattan is for sale at such times and God does not seem to care. A mouse is caught in a trap in exchange for a slight remnant of cheese and there is no winner either. The mouse may represent my father in hindsight. Meanwhile, the devil is now separate in time and Israel no longer pays for his existence which involves no money in the end. Africa will accept his existence as there own too. Satan remains in the ocean and this is like a blessing to the parties at hand. Bad witches embark on a journey to free the world of sin. The devil, meanwhile, is a living manifestation of a sin that is not redeemed.

The Illiterate Symposium continued: "Sex"

One: A Ride with a Truck Driver

The sky is raining cats and dogs, and the truck driver pulls up to the bus stop. Here in Chicago, a young girl is hitchhiking and hops into the vehicle.

"How much do you charge lady?" he asks.

She falters a smile and says, "Where are you heading?"

They do not have a mutual discussion, but rather stare at each other not knowing where this will go. Heidi gets into the truck in the middle of the night, but does not know where she is going. Though, she does have a friend just down the road. She puts a mint in her mouth and he thinks this is a form of flirtation.

"I am not a sex demon, really, I was just wondering, how much do you charge?"

"Oh, for that, right, I suppose I would charge a hundred dollars, but don't really know as I do not do that sort of thing."

"That's good, as I have a daughter that sells herself to the night; imagine that, I saw her on the boulevard, hitchhiking, and you know what that means!"

"Well, how old is she?"

"Oh, Lindsey is sixteen almost seventeen. That is my baby. By the way, my name is Frank Lloyd."

"Lindsey Lloyd? She was in school with me at Havershire, two grades below me. She was a real sweetheart."

He reaches out and touches Heidi's hair and presses his fingers through her hair as gently as a mouse. He was not a creep; he felt it like a father would.

"Why do you pick up girls like me?" she asks.

Frank replies that he is curious.

"Does this mean that you sleep with hookers that you pick up?" she asks.

"No, I am not the type, but I wish I could change my daughter; her mom, my ex-wife does that sort of thing too."

Heidi speaks, "I just never thought to charge for it."

"That's good," he expresses further, "good girls are like that."

"It is funny. It did not bother me when you were stroking my hair."

"I do not think I could do that sort of thing with a girl as young as you anyway. There is a truck stop over there. How about some breakfast?" he asks.

She feels sort of insulted and wonders what might be wrong with her. *Don't you like me?* she thinks. She likes older men and does not reveal this secret to her new acquaintance.

"Why do women go off and sell their bodies to complete strangers?" he says out of the blue.

Heidi looks away, not to show she is blushing. She replies resolutely, "The devil likes it that way."

"I just do not understand how someone could be such a pervert and pay my own daughter for this sort of filth?"

Heidi nods as though she does not have a reply. "Money goes a far way even for sex," she adds, and is careful not to word it as though she favors sex even though she does.

"I work hard to put food on the table, still she will not abide by me, my little girl?" He begins to cry.

"Anyway, girls do not always think about sex as a big deal."

Frank, as though shocked, shouts, "What, how can you say that?"

She makes a leap for the door at the red light and, as she walks away in the rain, her mascara runs on her face and she thinks nothing of the conversation she has just had. She reaches out her thumb and hops in another truck and has sex with someone that night without any regard to what she would consider ethical.

Two: Ping and Pong

Chinese girl one speaks on the phone with Chinese girl two. One speaks to two and two speaks to one. Neither knows I am listening to their conversation? They are gay, but I would not go so far as to say they are lesbians as physical sex seems natural in their culture as much as between a man and a woman as two women. They find each other attractive, but never go so far as to say they prefer one sex to another. In other words, they are curious about each other and admit their attraction, but do not make it a way of life. Though we do not make the distinction between being gay and being a lesbian in our culture, I hope I may interpret them differently in a way that makes sense? How does one talk sex in Chinese?

There may be little known about China as opposed to other places on the globe, because how we access sex in different places is assumed to be the same. It may be that in China, where we know the population exceeds a billion persons, is due to some sexual mutation in respect to the social dynamic the people transcend. Not that the people are more promiscuous than others, but the fuel used to produce offspring may be more efficient. Therefore, like playing table tennis at a higher pace than other places, they procreate at a faster rate as well. I think these people maintain an abject disparity that resonates as an inferiority complex toward the moon, which increases production. They are not making sex a way of life, but are absorbed by rather a dislike of it, which propels it further.

*

Girl one: "My mother thinks I need to find a boyfriend, that I am so beautiful?"

Girl two: "You are so beautiful, I am surprised at you not wanting to get with that black guy?"

Girl one: "Why don't you go with him? I do not like blacks or whites; I want to find someone from Taiwan."

Girl two: "I don't like Jamal either, but why someone from Taiwan?"

123

Girl one: "I think they are the same, but different; I don't believe in crossing racial lines, but just someone different, you know?"

Girl two: "You are beautiful, I am ugly."

Girl one: "No, you are beautiful, I am ugly!"

Girl two: "What does your dad say?"

Girl one: "Both parents want me to get a boyfriend; they say my grandmother wants to live to see a great grandchild."

Girl two: "That's so weird, my parents are the same way."

Three: Black Labrador

(The dog has a problem with sex.) When the family, living in Cape Town, is away at the beach; Nelly, the live-in maid and Walter, the gardener, go at it on the bed of Mr. and Mrs. Johnson, who are not aware of the relationship. The dog cringes when they close the door to the master bedroom and they have only three hours, at the least, to conspire in heavy sounds of passion in the privacy of someone else's home. This is South Africa, "Hey," what do you expect and these white people need not know what is not their business? When a man and a woman have to go to such extremes to hide natural intercourse from that which is the dog's masters, there is some injustice at hand.

The sound of hot sex is penetrating and would seem too raw for their white counterparts then to go further and place the dog in the garage to hide such a rendezvous must be some sort of crime here. It is not certain if the dog gets excited? But it makes a noise that sounds like a "jungle fever," pitch when the sex is added. Does one have to take a precaution to be alone, as Walter lives in a sort of shack in which ten family members reside? Being their own country, that which is white and black, such circumstances justify the covert situation. It is angry sex; the kind that defames their professionalism. Making them hide just evokes a mystery of the people in general. It is not being embarrassed by sex, but rather a zero tolerance attitude that even a dog should participate is natural intercourse? Sometimes space is limited, even in your own country, but something about a black Labrador watching seems a shame.

Four: India Libido

In India, there is a differentiation between the male and female sex that is so severe that it is assumed that woman is naturally evil. A man, and in this situation, a weatherman, feels there is no escape from her nuances. There is a toleration that demands that every aspect of life must be translated to relate to woman in some way.

In the studio of a news broadcaster it is a Western thing that women should be hired in the work place, which to the Indian male is discriminately a bad idea which he resents.

The studio manager is a female in this case and she denotes that he is on the air and he calls for rain and "hot sweltering heat," and the woman just laughs. (Not that she should read the forecast as any different than any other woman.) Still, he wonders what the two women are discussing "business as usual," in the corners of the studio? The manager, a woman, goes up to the weatherman and exclaims that "hot," should be pronounced as to expel it in a more sensual way. "Just say it differently," she adds to finalize what is hardly a conversation. The other assistant says she thinks "hot," should be said sort of sultry like the way Latinos sensate the sound of the word, "Just isolate the word in mid-sentence," she envisions as it would sound better.

Though he really does not know what she is saying? Actually, it is determined that more women are at home during the newscast and, therefore, business has changed drastically in only a few years? Even the wardrobe person likes more soft color ties such as magenta, light green, or at the least, beige. The country is changing drastically and it is not certain who is in charge? It does not matter if Satan resolves this mess in the form of a woman or a man, but most men think the other. Part of the blame may be attributed to super stars such as Tom Cruise and Leonardo DiCaprio, who are plastered on videos from the West and women respond in the bedroom for men to act differently in the way that they make love. There is an earthquake in India; men on one side and women on the other and the snake's skin is left behind only to separate them more?

Five: Black Girl

A black girl is selling candy at the bus station in some seedy place in Brazil. This may only be characterized as like the ocean. Without a father to guide her, she has an enclave of other family members who work as a team to solicit money from their base. Her mother fries plantain in a shack next to the station, as well. A black girl does not seek sex and her animosity to the disgrace it may entail makes her even more aggressive in her sales strategy. When an unsuspecting tourist gets off the bus, she accosts them like the assertiveness of a black panther (really). And, as they disgorge into a frenzy, she engages the clientele in the shadows like the panther making a kill until the next wave will occur. It is not that sex is foreign to the girl, but she recognizes the hope of getting ahead and with such diseases as Aids etc. She knows the sea like the money that will engage and recede, back and forth. She knows her father's plight which with children from several relationships, he is at a loss, in a sense? She would not play out her father's falling on another boy, as she knows that young boys may be foolish.

When she turns eighteen, sex is more accessible as she is pretty and candy sales seem so lacking in potential. Her body echoes to be touched and she plays her role by moving her business to nice hotels where single men will notice her. Her family sees her every morning when she is done with her business. Then, like a business executive, she invades this space and tolerates men doing things on the confines of her body for money. Soon, the family will be able to afford a small apartment and her strategy becomes a way of life. Where there is demand, there is supply. She has American "clientele," if you want to call them that and she calls her male counterparts, confidently, "sweetie." She did not know she would grow so much, in such a short period of time. It is considered by those around her as somewhat of a glamorous life; staying at nice hotels and sometimes getting a good meal. Things have changed in a short period of time; she had no idea... But, someone has to pay the bills, she thinks.

Six: Singapore Airlines

On Singapore Airlines it is not to engage in sex, but rather to sell it. Men from all over the world hit on flight attendants and even the males feel this sort of ill-treatment. But though Chloe, the head stewardess on the flight from Singapore to Bombay, feels the pressure to cross the lines. She knows, however, one of the main rules in the business is to be sexy, but not to succumb to its temptation. She knows this from personal experience, as her mother was a flight attendant and met her father when flying to Paris. Her father is a French man whom she has never met. It seemed so natural for someone in the trade to engage in sex as you are trained to please the passengers at any cost.

However, money is gained not by the act of sex, but the possibility of sex. Most professional flight attendants for Singapore Airlines do not cross the line, but there are the exceptions. On the other hand, she will go to great measures to please passengers without having physical contact. It is like putting a quarter in a slot machine; the flight attendants keep the men guessing, but hardly do you win in the end. I think the principle is to play in the rain, and not get wet. The women attendants on this flight must be assertive towards the passengers and not allow it to get too personal. Everything that transcends lines on the flight may be sexually motivated even if it is just a business. You would think that some of these women are like sisters, but Chloe is different. She stands out like a pink carnation and her father is a reminder of what could happen if you cross the line.

Seven: "Impulse"

On the Navaho Reservation, it is clear that when meeting a mate, character is first and sex is second. Girls look to find characteristics that their ancestors possessed, but not to assume that attraction is the only trait in finding someone? Children laugh at presumptions and would rather feel alienated from the greater cultural landscape of the nation; as a nation inside a nation does offer to some humor? They suppose it is like one wanting to live in someone's outhouse. (When the two cultures mix, it becomes an ordeal.) The two Navahos consecrate their marriage, I think, but little one knows from the outside of what steps are taken to get to this end? I think the Navahos believed in being one with nature, but to come here and call the land their own, seems presumptuous as they were here first? They want to stay here and marry in order to perpetuate this end, but one may suspect that anything taken at face value is not necessarily true?

The high school football team meets for practice after school and the Wildcats, are something worth watching as they epitomize the term "teamwork." Native Americans are naturally inclined toward this trait more naturally than those who came here after they were here. Still, things like libido are something private. One may see the game and is looking into an illusion that is vacant as new cars are in a used car lot. The phantoms of the land must subsist in order for the land to survive. They need not even show up for their own pageantry as if they subsided, so would those who live on the land, I think.

Eight: Barbie Doll in Finland at Seventeen

Dating is big in Finland. A girl meets her acquaintance on a Friday night, who is some guy in this case. First, she does the preparation that includes combing her long blond hair and powdering her nose with a pink fluff that finalizes it as such. Really, girls from Finland are by no means dolls in any sense. But, the result from a desire to please the opposite sex makes her prone to a more meaningful relationship. The evocation of the date reserves the notion of no sex on the first date, let alone a kiss maybe?

She goes to a restaurant to meet this guy who is a nice guy. It is not surprising that the classic date renders itself in Finland and the idea of procreation dwindles in an oasis that is calm and calculating? When they sit down for a burger and fries, the bill comes and she pulls out a calculator to make sure the calculations are correct? He is impressed with her ingenuity and gives her a pat on her shoulder. After dinner, she pulls out a cigarette and this is bold to him, though he does not smoke himself. He plays soccer and must be careful of succumbing to such behavior.

It is a mirror reflection of any date, except the models denoted in this case are not at all insecure about it and maybe it will lead somewhere. That is all. (Sex in Finland is like Japan, just more casual.) There are no insecurities here, rather somewhere else someone is playing with dolls and hence the name Barbie and Ken resounds.

Though, if Americans are young girls in sophisticated development, the Fins are more advanced and would render as late teenagers in comparison. Some girls are like dolls and do not mind others playing with them as such. It is not that a Fin girl looks different; it is just that they are different. Americans seem like such mongrels. She dreams like foreign episodes of a soap opera and thinks Ken is swell in this scenario. There is no reason to be any different from what their culture is inclined to, rather than the festering fire of a melting pot that adheres to insecurity in such places as the USA. They are models of what is an alternative lifestyle, but I would not go so far as calling them Ken and Barbie, (but their features resonates such).

Ken says, "Shit, I left my condoms at home."

And Barbie responds, "That's okay, we should wait."

He adds, "You are right."

(No sounds are heard in the night of a northern stratosphere! And the animals can sleep peacefully for once.)

Nine: Japanese for Sushi Episode

"You are such a tease!" Makiko tells Ayumi. They both engage in sex from time to time and sit in the park in Tokyo so as to not draw attention to themselves. "What does this man have that any other man does not?"

"I think he is gay, what other explanation is there, after we went out, he said that he did not want to jump into a full-fledged relationship?"

"I agree with you, besides not having much luck myself, it is just not becoming to attractive women such as us."

"We went to a porno and after it he wanted to eat sushi off my breasts, but no sex!"

"That sucks, as I am tired of these drawn-out episodes without fulfilling what is so natural anyway?"

"The guys have a complex of which their mother would not approve, I think."

"But I hate the old guys who want to experience a Renaissance of promiscuous behavior in their old age."

"You are right, it is like sleeping with your grandfather; they touch you so gently and then acts like a tidal wave of emotion and it lasts maybe ten seconds."

"That is not good."

"No."

"I want to meet their grandsons rather; it would not seem so perverted as sleeping with your grandfather."

Ten: Loving Devon

His younger brother William looks up to Devon, the way a boy does. They are brothers. They are like girls, but do not let this phenomenon hinder their relationship. Brothers in England are gold and they feel special as opposed to their sisters, who do not get the same attention they do. At age twenty, Devon gets cancer and brother William wants to do something special for his brother who is dying. William marries a girl named Lucy and they have a child whom they call Devon. Devon, in the hospital, holds the baby and cries, knowing that he will not live to see the child grow.

Devon and William think sex is a lot like death. When someone is born, someone else is dying. It is natural, of course, but they wish it would not plague them so vehemently. In England, sex is more a process that allows their lineage to prosper into the future. Devon wants to hug his brother, but loses his last breath so that William's son Devon might live on. Young Devon will grow and prosper in a culture that does not define a sexual relationship, in most cases, for women as opposed to their male counterpart.

Eleven: Camels in the Distance

In the white slave trade in certain Arabic nations, I am told that a person is kidnapped from Eastern European nations and held into a form of bondage. Here, they begin a life so foreign to them, that it may only be referred here as sheer slavery. Though, not common, it does happen possibly and children are bred to produce an offspring which may further result in marrying young girls to husbands who treat them as subservient wives. There is no proof that it does not happen, and blondes have a special superiority in the ranks. In some Arabic countries, to get lost might be the last time one is seen in the civilized world. I do not know what occurs in countries so austerely different than their Western counterparts, but a man in this part of the world may want to prosper through such means. I wonder who that girl who walks in the shadows of a newscast by CNN is, in a world that is all one may know? There is no way out! (Do things such as this happen?) One may only ponder such a scenario as the zumboorukchee is seen in the distance. There is no passport in such cases.

Twelve: Indian Sun

A Pakistani woman walks on a road that exists north of India and such women may be a model for other women in such parts of the world. She is called the "Indian Sun," and she, though living under somewhat extreme conditions, has found an escape which in other places is nearly impossible. A woman is someone the male counterpart respects enough that when posed with the question of sex, she is able to decline. I think here, there is a window of opportunity that designates women with an uncommon sense of pride. Why has an "Indian Sun" risen to meet the demand for a need for hope which is not yet possible in India? She walks onward, with dignity, along a path of rocks which she is not bothered by and may subsist further. This is phenomenal; imagine that, a slight light of hope shines for all women? Why did this not occur first for women in America? During the woman's lib movement of the seventies, women, in America, are not taken seriously enough? Rather than a woman, she is the protégé of a male world? A woman to be a woman may never be touched by her partner man and that is respect.

Thirteen: The Rocky Raccoon Road Race...

French women are different. Even at an early age they seem more playful and therefore more daring to challenge the male persona. At a café, a man and a woman meet, and on an even plain; it is certain that one or the other will win, but it is not predetermined either? Women feel they are the daughters of the father, but challenge this notion at every chance. The father holds the daughter and whispers in her ear that she will get a fair shot at life, that she is special. Women respect the father, but have a bloodthirsty propensity to prove to him that she was made superior. The model walks the runway at every hour of the day and there is no end to this road race, and she manages to have some fun in the process. Sex is just the waste that their life should plunder along the way and like a dog is not really taken seriously.

Dr.Kraus: Life on Mars

If there was a saint on Mars, Dr. Kraus would be it? Bad kids end up in his office, though, and it appears the epitome of white. Some kids have done bad things and the last alternative would be unconceivable. But, as there is mercy even on Mars, the process of doing bad things may be slowed to a point? The parents leave their child at the center with teary eyes and feeling very guilty that they have done something wrong. It is Dr. Kraus's job to find the antidote to that which is dysfunctional behavior. Afterward, if the young person is willing, they may adjust to something that is less ill-fated and become productive individuals.

There is a lake on Mars where some of the kids who pass the test escape on a boat through a foggy environment and return to their parents. This is only a dream and they wake as though nothing has happened. Those who remain in Dr. Kraus's care are fully adjusted and would rather not return. I think some of them eventually become police officers or join a rock band. Whether a dream or reality, there is truly God on Mars and Dr. Kraus is commended for caring enough. The great white hope is that wherever you are, God is there!

"Ferocious in Hollywood and Christmas Tree"

The walk back to Georgia is long and tedious. When I last spoke to Ferocious, my dog, (though never to actually to embrace,) he mentioned something about wanting to become a film director. This was in Malibu, (before he ran away.) Here, in Malibu, cars pass like film rolling and, by the time I ate the dried leaf from Diana's tree, it was too late and he was off on his adventure.

Here, on the road in Malibu, I saw his last defecation on the roadway from which he ran and I thought twice about eating it, but the sun got to it first. I would not have eaten it anyway, but it was sort of a dare to free Ferocious from this earth. It was clear it was a fully conceived choice, though he was not a rogue, his adventure was fully paid for in dollars fit for men. On his way, he saw many kids who were passing in their sleep back from their journey under Dr. Kraus's care and he felt sorry for them as they appeared remorseful and lonely, not like bad kids at all. And he wanted to tell them that this is what he does for fun.

Ferocious worked through charm alone, which is to say a lot. He had no enemies except my father, who thought a petty dog that commits suicide in space is no match for a lion that is killed in the process. The distaste for him was beyond repair and Ferocious knew this as my father was flying out to L.A. to see me and this may have been why he left in such a hurry? I empathize with my father and say we will have to wait and see what happens in this play Ferocious is directing?

A squirrel nearby sends a message that Ferocious had made it to his next engagement? Ferocious is subtle and does not tell anyone he is a step ahead of the culprit, who looks down at him as though what a cute dog. Back at the Malibu Inn, I turn on the TV and Larry King is interviewing Ferocious saying, yea, my first film is sort of a Western except the hero is killed by a Mexican in the end. I thought maybe I could get my dog back, but I doubt this would happen anyway.

My dad arrives and he is tall like a Christmas tree, and he does not know that somewhere Ferocious is barking at a "Christmas Tree," thinking it is him. Meanwhile, my dad stands with an umbrella in the rain in Malibu.

Ferocious and I have traveled from New York to Montreal, then to Vancouver, then to L.A. that winter. On our way, I resumed my work of one of two books of poetic free verse which the first one is called *Dry American English Verse*. Along the way, which is basically snow drifts and deserted highways, I saw a turn off that leads into a dead end, and photograph Ferocious on a stump of a giant redwood tree. You could tell Ferocious resented this very much like a child dressed up at Walmart for a photo and I sensed the end was near? We left Canada at the checkpoint into the U.S.A., leaving the bear's mouth that had absorbed us through the last week. (Though the redwood came earlier.) It was clear there was nothing I could do, but thought the Christmas lights in the night sky were peculiar in Canada and thought for a brief moment "Martians really know how to party," and I was back in the old U.S. of A (I think there was some sort of Martian refuge in Canada?)

"My parents were married at Sea Island in the summer of '48"

I suppose the reason Ferocious commits suicide out there in space is to avoid the life that is not his; you could even say Catholic, but I do not hear any Catholics making any complaints? Actually, it is much too "WASPY," for those who visit Niagara Falls on road trips through upstate New York in the summertime? Somewhere in between the Catholics and the Wasps is Dr. Bullard, though he and his wife lean slightly toward being Wasps. Mr. and Mrs. Bullard have one daughter together and she does not understand her parents at all? Her name is Mildred.

Mildred protests, "Why must I begin studying for the bar? I have two years left in law school."

While Dr. Bullard retaliates, "I have worked hard to send you to law school. An appreciative girl would do what her father says."

And Mildred asks, "May I get my own place? I met a boy from Honduras and thought we could share a place. He is also two years into law school at George Washington?"

Dr. Bullard responds, "Your mother and I will think about it. We will have to meet him first."

Her parents talk about Sea Island often and listen to old records too old to even name in the living room. They are so happy together, which to Mildred seems plain weird. The furniture is predominately classical and neither parent ever smoked. Her father has a tic which is even stranger for a psychiatrist? He uses his den in the basement for work, meeting patients in his late sixties, though partially retired. He is the type of father who would not know what Benetton is should you tell him you are going to the mall? However, he may name in order every opponent he boxed in the fifties?

His wife is worried about the tic as it gets worse over each year. His boxing gloves still hang in the closet and as though a secret, his eyes are fiery like that of a dragon. He has now passed on. I had been a patient of Dr. Bullard over the course of about a year, meeting in his den downstairs maybe twice a week. Later, I thought to ask about his boxing days, "To sir with love, did St. George kill the dragon or did the dragon kill St. George?" It is too late though, as time passes and there is nothing you may do about it.

Staring into his eyes, he blinks once and it is the only picture of him that is left to me. Sometimes, the cobwebs induce Mrs. Bullard to listen to an old record, though she thinks it is not the same. Mildred is now a lawyer and drives a BMW in Washington, D.C., but we have never met.

"I read the paper today..."

The sixties came too fast? I was born in 1971, but remember it as it seemed to drag on into the eighties. People are more conservative today, suspicious of protests and such. In boarding school, I felt that my class was the last to even know what the sixties were about. Rap, in the late eighties was closing in fast and Dead Heads in my class seemed sort of dorky and out of place.

"Give it up, this is the eighties," a later class might taunt us.

My roommate Ham listened to Guns N' Roses, which was another sign that the sixties was over. The new conservatism was heating up in young people everywhere and, though I read the paper today; it said that Jimmy Carter should have stuck to peanut farming and I sort of felt sorry for the breed entirely.

"Cockroach Parade"

War brings out the worse in everyone. Somehow, I think John Lennon, in his death, was the only Beatle to make it, so to speak. He was freed of the world in which he opposed. One night, the Beatles came to me as cockroaches. They were singing another sixties motif, "All you need is love" and I think it was their last time together. Paul, George, and Ringo were leading a parade that beckoned me to "smoosh" them on the kitchen counter. So, I did, (they were full of joy) and though cockroaches, martyrs just the same I think. The next morning, a giant cockroach rested on its back, on the floor, dead. John Lennon had been crucified that night and I am sorry this happened.

"Will"

By this time, I had finished my second book of poetry called, "Tiger Lost at Sea." Will is a city kid and represents everything good that liberal parents have to offer.

(Insert: "God Bless the Great American Hypocrisy: Part One")

My parents never explain to me why some people are rich and other people are poor. Our society may impel me to use a euphemism, if making a speech for instance, by asking why some people are wealthy and others disadvantaged? If I was a priest, I might explain to some children that some people are well off and others less fortunate. The president of the United States may exploit the scenario further by focusing on the void, the neglected middle masses?

Ask a collective of dairy farmers perhaps in western Pennsylvania, some of whom still hand milk their cows, "Why should you have to suffer?" Spoken at the local vocational school, some of the sons and even more of the daughters attend it. Maybe, a few of the children are embarrassed that each morning their fathers lean up against a cow and pulls on its tits for a living? But, even worse, is to lean up against the president's words, pure rhetoric, as though he does not know what you want to hear? Then, you think, why not, take whatever compassion you may get?

You spend some money on pool and beer on the weekend, and later at home, the tolerant silence your wife pervades, makes a little sympathy from the president easier to lean up against? But, there is one man in the back who has only an old rusted Chevy pick-up and a mule, and he is thinking that this guy does not stand for anything. And, before he finishes the thought, the president says between belated pauses of passion, "We must try to break the horrible cycle of poverty." The guy in the back who is poor, is wondering who he is talking about and figures he must be standing for someone?

This leaves me to fend for the rich or at least for myself. I grow up confused by menacing contradictions. My parents do not tell me a whole lot and let me explore things for myself. However, my mom does say that when she was young, she did not have nearly what I have and that I should feel fortunate?

Maybe, the fact that I have all the material things I need makes me weigh material objects less? This is good. Maybe some kids do not have anything but love and consequently never form the need for material things? My mom may have had one or two things, but the things she does not have makes her crave material things even more. She never uses the word "poor," to describe herself, but I remember hearing in the car when visiting her old neighborhood in Denver, how all the black people have moved in? All sorts of insecurities hang on this statement. To my grandma, their family works hard and moves into a better neighborhood? To my mom, the fact that her old neighborhood is now a black neighborhood means how dejected her beginnings are? While my grandma describes a brighter picture of my mom's humble childhood, and says there is always food on the table? My mom, however, weighs material things more and in retrospect, feels deprived? In a good sense, my mom wants to give me a realistic point of reference of who I am, that I am fortunate.

I grow up in a big brick house in Georgetown, Washington, D.C. We have a big back yard with lots of grass and two little hills. There are trees to climb. Nicole, who is older than me, but not the oldest sister, used to climb one tree in particular. She was sort of a tomboy until she grew out of it. My room was on the third floor of the house. I remember, in third grade, lugging my school books up the winding stairs past my parents' room on the second floor.

That was a decisive year as it was the last I remember my parents together. I do not have many memories of them together prior, with all the distractions.

My room was covered with wallpaper of the first aviators. My mom picked it out especially for me. I had two antique wooden beds that belonged to my dad when he was a boy and he gave them to me. I had collections of all sorts, including coins, stamps, wacky stickers, and about fifty National Geographic magazines. In the room connecting to my room, I use to keep toys. I sometimes pasted Polaroid pictures I took on the walls. It was sort of a wreck room. There was a large yellow metal plant holder that I put against the door, because it was the only door to my room that did not have a lock. When I had a fight with Nicole, she pushed through the door to get to my room and scare me. I forget what we fought about. Anyway, next to the side room was my own bathroom. There was an old-fashioned beauty salon hair dryer and I turned it on and pretended to be in outer space. There was a big bathtub with legs. Nancy, my oldest sister, Nicole and the governess all had their own rooms on the other side of the floor, but they shared the same bathroom. My sisters were a little jealous that I had my own bathroom.

Will, my best friend, was really out going and has red curly hair. He lived in a much smaller house than me, in Georgetown, and was always at my house. We played in the backyard each day after school. We played tennis, soccer, and football. I had a K2 Jr. football and, often, we threw it. I was mainly the quarterback and he the receiver. We tackled each other. Sometimes, we got into fights. Coincidently, we first met by fighting over the backseat of the school bus when we were five, but soon attended different schools. We played until it got too dark to see the ball. Sometimes, we even played into the night, using the moonlight to see. Will was a better athlete than me, but he played to my capacity. On weekends, we explored Georgetown. We went roller skating at the Boys Club on Saturday nights. Will always slept over at my house and we watched TV late and played Risk and Monopoly. On Sundays, we sometimes started little businesses like shining shoes on the street in front of the house. With Will over so much, it was hard for me to always do my homework and I complained at eight 'o clock on Sunday night that I have homework and Will finally went home. We always had a good time. We are still good friends today. I feel lucky to have a good friend like Will.

When my parents got divorced, my dad moved to the other side of the house which we had previously rented. My dad lived and worked there. He had an office on the third floor which divided the house. He lounged in is his big brown chair, smoking his cigars and talking business on the phone. Sometimes, I think he watched me out the window, play with all the freedom in the world. He was a soft-mannered and loving father.

My dad came from an affluent family. However, his lifestyle growing up was formal and sort of rigid, not free like mine. Still, my dad never complained. When I looked at pictures of him as a kid, he wore sort of formal dress. The pictures gave me the impression that he always wore this around the house; to tea, that sort of thing? I guess it was the time in which he lived. Maybe, seeing me wild and free in the backyard reminded him of his self? Maybe, it was what his childhood lacked? From the pictures, his childhood seemed sort of cold? He rarely talked about it except his glory days of being captain of his high school basketball team. It is clear that growing up, I had points of reference. If I am going to write, I want to give you, the reader, a sense of where I am coming from.

As a boy, I attended an elite grammar school in Washington, D.C. One day I was walking alone, as usual, from sports after school. I was pretty quiet at this time, as my parents had just divorced. I was about ten when this happened. A kid my age, from an upper class family, came over to me and slurred the words at me, "rich kid." He did not even look at me as he passed. I suppose, at impact, to someone who experiences a put-down for the first time, it is as if someone calls a black kid the "N" word. The only difference, I suppose, is the social and historical differences. When I got home crying, and told my mom that evening, she laughed. She balanced my insecurities by saying that I was a "rich kid," and I should learn to live with it. She laughed further, telling my older sister who, at age thirteen, was extremely mature for her age, that there were a lot worse situations than being rich. I suppose to a young African/American who is proud of his heritage, it is a turning point where he must face an uglier side. I am sure at the prospect of having to reveal this side, the parents do not laugh.

I think it is more difficult for a African/American person to survive, in our society, than it is for me? While, we are not fundamentally different, how many African/Americans may claim that their ancestors come to America willfully, seeking greater opportunity? Still, society, maybe for the better, claims everyone is equal, having the same opportunities? Maybe, by saying this, it is easy to obscure the truth and say we are the same, even though the greater population knows a much more private past. Is this fair? I would rather say simply that we are different and hide in the anonymous blameless white cloud America provides. However, I want to say, if an African American person who experiences this sort of initial blow, if he wants to, if he can isolate the pain in the rawest sense and not allow the psychological repercussions to fly; if I can, maybe we may say, for just one moment that we are the same.

"Indian"

(There is a tattoo imprinted on his right and left shoulder. On his left shoulder is a print of Geoffrey Chaucer and on his right shoulder, a tiger.)

In early November, it is seventy degrees in New York City. A kid from Queens finds in his prospective customers that are vacant cars a gizmo of sorts; it looks like another electric back massager from Sharper Image he scrutinizes further. Yesterday, he found two electric tooth brushes, a his and hers. The kid, barely seventeen, is surprisingly also an artist and puts some of the things he finds in his artwork. He is Puerto Rican and does not feel guilty for finding things that he puts in his scabrous artwork.

Survival at best is to find some lose change in the car seats and ashtrays. The winter is nearing and he can't afford an electric blanket. Really, it does not matter as he squats in a dilapidated building and is without electricity. On the Lower East Side, it is rare to find an artist so young. Keeping in shape is also important to this young person, as he goes to the YMCA and practices Tai Chi in his spare time. Wandering now on the Upper East Side, he will find discarded old lamp shades in the street then he hops home with them in a downtown subway, where he skillfully jumps the turnstile. His mom, who was not around much when he was a child and his father, a crack addict, display little hope for him, though somehow he manages not to be self-pitying and avoids drugs as well.

This is his reality, and he and his girlfriend are rather adjusted as such. He sees an Indian painted on the wall of a building and decides to do the same on the lamp shade he found. A pigeon poops on his head and he is not inspired as such, and he wanders the streets which he never left?It is an artwork in progress and he feels a certain pride in never finishing something; it just leads to something else. Standing on the long lanky figure called Manhattan he cannot see, he returns what he takes; a work in progress. The pope might be proud that he is also a Catholic.

The Illiterate Symposium:

What walks on four legs, has three eyes and talks like a snake? The non-factual description of a post age mythical creature is nothing more than a prefabricated vamp to effloresce like notions the counterpart to the male protégé; a woman, yields looking through her dark spectacles which may see everything in hindsight should detest and deplore? Between a brief intermission, a construction worker on the street commands such a title by the light which invites a view of two scruffy hands signaling a "T" for timeout to imply a set change which capitulates the time sort of flushed between two markers?

Meanwhile, in the time allocated, the sushi chef cuts away at the miniscule bit of fish that is considered inedible, like a tidbit in time to feed the cat. The proponent is this now-visible figure in summer Armani business attire, possibly a day in Venice, he sits down at a café in Lower Manhattan. From whose view may one see the passers-by of two opposite sexes willing to face one another in the light of day? And, for the breath that signifies the time at hand, he an Italian textile-pod, is willing to penetrate such a saving grace? He holds the reins to master the light which resonates the fashion manifesting itself here, and is exposed entirely from this one zetetic point of view.

"May I have a brochure of the lovely island?" the man in Armani attire states resolutely.

"No, a menu you mean?" the waiter infers.

"A menu, of course, a menu of the cake on this lovely island?" he says most blatantly as he absorbs the sunlight in Armani attire that a water with lemon might detest.

"Do you want a brochure too?" he addresses him as though a wowser/yaffle/sialoquent, the waiter slightly factitious.

"No, just a menu will be fine. Does the cake come with coffee?" he says this outright. as though in Belgium maybe.

"Yes, but you have to pay for it twice," yatter, yatter, the waiter infers.

"Then I will have cake twice, without the coffee." the man in Armani attire envisions as though a perplexing dilemma.

"I mean you have to pay for the cake once and the coffee too They are separate." The waiter thinks this is some kind of joke but remains stolid in the face.

"How about a course of soup?" The man in Armani attire beckons to change the line of inquiry somewhat.

"Okay, but that will cost you too. Our soup, chicken noodle and gazpacho is very good." The waiter is refreshed that this man actually orders something.

"What may I purchase that comes with my brochure?" This man displays a serious face.

"I am sorry, but you are in the wrong place," the waiter says while fiddling his mustache and quite annoyed.

"No mint?" the man in Armani attire pleads like a mouse to a cat.

"No mint," the waiter says like a cat bothered by the fly pestering it, but even more so.

"How about a water with lime?" The man in Armani attire is hanging on to this line of inquiry and slowly fading.

"I am sorry but you are going to have to order something. This is not France?" he, the waiter, responds to the umbrage.

"You are not French are you?" the man in Armani attire asks out of the blue.

"No, I am Belgian. Do you want a Belgian waffle?" the waiter says, as though insulted and his face turns red.

"What does it come with?" the man in Armani attire asks now, like a child.

"Nothing, the syrup is separate, (just kidding,)" But really, the waiter thinks.

"If it is not too much trouble, I would like a piece of cake on my waffle, but I will have a brochure instead?" The man in Armani attire seems more than ridiculous now as he states an impossible inquiry.

"Maybe you want to go to Times Square where there is a new Disneyland gift shop, it is free, okay. You are going to have to eat at some point and, unless you are willing to steal breadcrumbs from the pigeons in the park, it will cost you?" the waiter tries to conclude.

"That is offensive!" the man in Armani attire states for the record.

"Sir, please, I am busy now," said boldly. The waiter is beyond flustered.

"Gigolo," the man in Armani attire snaps at him.

"I will call the police. Don't test me," the waiter talks down to him.

"Fine, I will have your most expensive soup." The man in Armani attire finalizes the discussion.

The man is irritated and wonders if his spoken English an attribute and conversely strokes his mustache at a curious pace. What is so confusing isn't his mustache or the fashion of the day, but the sheer coincidence of being in Manhattan at any given time makes? Not to mention that there is a further ridicule of the illiterate symposium it may foster out of a ridiculous imposition of dialect, two sexes, should one face may menace in its landscape? Imagine, the construction worker flagrantly wearing a brassiere outright. What would this say to a male police officer who should pass leaving a gaping hole?

Or suppose a sushi chef wears a napkin as a hat? Do you think anyone would notice this is not part of the traditional dress attire?

"The man wears an Armani suit, question mark?"

"Who cares?"

"Still, he is continuing to rub his mustache with his finger after all this time?"

"Who cares?"

"He is rubbing it with a fork as though to spike it?" (A short delay in response.)

"Who cares?"

"The president has been shot (just testing). He likes to shave his pubic hair to make a statement about such private and public rights we must respect?" This diagnoses a velvet underground, I think.

"Who cares?" The respondent acclaims up in the air. He infers as though clearly mastering the proponent's message as a witwanton may elude?

This may convey everyday "jargons" that effectually stimulate, divisions among the different sects of persons and people throughout the metropolitan of Manhattan? A lady wears a delinquent jabot that represents her unlimited disposition towards fashion in the day? She need not define the moment with any further expression since the capacity of mood is magnificent with a simple variation in clothing? But, what does it all mean? If the answer is nothing, then what would a similar display imply from another slumgullion? May the instance merit an electrical impulse among the two which resolves in a bashful familiarity or acquaintance?

Unfortunately, the answer thereafter is "nothing," an imposing nomad of latent kinetic reality? Then, if the two were to undress or for that matter, rather than wearing such motifs of intrigue, to wear one less item on a grand scale, this might become an implication of archival infatuation? It might be rather than a display of implications, a lack of it thereafter as the reverse feigns of the presumptive measures to assume whatever?

"Why not, not wear clothes?" someone shouts on the street, causing a chain reaction of tidal wave proportions leaving every person slightly less dressed? It might have some sort of significance somewhere like L.A. for instance, but here in New York City, still, no reaction to wearing less clothes? As opposed to the fashion implications abhor to inhere while wearing different pieces of clothing garments etc. – nothing, no one cares if you wear less clothes as opposed to more?

The man still sits at a café and his Armani attire conveys little style suggestions for the present moment. As the person sips his gin and tonic with a twist of lemon, the napkin formerly resting on his lap now falls unfaltering to the ground. This is what fashion must imply to ants scurrying about in the cracks of the asphalt and concrete made up in the street configurations? Fortunately, there is no notice of this as he reaches for his wallet in his coat pocket and places a credit card on the table to evoke the waitress, now wearing one less garment and the red leather tie sort of naturally hangs from her neck, straight and downright what is sort of a response?

With a further characterization of mood imbedded in the dichotomy of a response and a tie that may only hang as straight as it is made, toward the ground; she reaches down to pick up the napkin that fell? And quite comfortably, she scratches at the strap that irritates her back and has a lighter response no longer hanging onto the shirt that once warped the sensation of the moment? Now, the man in Armani attire rises to his feet and offers a gasp of breath like insinuating a rest for a short time and the waitress, is actually a man named Lola? He, in a display of affectionate condescension, clears the table with check like a vulture swooping down at dinner from above. When, actually, the activity is dispersed among a group of vocal women marching down the street in different butch hairdos and further displays of loud demeanor of intrigue to dispose at the public further through combat boots to shuffle the discourse of their voices becoming louder and louder?

Now, this man, standing in an Armani suit seems no more than an easy target to this slew of women, without any representation of themselves beyond the obvious implication of flagrant disregard to this person? He stands upright like a man does after having sat at a café on a New York City street? He feels completely quenched of thirst and other, and to stand showing a sign of satisfaction to become smaller as a trolley comes charging horrific sounds from away, away?

In juxtaposition of the energy indicting him by mere contrast may falter this grown man weighing himself slightly off course and on the wrong foot? No one would know, at such a time, a brief intermission, who would pick up the napkin? Maybe, the waiter, as an implication of courtesy, certainly not out of courtship or further sentiment, he reaches to the ground? At such a time, having a group of women facing you while alone on the street; a man's best friend, a dog, but the waiter will do and he stumbles with the weight of one foot to another? He does not know what a march on such a pleasant day should mean?

The women pass in their belated attire and show little sympathy for this man all alone in Soho as they head downtown? The symposium marks a passing that does not have much consequence or meaning. Further, it invites a lesser imposition among those who should pass with loud voices almost like a chant, and the waiter clears the table completely. It does not imply any assertive implications of comradeship among friends or even a smile among strangers? The man in an Armani suit stands alone as they pass to invite less of a parade of warmth and compassion that this point of passage should render? The crowd is now gone, the waiter not present; the man stands alone on the street.

As though it were the last day before the fall of man, two Jews meet at the bus stop in Hasidic dress? Here, they discuss matters like it were just another day, but really the occasion merits more ordeals that threaten the faith on the sixth workday of the seven-day week? The bus stop is a secretive spot where the two men meet overlooking the Hudson slightly north of Manhattan in the Bronx? It is certain that the two should meet like the regularity of early morning sunshine; a reminder even in the nineties of summers past? It is as though taking a Greyhound from some meager mom-and-pop rest stop from the southern drive from San Francisco to Los Angeles? It wakes the senses for a while? Maybe of yippy love and the movements that should coerce across the land from the sixties to the final addressing, a quiet place to meet? The bus arrives and the two persons enter it like children getting in a bus to go to camp?

The bus driver speaks the same language and smiles as the two pass, paying the fare and moving a few rows back to sit together. Here, they continue their discussion in a language spoken only by a few others there. A woman of another temple smiles as the two men sit. She has a sort of stolid dignity dressed like a tradition that merits some attention and the woman is wrapped in a casual flower garment which was made from one's own hand rather than machine?

The time that passes is pleasant, but slow. No offensive words are spoken by anyone on the bus, including the driver. In fact, the bus driver continues to be a primary facet of everyday life in this modest refine. First, they wait on a sunny morning at a bus stop overlooking the Hudson. Then, the bus carries passengers, mostly Hasidic and other consenting individuals from the designated spot to another. To confirm in one another their vows, which seems to be a hallowed ritual among the sect of Orthodox believers in the Jewish faith, it does not seem unusual today or any other day.

It is just a hop, skip and a jump; heralding some more individuals before engaging in the final dissent to the island of Manhattan, at which the bus makes its final stop at the port authority? As the two holy individuals, one might describe devout members of the Jewish faith, depart from the bus that, prior, pulls up to the final stop like a winged dove, it is caught in time, but carelessly unaware of the set that binds them in all directions? The bus gracefully pulls up to the curb at a minute approaching a time as always and the two men get out. This is their routine. They walk effortlessly as though the air of the pope separates them in trust, and the drag of their black garments just a practice that mirrors their daily fortune out of consequence that the two should maintain a leap of faith?

A few blocks from the station, they arrive at the shop in the garment district where they maintain their shared business of call. It seems at this time the work begins, but it is not really clear if the workers, who arrive a few hours earlier, a little less formal and have names like Ahmad, should begin the work first? All that is investigated here is that the sweat from one Jew's face, at the early hour on a summer morning is fake? Really, it resonates a nervous insidious disposition that mimics what Jews do as a general practice regarding business and may be effectually resonating of some facet of a family line or a character flaw of cultural and historical menace? It is at this time that Christians ask questions like why we decorate Christmas trees or why Santa Claus has a red outfit and climbs through chimneys while people are sleeping?

Such menacing questions creep in the negative space of the world which would otherwise be a perfect Christmas? And the decorative pieces hanging from the trees stare at one another in this space with the innocent glare of the child's eye that sparkles in its presence? What may be such a menace as the sweat that drips and subsides from his face or for that matter, from the workers? With such a long history between the two – Christianity and Judaism – it is possible that Santa Claus could use the reindeer through such spectacles of glitter and sanctity, only to sell it the next day for meat at the butcher's shop? The possibilities are propulsive, similar from the light that shines from Rudolph's nose, bright? Still, no one at the shop may answer such questions and look as muddled as the children that dance in his wrapping of splendor?

To travel the distance here, a boy and a girl stare into one another's eyes with the same clarity that the future should swallow the past in the meeting to render no memory of it thereafter? After the workday which is like almost every other day except the Sabbath, children step, standing back to back while taking one step forward and one step back. Like the synchronicity of the work day, we breed such children with no knowledge of the past and no morality for the future?

The Jews in black dress wander the boundaries of such questions as dumbfounded as the children who stare into tiny colored balls that glow? Here is the end of the beginning and the beginning of the end, all in one space? Among the decorations the illiterate symposium is a child sitting alone, which in the light of its face, obtains the wisdom closed like the legs crossed and the arms folded that infuses a question without any reply?

(At home, the children play like anywhere else at any given time and with no knowledge of where the path may lead to; this is just a trifle that an adult should pass with no knowledge of its whereabouts either.)

Here on the streets of Manhattan, it provides an excellent answer to those wandering children whose curiosity, in such matters, may impose further inquiry? They absorb the streets of wandering items in an all out closing sale that ponder no reply except for a shake of the wrist to buy merchandise? What numbers arise are as vague as the temple implores to those believing in the cause, an avenue of prices tags that illuminate the way, the way in which matters of unsubstantiated finality are resolved? Random numbers, like the persons riding the train from one place to another of those subsisting on the bread fed to pigeons in the park; not knowing to know otherwise and now the two Jews are in a fabric of a much more complicated pattern while exiting the bus at the end of the day? Counting one then two, like the simplicity of the scenario, they have no trifle regarding this? And their dark attire invites the night and the questions are put to sleep as they disappear into the sky? Taking flight from it, just like this, there is a little island in the sky that no one really knows of, yet still it is there.

On a downtown street, a person of English origin and nationality hails a cab to bring her uptown, near Columbia University. She orders the cab driver to go to one hundred and second street, between Manhattan Avenue and Central Park West. At first she stares out the window looking to see if there are any pigeons wandering the after-hours set? A few pigeons are wandering about, but do not provide enough interest to continue the spectacle? She is more interested in the lights that glow transcending messages of anti-religious slogans? She rides through the garment district that absorbs the frugal hints of disorder? Right, left, left, right; up the Avenue of the America, she pasts the pigeon parade at Bryant Park? There is a slanky stewardess of horrific proportions there as they pass on 42nd Street and head towards Columbus Circle.

At such a time, she reaches for her pocket that carries a handful of glitter, throwing into the air in a ziraleet zombie response. With lights glittering the late hour parade, newspapers line crevices in the street with no home. Women standing at the pulpit of their religion, assure, in naked view, of their best attire; right left, left, right.

What may you expect when riding the late hour fire truck up "the avenue of lost dreams" which might stand for the very best the city has to offer? In the pigeon assemblage, children sing songs to lost heroes of yesterday and refrain once, twice, and further? With a twist of night, it is glaring and provides a collage of florescent colors that stick in the mind a still life, past and no more slanky figures riding like cans hanging to a wedding procession?

You hope it is a long black limousine with a sky roof, not a meager yellow cab again, for the best America has to offer, yes? Up along Central Park West she releases the glitter, into the air, as before? Up, toward Harlem, the cab stops at some dilapidated mansion, which never was, really, and she gets out here.

"You all really know how to party," a dog invites at the prospect of Prince's bright purple guitar? The woman walks to where an "x" is marked on the ground and not to seem desperate at this time, she waits, but her father does not show up.

The cab driver makes a U-turn then invades the park to return to the garage where he, an Arab from a Moslem-predominate country in the Middle East lives post-Gulf War in synch with the American way of life in New York City. At the garage, now in Queens, the other Arabs are arriving from the night shift. There is a woman dressed in traditional Arabic clothing including a head garment which is a rare spectacle to see? Meanwhile, men are dressed like any other with pants and a shirt. They discuss the evening in terms of money. The man who has just finished his shift implies it is a bit slow, but does not reveal how much he pocketed. No one really wants to know more.

Despite the goings-on of the Gulf War he reverberates a sort of brave stance that it does not matter here in America? What kids won't understand, they will never understand. The sixties are now over, as the woman in black Moslem attire scents the wind's demeanor in a cab on the way home like any other evening for that matter.

He thinks New York City is a strange place and he folds his money wad and puts it in his pocket, but "America is even stranger as though money is paid in yens. New York City seems like a giant seraglio, for whatever that is worth?

The Color White:

1. Hospital

The nurse opens the blinds to my room. The darkness, as it elopes with the sun, nurtures the children huddling in corners that compose a nightmare set that they will not wake from. I leave the room at a sleepwalking pace; while my behind is exposed thanks to a garment I wear. The light flickers in their eyes as I salute the witch to offer mercy so that only the window is a source of what otherwise would be artificial light. They hiss like a black panther as darkness confronts an intruder and offers a compromise instead.

I walk like a zombie down the hallway; it is a corridor to my sanity and even Benny the Fly finds the light too blinding in aura to penetrate. Children of this dark configuration stare at me from every corner, providing minimal mercy as darkness is left behind me and they hiss as each light is turned off one by one. I see a table in front of me. It beckons me further and meets me down the corridor. I am seen from behind while each light that I pass extinguishes a glow as I pass it. There may be a cross that the halls configure, at its epicenter where a table; a plain wood table that is modest, even painfully rigid, holds a glass of milk which I drink too.

The children are no longer hiding in corners, but embrace the cross that I meet, ignoring the camera that may just be "big brother watching." They joyously try to infiltrate it with smiles that may be a sort of baptism which they adhere in me. They are less of an entity separate and join together in the hall to refuse mercy with a rather sense of stolid patience instead. Three red devils appear and confront them to deter the lights shining in their faces. But they will not touch and they make a sort of bold "ooing" sound to absorb the fire, canceling out what seems to be a primal deficiency in other. The red entities or devils fall to the ground like flies while a candle is lit and draws them in closer and closer. The light is good and they tolerate a slight notion of pain as the wax melts slowly and is a metaphor for the Virgin Mary and a tear protruding out of her eye. The fire burns on the outside, but they will not meet and they remain good still.

It is not unwarranted to say that every aspect of the hospital will take the form of human sacrifice. The witch tempts me to eat the apple I represent, and she may be wicked. But, she turns dumb and dissipates like a cloud and the apple falls into my hand instead. I eat it, of course, but first I must find Jimi Hendrix's guitar? The hall monitors who are black seem sort of arrogant, but Marvin walks on the walls and the white paint may be the moon. Marvin is in his own element and leaves black footprints on the walls and ceiling. He detests the vanity of others as they listen to hip hop on walkmans. He plays the guitar in an intermission that mocks the vanity the moon possesses. The Vans on his feet squeak slightly to verbalize the cow's dismay to an offspring that does not recognize the water caught in the spider's own web to meet at Benetton and not go in.

But, the sentiment befalls as a Snickers lands in a vending machine and counts the quarters left falling like the smiles in their light. To open the wrapper is now a lie, and I wave at the camera as though I am home now too. The light flickers and may be a sign God is now watching as the black boy eats the Snickers without repenting, without the modesty of a white flower once picked? I will return here in seven thousand, nine hundred and seventy-one years.

2. Friend to God

I do not think God created me, which makes me ask, "How did I get here?" (I do not know?) But, at the very least, I am friend to God. As our paths divide, he may not like the security system I play into his life? He will be born in another soon and I pick up the flyer from the ground in New York City. The flyer just says, "Do not cry in the rain, smile at the sun, and let the wind blow through your hair." The anonymity that God may be an entity at any given time makes his demand even greater. Still, there are a plethora of messages. On the front of the flyer, it says that The Ramones are playing at CBGBs tonight.

We may be separate entities, but we are one and cry to show I am home too, and the white picket fence hides the blush on my face. Meanwhile, the Bee Gees pass so with bravado singing *Staying Alive*, which is a way to envision God in the new life he leads. To clarify the above, one way to help God is to recognize you are not. By doing so, I free him to a life that is becoming of a great person sitting in his boat somewhere like Mozambique. He is alone on the boat, and this is an oxymoron to everything around him. The answer finishes the Trivial Pursuit question as though his life is greater than himself. Like a blank page, he is now in his own element. His life is separate and he pays the bill with his Mastercard without presuming anything else.

We may be pawns of a remembrance of lives we may claim that may now belong to him and the storybook now has no ending. They join hands and wait to be one as those who died at 9/11 become white balloons released into the sky. It is a glorious day! I am friend to God and how may that be? He sits in darkness so that we may ponder light. As though a polar bear, in his own element, everything appears white from this perspective. When it is time to sleep, he will clap twice and this is when I awake. We have a symbiotic relationship and I am not alone either. He has no memory of 9/11 still he may see the balloon that rises from a cloud fixated in a dream. You may not touch him, but to embrace one must meet him halfway, and know that the white jeans the devil wears is a good thing. Opposites do attract? He is a light that blinds. To understand infinite space and tennis shoes, one must look at the face of a newly born baby as it drinks milk for the first time.

I see God in heaven sitting in a recliner chair, smoking a cigar wreathing inward and wearing K-Swiss tennis shoes. I do not mean that God does not care, but there is an air of what white conveys is of passivity? I do not see him termagant, red in the face, and enraged at anyone? It is more like an air of what does it matter, indifference. In this sort of objectivity, heaven is conceived so that space is not an object of interest. Not caring is infinite space! There is no need to be somewhere else as everything one needs is there as the limelight wades? The clouds curl inward like cleft milk in coffee and he calls this home.

3.Déjà vu with the Eternal Light of a White Sun

Which came first, light or darkness is the question I ask? At a high school dance that configures nuclear equations, it allows for some bodies to bump into each other in an eternal play that will not escape either or like a sub-atomic equation? There are two unprovoked menaces and the sacrifice of a perfect white sun in hindsight? God likes to watch from a distance to think as the ball flickers light like the little boy's hormones. Like ping pongs bouncing off the walls lighting up, what is there to be "Rock Lobster;" he plays along as though the first time too.

An image of Nat King Cole eclipses the moon and the sun will die sadly. The children lock as pairs kissing as a notion that those on the outside will die too, but not without an equal fortitude of energy somewhere else. The flower smells so ripe that it may not shed a tear. Just callous reminders of lost love that deter its quest in a suicide.

Years later, I may not play as a chaperone as I know the tear is not for me. Mimi and I will meet once again to seek a mission to understand the unprovoked menaces and the suicide it represents. God says never again and the fruit punch is spiked with gin or vodka? They envision a world where animals remain separate and he rather enjoys the punch still. Who would point a finger and he who gives so much? He, rather, considers himself an independent entity and I may just be his lamb?

Some kid is alone with red hair and plays an electronic game device wherein darkness no one would see the pimples that infiltrate his expression. God may feel sorry for the boy who is a lonely picture of himself too. It is a false presumption that the sun has no friends and God is a friend to the young boy just for a moment in time. A girl with blond hair goes up to the boy and asks him to dance. This is better than other and I am not God either? I play into the explosions that would recede me.

Mimi wears the devil's white jeans and asks me, "Where may a flock of seagulls embrace the sky?"

I do not know, as it is on the outer fringes of the reality at hand? I promise to return her shoe that has found a home somewhere else so that the blisters may heal.

"Nothing," is the answer I relay.

If not for the dance of callous reminders of a nuclear equation in the past, I am driving a yellow cab in New York City. I find myself part of a fabric much more complicated now. There are no answers to the questions that may be forgotten if not so evil of a journey, not I? The boat leaves from point A to point B and you will get to where you want to be in the end? I am a slave to the notion that these points meet in the sky alone like an art deco Oreo.

I say here is your shoe Mimi and, like Cinderella, she will call New York City home for a while, but the apple in the past is wicked. Satan represents a vision that should not be remembered in the future of tallied mushrooms she bears picked while man is framed by deer who deny it too. The white mushroom is so pure it will foreshadow the flower too and there is mercy here for a time. In their homeland of Japan, it is not their fault that this white flower is picked. Still, they suffer from the unprovoked menaces that will rise into the sky.

Gold is relayed when the two meet and I will go out somewhere else, but still innocent in this light. I hustle the streets in a yellow taxi cab and provide nourishment in the evil conquest, and I search for Mimi instead. I did not know prior that Mimi had a sister too. We just meet on that day that frowns on the sun one time in the past and this may not happen ever again? The apple is sort of a metaphor for a love extinguished in the moon's own salty tear. Then it happens! I do not feel the energy again like an explosion in my loins.

On the third day, I enter the park on the west side, the exact same place that I had been two days earlier, and it will explode again, manifesting somewhere else like a suicide. I am free and no longer a slave to this notion. Mimi's hair is like Stew's emission in the wind. It is sacrificed in the night sky only to be born again in the light of a white sun that will rise the next day. The children will inherit a white horse too. We represent stars in the configuration of diamonds that light places forbidden that we hold dear, and God is alone in heaven at the time. White is not a color, it is a way of life.

4. Confessions of the White

While in L.A. I was carded for cigarettes and I felt insulted as I was over twenty-five. Still, I showed my license. The next day I walked into a Korean mart near where my car is parked in Santa Monica, and I took a bottle of apple juice and left the scene. (I felt like they did not accept my money.) Like an impulse, I walked out and before I could go back and pay like everyone else, the police accosted me. Eventually, they would let me go. My car had been disabled and the tow truck driver let me out in front of a Mitsubishi dealership and garage. I could not find the right repair shop and slept there that night. I thought they might help me the next day. My Blue Eagle Summit, was actually made simultaneously by three different makers which included Mitsubishi. (It is confusing, I know.) And the next day, they said they could not help and I called another tow truck and they brought me to another garage down the road. So, I walked back to the German deli which was around the corner from where I parked the night before. I guess I needed a friend at this time.

But, I did not know I was homeless until someone in a car handed me two twenty dollar bills? Though, I did leave my wallet in my car back at the dealership, (for whatever reason?) But, how did they know this? This happened later. First, a girl at the German Deli brought me to a really sleazy motel and paid ten dollars for the room and also gave me a sandwich. The next day, I went into a store and again, on impulse, grabbed a pack of Marlboro Reds and walked back to the German deli. Now, I am homeless. Actually, the forty dollars came thereafter. Still, the resipiscence I feel is real and this is my requital.

5. The Judge in Elmira, New York

The honorable judge asks me (not in court), "So why did you steal the apple juice and the cigarettes?"

For this I do not have an answer. But, I suppose it had something to do with my money not being worth anything in L.A.? So, this is how it felt, though I did not wish harm on anyone... I suppose if I was black, I might blush. It was that sort of thing. Maybe African American people find themselves in their own element of what may be a venue for this outlet too? The judge says I am free to go. The KKK anoints the devil's head with water and money at such times seems worthless...

6. Lightbulb

They say it is a wonderful life from where he stands on African soil. I think an afro is energized to a certain point like a lightbulb. They would rather not confront trivial questions why the lights are so dim, but shed questions that have no answers instead. They say opposites attract? But, there is no answer to the setting that should profess the bun separate from the burger at Jack in the Box?

Why, in America, does the old lady cross the street when seeing a young black man heading her way? There are no answers, but to confront your inhibitions that find the truth dangerous it merits some respect. The children of a dark rose will embark on a quest for fun and ride the Cyclone at Coney Island at night. They want everyone to be free and their smiles are lit with the freedom on which they embark wherever they go, as though brighter than the lights that shine whispering secrets in the dark. The smiles on their faces are just scars that need not be addressed now.

A camera permits a flash picture on the dark side of the moon that contends the prospect that there are places that dark? They see the swans in the park as their parents, and the moon is forbidden to participate in the pageantry. A boy stares through the glass façade of a tuxedo shop and thinks it is perfect for the prom and cotton is accessible to those who participate now? They do not blame others for their plight, but I guess with responsibility there is room for some repentance too.

Michael Jackson watches from a cloud and feels slightly jealous of his brethren and this is a good thing too. Two lovers meet behind the bleachers at the high school and are commended for bringing light to the darkest of situations. They think it is funny that you do not know this and the moon might be their mother too? He is my brother and God fills the void in darkness as well as in light. An afro is one way to see what is a lightbulb that lives on in someone else's sense of fairness. But, the children are free and I am dark matter that will join them in this light that lives on in this human form.

Satan may be afraid of the dark and light will penetrate the void as the doctor orders an acquittal at such times. I may be darker than clouds on that gloomy day. My father is not present.

7. Santa Claus

Santa Claus' beard is a white as the snow that manifests here as sort of a picture. He is second only to God in his light. I transcend the realm of the cheetah from where I once stood. It is March in the North Pole and he eats a slice of cherry pie that his wife prepared for him in a brown paper bag. Now, the UPS men form an army of believers in his cause that rumbles like his belly from every corner of the globe except Mozambique. He may no longer keep it in and he soils the snow with memories of children who may keep a secret instead. His joy is only physical and he laughs at the presumption that smiles toast the stars at hand. He drinks a glass of sparkling apple cider that his friend sent all the way from Minnesota. He thinks every snowflake that falls is like a child, each being unique. Also, he loves children through his belly which will grow three inches before Christmas.

Sometimes, in the North Pole, the sun does not shine and the moon provides some light instead. One winter was particularly cold and Santa became frozen in a witches' spell. He managed to escape the evil curse and, when most of the snow melted, he woke up.

It was a time that my father should enter heaven and things will continue like this. When someone enters heaven, Santa Claus must win at staring match with a black snake that he always wins as he sleeps from within. All that is left is the white part that forbid others to penetrate. A hole remains in the African Congo and children escape the fate of dark entities here. They think darkness is being frozen in time and they would play with other children outside the still life that resounds.

A dark man in the Mississippi Delta puts on a Santa Claus hat at Christmas and brings toys to a few special children there, that is if you believe in Santa Claus?

8. The Witch's ' Toad and Eleven White Rabbits

Beauty and the Beast transpires in China as an authority figure in which compose the eleventh dimension. She is the witch to all other witches and they are subordinate to the cause without denying her role as a mother, and the toad may relay as a lesser, her husband. The design of a perfect white sun is her purpose and the eleven white rabbits ponder her nuances like pets. The scenario dries her tears and may ride a phoenix in my imagination. Meanwhile, her husband is a toad and will not escape the wet landscape that denies him of luxuries she invites. Here, the children will inherit a white horse and her husband smokes someone else's Camel Light cigarettes, and the tiger finds this at best to be a test.

Meanwhile, her long blond hair falls in sunlight which merits respect like tattoos now hidden. She escapes a fire which the curse is bestowed on my left knee, and flies into a horizon that will not meet the ground. She inherits the knowledge that detests good witches from bad witches, and she would rather diagnose herself as other. Nancy walks on the beach and dreams a better dream which is real. The sky is white and clouds will not penetrate her domain as though the devil is out of reach and considered by the eleven white rabbits as futile in her cause. The toad sits on a rock in a still life and allows itself to be present at a ceremony, though I am not a Jew. This is rather her domain.

Her child will walk on toads leading into the sky and joined as a family and such. I would not know otherwise, but see from my motel room in Malibu, a perfect white sun which is her creation. Like the Jews, the devil is not invited to the ceremony. Instead, the toad waits in a lake so that the eleventh dimension will explore its boundaries of the different sects of witches that resound. The devil is now a toad and the white horse something else entirely. Bad witches subscribe to other and in their parting, the white horse gallops on clouds in the sky which she now owns. The Jews are free to dream a better dream and she will meet our father in the sky too. The devil is bored and a giant white goose carries our father to a bar where he orders a scotch on the rocks. Their paths will not cross either.

9. Woman in White Lace (the twelfth dimension)

Woman has earned respect and falters on the ground like a cup of coffee dispensed in milk, which is a vision of Alanis Morisette riding a white horse while naked. She is not framed by the ordeal, but represents the twelfth dimension, which is the last natural form and rather remains on the ground for the sake of man, which will envelop visions such as this. The curtain will now fall as she wears white lace to bed and the show is now over as her daughter prepares for a spectacle that is other, where poetic champions compose. I may be neither man nor woman, but maintain an animalistic instinct that allows me to persist further. It is true that woman does not conspire, but rather shares information instead. She does not deny herself having fun in the process. A man may not touch her long flowing hair in the ordeal and he is a testament that she did exist too. Man is subordinate in the cause as she enters a different domain. Man may not be as lucky as the white lace she wears enveloping the sky in darkness. With the help of two white swans, she creates woman from this perspective. Meanwhile, Nicole holds hands with our father in the sky to not reveal secrets made in the dark.

10. Polar Bear

A polar bear is a cold element if not for the ice, which is so unbearable like a fire if not for their fur. They are in their own element. They are so naked to the landscape; that you might say they are ghosts which should not be penetrated by man. At the least the ice and their fur absorb the landscape so that one would not notice them at all. Like other animals, they are invisible, but even more so for polar bears.

It stands up on massive paws and finds itself as slightly off balance, and this might direct it where to go. Animals are out there in space. To kill one is taboo as only the ghost of the carcass remains. And it absorbs the infiltrator's soul it consumes, which decomposes in the dust that remains from the first kill. I think God meant us to be vegetarians? But, there may be exceptions. Native Americans understood this somehow and, as shooting themselves with a bow and arrow in a kill; there was enough respect to make it an exception. They are now gone in animal heaven and God permits this. The polar bear feels naked in its environment while animals deny their sin too.

11. Broken Glass

Walking in a place that is no more than forty miles outside of L.A., I wear my penny loafers. The black rock I carry is no more than a pebble, but may have significance in how God created the world. In the shoe, I took it out and put it in the tongue where pennies go. I thought this rock is a remnant of that which merits some scrutiny in God's greater plan. When the three of us arrived here, a small black rock like this one was possessed by one of us and thrown from our precious existence like a photograph that is all that is left us? And hence, God had a point of reference to create a world that only once was and so it be.

Walking to Niagra Falls would be too far and I pick up a jug to walk to the nearest place to get water. But, first I leave my stinky shoes in the grass of a friend, Jamie, who died but is remembered as such as a pair of shoes. As I say farewell to a friend, I hear God tell me to walk barefoot on the streets and the shoes are side by side in a grass patch which reaches to its boundary but no farther. This was a test, as I was to go past the boundary of which I am allowed. But, God would not let me down and proof is no glass should pierce my bare white feet and it did not either. As for the tiny black rock, I left it at some construction site I thought God would approve of.

12. Albino Superman

Superman is the epitome of white. Despite the movie that expresses otherwise, I think he came from a dysfunctional family and beyond his crystal palace is a migraine oasis that will not allow him to be free of the past?

156

Though he possesses super powers, in a persona outside of this realm, he is unable to change his world and seems, in effect, powerless. He feels mocked by the environment that denotes him as Clark Kent and from somewhere else really. While I call this home, he is left biting an inferiority complex in reverse. I must admit, I would not want to be him. His situation leaves him in a schizophrenic disorder and all he really wants is to be set free from this, but his parents do love him still.

13. Superfluous Camera

A photograph denotes a hope to communicate with God and confirm our existence. Somewhere in creation, a camera plays a role in people's lives, but is it superfluous? I think yes and no, like picking an apple; it depends on who is taking the picture. To actually render this machine, you must be of the light and, if not, the picture will turn out all black. You will hold onto these pictures like your favorite torn jeans, and not know that they are never to be unfortunately. God takes photos, but are they superfluous, I do not know? I took a bunch of photos of my apartment where I met Mimi on East 80th Street, and they came out all white?

14. Stranded on Bird Island with Steve

Sometime in the eighties, I crossed the devil's path with Steve, stranded on Bird Island off the coast of southern Georgia. It is a sandbar off the coast near Sea Island. Here, our boat drifted to sea and all that was left in this hell were a couple of warm Budweisers in cans, sea shells, and a lot of seagull poop. This is a photograph of what hell is like.

We made a display in the sand with shells that read "help," supposing a plane would fly by. It was getting dark and we did not know if we would be rescued? The thing I learned about hell here is that hell is not the propensity toward life, but death thereafter. The fact that I will be born after I die is something else entirely.

Next time you are at Uno's Pizzeria in Georgetown, Washington, D.C., ask yourself what raw remains of a seagull's waste would taste like and that is hell, it does exist! (All that is left of the devil is the foam at the mouth of the ocean floor.) Slavery was wrong no matter how you enter the door so it is and I was wrong too.

Adam and Eve Hotel Theater Productions

"Sequential Mathematics" (part of the Illiterate Symposium)

"32" The Jewish Potluck Dinner

Death (like dinner) is a phenomenon that Ferocious might know, though I have not been born yet, I think. He may, at such times, be adopted by a Jewish family in Omaha, Nebraska and be loved too. (And mazaball soup tonight, his favorite.) I promised that I would refuse porridge at all costs, but this is kosher anyway. Ferocious is an entity who died and was re-born and, therefore, never had to face a fate that many fear, including my father who died and continued thereafter. In a short delay, only to continue as though without any change, he feels inclined toward supper rather than dinner. This is a rare occurrence when the two share a dinner table, despite their separate fates still. If there is any entity that is inclined toward death in the end, it is my father, but he does not seem to notice.

However, Ferocious is born and re-born in death and, therefore, the fate of my father may be more attractive to some. Ferocious would rather be a ghost like Michael Jackson is to God and, as a result, has the grace never to die which is a compromise with which he is able to live. Even in death, he has one life to spare which he fathoms is like Mickey Mouse standing in the shade on a sunny afternoon. Ferocious will not sacrifice his loins to the fate of man.

The number 191 is ironic and belongs to Ferocious despite my grandmother's phenomenal dill pickles which she grows outside in her garden. And, here, the numbers 191 and 32 are the same and breath life instead of death. Dinner is composed of mathematical equations which I refer to as sequential mathematics. [(38191)=death=2=square root of 2]. Therefore, comments on black hole #1: "In the universal scheme there may be two layers of blue like a polarizer lens? When the horizontal and vertical lines are perfectly parallel, one sees something like lights at the end of a tunnel in death. There is light in darkness! What we may see makes us more blind relatively in what we call "light," (in our ordinary lives).

While comments on black hole #2: "No to number five and 24 represents twice of the concrete dimension 12 which may be the last conceptual dimension. There is "the end" which cannot be naturally seen like death... Three to six is divided and equals two which is also zero.

"Black hole #2 continued:"

"Why we cannot touch death is the same reason why we cannot see death." There are three ways of proving this as denoted formerly. First, if God represents the fifth dimension which is also the center, to say no to it is to deny the part of God which is in every one of us. This is also how we know something is out there. Second, then, if infinite space is infinite, the last dimension 12 which God created in the form of a woman, is also the same distance from it as 24 which is twice of it. This adds to the proof that we know God is there (from within). Thirdly, six divided by three is two which is death which is the same as zero.

"Comments on Black hole #1 and #2": "Whether from the outside or from within, there is more than one way of seeing too. Since (I believe) if one is to split an atom, it is only in my view a form of rejuvenation. Therefore, this, what I call sequential mathematics is just a new form of relativity. The fact that we may play with electrons and protons, means God is among us. However, since there are still mysteries means there are some things we are not supposed to see or know too! I still want to ask, if there is a blind spot in the universe, somehow, we know what we need to know? (Why can we not see the spiritual world? Blue is empty of color...) and Hitler died on a cross just like the Jews (metaphorically speaking). Porridge is mixed at the table and I decline to eat with him. I may be a lover at such times, but not really where water and milk find common ground, I am inclined... and our paths part for an eternity, we never met, I think. I see through Jesus' eyes and there is death all around me that the number 32 predisposes.

The point is that a prince may in fact see through death's eyes . If blue is empty of color, there may be more than one way to see in darkness too. God interrupts the dinner and prays for Jews who remain in a sort of quagmire. Death is better than the alternative sometimes. It is like wearing your favorite jeans without getting dirty in the process. The meal they share is components of last year's war. I see through death's eyes and succumb to its allure. I take the dog out so that I will not get wet in the rain which may be the Jews too. The rain to me is calculated sloppy kisses from this dog who escapes a lesser fate and the rain will not penetrate this domain either. Sorry, but we have never met.

"65" Homeward Bound

Where Africa/six and God/Five meet there is an eternal play that diagnoses a center which the players invade the space as though to enter it in the middle as one thereafter. "Who is the real God?" One may barely hear the Simon and Garfunkel tune on the outside as it is played for "the Walrus." I think like melodies of lost love, they do not meet. I provide a dark cloud where we may meet, however. Where the poetic champions compose, God enters here as though his own too. The black stallion does not know now that it is not of the earth, and the milk turns in his cup of coffee inward and no spoils to account for, and the black turns outward as well. This is where we will meet, I think. He may have friends which calculatingly deplore the play at hand, yet still enter which he had done prior. They will call this home too. A giraffe stands erect to watch over the children at such times. God is one with the people at hand.

"42" Hitler on 42nd Street (lettuce and the lie)

An army of blue soldiers with glass eyes is erect and in motion like the layers of fish that occupy the ocean. They believed a land without a tolerant god does in fact exist? The lie exists on shores of sea lions bathing on cliffs as though next to the sun and seaweed is food that satisfies their soul, though God is not present as well. The lie is that this tastes like lettuce and one walrus plops in the ocean and makes a splash which negates a sanguine tolerance that would not exist here without a god? The blue soldiers lock arms as though an existence is tolerated in a chain that will live in a soulless realm as though not to care either. Water may exist further as without tears shed in the sky? (Hitler's unnatural sin may not be unlike the tear that fell from God's eye.) The rain will come and go at such times. Marilyn Monroe sheds a tear too at such times, while men of a dark land trade their wares of wooden statues and the pharaoh's gold is worthless now, in contrast. Hitler is a false god to that which is "money" and "lettuce" in the exchange.

Forty-two is a sentiment that is twice the dimension of twenty-one , but is foreseen as existing without a soul too. Renata, as twenty-one, will not shed a tear in the process of this artificial passing of the devil. She does not know where the path she follows in Nantucket will lead to? But, I am walking next to her in this dream! Instead, I eat a salad at Howard Johnson's in Times Square and leave a tip from a twenty dollar bill as praise for my dad for just existing. His soul, like "the brats of doom," will take on the form of a dime which is redeemed in New York City. In memory of the Jews who died in the holocaust, New York City is for sale at such times. "The Unbearable Lightness of Being," is a reminder to him that he was here once just like his idols the Yankees represent with signatures on baseballs left to me, and I will not pawn this memory. I continue to drive a yellow taxi in the rain in N.Y.C., but like Hitler's private island, it is a mirage and I escape the fate of the brats of doom and the sun is shining outside too. I will not leave until my dad enters his domain in heaven and is forgiven for things like the holocaust too.

"55" Africa for Sale

The cat's tail is severed from one's body for an eternity. She may well not have the best of intentions at such a juncture. A black snake remains on a tree dangerously close to the sun. She may well have a primal instinct which allows her to tempt the other sex, but seeks greater control over the land she will inherit. The market propels her to sell all of Africa at such times and, coincidentally, this frees my soul as well. Whether good or bad, a cross remains at this juncture and he will die for this sin. She will sell her rights here for some cheap jewelry and is battered in the process.

In her death, a queen is born in Africa and they regain control over a land with dark tendencies; for a lie which is not hers and for a sin which she will embrace as her own most affectionately. She thinks this is better than having nothing anyway? At such times, she may buy all of Africa and trade it for a sin which is not hers. In closing, she joins all of Africa in prayer and she clasps her hands together like a testament to this at church.

"33" Ferocious Again

Ferocious inhabits the dimension of children which is diagnosed in the number ten. My mom creates woman in a guise as though without it thereafter. She is an orator to this play with woman being her creative pursuit which man will never understand. She escapes a fate which Satan inherits while he is resting on the boardwalk of Venice Beach in California. He is kicked by those who remember a time without this imposing element. As though to take responsibility for it all, he feels the soulless waves that crash to the shore as God has left now, as well as Mt. Fuji, who was afraid of the sun.

This is really just a mirage as Ferocious finds an alligator skin wallet and claims it as his own. The camera follows the other wherever he goes and this diagnosis does not find me damned at such times and the blisters that formed on my feet are now healed. The ocean is left with dark tendencies which will escape God if not for three lions and the "half-moon and red tide..."

Seahorses dance in a bath of fish urine forever more and Will has flat feet that stand on ground that is flat like his, too... My dad, with surfboard in hand, asks his girlfriend Mimi to take pictures of him on beaches to appease his giant ego at such times. Otherwise, he is a tow truck driver in Malibu and the rain subsides for a while at this juncture. Meanwhile, my Jewish grandfather stands on a cloud in the sky with a blue umbrella too, in hand. My sisters walk into the sky to meet him, while holding hands. The number eleven represents the dimension of witches. I feel inclined to live near here, though.

Ferocious is born from an artificial sin. Meanwhile, the kids play in the ocean without any fear of Satan who is left behind without any consequence to the sins that resound. He is God's waste in hindsight, if you want to call this a blessing? The children build sandcastles in the sky and God is always watching too. I think his mother is Mars. The color blue elopes the sky out of darkness and he knows why the caged bird sings? Africa is his soul and is freed and overcomes the emotions of that which is the devil. They will not meet either, and Satan is now considered separate too.

"13" In the beginning...

There may well be three blue devils who worked on the sky...where one through twelve are natural dimensions and the number 13 begins again as one here. Mary Magdalene may well be his sister, but, while my sister Nicole is definitely in her own element here too! A mother, father, and daughter exist in India and are exonerated from the sin that would manifest later, too. The triad that would manifest here to this isolated family diagnosed their innocence while deer deny it. God asks from the inside of what became Africa, who ate the fruit? The Garden of Eden would decay with the sin of others and the land became a crime scene which demanded the suspects to leave for a time, I think. The animals may have had a choice whether to leave and God may have made this his temporary home in a distant land, this is just a procedure really.

Meanwhile, two blue devils were infected by the sun and became my eyes, while the one left untarnished was spared and became his own, which could not be penetrated as God may see differently than we do. When water falls from rocks above he is absolved by his creation and the venue tells only the truth. Rainbows seem like different colored soldiers holding hands in the sky! A black Labrador smells the butt of a poodle and this is a façade which is not far off from God; it is a farce of what is God and we do not even know he is there.

My sister Nicole represents this dimension which is where man and woman find common ground. I think man was created in God's image too. Nicole has a connection to God through this guise which is man. Meanwhile, Bob Marley returns to Africa (if he was ever there?) and sings Reggae motifs and asks could this be love? Our parents and Nicole walk with Nelson Mandela to freedom as the sun fades. Nancy and I escape this fate and walk onward too… We listen to "dreams deferred," not so far away either. (A gay man knows his life is not over yet.) I am not the very last person here as God's life has just begun. The clouds form at his feet so that the sand returning to the ocean is forgiven as well…A rastaman is born like sand in the ocean which is better than what Satan will inherit. South Africa remains "out of Africa," as a metaphor for a bear detached from the forest. "Out of Africa," might mean you are not God either? Satan is a weed that is detached from Africa's infrastructure and the devil is broke at such times. Satan may have one dollar which is to say he is rich in the eyes of God. Africa will inherit God's love instead. The slave knows that freedom is not gained on the African soil. They are slaves to God's love and like the number "33," it is a deal Ferocious may live with. Freedom is gained from this knowledge too. Beware of the female tiger as she is woman too! I am no longer a slave to this notion. Satan and Lily remain in the ocean as viaducts in my eyes of all of God's creation. Satan looks through the devil's eyes instead. To see you must recognize you are not God too.

The mirage of God smoking a joint is actually an illusion that the devil may have alluded too. The devil has many faces too. I also do not deny God's creation. I ask, does God have a sense of humor? On a serious note, seeing through two eyes is different than the way God sees. Though, he will see through us too, he accesses one of the blue devils that is pure. All that is his creation becomes invisible in respect to how we see. You may say we are blind in respect to the way God sees, for the most part. The illusion is that the model T Ford has only one headlight. It is just a different way of seeing anyway. Meanwhile, a deer caught in the car's headlight sees only reflections of what is God and that is all. It is a blessing, I think, that Stevie Wonder may ponder what this is like. Meanwhile, a dog chews on a bone and wonders what it would be like to be a man too? Anyway, there may be many different ways of seeing. Through hazel eyes, Mimi sees the rain falling. Her tears dry as the blue sky unfolds like an island in the sky. She will not claim them as her children at such times. My dad with blue glass eyes watches old episodes of the Honeymooners while eating his soup with a silver spoon and he is not Hitler either! My dad sits on cloud #42.

"21" Like a tail of a tiger...

Hell is not a punishment really, it is just "other." The fact that I do not recognize the Holocaust does not mean it does not exist. It is just that I see those who died in the spectacle were re-born (including myself maybe) and therefore did it really happen? Dead cockroaches form united in strains in her sister's hair, but does this mean that cockroaches are re-born in this form as well? I ask does kangaroo excrement live on in a different form, I think yes too? The apple that fell landed calculatingly in God's hand, but I accept this as part of his greater plan too. Meanwhile, bananas and pineapples are two different fruits and he lights his cigar with like a tail of a tiger. Even fire is accounted for as he might call this heaven too.

Mimi's sister has a tail that sees through God's eyes and this will not deter your quest for an eel that remains in the ocean. She will not die like the eternal clouds in the sky. The Jews who died in the holocaust will not die again! Brian sings a song for Mimi too...

"22" Where the fourth dimension and Satan's End #44 (John Riggins) meet...

Number forty-four is twice the dimension twenty-two which designates an artificial sentiment really. If he does exist, Satan lives in California really, while John Riggins #44 of the Washington Redskins is my bodyguard at such times. They are three squares compiled on one another, and this is the fourth dimension. He may not enter within, but rather propelled farther outward like John Riggins' belly, I think. A Catch-22 is being trapped in a square when this is all your existence may produce. John Riggins eats baby back ribs and drinks a red Merlot to drown his disassociation with that which is Satan. He rides a sailboat on the Chesapeake at such times.

Satan's End is when the tail of a blue eel conspires with the once salt in his tear, and sandwiches crusts are cut off to deplore a demeanor of seagull waste is edible at such times. He will not escape *The Catcher in the Rye* at such times and throws the football with Joe Theisman on the beach which is really some sort of mirage.

I serve as a spy for Obama's foreign legion when my belly is propelled outward like the poisons the ocean possesses. Satan finds comfort here in a moonstruck place which diagnoses his life as nil, but he makes a deal to carry on his fate further still. The waves crashing to the shores in the ocean are the metaphysical reality my belly endures, but I may not escape this phenomena which is Satan. I digest the ruby, instead of the emerald, and this is my destiny like a goldfish trapped in a bowl is the incognito of my belly.

John Riggins wears the #44 on his jersey and this is enough to keep Satan at bay somewhere else. He attacks the line of scrimmage and does not digest the ribs entirely, rather some of it remains in his colon. This designates something dangerous here, but he may press onward like the eternal ocean.

Yet, it is the lesser danger merited by a tail of a blue eel which sees everything through my dad's eyes and never sheds a single tear though. I ask, which poisons do exist as milk from the moon may exist in the ocean in the form of malevolent spoils of a spider's fruit, that which is her sister? The number two may never enter another two at such later a time, I think? Meanwhile, I may call Madagascar home. Like three squares (the pyramids of Egypt will not die) even as it turns to sand, she mourns the death of another at such times. This is the entrance to the third world and I call Finland home too. Mimi mourns a loss which is her own tear and this is a beautiful thing too! Will represents Denmark which is the fourth world and it is now separate. Norway and Sweden divide like sisters holding hands and represent a division of the first and second world too.

"23" Marilyn Monroe

Marilyn Monroe is a metaphor for how fertile a flower may be if not picked?

Her dimension is as real as the milk from a desert in the ocean. She will die on the four corners of a bed and she lies naked here with no shame of that which the candle experiences while fading in the wind. She diagnoses herself in the corners of a square; still she finds the hotel comforting enough to stay a while thereafter. The window is left open and pigeons make profane gestures with the cold air of the mortician's spine.

James Dean sleeps in the next room next door and Ferocious collects the red down jacket I left for him, yet the two will never meet either. A woman exists in this trance for that which she is a muse and within the number twelve there is a mystery of the last natural dimension. The number eleven is reserved for witches who comply notions of 55s and those good natured within further, I think. I find it comforting that the #23 may not be penetrated, but on her way home, she is kidnapped by a dark land for ransom and a handful of colored jellybeans. Children collect them on Easter Sunday in the rain as they are within their element too. She will come home when she decides to!

"24" The Lion

My father sheds the blood of one thousand coverts in a distant land. His fear is resolved in the loss of heaven; here is a deal he complies with (different colored jellybeans on Easter Sunday) and the raccoon that exists, he is scared of too. He will not penetrate God's realm , but manages to buy a cloud over Yankee Stadium instead. He is a lion that through things such as peer pressure actually fears heaven as a toy he is not inclined toward and rather not play, despite the bee buzzing at his disposition is artificial. And he is an exception and, likewise, when it comes to heaven, he would rather not, but this is not hell either. He finds the notion of tempting the devil a fulfillment which his mane endures as royalty and he too is in his element. Though, he is a man, he is like man as well and women seem to like him which is the next best thing, I think. However, the other would not rather deny him his manhood really? His stature from where he exists is somewhat like the pink panther, I think. Time plays a game with him and denies his existence though God's own creation; he may be a man too? Women like the fact that he creates his own destiny despite the fact he is not God either. Note, the number twenty-four is twice the concrete dimension twelve which is also woman.

"25" The Gay Quarter Show with Stew the Racehorse

The play is prolonged in this display of twenty-five entities here that sequential mathematics may foster. It is a dress rehearsal for affectionate characters displayed on the outside. They show a longing for those co-existing in Adam and Eve Hotel Theater Productions, to show their demeanor is real, but the garden now long gone. A garden with a harmless green snake exists in

China next to a spring and giant pine trees that absorb it and infiltrated by goldfish, where a black cat once stood, too. Within Africa a trade is made with many a child's poor pennies to buy a beautiful white horse. It will remain outside this scope too.

The legend says that he never drank water and only drank wine, but I do not know which is true? Meanwhile, a rainbow spans the ocean from South Africa all the way to Australia. When the exchange is made like bread for wine, there may be no entrance within and the play merits the sympathy of the devil as it does dry the tears of many kings that occupy foreign lands. The stage is set on the East River, way uptown to propel notions of eternal life through the guise of this play which ends with the beginning of another more challenged display of affection to a dying sun. The horse is displayed here in a cage of children's eyes that dooms the subject to an existence that may be only be interpreted as a compromise.

Ilius shed a cross in Mozambique for the life of a horse which they call Stew and he enters the sky with a functioning capacity to spawn a longing forever more. Indians are spared a lesser fate. A princess rides the horse in a distant land of Lepure and finds an affection for it usually reserved for a father. Lily, a crooked-toothed tiger shark eats her lover Fidel in a dream too, if she was so inclined? Her jaws are displayed in hindsight at the Museum of Natural History. Showing a strength women rarely possess, she escapes a fate that is less than damnation and visits the gay quarter show with her sister.

She swallowed her lover and, in doing so, escapes a fate that Satan will inherit instead. The *Gay Quarter Show* plays out in the sky of men who are born once again, and my dad says he has a good seat to view the display at hand.

"26" The bear dance and hat #324 (Where two 13s meet in the sky, I think)

Nicole wears hat #324 and this is the dimension where psychedelic bears dance and the ocean divides in happy plays where thirteen and thirteen meet(as 33s go so far before they head back inward again like sand raked in by the ocean, which is in fact her father.) She is an only child, and Nancy and I escape her fate, which still is a gift. We watch her from a nearby cloud, though. Thirteen is like a grand entrance that tests our father's fate and begins again at number one. Two thirteens mark the capture of this time. My sisters are the gate keepers in the form of 33s where the three joins from three hundred and twenty-four, and eight hundred and eighty-three.

Once the play finale begins there is no way in from this point of view. But, children allege that the play reveals crimes of the past, though. Those guilty of unnatural crimes will deplore the ongoing play and fetch those guilty as "out of Africa." One may enter here to fulfill the seat vacant, like 10,000 maniacs do participate? In the intermission of the grand play at hand, Nicole wears the hat #324 while the doors are open to view the dancing bears performing a skit subsequently as though an intermission. Those guilty of unnatural crimes here will exit from the back. Witches in India exonerate those without blinking an eye while children play and play. The sport here comprises three different teams. Chinese witches comprise skits of beauty as 10,000 entities at hand, and they are the preponderances that propels the clouds onward forever. God may leave anytime he wants to, though. Those who are waiting to participate in the show fill vacant seats from the venue of South Africa too.

"27" Three Nines and Redemption's Alter Ego (blink 883)

For this play to exist, man must prove himself stronger than his sins on the outside. The lizard blinks only once and three nines divide the #27 equally so that those on the outside who do not find redemption by three AM the next morning are subjected to a punishment. In exchange, the children are rewarded as to know themselves. Redemption does not occupy the fourth dimension on the outside of Africa and the punishment is like the children who will know themselves, but this is a punishment, I think. Only God may free such subjects of this destiny. People like Louis Armstrong and others are friends and escape a fate and are re-born in places like South Africa where those who are resting find this is an escape which is more than hospitable. South Africa is severed and is not really part of the grand play at hand. It might serve like a brother, in such a situation. Benjamin Franklin and Nelson Mandela may co-exist here, and are best friends, I think?

"28" Four Sevens (the year was 1952: the beginning of time)

Albert Einstein created South Africa with "the four winds" (reference to Joseph Hurd) to know that the four doors here one may enter may also be used while leaving. It is a vacation spot of Americans who enter a square to escape an already tolerant world that bequests this luxury on their own subjects. A tolerant world is enough of a reason for this place to exist, I guess. Poetic champions compose here while a light is left on at the kitchen door, I think. An energy exists here that merits a respect of those who live outside the scope of what is Africa. Animals are not welcome here, though they come and go, too. Energy professed in the bombs is reinvigorated in time again, but may not die in the sport. Where human hot dogs exist upright and Mt. Fuji practices a rare martial art to capture lions in a sort of trance. A giraffe seeks another respect to foster the care of the children otherwise, and soccer is a popular sport as well, but, the animals do not participate here. A zebra kicks as to demonstrate that Eve still has maternal emotions and a cheetah is a soul of the wind and may capture a gazelle, which is a sort of a sport Jason tells me and he gives me a photograph of this instead.

However, a society of gorillas does exist in the rainforest of the Congo and represents dead suns from afar to merit life in death, it is true. If you are lucky enough to visit this land, you will find a leopard on a tree in the savannah does smile as you leave. A tiger is now at the center, but part of the sport is keeping it separate from leopards, while bears are taboo as well to the sport and land. A Jewish cross forms at a crossroad and the devil is not welcome to enter within. Meanwhile, Satan's punishment is to remain in the ocean forever, more! Though, snow leopards are the devil's pets in distant lands, though. God waves to Simon at such times, singing African American spirituals, "All things are possible," "Swing low, sweet chariot," and "That's alright," as to signify their existence in order of Will, Joseph, and my dad (who never left). The children now ride a great whale in the distance, waving now back at God.

The beginning of time began the countdown backward in 1952 and an explosion occurred in my posterior when Simon is freed in the ocean and the garden which once was is reinvigorated, while all friends of God are welcome as well, now. Simon lives in the ocean as though on land. Meanwhile, America represents the number seven and gets lost like the wind in her journey to meet her sister somewhere else.

"29" Poor man and Satan's End: (Bring tea for to man in China...)

Satan still remains in the ocean for all this time. He carries a CD in his leather satchel *Tea for the Tillerman* by Cat Stevens, and may be forgiven for crimes he did not commit in the past. He is a poor man and will never know what it is like to be other, and this is his punishment for the act of just being? God and Jesus may join hands while Big Ben stands erect in the rain while holding an umbrella at such times and this is his punishment. God is everything, and "other" means you are not God, however! God looks dark from this perspective and Satan's skin color is not an outlet for what cannot be seen as a sort of an oxymoron.

"34" Phoenix at Witches Door

My sister Nancy absorbed a dying sun and its sacrifice allows it to exist further in this light. She represents the eleventh dimension at this juncture, but only in my mind though? She divorced it to marry another. She no longer works at a "Red" McDonald's somewhere on the outskirts of Pasadena. The fish sandwich is not hers, though, as there is only one moon, too. Here, the Earth dances with Mars; "if you ever go to San Francisco, remember to wear a flower in your hair..." and that is enough to appease her from her trifles, I think. She is what is left of our father; a lion like sand raked up by the ocean.

"14" Puff the Magic Dragon and the children play and play...

Will is from Mercury, but escapes his fate for a better one in a metaphor of a record player that skips over that which is the earth to land on Mars. Really, Dr. Kraus tells me that it is possible. A man with red hair ran naked through the woods over there and a bear is the only entity who kept record of this occurrence. The children on Mars sit around the campfire with the likes of such specimens of Ziggy Stardust singing songs like "This land is your land." Smores are plentiful like sunflowers are to the sun, but we are able to sneak some of its seeds to provide some otherwise nutrients too. He does have large feet! "Puff the magic dragon," seems déjà vu at such times. The tiger lost at sea is now found.

"54" Woman Riding a Unicorn

Woman is twelve and the last of the natural dimensions. Two sisters from India occupy the halls of the hospital and serve in the creation of women thereafter. I see a raccoon on the road and know at this time that I am hallucinating. Raccoons, like children conceived in the dark, are able to maintain a secret well. She rides the white unicorn naked and is not ashamed of her creation of woman at such times. She rides with her alter egos, including Alanis Morissette and she listens to Simon and Garfunkel's "Cecilia," on her walkman. A unicorn is a vision of a bear who detests Jupiter on Mars in this perfect embrace.

"136" A phoenix, a dragon, and a unicorn join forces in my mind, a bad-ass Martian brain, I think…Eight "17s" form a circle in the rainforest in Brazil, a dream from which they will not wake…

"123" Reverend at Heaven's Door

Christianity is in the form of the combination of "Black," "Jewish," and "Chinese." A combination of these entities is Christianity in the form of a "race," "religion," and "nationality." I think Christianity composes 30% of mankind in this scenario, or at least of the wealth? Though, I refer to "Black" meaning those of African American descent, but this does not include Africa. As a Christian in this scenario, I guess I am doing pretty well. The Reverend, of African American descent and I may be one in this conception. He never asks for reparations from slavery, but knows his ugly past in a stipulation where the man warrants only respect. In the southern coast of Georgia (an island called Sapelo) as well as parts of South Carolina, there are the Gullah and Geechee descendents. And I guess it is sort of ironic that these people do not contest any separation from their homeland which I will be so bold as to refer to as Africa.

"10" What will we leave future generations?

I guess children are free to dream another dream? The children occupy the tenth dimension, which I note are remains of roadkills on desert highways. They do not die is the point I am trying to make. Still, we act like lions in car contraptions and they ironically are not our prey anyway. Still, there may be a choice to leave this great land should the blinking lights shine their eyes upon one? Other than a colossal network of fast food restaurants and theme parks from where children barf their lungs out as they leave, we are a rich land.

We are pummeled by this disease in the outreaches of our existence and the door is open to exit likewise. Some may follow Steve, and they follow him to different lands, but Africa is forbidden in his quest though. You may well find yourself at your doorstep a thousand years in the future? Like the two doors the panda bear's eyes possess, there is a choice here? I promise to return to the hospital in which I was a patient one rainy winter night in the future. And I said seven thousand, nine hundred, and seventy-one years from the time I entered here a few years into the second millennium. As the countdown is now begun inward, I think? I left June a steak dinner, and Marvin, Jimi Hendrix's electric guitar (which I could not find) so I sent some Vans (sneakers) instead, and the black kid inherited a pink rabbit Volkswagen too.

"56" Lucky to be American/Italian

Though I am born half-English and half-Russian/Polish Jew, I consider myself lucky to be American/Italian in hindsight. When Gianni Versace died, I felt a connection here which is not far off as the end of the African continent forms as far as away as the Alps and therefore Italy is really part of the African sub-continent. The riches of the world may well shine down on this land in which history should revoke their participation in this play of sorts. Really, God loves this land as his own son. The number "56" is a weird way of expressing his love of these people which merits a cohesion of sorts in this scenario. But, really, America is very blessed as well. The former is a strange sort of love I think, though. Africa does reflect the sky and I thought I should say that.

"64" Still life at Graceland and a picture of Elvis too

There may be a picture taken in my mind of my earliest assembly of my father, though, likewise, it is Elvis too. I see things in motion and this manifests itself as something bad when taken out of the context of what was once Graceland. When I see motion outside the confines of a still life, a picture is taken of God. My parents may have conceived me like Elvis, and Pricilla is royalty too. The former are left in the darkness thereafter. My parents did not conspire me, but injected love in my soul to free their dark tendencies and, likewise, they are free too. They only need love me once and this is enough for our paths to part and they will curse those who revoke their passions in a dark land I think.

They made Graceland for those who would rather not, though. Black masks debauch their demure as something bad in Africa and this demands a certain degree of respect, too. They do not want to co-exist as something bad, but are inclined as such and blame others for their plight. Pricilla combs her hair while holding a sterling silver mirror and sees my mom instead. Elvis may be suspicious that he is not God at such times, I think. His mortal life is not far off from that of my father. There is a set change in the Garden of Eden and the diagnosis requires all those present must leave and I took a picture of God at such times. I manifest it as a dark entity really, but it does not fade either.

Graceland is my dad's second home, and is exonerated here as he makes the pact to not be God, and this is how I see my father. My mother and father, though dark in intentions, do not belong to God, but still act as vestibules to serve him despite their diagnosis is not good either. The wooden masks they sell at markets are not theirs either. They may be an extension of God's hand, and this seems to God as a compromise. He sells bananas next to their stand and this is my father too. My dad is somehow connected to God I think?

"17" Pattern of the marmalade

The number five is subject thereafter to the dimension seventeen and forms a pattern of a lion here.

"18" Pattern of inside a pack of Camel cigarettes

The number six is subject thereafter to the dimension eighteen and forms a pattern of a dog here. Inside a pack of camel cigarettes, he is the devil too.

"16" Pattern of coffee dreams

The number four is subject thereafter to the dimension sixteen and forms a pattern of a black panther to invoke drinking the blood of another which is coffee too.

In these venues, there are three tribes that compete in Africa so to join God in heaven. A play is made to a dying sun too. The first tribe is represented by the number five which is a lion. The second tribe is represented by the number six, which is a dog. And the third tribe is represented by the number four which is a black panther.

"Sequential Mathematics 101"

I am perched on an artificial dimension represented by the number twenty-two. While one through twelve are natural dimensions. God speaks to me in many ways which includes my sisters. Like eleven, it is a realm which she demands the respect of witches; good and bad. My other sister Nicole would rather speak to our dad, which I address in denial of his greatness and she is thirteen to form a cross that begins again as the number one too.

In space, I am in the center of this artificial sentiment, between my grandmothers who may be other too. I represent the 22nd dimension and the cross forebears the number twenty-one on the left, and represents my mother's mother and twenty-three as Marilyn Monroe represents Mimi's ghost on the right or my father's mother. I remain to oust Satan #44 from the garden so he may remain separate from God. A bear remains for those who must believe. This keeps Satan at bay. "Kelly's Eye," is the number one, which like Manhattan, is a prostitute which may not be paid for in gold.

I call New York City, "Adam and Eve Hotel Theater Productions." Here, God and the devil share common ground. Through Kelly's eye, she views "the Gay Quarter Show" which is the exact opposite of the Virgin Mary. My dog belongs to the good witch to man and she keeps record of the time as it counts back from 2000. Ferocious is out there in space and is my companion too, like the number thirty-three is "from here to eternity," like my father. The gay quarter show may be a prep for this show in Africa exposing the sins of the father and a dying sun as well. My mother may not be present while I lean against the base of the Empire State Building after taking a picture of my dog "Ferocious" on a redwood stump. From here they sing, "This Land is Your Land."

Meanwhile, my dad may exist on a cloud over Africa where he may see the New York Yankees and they sing to a tolerant world, "The Saints Go Marching In." One may exit the door while entering as God prescribes. I really do not know what nature is?

Dark Star in Nine Parts
who are you? Five: God
(Jamie Daves)

The folktale says that he shot the sheriff,
but was really not him. Only a bear remains
for those people who must believe. But, the
children believe he is innocent. To make
the world a better place, someone must be
tested, but he is just where the center is, let go!

Part Five: Lost in L.A.

From the climbing street, the spring crosses under into a vista like a painting and falls upon a river in rich foliage of mostly green in summer. To trek this virgin soil is like staining your best pants before church service on Easter Sunday. It does not know that it is untouched and, with the spring that crosses over its natural serenity, it cautions the vagrant to let it be. The smell of musk and the water making a small path leading the way, it is not sure if it will actually make it to the river, part of the larger panorama down below?

Entering the terrain, I must cross a small fence, where a garden of rocks manifest their holy remains, from the mountain that fell years before. And to pass from the street on the other side of the fence; a collage of densely situated campers of whose grateful denizens form in their abode a pattern, in sunlight, of a glimmering white rose. Sort of a maze to enter the center where conceivably the most life is; the outer fringes contend that it is dedicated to the community within and not the lonely Indian who passes on the other side of the fence.

On the street outside the mesh of residing campers and such, he passes on a narrow path along a quiet, well-kept road. From this viewpoint, he may see the more affluent homes wedged in the cliffs so natural. Here, he walks, I think a shortcut in the wilds, like a small desert shrub spared by the metropolitan's terminus dynamic on the way to school. Over a small gate he climbs, with a sign that says, "private: state run land," and so on, unlike the camper community he passed prior to this.

The cliffs above occupy a few wealthy landowners in lots reserved for those Native Americans who in rare occasions maintain the capital to do so. Farther up the path I follow; I concentrate on the sharp rocks that compose the way; and huge, forty foot electrical poles are maintained by the state, sub-sequentially. The poles make an ominous sound like a vibration in the wind and, like the great Native Americans who lived before, they offer a powerful, imposing feeling. Behind this is a rock thrown to the glimmering white rose a veranda in the sunlight which weans as it is too far to reach, but represents a progress of sorts.

I pause before releasing the rock, then hurl it high into the sky and it falls somewhere on the footsteps of the path behind. On top of the hill where the modern day Indian stands upright next to the gigantic poles, their great ancestors trekked at such a place. Here, are an assemblage of rocks; fertile and energized, but the sounds taunting. The sun beats down relentlessly and maybe this is a holy place to leave such artifacts of the land which may be the last remnants of a heritage an Indian might detest to. And, in the distance, there is a hill that climbs to this height in perfect symmetry, like, maybe, a burial site. To not touch the beckoning rock that has an imprint of the sun and calls like the wolf to feel, I leave it to be the skin of the wind that puts it to sleep with every sun falling like it has been always and therefore, should be!

It is visited by three spirits vibrating with their voices in metal beddings in the ground and the rock bakes further in the sun as it falls in the sky. On the other side, there is another fence which I study to find the best place to climb over. There is a small designated area here like a bear's resting area and tires which in the opening might be guarded by some junk yard dog. On the other side of the fence, the freeway restricts the area.

A funny thing about this place: one second you find yourself in some desolate place like a walk in the desert and the next moment one is submerged by winding freeways that coughs the black bird's lungs in this terrestrial display. Surprisingly, no dog; just a slight ripped cloth on the fence which may have torn from someone's shirt. The tires remain behind me as I attempt to climb the fence and I clear it. On the other side, raw freedom processes me. I think to ask a stationary truck driver where I might go from here? I leave the space behind me relatively untouched and do not rip my shirt on the fence. I pass the truck that is loading twice the nothing it openly shows and I think the driver has a funny resemblance to President Clinton, like a fuzzy animated character.

I do not know the omen or occurrence should play into what persons in L.A. may resemble thereafter. A police officer waits on the freeway along which I walk. I have done nothing, yet, I think to myself. He poses like a movie star with a shiny badge and high, worn boots, as black as the tires that spin on rigs passing. Burning rubber, so to speak; I pass this confrontation. I think of how I might have worn the paper box as a hat for this journey, that which I saw before.

But, there is no way to turn back, now. I might not have thrown the rock at the backside of the vista, at the community of campers. I left it almost as a farewell offering. I confront the cop, who does not look quite as polished as a movie star. At the meeting, I feel an unusual guilt sort of harbored inside me, away of view. I should not have thrown the rock at the community. Though not nearly reaching it, I still shatter something like my mom says, "Don't throw stones at glass houses."

But, before entering the marked-off space; walking on the road next to the community fence and along the path before it, there is a parade of purple flowers on a quiet street. And on the other side there are cramped campers set up like houses in a destined and systematized configuration in the sunlight. But, here on the other side of the fence, there may be a wealthy Indian or son of a landowner walking to school and the purple parade of flowers all talking to me in the breeze and the last one tempting me with its beauty to pick it.

I had picked a flower earlier in the day, near the overpass where there was a hill of baby cactus and a yellow flower. A dandelion it was, or something common that wakes somewhere else like a small grow patch. But, I did not pick the purple flower.

The police officer checks my ID and I move into the vista that will take me back home. I must make this journey as I have left my father behind me; I must find a way back alone. Coming upon the vista, I am beginning to regain my memory, the memory of the "owl rock" that is bestowed to me by my grandmother as belonging to me after Stalin's millions.

Only a trifle said Mike, who was like a friend to me and, in one of his many baby cactus gardens, there is a special plant that is grown along highways, and I stare at one of his many possessions. What is a little yellow flower? I sit, as to think, that this is the garden he wanted me to see. Without telling the ending of what happened, I am gone. So, I should wake, maybe, the same as a yellow flower and maybe on some cruise ship out at sea, under a yellow-shaded gondola and sipping a virgin strawberry daiquiri, (just as you asked). On some crinkled paper I wrote this poem as a gamut and one of the few things I learned in high school; it still haunts me: "In the Valley of the Dead..."

*

Flowers grow in the valley of the dead.
But, not so pretty though, people hardly notice me...
Season upon season, they flourish here upon this rock.
The wind crosses to awake their eternal fire.
Sing, song; the birds chant at spring's waking hour.
The rock is cold sadly and the birds fly south for the winter.

And the animals surround this place, white modest flowers for this honor. This is new for some and old for others;

And maybe it has gone a bit too far,

For everyone to perish for this one tiny flower.

*

Through the magnificent passage to the most holy of sites, it promises never to be touched. Then, stumbling on rocks I slide down the steep throughway as the dusk air and the stridulation of the insects imply the outrage of the obstruction. It sounds a fury and an odor of the musky water it is intruded on by another who would impose. A strange croaking sounding creature like that of a toad, it is one particularly disguised behind the other's chorus it is dressed in such vespertine. As the musky odor rises with each footstep, on the soil it is untouched at least since the last rainfall, or longer.

She speaks through this guise as its long lanky body confounds in her voice, an echo of its lonely history of deprivation and pain, and may only utter the words, "I do not like you."

Even if it might be your own son, her voice echoes like someone who really means this, but does not know what she says really, more lonely than spite. At the base of the hill where the picture-perfect canvas of nature meets the dimming lights, this happens every evening and the further cooling of the mist above. A flat hundred yards to the river, but wait; it is bulging now and may calm to pass in the morning, I think. In the grace of a metropolitan area, wild lettuce is grown here in the swale. And there is an abandoned car here, rusting for a decade as though a meteorite falling to the Earth and how did it get here?

As I wait at the banks for the entire evening, it occurs to me that the wind will crease the sand as I lie on bamboos that hold my weight like a bed next to the raging river. My son waits for me on the other side and I wake in a chill. To step the stones, is still premature, but if we could talk maybe a path would form, joining us, and I would say it has been a long time.

Another long day is ahead the next morning. Mike shows me his rock collection. He is someone, I know, and the ghost of my son falls with the moon and as I wake with the sun; there is Mike. I hesitate to pass and wait for a sign of the water slowing, which does not happen. Around mid-day, I cross, without the water falling below my knees. Another person who is real, across from the river, walks on what I call "the road to nowhere." Meanwhile, Mike contemplates how he would embrace his son as Jim Morrison? I do not claim to have any children of my own at such a time.

I decide to try to catch up with her, but she disappears as she is walking at such a fast pace and is now gone. Like the strange drivers passing into the night (hound dogs from hell) on this desolate road they disappear, but I can't say they were not there! I come to a passageway, behind an electrical facility, and there is a path there before me, away from my estranged father who I left before. (We were driving to the psychiatrist's office in Thousand Oaks when I jumped out of the car.) I am possessed by this ghost, not that I have a son anyway. But, I should have known that my dad and I would part, not far from where he had met my mom in the greater Los Angeles area. I knew, if I did have a son, he would be waiting for me on the other side.

Despite losing my dog, my close companion, I was ready to go back home, back east to Georgia, maybe even if I have to walk part of the way. My rambling thoughts expire here like the rambling path before me. I do not know at this time that L.A. is five hundred square miles and it is easier to arrive than to leave.

Along the path I walk, I come to what may be described as a scaturient Earth Goddess of some kind. It is a sort of tree formation that if it weren't for the credibility issue of tabloids, this might be a natural wonder. Here, on this path that leads to what looks like a path in the wilderness, there are hills leading out of the outreaches of suburbs to the city.

Here, there is a large electrical facility in which I press myself against a wall to meet it. I have no idea where I am and I think of erotic poses of the superstar, Prince, "Under the Graffiti Bridge," or "When Doves Cry." Actually, it is astounding, the writhen form of the tree with such development and fertility. Its limbs transform the imagination and I almost feel different after leaving and parting with my dog, Ferocious, in Malibu.

I remember that something told me we would part and this would be how. Also, I should not try to fight it and I did not. I suppose in the back of my head, it was right; just to be not death do us part and how. We are still together in some way. I decide to walk on the rocks surfacing upon the waterway; the low path. Rather than the high path that seems evident of glories of such land masses, the Andes foreshadow, following an Indian named Keto and his llama. No, here, birds chirp in a backwoods rivulet that smells like an abandoned sewer. Still, the birds chirp. I think it bizarre that a plastic globe, about the size I might hold in my arms, floats by. I throw a rock at it. This time I embark on a voyage with a positive feeling, as though not a trace of bewilderment at the intriguing setting and bizarre occurrences.

Okay, so I will stay the night where the lush mud of the earth reaches out of the ground from where I crouch, a few inches from my behind. What am I doing here? This may be a sacred Indian burial site or the back set for Universal Studios. Whichever, I am in the outback of some deserted place and I need to get back to my car in Malibu, find my dog and go back to New York City. Still, something bewildering, in my head, evokes me to take the long way back through the countryside, back roads and river divided scenic vistas.

Something says to stay here the night and I assume a loyalty to this place where an old firebird was rusted inside and out and landed from the moon in the seventies. Furthermore, lettuce grows wild in a vista between a freeway polished by an officer's movie star shiny L.A. boots in my back hospitality. Part of me wants to walk and the other part tells me to return to my car in Malibu. I retract my steps taken before On the other side of the river which I shall pass in the morning, a country road exists and I am lost for better or for worse. There are no people around to bring me back and the stars look so far in the sky and I wait. All I smell is the sort of musk that could only be a set of some movie production company. This is such a prefab sort of nature and I wait further. I nestle my body on bamboo shoots, hanging like a hammock over the river. The river intimidates my senses and I know I must wait while the sky passes overhead and I sort of drift away. Later, I wake much colder and find I am in some moonstruck place. In its light, I find a garden of rocks that I jump from one to another increasing the warmth in my body. The rocks just glow. Whose rock garden does it belong to really, God or Mike, I ask myself?

In the morning light, I think the river wild might calm around noon. Though it does not, I have time to spare anyway. This leaves me with my curiosity among the rocks now visible for exploration. At first, it is not the interest, but the spectacle guarded by Mike who now implores my curiosity further. I lift one of the rocks out of the bank of the river and into the sunlight. The light ricochets off of the rock and into my eye, causing less of a sensation of guilt.

"No, not that rock!" Mike nervously forbids these rocks to be observed at first. Of course, this is Mike's rock collection and just like a child hanging onto a toy eventually gives into the temptation to show them off. The guilt I feel is only brief, but I would be careful to place the rocks (so natural in splendor) near where I find them. Eventually, my curiosity has been evoked and I dare touch one or two more as though virgins on the earth.

By noon, I pass the river and at the crossroads, so to speak. Here, I offer the river my New York State Drivers License. It catches the wake of the current, like a leave falling. My identity is now gone, as the photograph inscribed within its voracious appetite floats away.

Roads in L.A. and its outer fringes are strange. Some roads are fire-hot freeways and others winding destitute passages to nowhere. And at that place behind the electrical power station where the Goddess poses truly in the form of a tree, it is clothed only by previous vestals, who should leave white pieces of cloth hanging in nearby trees. And, of course, there is the woodchip I left behind which was once a part of this magnificent sculpture.

"Will I ever get out of this place?" I should think. And in this awful waste channel, there is a sanctuary for birds that find it more like hibiscus petals in spring. A strange occurrence, or how about the cave that I dare not enter, but it is visibly empty of bear. And "the owl rock" rests on the ground. The energy it professed is good rather than the millions that Stalin killed. It forbids those from entering its sanctuary. A strange croaking sounding creature like that of a toad, is particularly disguised behind the other's chorus, dressed with the musky odor that rose with each footstep on the soil. It is untouched at least since the last rainfall. Saying, as it hides its long, lanky body, in its voice; I hear the echo of its cry.

In its lonely history of deprivation and pain she may only utter the words, "I don't like you, I don't like you." She taunts innocently, in her untouched space, even if it might be her own son. It is a mystery of what propels me to throw the rock into the sky, back at the glass façade and I dare say the glass was not broken even in the slightest. And I shall not touch "the owl rock," from which it sits in the back country of nearby Thousand Oaks Mall, and God shall prevail for once.

"Closer to reefer," is like how the fish should speak as the ocean is sort of a tranquil drug which condones their tactical demeanor. Is there a voice at all? "Closer to God...what?," it says. The fish swim in ordered shoals not unlike the German militias of the Third Reich. And breathe in the cool blue air and allow the scatological matter sit in your chest for a while.

"What blue cloud of air?" retaliating further, "liar!" blue is empty of all color like a polarizer that divides two plains, it is just an illusion. This is a fact and didn't you know that? Where are your toes and the tingling sensation that mitigates the cool breeze around your face? Partial dyslexia awakens you and the ocean current fizzles on your tongue and resourcefully returns everything to the ocean.

Then you ask, "Do the birds not resent the smoke in an unlimited insane chaos only heaven should speak? Out with hell, it embarks from the tree of the filtered joint?" It does not matter what the tree says whether there is a heaven or a hell for that matter. To patronize the notion just for to carry the bread home this one more time, with burning sensation of my cigarette at hand, "is this not love?" The clemency portends discussion further now as I sit and watch the ducks assemble at the fish pond. Leaning your forearm loosely on the park bench it is lackadaisically visible. And with its gloved, calloused hand, you ask the same question, again and again, to create the god only one speaks about at such times.

There is more to this equation than tree markings on a limb made by a bird, or the ants that scurry about in an intense fiery trance, or even the caution a wave makes for a brief intermission before crashing to the shore. Here is where I meet God in its many disguises, but not to touch once. Not even a hair from my own head may be sacrificed so to offset the dichotomy. And you ask how one spells the word "trunk," like the trunk of an elephant or a trunk of a tree or maybe a trunk like that which holds gold and so on, on the bottom of the ocean floor. It is a misnomer that one should not obtain a single definition for a word as simple as "God." To interpret this paradox, I must first dispel the notion of Satan's stare and ask my dog for a different point of view. This is a relatively easy task, with a less than easy answer.

The doctor arrives to prescribe the medicine. I wait in the dark shadow's forebode, in the wake of the nearby ocean currents. What makes my dog freak out, that day, on the beach parking lot? It now settles with ominous undertones, foretelling a story that may be traced in the gold tears of my sister's eyes. And to know I am alone now, as the dog ran away somewhere. The undetermined air wasted by the current's sick mouth now settles as I sponsor his sojourn further.

To study the ocean is like studying the eating and migration patterns of sharks. Instead, I will study the digestive track of my dog in the previous six months. The pride I feel as Ferocious fetches the ball a few weeks earlier, in Central Park or the feeling of lifting him on a redwood stump there in Northern California; these are some photographs I take of him before parting. I do not know them to be the last, "Ferocious naked on a redwood stump?"

We sit together in the unsettled air under an overpass ramp near Pasadena. The broken car is parked nearby and we clutch one another like the end of the world is coming in this terrine display. What a fine place to break down on such a night? (on the L.A. freeway) after leaving the Thousand Oaks Inn that Friday.

"Let's go back to the car." I carry Ferocious, like a baby, to the car and to think of a new plan. The end of the world pass by like dark clouds above, not to wake from the dream or nightmare, may it be. This is a serious edge of the night where one finds their worse and best of friends. Maybe one of those "blue devils," will stop on the road and give me a jump start? We coexist here in the night and in the morning light, the cars whizz by like red flashes in the distance.

"Blue devil" is a funny name for a police officer, I know, but it is not too late to begin again. This is where old and new worlds collide in a menace and the ant's path foretells the light of the future day. Why not stay inside, for now, and breathe a little warmth for a while? Or, should I be frantically hyperventilating, as to show my thirst for getting the hell out of here?

It had to be a Tuesday night alone at home with Ferocious. Watching the TV and changing the channels like surfing a wave and before it breaks, changing the channel again and again. Ferocious curls up on the corner of the couch at this time to show a protecting pretense a dog should always show to its owner. However, he is the witch's dog and I watch him for Diana at such times, she being the good witch for "man." But, more curled, he is alertly posed and singularly available.

"What is he thinking?" I wonder and it occurs to me he already went around the world the previous night as he is not of this world like you and I. What he is thinking when I am gone is left for the birds? But, he probably has gigolo aspirations, so not to feel alone, I think. One Saturday afternoon, a small bird flew in from the outdoors and perched itself on one of the couches as though a friend to Ferocious (coming by just to say hi.)

This occurrence conveyed that if there was a heaven, he might say between channel changes on the TV, "Heaven...I have already been there, maybe somewhere else as I am bored."

While heaven might be very appealing to Ferocious and he might jump at the opportunity like a teenybopper fan at a rock concert just to meet God? I do not know what Ferocious thinks about there, floating between the world and heavens above? But, for a dog, a chance to go to heaven is more like a temptation from the devil; like the perfume scent fragile on flowers below in the morning dew; it is a menace, but a reality? Yes, to go to heaven and meet God is all he thinks about and his next meal, of course, dried dog food, a mixture of lamb and rice. Otherwise, when I get home, he thinks to shut up and be good for now.

A devilish mind, a dangerous body, and a contorting bark; all these things and more embody Ferocious. But, to meet Ferocious you might think of his fragile demise and brindle coat a combination similar to an old blue leather piece of luggage rotating tirelessly around a conveyer belt at the airport. Even worse, unclaimed he resembles a lonely and soggy hot dog at Shea Stadium in the rain. In other words, he blends well with his surroundings, but feeling sorry for him will go nowhere, as I have already tried.

Instead, a woman in the street reaches down like so many real estate sales pitches before, to allow him to smell her perfume-scented wrist and clutching his neck in a subtle motion as not to be rendered publicly. This is routine and Ferocious enters a place in his mind. And, so, he introspectively checks in at Mt. Sinai Hospital, like every evening, and finds himself on the eleventh floor before the door to the mental ward closes around nine in the evening. Ferocious conceptualizes on the eleventh floor, in the corner. Ferocious checks in here every evening in case someone, by chance wants to find him or maybe it is a strange habit and his obsession with this place is similar to how some find a particular bar enchanting.

Maybe he finds the head nurse pleasant to be around and travels in his mind here every night, making a point in particular to stay out of the rain. To chase taxicabs by day then to retreat each evening here is a discipline innately peculiar to the breed, a Cairn Terrier and, even more so, Ferocious.

Women's scented wrists may be a third obsession and by the time the day passes into the evening, thoughts of God become more a spectacle of passing curiosity. If not for the fire that feeds his imagination, much like the bird that visits from time to time; Ferocious spends his time walking down corridors of patients, hoping he might talk to someone. Ferocious figures this is better than standing out in the rain and besides church is for losers, he thinks. Light invades Ferocious's space and reveals aspects of his personality, when TV is a bore and, unknowingly my path crosses over his.

In fact, Ferocious is present more than just in the park on Sundays, and finds himself in other roles that embody my every day. But, he is most loyal to the eleventh floor of the mental ward at Mt. Sinai Hospital. But, primarily, when the doors shut at nine PM, the mind of Ferocious closes as well, saving a smile for a sunny day like all good dogs should do.

When Ferocious undertakes a sleep, all I hear is a bird's eulogy spoken eloquently at a pitch like a ball flying into the catcher's glove or an old couple lifting a blue leather bag off the belt and leaving its tag in the airport. A mental hospital might be an appropriate place for the fixings of a dog's mind such as Ferocious. Here, if he was the fixings bar at Roy Rogers he might embody an onion on the side, a pickle and some ketchup. Why the eleventh floor of the mental ward at Mt. Sinai? This is just a place like any other place that Ferocious might find himself. Maybe on Friday afternoon you might find him chase a fly ball at a softball game in the park. (He always plays right field.) Yet, he returns like clockwork every evening to Mt. Sinai. Here, he is much respected like an on-call doctor. In other words, Ferocious wants to be appreciated and, in his mind, he is accepted at the hospital as such.

The night, maybe six months before our parting in L.A., I feed Ferocious his first blueberry. It seems appropriate as I may have been dreaming of Russia and, for no reason, I urinate in bed while asleep. And having come to terms with this fact, I spontaneously dropped one of the blueberries in Ferocious's mouth. This may represent the blood of the earth and his first taste of the "Big Apple" so to speak. While urinating, prior, may mean that there will be parting. He is neither repulsed, nor abducted by the taste. Instead, it represents something marginal of a quest, and he can digest it fully without facially disagreeing with its harvest like wine. The blueberry represents the earth that he may or may not stand upon. For a dog, the step this entails is like man's first step on the moon. It is further removed than that which Adam graced from his loin and ultimate fall. For a dog, this is like the beginning to an end or a suicide in some respect. The question remains, will Ferocious digest the fruit's harvest in full without experiencing it as a drug and toxic demeanor bequest upon it like wine? This is an ultimate test to determine the place of his existence should he ever arrive at God's house. To know this bit of information is an opportunity.

I drive with Ferocious that winter, north to Montreal, where we collect ourselves. Then we journey west along the ridge of the Northern Light, then south from Vancouver to a little place called Los Angeles. Besides the snowy drifts and bear claws along the way, there is a generous supply of Mike's donuts. Christmas lights illuminate the towns in splendor or redwoods and are nearer to where Martians first trekked here on Earth. Then, we finally arrive in L.A. We are here! On a hill overlooking the evening lights across the city, a sort of truck stop; a young girl tests me by asking for a cigarette and I reply slightly indignantly, "No." But, I cannot bother to confront this test of moral capacity anyway and give a shrug motion.

I remember now giving Ferocious a blueberry as though it a dream. I take it with dignity that seems characteristic of Ferocious, a small dog over whom one must watch, similar to children. His staunch and well-toned body stretches to the ground always, if it is not the sky too. He is at a disadvantage, as a dog. But, still, he is entering the human race as though late for his own initiation, and maybe thereafter his reincarnation in which it unfolds. Images of him are like tears his mother shed.

Now, the competition has risen one level and he does not hesitate to accept the compliment. Still, evoking the sentiment, he cries, "I am not a lion!" Without a loss of a single breath he subsides, "I am a dog." To drive the L.A. freeway this evening, the car abruptly breaks down near the ramp leaving Pasadena. To see his face as I leave that morning, he is destitute.

"Why leave me at this time when the roads part so vastly and take me into your arms to arrive at the end of the world, here and now?" Holding him as to forget his father's wrath or even that of my own father, it comes with sweet comfort of holy light and something greater; "It is not me!" Ferocious plunders as I leave to find a gas station. Leaving him all alone in the morning light, I leave you as the parting sun rises and is now my father, innocent on all counts? And I am the same?

"What spell of the evil Witch should drown my path out of darkness and spare this one dog, but not my brother?" I feel remorse at the underpass at night's request and "know," at this time. The way of racing cars in a "coma zoo," trance, the night prevails here. It does not retaliate, but vibrates in a sick engine's transmission. Finding its tongue as it feels its way through the tailpipe and along the pipe where it shuts off the engine with a quick tongue action.

The war between Godzilla and King Kong is a stalemate. And where it began, somewhere near the George Washington Bridge in New Jersey, heading north, is now over. And to leave the luggage behind and not my good friend, Ferocious, I compassionately refer to him as the Witch's dog or of that of a grizzled homeless woman who I had met in Central Park years ago. Her name is Diana, and in remembering the plight stricken from Adam's fall, man should subsist like this if not for this dog.

After leaving the Thousand Oaks Inn, I find myself naked on a beach in Malibu. Here, I am naked to the sun with my back to Mt. Fuji. With my back turned, I am less of an outcry and more a spectacle on the empty beach. Here, it is my turn to speak to the children abandoned by the sun. Having overcome this passing in its naked light, it chants to me for the dog, which having overcome this passing, should bear their tolerant bending to the sea.

Where, he, (Mt. Fuji, maybe a lion and not a dog, I think,) entered the ocean to hide from the sun, Ferocious commits suicide. By doing so, he killed the lion, I think. Mt. Fuji remains for all to see that someone may transcend this oasis. To rise from the ocean, he confronts the legacy of which Ferocious must bear.

Alternative to the dog, lives this person who bikes to the rhythm of the red sun. He practices martial arts, like Tai Chi, in this distant land that resounds as bumble bees in the wind of a lion's nose, which is so far away from where he stands. As he left the ocean, the masses tread on beaches to find the spoils of the ocean's trinkets it sheds in full. My dad is just sand raked up by the ocean; a reminder of what was once there. Here, in the morning light, people internalize their harvest to drink a beer without any fear for the plight of the rising sun. They say their mother is a "magnetic hoe."

Furthermore, I arrive at the Thousand Oaks Inn and find the people working here most opposite of the strength and wisdom, I remember of this woman, Diana. It is an omen to see this feminine outcry without the love endowed by God. To see the sun in its nakedness and where the hedonist pray upon the ocean to waken him from behind without an ascetic blessing of the Buddha? To see the dog naked on a beach in Malibu here, they pass without shaking hands? Meanwhile, the Witch blasts off in her spaceship as she heads toward the sun, which will eventually subside. Even with the whole world at the Witch's mercy, she is not able to see the dog once.

As I eat the dry leaf from her tree I feel its slimy body rise to the corners of my mouth, as to show some sympathy and to see her son one time before the ultimate resting, just to say farewell.

But to say "no," and find a world callously opposed to her belief, it is a cruel disposition toward light. As I promised, I will see him off to his last breath, and I lift him into the sky at this time, while eating her body in the form of a leaf, here in the parking lot to the beach in Malibu. And very naked, Ferocious stands here fulfilling all his promises to me, three things too personal to mention. And, I stand naked too. For a brief intermission, if for the sake of compassion in this cruel play of life? With all the energy of that which is good, the dog runs wildly like a hurricane wielding his true mother's mercy, which is surely good in the eyes of the dog?

But, with this visible of weakness, he now must face the realness of life when gaining this spectacle of a second life for one undeserving? But it is just a trifle of the good witch to man's sorrow. What may it be that Mt. Fuji should catch the orgasmic reply and at this time, return from the ocean which wept one too many times. Now, simplicity is the outcry and Ferocious is a gift which is the legacy of his father; a dog with three hearts and a sharp impulse toward winning at Russian roulette. Now, Ferocious is the property of the agents of darkness and the ocean sighs in the voices of bread for wine. Now, the dog is no longer what it was, "the Witch's dog," but I do not know for sure as I should never hold him even once.

A few days before this parting and before the breakdown on the L.A. freeway outside of Pasadena, I find myself watching movies in my hotel room on the ground floor. And, upon leaving, there is an atrium that tiger lilies climb around and around in this ceremony for its lost brethren. A tiger swell is in the air and the crowd cheers the tigers, while I lie oblivious and naked like Ferocious. Seemingly unaware of the voice, the movies cannot penetrate our surroundings. Aware of what they call "tiger swells are on TV," and that which fades in the level of volume and then fading entirely, "tiger swells are on TV" they chant.

Still, Ferocious on our journey remains completely unassuming and would feel comfortable walking the grounds naked. He is not bashful, using the bathroom in this spectacle and sitting on the toilet seat to go like eating a piece of pie and fully enjoying it. We are like college buddies hanging out in a dormitory. Still, the audience or the world for that matter, watches with non-penetrable eyes absorbing every motion of the light we invoke without any mercy. Tiger swells are on TV and that is all that is said, but audible enough to hear this anyway. Around and around, the atrium invites a spectacle for Ferocious, a large selection of virgin flowers to invigorate at his will.

Maybe, Ferocious is becoming aware of something like waking from a dream. If tiger swells are on TV, he then asks, what does this make me as a stealthy joke; with himself as a smaller traveling companion? Still, he remains abjectly unaware of anything else. And as the stakes increase, Ferocious figures, so does the reward.

The stairs of the atrium turn the corners from three sides on four floors where the cleaning ladies should pass by in the roundabouts of the work day. On the ground floor, the flowers are most potent and the odor is aromatic with also some greenery and a small gazebo visible from all angles of the hotel. In the building next door, one may pick up movies, sit and read in the library, and dine at the fabulous Dupar's Diner which is famous for its homemade pies for more than fifty years. When not participating in the tiger swells, which is entertainment for the work staff of the hotel, the time passes and other clientele bear false witness on weekends, having the title of some conference. Dr. Emory sees the patients who would otherwise complain at such times, knowing tigers only eat red meat.

Having participated in the events and having a pet dog to entertain the staff, it becomes clear that they did not need me. I do not want to be a poor sport and they simply aggravate me so that I might leave. And the hotel for which "tiger swells" are prominent mean some fresh meat might be an alternative? I sense the inconclusive and bewildered energy of the staff and leave without receiving my deposit. I am a bit irritated by the hoax, "what a strange place?"

Ferocious likes the flowers and selects one upon which to urinate. Also, he finds a soda machine, which might be a sort of business he adopted while I was fighting tigers on TV. Where am I going to find another hotel that permits having a dog? I am more than irritated, at this point, and forget an appointment with the already prestigious Dr. Emory of whom both Ferocious and I concur to be somewhat of a flake. After twenty minutes on the freeway, it soon elopes as to a few hours lost. Besides forgetting my appointment with Dr. Emory, that Friday afternoon, I find myself on some road like being lost in the desert infiltrated with beautiful orange groves. Furthermore, I have no luck in finding another hotel. It seems the dusk passes into the evening quite decisively. No one knows how tigers really hunt? But, based on the expression of Ferocious's face, the tiger lilies are smiling when we depart from the hotel. Maybe, this means that the tigers have already eaten, and I being so tired, will be easy prey in the future.

In the meantime, it is easy to get lost on the winding freeways. When the car finally breaks down near the underpass to a Pasadena ramp, the cars at this time are whizzing by. By the time the morning comes, I decide to leave Ferocious in the car and walk to the nearest gas station for help. Along the way, I am picked up by someone that has a "bear" resemblance. He is scared that I would tell someone that he is out of the woods and metaphorically speaking, naked. And not having Ferocious with me, this is not a problem as I guess bears do not like dogs. He lets me out of his car, hypnotic and slightly neurotic and otherwise how a compliant bear should act. I think at this time, nearer to the next exit "lions, tigers and bears."

It seems to me that I am now fully in the swell, so to speak, and being observed from all angles and such. Now, this police woman finds me off the ramp of the next exit. She, too, reflects a certain animal temperament (is it just me?) and she frisks me before giving me a ride back to my car. She is not sure if I am from around here and tells me she is originally from back east as well. Besides being red-haired, but more orange, she is also near-sighted and squints in a sort of cute fashion as she is in full uniform and carrying a gun. If she was a tiger, she is scared of something and I sense this by the way she talks nervously. I don't suppose she is hungry and even if she were, I wouldn't ask, but she does manage to ask me if the dog in the car belongs to me? Otherwise, she tries to give me a jump start and, without any luck, calls a tow truck for me. She smiles, in parting, as though I am Dorothy in *The Wizard of Oz* and so far from home. There is a certain degree of humor here like when passing the orange groves the day before, the pensive look of the seemingly Japanese or Korean lady is so sublime and I am lost anyway.

You would have to ask me "where I am?" if confronted with me. Around and around the stairs revolve at the Thousand Oaks Inn, and such at the mall and so on where I told someone I was homeless for some cinabuns. This occurred later, after leaving my dad's rental car on the way to Dr. Emory's office. Or here on the swerving road among the orange groves of which the oranges are actually stark white; I think, what an ugly colored garment the lady walking along the roadside is wearing; almost puke pink like a bottle of Pepto-Bismol. I am now free of tigers and further, with the acknowledgement of being lost, I throw my medicine bottle out the driver's side window. And, this leaves me with one container of the medicine still. I am certainly lost, as I know Los Angeles covers a good five hundred square miles and I do not know where I am anyway; probably somewhere far from home. Perchance, the car breaks down and it is not until past noon the following day that the tow truck arrives. That night I am caught figuring what appointment I have missed? This is pointless, because I do not want to return to Thousand Oaks where Dr. Emory's practice is and he may be acting as "the Wizard," in this case. Furthermore, I place two rocks along the road together to signify my friend Sierra, "a desert in the ocean." (Should the rocks separate, so would the ocean.) There are no tears here, with the exception of tiger tears, which no one sees from this point of view.

After they have eaten, and to dispel the notion that I am leaving, I have the tow truck driver return the car to Malibu where Sierra lives. I have not eaten and feel my face which is true. But, first, I pour some water on an oil slick by the car as though to preserve the medallion, the face implores, as I leave. Now, the chant becomes that of returning to the sea and the cars around me seem to be chanting Sierra's name and I take this to mean something good, like when children find out they are going to the beach.

While they chant, "Sierra, Sierra," Ferocious is the pilot in the back of the blue Eagle Summit. Behind the tow truck, he witnesses complete nuclear obliteration. Meanwhile, being one of only two survivors, I sit in the front with a dead driver. We both subside and listen carefully as the car becomes a nuclear waste with a flash of light. The annihilation of every race and, starting there in the mid-day light, to hitch a ride in a tiger lost on the highway smiling with a badge, a ride to Malibu, where else? There, to get rid of the evidence, Ferocious is in my arms, exhilarated, thinking he does not know how fun death may be. Ferocious is in my arms to the sequence further and he is released by the fading conquest, to die in the end. The car admonishes there with salty tears of remorse, kissing the tow truck and two hundred dollars goodbye. Ferocious, the pilot, is the only witness of the death wish of the human race to end in a stalemate; all in nothingness and he breathes the craze of the lunar wisdom up to a new race of poetic champions. It is a dry mixture of rice and lamb.

No, the smell of the ocean and its waves breaking on the shore is welcoming to a dog to forget his father of vengeful reprise? And to swallow the fruit that tastes like home long enough to forget his face? Wherever he wants to run and land on the moon; the switch and take-off and never return? Never to see again, never to run like a blue dolphin hurling through the air.

Ferocious's black Harley Davidson arrives confidently and I find myself on the eleventh floor of Mt. Sinai Hospital to pick up my dog that ran away. But, coincidently, he follows this random elevator to the eleventh floor, like any night just to get off there. Always volunteering, he finds himself stuck on the floor of the mental ward, somewhere; if not for his mind at least. Ferocious thinks that riding the elevator here is like chasing a ball into the stands and falling asleep in an anonymous cloud and smiling at the rain. I must jack off briefly at this time; around and around and smiling too.

In Malibu, this is where he ran away. "Sierra dear," I implore desperately, "will you spare a fake tear in the whole of the ocean and embrace for this one dog, the Witch's dog, sent maybe from heaven and lost in a handful of sand in this manic episode at the beach and watch him for a while, he is not eating right?"

But she must work and California seems so cruel. The piece of chocolate is in my hand and I am about to feed it to Ferocious. In his mouth, a suicide is played on tape one Sunday afternoon. In the hot sun in motion again and again, someone called "the Woodpecker," finds him on the beach parking lot and lifts him in his arms. He promises only one thing and he is going home.

"Sierra, will you take this dog, before I feed him chocolate, your fruit?" It hangs off a Chipwich while the dog stands alone near the beach in Malibu. One breath, like the fake flowers in your hair and everyone chanting her name to the sea. They call and beckon the tides rising in the ocean to the desert that exists there. This cruel situation makes me feel something which is cursed by a loving father's hand. But I do not feel it, as the rocks joined are now separate. They are never to join again for the eternal desert in the ocean? I know now what is to come as she takes me with dog to the Malibu Shores Inn and he eats the chocolate in my hand. I feed him this and I eat the dried leaf, the fruit of the Witch Diana who sent this vestibule of light into the realm of darkness and he ran away.

But, suicide came first and he must leave and arrive at Mt. Sinai on the eleventh floor where a warm bowl of porridge awaits him like every night. He travels in his mind to this place that yields at least the dignity a dog should think a snail makes for its tiresome work and payment as such.

Now, I must find my way back from where I came. Does Ferocious care that he does not know the way back? I find a purposeful equation to the soil in which I stand; it is true that Ferocious and the direction in which the currents in the ocean press now are more twofold. If it were not for death taking the form of two heads of a snake, it is apparent that Ferocious may not eat and either direction might seem the wrong way, like a double whammy. In the schizoid nature of the demised coalescing fornication to where the currents press in the spirit of the light and it is too dark to froth at the mouth of an ocean?

And more apparent, like a day infused in a distant mirage where naked women walk in full form, it has little shame to merit any confrontation. Would not Ferocious embrace Sierra at this place when the opportunity presents itself and find an end if it were not more noble otherwise? To take him to the Malibu Shores Inn which I think was once called the Blue Oyster Inn in light of the broken neon façade hidden from view to most, we seek some form of help. Similarly, the ocean should divide in a manner when a sane person realizes his deeper madness and the place placates a lesser phenomenon to embody the form of division like so much of the ocean?

Unlike sweet chocolate demise, the brother who should lift him into his arms, a shade lighter, but finds comfort in it anyway? Here, Ferocious rather offers a farewell as though to see me soon. Maybe, it will be like a vacation. It does not resolve any dispute unsolved and the fading image of his mother in the reflection of the ocean seems now a bit dumb. More importantly now is the car; whether it be a nuclear waste and the question is where to dispose of it? And to save the battery, its heart; I wanted to throw it in a river leading to the ocean; a spectacle to resolve the clairvoyance now fading. The ocean is spellbinding and increases in a voice long lost. But, in its fleeting that does portend; it is of his father who does not recognize him as he is now gone? Ferocious, on the beach, expresses the greater notion of living through death in order to beckon the long lost life from which the ocean's sick tongue exists in this sort of rut.

This is where God may remain. He is there, as I feel his presence, but I am not alone, but am I alone? And as the ocean divides in two forms from which creation beckons with wind at his back and I feel its presence. If not for Sierra refusing to watch over Ferocious and someone otherwise claiming him, is he not found here finally? But, he thinks it only an adventure to explore further. The ocean is truly a voice here, but not heard as long as the light seeks that which is in the form of a dog it resounds in? Glorifying in this instance, to see him look at me through glaring eyes and the creation a mere second to the spirit bound in the phenomena? Can a dog have three hearts? And, further, the fire that beckons Ferocious is now at bay and the doctor comes here to give me my medicine and Ferocious is gone.

From the shore on the beach where I stand, the ocean beckons me to come near and touch the foam slightly with foot bare in the sand. I retreat slightly, not to scold so much as the poison it represents and it will not hurt you. But, the makeup of the two heads of a snake, divided like the moon is a loaf of bread cut down the center. Where do the tears that form from below manifest this poison on the beach with little suffering of those involved?

But, like a natural underwater spring, it dictates the progression in salty tears below from where? This is decisively awakening and along the beach, one may reach this wonder at any angle and it deploys a warm retreat for those who want to tackle shallow water. As the surfer enters the wake like a knife slicing a ring of cheese, it is more decisive to the point where one becomes object to the conquest of what the ocean swallows. From below, where Mt. Fuji's mythological hiding from the sun is in the ocean in which he later leaves, there is a step foot that represents an active motion of those otherwise unclaimed by the sun? Then, to divide into the wake fully, he tracks his path overlapping like sharks and then to smile in its salty ways, he penetrates the air above like a dolphin.

Otherwise, unlike the others, a whale should remain and represent the ocean and the greater quest at hand. Then, there is a lion that swims in the ocean and is returned to the shore. Always somewhere else from where it drowns and more plausible saved, there is the good intentions of that which lives there, it is a force bound in the breath that separates the ocean from the sky. Maybe, as the dolphin jumps from the ocean; the shark penetrates a lost blue fish to organize a path for a whale. It need not put on a show with its still mammoth power which may endure to a greatness stronger than the ocean in which it swims.

From the many layers of sharks that divide the ocean in different overtures (that the dolphin flamboyantly hides its greatness) to where the ocean meets the sky; the whale like "old faithful," squirts water from its spout to motion that it speaks with a greater tongue, here and now. The ocean has a powerful voice here, and speaks a language that is mostly old. But, at times, when a non-welcomed guest infuses itself in full, it is not to be a detriment and he wakes on a different shore, in a distant land and always waking from a beautiful dream.

Why would someone trek into the ocean and return somewhere having drowned, but also saved? Here, the whale remains in the ocean to suffice the greatness of the voice of layers upon layers of fish which the sharks patrol on different levels and aptitudes. Dolphins regulate it further and the whale, which is already too big for its own good, does resound. A large array of ocean life which makes for a complicated dynamic is further transmitted to degrees of blue lost in the salty tears where lions are at play. And to think, why do the tears drown in its waves and then save a complicated life oasis?

Here, on the beach in Malibu, I stand naked and alone like a wet shadow that never actually touches the tears dry upon my skin with salty recourse. Does Ferocious run away? While on the one hand, it might be true that Ferocious would feel compelled to embrace Sierra's arms? For being Sunday, it is not. On the other hand, Ferocious is not regular and since leaving New York City a few weeks earlier, eats at a minimum So what opportunity poses itself; does Ferocious attempt to escape his responsibility so as to run away? Since Sierra is not willing to watch over Ferocious, I feed him a chip of chocolate and we resume at the Malibu Shores Inn.

As the currents are purposeful and the flower's allure scathingly indignant, Ferocious is apt to run away and leave me in the dust. Furthermore, the wind makes for a run around on the beach first. To count one to nine and turn around at this time, I find Ferocious exploring another more lavish hotel across the way. Then, carrying him back, I see the withering dry leaf of the good witch Diana, and I reach for it as we pass to eat it. As I tear it from the branch from which it is hanging, I eat it as though her body and also respectively "man," I prepare to presume the freedom over my dog. But, first I have one trifle to settle. Counting one to nine, I let Ferocious go, and by this time I count backward from nine to one, a man of dark complexion, but relatively fair still, picks Ferocious up then sets him down.

At this point, I know Ferocious, which is now my dog, is unreachable. The man I call "the Woodpecker," has come to take Ferocious home. This terse farewell becomes a condoning menace as Ferocious is free and "the Witch" has given him to me. Three things must transpire before I let him go. He must show the spiral of the wind that reticulates behind him, he must explore the bounds of nine steps that precedes this voyage to L.A. and, in respect to our experience on the freeway, it never happened. The bomb never occurred, because while an atom may be split, I think it always regenerates and therefore never happened.

Consequently, with this knowledge of death, but still being alive; suicide or not, it is old and in the past tense and not beyond God's greater plan, but thirdly, he must smile. As for these three objectives, otherwise, there is eleven sparkler pieces. Without altering his freedom, I hope to retrieve nine of the sparking pieces on his collar, and the twelfth, I disposed of already in New York.

I hope this man, "the Woodpecker," will carry him back the way he came in a camel's eye in hell around and around, at the same time smiling and from one to nine, arrive in my arms likewise. This is a play of sorts and I want to take from the original twelve pieces and leave only two, representing each of his eyes. It is like a badge and, hopefully with this collar, I might find him on the other side and the quest has begun. The first thing "the Woodpecker" does is to wither a faint mark on the redwood stairs leading to the bar then he begins to take the dog on the voyage back in his car.

I first ask, "Where are you taking him?" and prior to stomping on the wood and marking it with his foot. First, he passes me at an arm's distance and he responds that he is taking him home and I believe him. He walks to his car and leaves me in the beach parking lot across the street. Now, sparing two hundred yards between us, Ferocious is smiling the way dogs do. Also, the three tags on the collar are all in the shape of a heart representing Ferocious having three hearts.

Is this possible? You will have to figure this out for yourself. With Ferocious's departure; it is the beginning of a story which begins, "If the sun should fade..." and I walk back to the inn and look down as to see the sun should find Ferocious's schumber before me like a vestige of his existence prior. It does not matter, as Ferocious and I will meet again in this spiracle. This may be a token of his might and will.

The flowers around the inn are particularly contrasting to the hill of wild yellow flowers hanging on to a cliff nearby. Other flowers surrounding the grounds are more exotic as if to say if flowers could talk, "We have eaten and full, but do not tell on us."

This is to refer to Mike as being mad and angry. This is where a lizard and such tetrapods and the pun it stands for rule the grounds and you may find him bathing peacefully in this light under a Kleenex tissue, around mid-afternoon. What is most interesting about the flowers which a young woman named Leslie manages, it appears that the more exotic flowers deserve water and while the more wild flowers are not deserving.

This is an interesting phenomenon that implores a favoritism to the vestal of exotic flowers. The grounds are well watered, while the wild yellow flowers surrounding are desperate for water. This is much like the surroundings in the area of L.A. and from this viewpoint I begin my voyage via the thin blue flip flops I wear on my feet.

While I may be from a well-off family, the car without a house puts me on the lower level of the social register. Though, having a friend who lives here, I am still solivagant at such a time. Being stood up by a woman makes my social presence among homeless and weathered friends passing by, on the latter end of a favored role among my peers. My only hope seems from a rich kid's impulse to make acquaintance with Leslie, who runs the inn. I call Dr. Emory as I had forgotten our appointment a few days earlier and he rushed by offering me some medicine. I call him "the Wizard," I suppose as a sentimental perception of what a man living in Malibu acts among the elite who live there. In a strange way, he is sort of "cool," in my perception and this conveys this nickname.

So, anyway, Sierra, Dr. Emory, and Leslie are agents in my life here. When Dr. Emory is "the Wizard," he represents a socio-societal role that maybe promoted LSD in the sixties and with his psychiatrist practice has profited greatly from the promotion if not calculatingly Ken Keseyish? On the other hand, the less hip and almost social dead head, Leslie, reminds me of the type of person who will make me ask myself whether Martians do inhabit the Earth. And, if so, why do we feel sorry for them, in this sense, as though they are left behind or something?

My friendship and the dynamic that presents itself from this point, is intrinsic and dependent as I stay longer.

After the sun goes down, Leslie finds time to note, "Did you lose your dog?"

And I reply, "No, he is just taking a vacation."

Later that evening, Sierra calls me as she had checked me into the motel earlier. I am nearly nude on the ground floor room. She asks for me to answer the pay phone outside or to do not call back and I don't. Anyway, with my message, Dr. Emory finds it easy to drive from his hillside estate and bring me the medicine. He charges into my room and tells me to take the medicine and I ask "Why?", and he replies "Trust me." When I am speaking on the phone to my dad, I tell him about Ferocious running away. He basically says he is coming straight out and the situation becomes much more complicated.

The mirage is visible from the beach in Malibu. Maybe two miles out, if I swim, the land will distance itself the more I swim out to it. This place seems to resemble an island and is visible in sunlight beckoning me to swim out to it. If this test of cohesion should drown me in a destitute place, then I will find myself lost in the ocean forever. As my father is coming out to see me, I think of the possibility of escape. When the tide propels this image in sandy beaches and palm trees on a private island in the distance, I begin to accept the mirage as actual. I imagine this place has women who walk around in naked modesty. Why are there beautiful places that disappear in your mind, and Ferocious, like this island, is fading?

The next day, some young adventurers want to take a walk on the beach. Crossing the highway that encircles L.A. in full, it placates the seagulls that become trapped here. I stay in my room and wait for my father to arrive. Here in this room, it appears that someone is spying on me and now that Ferocious is gone, it is likely that it is possible? My dad arrives and wants to go to dinner with Dr. Emory at a restaurant called Marmalade. As I sit there, I think of Ferocious as though the dinner I am eating is that of him and further my dad a 1949 Chablis?

It is an old-timers' restaurant and Dr. Emory and my dad feel right at home. The next day, my dad wants to show me where he met my mom, somewhere in West Hollywood? By the time we return, it is too late as the road leading to Malibu is closed as a result of mud slides. Consequently, we check into another hotel. I notice that my dad likes L.A. and I order some food in the Holiday Inn we are staying at. This is my time to explore, but I stay in my room. It is apparent that the hotels in L.A. are only concerned with turning a profit and it is becoming tiresome having stayed in a few places already.

Two other things I notice is how often the Holiday Inns have sealed-off windows as a precaution I guess so some poor soul is not tempted to jump and, further, the food is not bad. I stay in my room and, by the time my dad enters to ask me if I want to get something to eat, it is too late as I have already eaten. No butting heads, I guess this time. The primary lesson that all my experiences compound is that he always wins an argument and his rustic nature is truly his personality which I call "the African Jew Phenomenon." Much like a lion he is, his parents are both Protestant. My father, I must admit, is an institution of my curiosity. But, even more interesting than knowing how my mother and father meet, is to know about my father's childhood, if any? There is a picture in my head as though I took a picture of my father's foot in a lake before I was even born and this picture represents and signifies something innocent and pure about my father. Before he exits the lake his foot is but an alligator's blink rectified by a fish so he will never leave. Maybe as though the silvery fish in the lake offers its life for my dad and, as a result, he does not leave the lake after the alligator transcends the oasis by eating him in the form of this fish.

In olden days when my dad dives into this lake, from below, a picture is taken of the vestige as he tries to leave. What is it that signifies this still life photograph and maybe "a step," in a place not so different; that my father may have taken this step for me and consequently relinquishes me for all responsibility in Africa? My dad remains in the lake with the instinctual sensibility of an alligator. A fish in the ocean , however, propels itself into the sky to signify he is home and the ocean parts like that. Ferocious carries an alligator wallet to remind me that my father once upon a time, exist.

In the olden days when someone should pick a fruit from a particular tree, no matter how innocent, the picture is taken as to resound one who should take responsibility for the act. The step he takes for me means only that as I have never been to Africa, and he has never left and the ocean divides for Moses at such a time. Through the eyes of a lizard, from the beginning of time, "before the stars and after the dinosaurs" these natural photographs signify a vast historical account that resonates as prints compounded on rocks. Furthermore, the world that divides my father from my world, because of this occurrence, is vastly divided.

Back at the Holiday Inn, we check out that morning, I leave behind my red down jacket in my room as though a piece of historical paraphernalia; supposing James Dean should return to claim it? And my dad drives me to Thousand Oaks where I jump out of the car in a decisive motion to walk away somewhere and get lost.

What is so significant about this step as though from yesterday? And before "the step" where my father and I should part, we meet in the eye of history? More importantly, when a great catastrophe in the twenty-first century does occur and in the past, catching up determines a break from the past. Furthermore, when a rape may be forgotten (the nun is just a metaphor) a massive killing spree occurs across Russia. The ratio of death there prior, is so great in modern society that this loss designates and warrants a historical mutation to the world in which we live today. There is the responsibility of those who live according to the past.

In the beginning, the Indians may have been sponsored by animals and most innocently leave the garden and return without any damage. They redeem its heritage and make for a tally of mushrooms picked in distant lands by man and animals alike. The consequent annihilation of these people, as well as the ghost of a people that cover its greatness in spirit and blood, may resonate in the nine steps that is not foreseen?

What after the second tier of gypsies and such that safeguard the fortune designated and inherited in trust to those who believe in God? And before and after, they becomes an anomaly to one another in this great light and shame to those who do not comply in it. What becomes that which is most distinctly termed "Stalin's Daughter," (in respect to the killing spree,) is a nine-level rape that should be recognized by the church.

The Russian people may disagree and assume consequently, a massive suicide instead, and they do not want to be bothered by others who sin. Between odd-sounding cries and menacing facial stares of the people in the darkness, the sacrifice of human flesh reaches the sky. Therefore, they are most praised by those who should not benefit in any regard to the historical consequence and imposition? Stew the horse could not find the sky on that day. I want to ask my father if Stalin may render a relationship to this one dog Ferocious?

What might God have to do with heathen or military totalitarian movements? Nothing and neither does anyone else for that matter. As "the step" of my father who once indicted the innocent many, it now relinquishes these from the coup. It presents an agenda for all beings of the Earth with greater axis to those with no memory of the past. If my father is a step in time, what then must the picture frozen in the lake designate? The picture relinquishes me as well as you.

What name does a person have who lives in the ocean so deep that is not related to any other creature or species? Here lives a gorilla in the deep blue sea. What if God is to pertain itself here where no one will notice the tears that fall from his eyes? Moreover, if it were not for a lizard and wicked cruel son, this token of fate might leave as a choice to the higher stake calling? When, once upon a time, something should be eaten in full by a shark, and now it blows bubbles much like bubble gum to implement the surrender and retreat. With one bite, the ocean swallows something that does not belong to it and, consequently, must relinquish all its powers and wonders in full to the person it offended.

Also, Mt. Fuji is just an arbitrary factor like a dead battery in a flashlight for whatever reason? When the time comes, the entity that is so well in the ocean for fear of the sun is now sent as a wakeup call to God that it is time to leave. Once, the ocean ruled over much of life that precedes it. With scary resurrections of faces of the sun, it determined that these entities may not live in a singular world and must be killed and decomposed at best. When the fish blow bubbles and the sharks fight for space with dolphins and whales like its protégé "Old Faithful," sings the songs relinquishing all from the ocean, then a certain power will command itself to its own higher calling.

So, in a time, a gorilla fell asleep in the ocean so that, should its friends, "lions, tigers, and bears," form in respect to one body or agent of life? They are now confined to darkness only. That is the calling of "the Pharaoh Bird" which calls God to resurrect himself immaculately in someone's heart, but there is more.

The gorilla in the ocean forfeits all rights to light and that which stands beyond the parameter that yields the right to choose in life and death. With this sacrifice gains the power to do so in its ultimate will. So what is so magnificent about the timing when the ocean surrenders its evil ways to the light and, in return is only to be seen through darkness? A gorilla, likewise, is that which is a sun revitalized in itself in death. This gives an agent of life the purpose as to rectify all these wrongs. And maybe the agents of darkness may sit in judgment for all time. Yet, may you tell when one of these three entities; an eel, a spider, and a cat, wear one another's clothes in these forms? There is that which you need not know!

Deep in the ocean, lives a gorilla and it fathoms all its glory not for a single breath. Instead, it inhales a sort of glow from its dark surroundings and swims from one deep rock to another like the fluidity an octopus makes if not even more stridden. Then, alone in its solitude, a shark makes bubbles as a sign in the deep blue that yields a sort of forfeit. But, this is black waters and dolphins, again, in the blue compete with sharks for space. A whale is tired of telling those who should ask, "Are you God?" and replying again and again, with the motion of its tale no, no, and no... It seems that the waters have a nerve agent of something dangerous that lives there too.

The dark blue water is only mildly associated with black water of the deeper, non-penetrable lower ocean. It is the realm only visited by young children who tread into the ocean for the first time and feel that of fear or comfort in the tranquility. And in dreams one experiences, it is like one emptying a bath tub the size of the ocean and when refilling it, finding an entity unknown does live there.

Leaving the Thousand Oaks Inn, it presents a problem of where to stay? Surely, Sierra does not have the time to watch Ferocious, and I must at least find somewhere to live in the meantime. To experience the sun on Pluto is an experience that is not often sought. But, more, it is a place which at this point in the development of my relationship with Ferocious is a token of a vow that brings me even closer to him. What is he seeking at such a place whether it be Venus or Pluto? And I stand tall with my dog on my shoulders before jumping once upon a time and eating the forbidden fruit as though it never happened. Then, I walk into the light that its celibate passions are drunk for all time, like the fish that swim in the ocean, I think. Worse than anything are the annoying bugs pushing medications at every whim.

But, before the car breaks down on the freeway, Ferocious wants to show me this place in central L.A. that is the City Central Motel. I do not know why, maybe he has friends here. I was asleep for most of the eighties and do not remember much. And all this time he is accused by the high court of committing suicide and while clutching him on my back, "Ah, I have you!" and we go back to our room. Here, I sentimentally drop two bombs on Ferocious on the bed and laugh. Meanwhile, when the light is off Venus exposes the purple fields of Pluto; there are bugs there that live in an auspicious manner in Malibu.

The tides speak of a different tongue, telling the colleagues to take out the trash, and leaves a most noble sentiment forever in a tin can. Here, God speaks, but only for a short time. And I am neither Stalin, my mother's father, or the person who dropped the bomb. I find it blasphemous to be that which is a photo negative in the end.

Dr. Emory may be from Earth, but like a whale disassociated with the ocean, he resounds as such. He, in many senses, is subject to Uranus like a chance a squirrel should happen by its walnuts and eat them in autumn; this is a diagnosis of insanity here in California. Before long, in some distant cosmic infiltration, he is referred to as "the Wizard." It is even stranger for a once boy and now man, to have the result taking place when you are as crazy as the patients, maybe slightly less so. What do numbers have to do with prescribing medicines? With the exception of the number seven, denoting the seventh planet from the sun, the language of Witches has little significance here. As being prepped as a wizard, Dr. Emory smiles to see leaves change from summer into autumn. He constantly keeps nature in check by lodging that which might land one on Neptune and further. He opens the door to a feeling. When the tides become stronger than this feeling, the trash is released past the spectators and for a long time by a cat's tail on Pluto. And it dissipates as no longer, beyond such bounds, and is in the realm of where children dream.

Pluto, the ninth planet from the sun, alters its formation with Neptune from time to time and here represents a sad tide in respect to God. It is a place of persecution of those who would otherwise deny their association with God, while some maintain a good standing and consequently are not dislodged at such times. The planets exist like a cat's tail off Pluto and such a place does exist. More interesting than the ocean's tides and cosmic long distance communications; the order of the planets represents an analogy of the language God dictates to the stars in the olden days. If one wanted to associate Venus with Pluto, they only need to say the number eighty-two; with its altering with Neptune is in the light of Earth and melds with Venus for a short time developing a color purple?

For Chinese Witches of the ninth house, this house is associated with beauty. Here, the concept of beauty draws an eclectic group of individuals that, for the time, gives them entertainment without having to go outside. When this occurs for the dog, not Ferocious, it is held onto by spectators and then going out is somewhat innocent and the dog does not mind all the attention. This is a place outside the nine planets and may be heard as to resonate the cat's tail off Pluto and sometimes it is misunderstood as something else.

Here on the edge of the voice of God and whether Venus or Pluto, the two Chinese women who run the motel seem to possess the ramification that the evils that possess the night is no one's fault? And, in the spare time, they caress a cat that it otherwise might not have a voice at all. Unlike voodoo or spectacles of waste here on Earth, these informed souls hear a tumultuous twaddle that may be recognized through the ears of Venus and as far away as Pluto. From here a large array of trash is thrown away.

Furthermore, I might add this is hypothetical to say the least, but something has to happen to that which is discarded as pollution here on Earth? L.A. happens to be a hub from where the language is most resolutely heard and from this place, the most pernicious individuals have a voice which dictates the throwing away of pollution and its uninformed others. Therefore, to be a member of this club may be an honor here on Earth as it is on Pluto, subject to its light. An oasis, for whatever reason I think the Starlight Express, should pass Pluto in the night sky around Christmas time. These two young Chinese women at the motel salute the passage and their cat is barely hanging on at such a time. Those claiming right to Earth and its good light do with few exceptions, not throw away its trash, it might otherwise become material in a set of a Broadway play. This becomes boring matter for other entities, say for instance a tennis ball may be what it is on Neptune and the hand that holds it either a winner or a loser in the eyes of God.

The act of God's mercy on Earth does not dispel all responsibility for those who claim a right here, but rather increases the responsibility. For those who hang onto a cat's tale off Pluto, so to speak; referring to a dog now one might call "Pluto," as to have little hope. There is a spectacle where somewhat less tired individuals appear like winners. In this light, they are praised by spectators who claim no right in or out and sort of adopt something of their own. Others, however, take a vigilant composure to the surroundings and find themselves at the mercy of children, where in most cases, there is no hope of returning.

For example, if one is to follow the book which claims the Ten Commandments and always just follow nine of them; this person might survive on Pluto, provided he or she has not tasted blood here. This, in a sense, is a last chance for those who have fallen. Many find themselves trapped on Pluto and at the mercy of Chinese witches and it falls in the dimension of where beauty is found.

Consequently, as winners or losers, they are protected as such. Otherwise, the struggle is hard and tired too. But, the light of Jesus is stronger than most and may only be found here on Earth. As for Earth, "winner" or "loser" with the exception of my father who is neither, resounds little interest. I wonder if he asks himself, more than once, "If my son is truly innocent, am I a winner or a loser?" Or asking, "If I have a natural cycle, what about sin resound?"

He asks questions as such, but is really thinking about earlier that day when a parking lot attendant gives him a disrespectful look. Unlike children who bend down backward, with the sun always at their back; I leave no reply.

The winners are those who do not necessarily prescribe to heaven, but as a matter of consequence are not too sensitive to hell alternatively. "Pluto," the dog, does not let those from Earth down, but is unable to return from the plight he suffers. Therefore, Ferocious is a winner in respect he has experienced death and has lived long enough to know his life is not over yet. This means that he is in essence a dog, but he has experienced life in death and offered thereafter, a third life, retracing someone's handshake and redeeming himself in light of an alibi, my father.

There, in the lake, a photograph is taken of my father's foot and Ferocious will never cross his path again? Here, Mike lackadaisically sits in the shade of a Kleenex tissue surrounded by fruitful baby cactus and yellow flowers in a thick array of soil trenches in the hills surrounding. Maybe, the sun is young respectively, but has a certain degree of vanity in the light of nature. Maybe, like a film producer, he watches from such a perch. Interestingly, nature tends to repeat itself. Those agents undisclosed in the universe are not subject either as the soil that she walks is virgin matter, while otherwise everything else is fresh as the previous day's yawn.

The other controversy is remembering the order of how things occurred when in L.A. and the time that elapsed after leaving Thousand Oaks. Then to return to this place as though never being there in the first place? Should one pass through the passages of time and end up at this point in the wonder of God's glory, you will find it is old once you find a friend and you will pass by as though the first time. Then to predict the weather, a second time, as though to say not only to the tree of knowledge? But, there are two other entities besides Ferocious, a vestibule of light. He is unharmed in the transition. Only its ego should die, dividing into three parts and passing like the sun he stands for?

After leaving Thousand Oaks a second time, I must find a way back to Malibu where my car awaits (after leaving with my dad) but it is more time-consuming than it's worth. The car is a museum for my father as he touched "the nuclear receptor vibrator," and not I. I think the car might be radioactive and further think it would be a wonderful gift to throw in the ocean and provide a sanctuary for fish in the deep blue sea.

Meanwhile, the combative forces of Godzilla and King Kong now alludes me. As I am on the streets for a few days and Ferocious is gone, it is enough time to clear my head and think about what impels me to return to the east coast on foot. Meanwhile, Ferocious is on the road and so am I. The unfortunate thing here is being homeless, and there is little escape from the city that entrances me. I find little release and am often called upon by the police in different situations. Then, I find out firsthand how far I have fallen in social status. It may be appropriate to stay in a motel from time to time as I try to leave the city with my back to a thousand anxious tormentors.

Instead of walking, I find myself in a cool cab with the intention of driving as far away as San Diego, but at last, ask the driver to turn around and drive me to Malibu. There, in the middle of the night, I find the car sitting in the motel parking lot, a few hundred yards from where the tow truck had left it. I guess my dad had it moved? I check in again at the Malibu Shores Inn and ask for my car keys and they respond "no." Here at the motel again, I find a commandment for every angle that seems to merit a break in my privacy, or at least nine of the original ten. The one that is pending is to not kill, which when instituted in defeat, becomes a window of ongoing fatalism.

The room is small and the window in the bathroom is an audible studio for the ocean and a bird that offers an eulogy for those who care to listen absent of course of Ferocious, who is like the sand lost in the ocean. But, he is always accessible to me, still. The cars that pass the motel further are like a movie camera always turned on. As the cars spin along the freeway around the city it most productively tapes what is within its bounds. Not only am I one of the main actors in this ongoing movie which never stops, but the first scene is as I tiptoe to the ocean on bare feet and come a snail's distance from its mouth. It infiltrates its desire to see me naked on the beach, I do not know? It is apparent that the first take from the director, a squirrel having made many triple-X movies but never four Xes, is quite excited with ocean at back. Four x's refer to a porno that never ends at least anytime soon. My feet are becoming sunburned and as the first take occurs, the blue flip flops I am wearing are impaired on the bottom and I must ask the director to freeze action? But, the camera of course is still rolling; nine of the Ten Commandments still not broken.

The next scene is simple too and it is of my father, dating the like of my beloved friend Mimi. In the previous scene, he drives a tow truck and in this scene he becomes a surfing dude as well. After the take and the previous two in one of the former, I am standing naked on the beach after Ferocious leaves. What is so intriguing is that no matter how late, the camera does not stop unless someone is killed, which never happens as of now. Ferocious is the acting director from his perch in a car driving around the city, a metaphor for the film rolling, in a sense. He is with his somewhat dark-skinned companion, "the Woodpecker." Likewise, I watch the film roll from my car parked or the car inspected as "my dad's museum," and I pardon the radioactive waste as it is not mine. It could happen, though, I ponder? The nine level rape in Russia is created from a mutation of a killing spree which will not allow the film to stop as a result.

Likewise, my dad plays the tow truck driver who likes to surf and gets his girlfriend to take pictures of him, most hyper intensively, on different beaches and his ego is immense. And I watch his girlfriend, but we never meet between takes, as the cars are going through the drive thru at the Jack in the Box next door. The drive thru is always open and the film rolls around and around. In the periphery, it is as to merit some mode of fornication? This is a game which occurs when the camera is turned away from me and it becomes subject to nine of the Ten Commandments.

In the next scene, I become homeless and the camera focuses on my feet, in naked view, as they become sunburned. Ferocious is on the road and I must walk in conjunction with the promise of maintaining his anonymity and the camera side tracks the new characters and rather intensifies the wonder of my feet getting sunburned. The new character is the not so friendly and rather deceitful alter ego of Diana, Dianne? She plays a dear friend and is always in view of the camera, which implies ill-intentions, respectfully. My feet are rather blistered and cut up from my journey, after parting from my dad, and now wearing these blue flip flops. And to replace the shoes I wore for part of the journey, which becomes a haven for bacteria, I throw them in some dumpster.

Anyway, Dianne's role (and I am just kidding about her being deceitful? No really?) is as a good-natured person, who comes from Washington, D.C. to cure my feet from the blisters and also to mourn the loss of Ferocious as she knew the dog too. She soaks my feet in a bath of healing chemicals for the cuts of the previous day's journey. Two other persons come into view now that my dad is gone and he was never really in view, (I think he wants to make appearances for sake of his ego, which is seen from all directions as Mimi modestly photographs him as such) but in spirit of course. Alternatively, Leslie and Nancy are visible now too.

Unlike the previous film which depicts primarily King Kong and Godzilla in the engine of my car fighting to the end, I am now a character in the ongoing film. It appears that Ferocious has transformed himself into a sciurine entity and may be the assistant director. The less composed lizard is the evil director or producer of the film that prescribes the death of God. I think it is impossible and, therefore, the film has no ending and forsakes itself in the spirit of the sun. But, here and now, I am infiltrated with three women, Dianne, Nancy and Leslie. This is a good dichotomy as I am pleased with it as being enriching and the scene with my father prior is a disappointment. I understand it as "sand swept up by the ocean," in daylight and "shadows in the darkness," by night. Stew, the horse, may seem black in the silhouetted sky the way Satan stares back through the devil's eyes. Here, there is little mercy in the show at hand. Meanwhile, a white horse stands in command of the light of day too. But, Satan will not wake from his dream of darkness where he sees through the devil's own eyes too.

In the future scenes, a lot of work is coalesced in a secret as to not give away the mirage of an island and I act as though it is not there. Otherwise, my father disappears in the scene going to Dr. Emory's office where I jump out of the car after offering him a piece of candy, which he refuses and the camera continues to follow me and I am not impressed. Meanwhile, Mike floats about in the shade of a Kleenex at the camp back in Malibu, and he is most difficult to talk to, I think. There is an odd obsession with naked Swedish women in a compromising situation, and I look away as not to notice.

In this film, I am suppose to swim out to sea where two of my friends from Sweden are walking around naked on a deserted island, and it does not seem compromising to me at all. Mike does not seem to mind that I take part in this scene but, most importantly, he catches the prior scene of me confronting a young version of my father. But, Mike is watching the new characters and forgets my Swedish friends for now. Ferocious interviews me and wonders what a curious situation to have both a brother and sister on the scene? Will is not my brother, but escapes the fate of the ocean, and maybe at times seems like a seahorse from my eyes or a tiger lost at sea. Mike does remind Ferocious (who is really the secondary director and more of a camera man really) that the camera is rolling and Ferocious squints from the car he rides in. It moves with others around the L.A. freeway which serves as a thorough if not primitive camera with a quantum initiative to sell all, flexing particular muscle, in the light of day and perspective at night.

However, for now Dr. Emory is informed of my whereabouts and transforms into "the Wizard" who wants to give me some Risperidone and thinks it will help me with my performance. He promises a better view of the island from his house from what is like a vespiary to see. After Dianne washes my feet with some chemical healing agents, she accepts for us both to go to his house.

I suspect that Dianne is sent to watch me in place of my father and talk with caution to her. "I do not know why, she, (Nancy) is coming out all this way. Oh well, we will have to meet Dr. Emory," I suppose.

Dianne replies, "Brett, she is your sister..."

I reply, "I know she is my sister, but why does she need to speak with Dr. Emory, he is a weirdo after all and Nancy meeting him just complicates everything."

Dianne replies, "Brett, your feet are scared and bleeding, and I am sure she heard this from someone and wants to know you are okay."

I reply, "All I told my father is not to send her out and if she is to meet Dr. Emory, she too will need therapy as a result. The person is quite strange. What does she want coming out here? I suppose she is quite intrigued. I suppose she spoke with Nicole? Tell Leslie we need another room."

Dianne asks, "Who is Leslie?"

I reply, "She is the woman who runs the inn. She wanted to know what happened to Ferocious and I told her he went on vacation."

Dianne exits the room at the same time Nancy enters, as though already checked in and such. Nancy is further perplexed slightly and wonders if she had been here before. Meanwhile, Dianne is slightly perplexed by the fear moths superimpose here in L.A. She wants to leave and forgets about the butterflies, as it is dark, and she will leave sometime in the morning; something about work. Leslie enters the scene, something further concerned about two separate rooms and how I want to bill it and I reply that my bill is separate. My sister and I will join forces later to confront the darker tendencies that remain. She is intrigued by Mars which Leslie calls home. I sit in Dr. Emory's office and fear she will do the same. The whale contends its insanity to Dr. Emory from this point of view. It stares away from where I sit. It lives in the past and is now separate.

Why must I take Risperidone in order to swim the surf to our private island across from Malibu? What I do not know is the gorilla in the most awe-stricken composure lives most inaccessible to anyone and Dr. Emory warns that those who dare to cross its path, that it is impossible. Finally, I meet a sane person and look away. He becomes the agent that is missing as I walk away from the concept entirely. It seems he may have seen something in the ocean once and, since then, is a door to this place. Like that which always leaves some homeless person who dares to swim out; waking from a great sleep on some tropical beach?

I remember my back to Mt. Fuji, even though only lions tread in such space and there a tiger is that which is still missing, I think. I wake from a long sleep on some tropical paradise, but as for the gorilla, it does not leave the ocean. However, if the water was to be drained, then maybe the gorilla would be naked for all to see. People wander about collecting shells and arrive in horror! Before Ferocious leaves on his vacation, we see the black ocean currents breaking on the rocks below some deserted highway at midnight, but that is all I remember really. The next morning, I wake from a nightmare, as it is, and go to the coffee house down the street and Nancy is returning as though wondering where I have been? After eating, we return and plan the day's action.

Besides Dianne, who has already left, the other acquaintance, Leslie, acknowledges my sister and me, as though a Martian had landed on Earth and is consequently introspectively curious about such people. She conducts herself as a perfect specimen from the sweat of the spiders from Mars, like the statue of the David in Florence. Here, though, the lingo is slightly different, but she uses L.A. as a way to study human activity.

From a distance and in respect to the German militias of World War Two, it is the closest to her livelihood activity which is watering exotic flowers for someone else. She stares at the people and enters the scene as aware of the filming and is respectful and courteous as such. Nancy, however, enters the scene like a red fire truck and in a certain language expresses a desire to resolve something bothering her as well. I think I made some contact with her, which rarely occurs, and something repeatedly reminds me of her like the heinous woman serving fried fish sandwiches at McDonalds and she calls herself wife to the sun, if there was such in the heat of the day? But, moreover, Nancy enters the scene after waking or falling asleep rather to a perfect white sun, as the past is the past; forever and all its strife redeemed.

I have difficulty eating my fish sandwich and the white sun must be only visible from my slightly open shaded window and I look away through somewhat mesmerized eyes. All I may take in is that this is Nancy's doing and I fall asleep. Nancy, meanwhile, becomes acquainted with Leslie and the two give up enough to surrender, to not interfere with each other as women do. Meanwhile, Dr. Emory is supposed to bring me some medicine.

All I know is that no one will give me the keys to the car and it must be programmed already that this is a sort of universal roll call in which both Nancy and Leslie are included no matter how bizarre. As far as the film is concerned and the squirrel who is Ferocious' spirit directing it, there is the McDonald's fish sandwich, the almighty Kleenex and the sun. The rest of L.A. must be keyed in and some lizard I call Mike watches my every move.

As for all the extras, I am not acquainted yet. My sister is in her room probably watching CNN and smoking. Mike may have built my car so that it would deliver me the three thousand miles which it was afforded when purchased and delivers me the difference to the Inn most timely to the inexcusable farewell to my father, "perfect" Mike thinks. Leslie may well be some sort of Ziggy Stardust, a perfect specimen which unlike Nancy finds Earth to be dreadful and the world divided as heaven and hell. Dr. Emory arrives to give me some medicine like a skit to remind everyone of God; or the Father, the Son, and the Holy Ghost, and I think he can't act, but maybe it is me.

The promise is in black print. As though I am still in New York and, for that matter, still pre-occupied with useless variations of reason and in an otherwise cruel and unfruitful association with reality now for matters of the tide foretell something still missing and too complicated to presume innocently?

For this reason, my parting with Ferocious gives me ample time to correct the cursive "y" allowing the promise of this tide with Satan's imminent death, to froth from the ocean and line the sky with fruits of this risky association. It is considered only a vacation and a promise of bread for wine and in this order. Now, in an air that one deciphers black from white and, for that matter, color in general, it may decipher each independently without any reaction. It seems evident in premise that blue is empty of color and "black" is black and "white" is white. If God looks through blinding blue eyes and only sees light, should Satan be gone, its curse remains hidden maybe in a cloud of darkness deep in the ocean?

The three questions are new and most timely associating with the premise of lions, tigers, and bears. It is a misleading assumption of the three warring tribes in Africa and for matter of sport, a lion exists and the other two are a menial association. Like bread for wine or black for white, it replaces the other two with an equal unit lopsided in the equation for the truth merited, it tries to enhance? The number "three" pardons those active here where the Congo is and L.A. just a dream where Ferocious should part and Satan becomes obsolete. Still, my father's former secretary calls me out of the blue and I hang up saying wrong phone number. Still, there remain three questions and the dog that ran away.

It is evident that the ocean is a playground for lions that usually are like disoriented individuals drunk and find themselves in L.A. I am not a lion, but still I walk the streets in flip flops torn at the bottom where my feet rub and bleed on the streets of L.A. and nothing may prevent the ongoing and, like a native son, the sun beats down upon my feet. What is it about lions that feel so destitute and walk like the ghosts untouchable in the golden light the sun processes at such times? Like fleas embarking on a voyage to death, they find themselves in the ocean to detest the arm of time and wake on a white sandy beach like a dream of tropical splendor. How is it that such persons find comfort in drowning in the ocean and wake up in the morning sun like kings which are only attested to in places where such persons are a commodity like gold?

These persons came forth to Santa Monica and sleep under palm trees. They never worry about strife, as the city provides the essentials and detests these persons despite the awkward embrace as though a long-lost father unsure of how to hug his beloved son. For most, these individuals draw more jealousy than sympathy and, like fleas to a dog, attract otherwise only good tidings and free beer from time to time. However, the real kings do not participate in physicality and are talked about like holy figures having gone through a long journey like a child becoming a man.

The tiger swells at Thousand Oaks Inn bring on a different sun that when invited, plays in what is called such when one or more tigers cross over a line that forbids animals to commence in human being ordeals. The phenomenon is like a trifle of what to buy at WalMart and becomes a heated experience which is not physical, but its ramifications very real. Tigers then come in a heated frenzy and want to be taught how to behave in the ghosts that haunt those invoked to participate. However, tigers are not known to be vegetarians either. More importantly, is the design of the play at hand and knowing when to laugh and when to shy away? Tigers are adeptly sensitive to kinetic energy and are not afraid of isolating when one is not aware of this to be a singular bout. However, the outcome is left as a phenomenon pertaining to ghosts unless, of course, you believe in tigers? Beware of the female tiger as she is the epitome of what woman is to man.

The bear is the most distant of God's friends. They often show up at events as though invited and, more importantly, assume a special relationship with God. One might find one at a dinner party muttering to itself, "What is God?" and taking more than its share of food as well as compliments that it takes upon itself. Also, bears like to drive and so, whenever a dog is active like Ferocious in a film, a bear is not far behind. It is never formally introduced, though at such times there is an imitated confrontation, it seems like a scuffle which is really just the bear's stomach saying it is still hungry? Otherwise, you may have a friendship with someone and never know that the bear does not feel the same way a person does; hugging a teddy bear made of cloth is hardly ever confronted really, as bears are much too preoccupied with what is happening in the film that it follows on the road.

Behind the road, I walk to the outer limits at night from the home in Thousand Oaks Juliana provides for me, which is a temporary alternative to being homeless. People with television eyes who cut their lawns on Sundays seem to find compromise bearable. Behind this scope of lions, tigers and bears, people are more interested in home appliances than going to church, where Juliana is an exception. Reality is something more in the vein of the sun that shines in three different realms like that which the ego of a dog should divide. It dispenses the notion of what is absorbed by animals at zoos and gives you the chance you request even from a vending machine, each quarter counted tirelessly? From this viewpoint, I am more aware that these tides may be met from all three realms simultaneously, while the eyes of this dark beast absorbs the return of the enthralled creatures and does not respond with thank you or anything relatively affectionate.

Actually, it is more a coincidence that lions, tigers and bears subsist simultaneously, without any questions of whose sun dominates and nuclear physics becomes an art form.

"But, what would it look like if you could see?"

I am not sure what the question you refer to implies, still three questions remain. First, why does no person ever die afterward as though the film is mocking death and all its deficiencies? Does my dad commit suicide or like his alter ego, Hitler, foretell a truth unaccounted in the sky and is killed in reality? What happens to lions, tigers and bears; when really the dichotomy of Benny's painless existence as a fly; there is a mystery of a lost son in Aborigine time as compounded in a car and therefore left unanswered?

As though lost in a city where one may never leave, this is like a pardon from above to find oneself here at the dispense of the neighbors. It is a creative faction that the wall of death should be built here, and a play to see what is becoming of America in a foreign land that which radioactive hot dogs roam about upright in a placated neighborhood similar to ours and in full site of sin?

The owl rock remains nearby and is a blessing for most. I walk the streets looking for something, but still have scars on my feet and end up somewhere like 166 Siesta Drive and like before when wandering the streets of L.A., then stay with Juliana, but only temporarily. I am picked up more than once in her car that resembles something my dad had driven years earlier and I see the tag of a fish representing Jesus, though it is retired now.

Here in the bottomless pit, I listen to the ethereal music adoring Christ has risen, but would rather find me wandering the streets of L.A. on tiptoes searching for a lost friend. I think this must be some kind of heaven for cars which is stigmatized by my father's existence, false gods in peril. Sin is a game of sorts, I suppose, and Satan is gone into the sea. I am harassed by police when I do not find a home, but would rather leave an apple pie, tangerines, and nature bars with sunflower seeds for my father should he follow me.

But, to part with my dog and think where he must be as I walk now on the freeway at night when really some idiot should swallow "the Witch" is really damnation, but I walk farther anyway. Here on the street outside Juliana's treatment center and somewhere before when I am still with Ferocious, I leave this food for my dad as though the last supper.

There is a wall on the road where persons wail, when one wakes in a place and is scared as shit. But it is safe now and behind the wall which looks more like a seaweed palace, and I am standing on my tiptoes to see if I might see Ferocious? But, really, this is asshole's peak. Directing the slur at Joe, Juliana's husband, who resembles a snail, but really comes across as some sort of Doctor Dolittle, who hails the reckoning I administer. But, really, it is eaten in two parts where Makiko and Ayumi divide a Hershey Bar fifty-fifty, as though to find a soda with a friend and how to divide it exactly even and to walk onward as to realize you are no longer in danger and dinosaurs died out a long time ago?

Dark Star in Nine Parts
who are you? Six: Africa
(Peter Fenton)

On the other side of the devil, but good;
it is a blessed land and like America, fertile
to the future. When the land is one, the people
will stand proud with God. Redemption
is just a procedure, there was never any doubt.

Part Six: Saturn Man

Adam and Eve Hotel Theater Productions Prelude in Eight Parts

One: "Aph" (Childhood friend from Mars)

Aph is an elastic orange ball that bounces on the television screen to promote things such as literacy among young children. Sort of like Pac-Man, the ball is an energizer and, when an animal figuratively eats it on the screen, the creature becomes pink afterward. This is supposed to educate children about how adult issues such as the environment, for example, is a vulnerable matter and the pink resonates this. Children watch the pink and try to follow where Aph goes on his adventure. However, one stigmatism that Aph demonstrates is how Mars is depleted of the wonders the earth possesses. Thereafter, when an animal eats it, the entity becomes sort of conceited, in a way, that reveals the degree of fortune that furthermore dispels hypnotic powers. Maybe, if we were on Mars, a person should not care about these issues and humor is the primary method of this form of reverse psychology.

Today, two hippopotamuses are playing tennis and Aph is the ball they use when a crocodile swallows Aph and it turns into a pink Abraham Lincoln who declares that "black" and "white" are the same thing. The hippos detest that such is a quagmire that these colors are un-detested where they live, as all the hippos are pink and therefore there is no deciphering one way or another. Then, a snake slithers in the scene and is colored like a rainbow. It dithers that there are many colors that exist besides pink. According to Abraham Lincoln, who is still a crocodile under the spell that Aph processes, he says that black and white are just colors and that is all, and neither is superior. But, rather, they are the same thing, just that "colors"? The crocodile turns into a third juncture which is a newspaper and the two hippos are color blind and, as they cannot see the newspaper, this proves that black and white are just colors!

A yellow bird comes along and puts on glasses that turns pink and reads through Abraham Lincoln's spectacles (that are prescribed by a doctor) and the bird reads the newspaper which says that there is a new drug called blue air and children look at the bird which is now in a scholar's outfit and warns that "drugs are bad," but some are good too. The bird tells the audience that some drugs are called medicine, but you still do not take them unless a doctor tells you to. "Birdie" opens a bottle and out pops Aph and the bird eats it and turns into a pink airplane. It flies in the sky and creates clouds that read above "pollution is bad." However, the pilot adds that some pollution is not real bad, but the reduction is always better. The plane drops a thousand gum balls below and children run and pick them up and smile as though "yes, this is good." Aph appears as a girl chewing gum and blows a big pink bubble and it pops and the words say "moderation is good." Another boy is chewing a lot of bubble gum and soon his belly begins to inflate and the boy tells his mom, who is pink, that he feels sick. His mom is really Aph. Disguised, she says, in the voice of Aph that "moderation is good." The end.

Two: The Prince's Segue

While I may not be three entities, they are, my mother's father, Stalin, and the person who dropped the bomb. From this list, a prince is tirelessly born out of the dilemma. The inner trinity, that includes Bob Marley, claims that there is still a connection to the mother. In Jamaica, the storm fades and uproots it, a plant that is their mother too. A prince has only a symbiotic relationship to the mother, though Bob Marley denies this and he is born without their lack of recognition. He would rather not know who his mother is and claims a notebook instead with an "x" written on a page with red paint. She does not claim to be the "x." Still, there are nine levels to which a prince may be born.

She does not arrive at Ziggy's house after his father died. He is easy to find, as his house is the only one that is magenta on the street. Meanwhile, the birds are only partially a menace to those who live there. The storm had passed and Xander appears here in place of their mother. He is Caucasian with dreadlocks. Also, he represents a prince in the eighth house. The plant seemed uprooted and this is the next best thing. Ziggy will not know the viaducts of her eyes as a teardrop falls from it and she is their mother. Meanwhile, the children of America and those who have flat feet like God will claim the black rose instead.

Three: Venus Flytrap Murdered

The models line the boulevard into the heart of Brooklyn. She detests that there is a humility here that is not found in remote places. Still, there is danger too as to deny an allegiance to places like Africa. The diamonds on the soles of her shoes are fake, but she will not reveal it as a lost either.

She joins a date at Junior's, where cherry pie is famous. After dinner, they go to their high school football field and the bleachers are rusted and old. She does not know that the gun in his pocket is real. He lacks the pride that his predecessors in Africa embrace. The money in her purse is enough of a reason to shoot her. No one is responsible except a dead Venus flytrap. She may have an allegiance to the very Virgin Mary and God's mother is Mars. The man lacks the pride his predecessor in Africa glow and puts the gun back in his pocket. I cannot make out his face, but light infiltrates a black glove left behind and OJ is now innocent.

Four: Purple Popsicles from Pluto

Lionel's mother is a fourth grade school teacher. And his father is a city bus driver. He is attending a public school and is in the fifth grade. Upstairs, in their apartment, which is way uptown in Manhattan, his friends join him on his birthday. They enjoy purple popsicles from Pluto. Meanwhile, his brother downstairs smokes crack. Their parents are aware of the goings on, though they do feel some pride in Lionel, who represents some hope. Lionel loves dinosaurs and visits the Museum of Natural History often. Unfortunately, the older brother who remains anonymous finds drugs before they may reach him. The kids at Lionel's party eat purple popsicles which may or may not be a drug too? Purple popsicles from Pluto sheds some light in Germany. There may only be one God too. It dispels the notion of purple rain that divides the ocean at a loss. If there was something such as light in darkness, the brothers might embrace like this. This is just a brief moment and the wall in Germany is torn down. Meanwhile, Africa and America become separate entities. There is a choice!

Five: From where God should speak?

Jamie has a big heart. On weekends, he joins a multi-racial group to play basketball as a way to release tension that develops during the work week. It is never too late to be a role model for Jamie. After the game, Jamal tells Jamie that his girlfriend is pregnant and asks if he has any money to help with the abortion? Jamie chips in ten dollars and never responds by telling his view on the situation. It is better, according to Jamie, not to evoke an argument with personal views. There is a Starbucks across the street and Jamie also treats the fellows to a coffee and even a snack.

Besides basketball, Jamie also likes to play golf and loves going to the zoo, which is something that he developed an affection for as a kid. Animals are a wonder and, though he does not like the idea of captivity, he has overseen such as a sacrifice with which he can live.

I am certain that God likes pepperoni pizza, as does Jamie. But, has anyone ever seen God interrupt someone or even project his view, other than the Ten Commandments maybe? I think not, maybe? God talks through others by setting an example. There is no way to distinguish God from people as he is always present and does not envision anything that confirms anything other. This makes him invisible, but who would know when he speaks and when he abstains? The truth is, is that God sounds just like anyone and anyone may be God at any moment in time. The distinction, however, is when Jamal makes a decision that is not God (as he respects us too much) than to make a decision is that which is not his to make? One may only search oneself to conclude what is the right thing to do when it comes to for example, "abortion?"

Actually, I do not think Jamie is God, but he talks in an almost identical fashion and this makes him more coherent than most. Why not play another game of basketball thinks God and Jamie goes along and says, "why not?" The world of God must seem very surreal, as unlike Jamie, I think he may be in more than one place at any given time. The paradox is that God has only one heart and, therefore, the truth that follows him wherever he goes is something that everyone may interpret with their insides from only their point of view. From here God speaks?

Six: Gianni Versace

The death of Gianni Versace was a dismally sad affair. What is wrong to one person is taken with a grain of salt to another if anything? When

Muhammad Ali fights Joe Frazier, it is not a race issue; all Americans followed the story as patriots if not just fans. Here, I think it is fair that some degree of race may be at hand? The truth is that I do not know how to frame the question in such a way that race may be included in the frame of an incident that I ponder further? Jesus was a Jew and Gianni, Italian; but that does not make it a race issue except for the fact that if Italian, he is different in some way than other nationalities, if for not race? Gianni should not have been killed to be sure. But, how does race play into it? I do not know the answer to this question and further detached myself, sadly, from the story as it struck my insides like an opportunistic flaw that should allow such to occur, one race to another, I think?

I can't imagine what it would be like to stand in awe of our Christian heritage, yet, still be demoted by a death, in a siege, not unlike Jesus, in some way? Gianni is pleading for people to not be like him, but rather to be otherwise, and this makes the incident even more disturbing. It is as though Gianni was begging for forgiveness from God; still he does not receive the attention God would give in such a situation. I am outraged by the outcome and know some sort of wrong has occurred here. I guess it is just an innate psyche that leads me to such a conclusion.

Though I did not know him before he died, I think what he leaves behind is to be reminisced for years to come. God may forgive Pontius Pilate, I think, yet Gianni Versace is not given the same respect in the matter. I feel cheated in some way and, as a public figure, it seems untimely that his life is cut short on my watch. All I can say is that the beautiful shirts he made out of the finest silk are proof that his life was real. It was cut short and someone needs to be responsible! If those who gained satisfaction from his death are rats, Gianni would surely be a lion, one race or another?

Seven: Matt's best friend...

When I saw the heart to where grass should deploy, I did not think twice about picking it... It was strange that the land should prolong the nature of a sublime life so that it too has a breath, so to speak? It is not that the earth is not alive, I reminisce mostly and this falls in the category of fire, but it is not wrong, should it have a heart? In Poland, the dolphins penetrate the height of the horizon which may only be experienced by children. But, the milky froth of the ocean is a metaphor for the cows that produce milk from the grass it curiously chews. It is tears lost, I think. As for Matt, I am a friend and children may go to sleep at night and pray for a better tomorrow.

I feel bad for Matt as he never escapes Uranus and falls asleep like a Tic Tac in the devil's mouth. It is written in the stars that this heart be not risen from the soil it adheres to like Uranus. As a dangerous element if released, it is like a tiny green flower that does exist.

Here, in America, where children share the landscape with birds, cows, and a dolphin; they do not know other and Matt's best friend is like a fresh saddle on a horse that never jumps, but rather glides across the terrain. In fact, Matt is rather unperturbed and rather passé, and only remembered by the brethren of Indians, who subsist in its landscape, but in time somewhere else. Now, they are gone and children remain so that kids in grade school will learn something reminiscent that Indians once occupied this space and nothing may cancel this memory. Why would a heart so immense fall below sea level forever and it just seems natural that horses glide and not other? The dolphin flies through the air and Poland once was the heart of the ocean if placated to a space?

There is only one heart to the ocean and not even the Westerns remember why the Indians went away and a saddle is a ghost they leave behind. Matt is just the saddle, but like a dolphin to the ocean, it never betrays the horse to which it is joined. I think a cowboy named Austin had a knife and cut the metaphor of a cow to its mother just once. The children of many colors run in the grass "free," and never ask for another favor. (Remember, a rainbow is obtainable in one's dream and that is where you will find Matt.) A rattlesnake curves across the landscape and it is the door where one enters America and no one worries about being different here. I think the ocean from which dolphins excel are like the saddles that crest the wind of a cowboy's butt, and Austin watches the coyotes play from afar. A saddle, slowly wearing is proof that the Indians are still among us, but only cowboys claim to see them.

Eight: Battery Jack (India Sun should subsist)

The alternative to America is "Battery Jack." It is not that one is right and the other wrong, but should you see the sun fall from the sky, it is possible you are seeing "Battery Jack." Benny the fly goes out always and, when reaching Australia, finds the Aborigines are still there, should he ever want to go home? The dark star may be the star most prevalent to the Aborigines, but it is seen from the inside and outside in installations and such has been the way for millions of years. Aborigines are on the outside in reality and it is only natural to look beyond where they subsist, but Benny, their brethren reminds them that there is a realm within as well, and both dimensions may be visited. The Star of David is seen from within and this seems so far from them really, and Satan plays in the outback minimally, like flies hovering over kangaroo shit. Furthermore, the rainbow is not theirs to claim. One is foreseen asking where Benny is and the Aborigines fall asleep and Satan is not present, but instinctually such is propelled from their environment. It is an enigma to conclude where Satan delves from and I think "inward" from the outside. If it does exist, it probably would be found far away from here.

I think a battery could energize the ocean, but somehow it escapes me and one must be watchful of lost battles. Even if Benny is not evil, the Aborigines know this even though the flies swarm by the kangaroo shit? And, that in the ocean rain tears of something so evil? I do not think Aborigines are fearful, but should you become an inflatable dummy with which old men have sex, you probably took a wrong turn on your journey and this is not a worry for other? The Aborigines are like mammoth statues on Easter Island and they remain to look for Benny when he decides to come home. The dark star may be a flagrant lie that consumes us all. The Australian Aborigines are on watch in case an unwelcome visitor falls from the sky too. The Indian sun is the number eight and will eventually transform into an eternal plain. Until the show begins and ends; it being a show for the sun of yesterday, I too will stand outside looking in. While God stands inside Africa with flat feet, he stares here at the stars and has the best view, I think. Eventually, "Battery Jack" will subside like the ocean and the Star of David and the Dark Star may become one entity and this will free my soul in Africa too.

Saturn Man

Gary Coleman was accused and, in respect to America, convicted of the same charge as Michael Jackson's molestation case. While, I doubt that Coleman was at the Neverland Ranch at the time, it is unlikely that he did anything, considering the accusation dealt with a matter of race? Continuity in ethnic association is a complete exoneration of Michael Jackson. Talking to a cop is a risk for someone already guilty before charged and sometimes, this will lead to a noble act by the police officer? It is always uncertain, like a slot machine, whether there is success in the heart felt intentions. Regarding the children who are asleep in a dark room, it may backfire. It is clear that the media jumped on the bandwagon and in the case of Michael Jackson; he is innocent and time will show this truth. There must be some sort of diplomatic immunity, I think.

As for Gary Coleman, he is walking around unaware of the accusation that someone else may have made. At this time, dogs bark into the night to instigate their delusion that black is always bad and people of kind demise get involved in something that is none of their business. Then, the media propels this hysteria as they are guilty of not having a point of view (ironically) at all. America, at such a time is being watched from all directions of the world and shudders to think of the crimes committed here? Evoking surprise, police officers are aware of the contradictions and end up in relatively fair retribution. Anyway, the crimes against humanity that manifest themselves in this case, eventually land at your doorstep as though someone selling bibles and you smirk and say "no," but "thank you."

She does not know that the sacrifices abroad have interest in this matter and you go soak yourself in your Jacuzzi tub and tell your daughter to watch out for strangers on the way to the store. On the one hand, it is not a temptation to do harm, but rather a trade-off for a sin and, actually, while you stand in judgment, do you mean watch out for black people and all you want is to live your life peacefully? Except the person of dark complexion is not welcome in your house. But your intention is to invite him in readily, and he is welcome and watches cartoons on your TV with your children.

The children of the night exist here the exact way they would exist in Africa? Even children are responsible for their actions, black or white? The problem is that influences rub off and, likewise, the bad tendencies devour their innocence. To harm them here is the same as to harm them in Africa. When justice is served, they will have a choice to return to Africa as though they never left. The scars remain as well as heartfelt goodness and they owe a thank you as the gift is good, and those who participate positively are rewarded in their purpose.

One problem is when the prisons are overcrowded, the question of goodness is questionable. These problems do not hide in the cracks, but rather compound, and a loving embrace is always better than the other. Unfortunately, for adults, this becomes a menacing problem for those who know scorn and dissatisfaction, what is too much? Maybe disassociation is an option in God's world where saving a whale is the same crime as killing it? The untouchable is an element and therefore there must be a better solution than confrontation. One solution to the alienation is to admit differences and comply with the act of giving black people six digit phone numbers and white people seven digit phone numbers? This is ludicrous! What about everyone else? No one would like it, but it is just a thought? I think the political system is working positively, somewhat? Unlocking the mystery is worth the effort; "who is the wicked witch, who is the wicked witch?"

Last night, I was beheaded in ancient Rome in a guillotine and that was a good dream.

"Michael?" Gary Coleman infers.

"Oh, call me ghost." Michael says.

"Okay, ghost, I think I will walk to the trash dump to clear my head." Gary Coleman invites the notion.

"Oh, may I come?" Michael asks.

"Yes, you may come, but why are you following me anyway?" Gary Coleman asks.

"The same reason Jesus should wander helplessly for centuries in Africa." Michael responds, adding, "Don't you remember that, but things were getting bad and so we brought Jesus over on a slave ship to America and there were also six princes of black origin. And, though, we progressed, sometimes a person, black or white, denies Jesus in sin, which makes things worse."

Gary Coleman says, "Someone told me white people do not sin?"

Michael responds, "I was buried alive as some voodoo ritual and now there are only five princes and the devil replaced Jesus just to agitate us. We are responsible for our actions. Though, in God's mind, those who are innocent will, over time, find salvation through redemption."

"What do you mean you were buried alive?" Gary Coleman asks Michael, as though he is blowing in the wind as he is a ghost.

Michael responds, "The funeral was done out of hate, as to bury one of Mike's rocks and this is a crime in God's eyes."

Gary Coleman says, "Well, I am not looking for God, I am looking for cans that I may trade in for money."

Michael says, "Also, they fought a long battle for more than two thousand years to get Jesus back. Let's just say that he has been here a long time and two thousand years is just a drop in the bucket? Still, they have him now, which makes their responsibility even greater. However, like a stone buried in the earth, sin replaces time and therefore, in an instant, it is over, that is the struggle of good over bad. I probably should not tell you this, but Jesus is a bitmap for all that is good; and it represents three points in time that which is crucified not in the sun, but a photo negative of this, which is darkness. Therefore, it represents three points in time really; 'before the stars and after the dinosaurs.' I talk to him occasionally and he tells me that it is sometimes not bad to do nothing as things work out right in the end. He says, don't reject me, because I am good, but also, do not come to me in sin as it is an insult."

Gary Coleman asks, "So, what happened to all your money?"

Michael responds, "You know, a lawsuit here and a divorce there; they kept on taking and I kept on giving until I just had one dollar left; a rich man in the eyes of God, and now I am here talking to you."

Gary Coleman infers, "So, what happened to you after you threw that rock at a robin?"

Michael asks, "How did you know that?"

Gary Coleman makes the statement, "All black kids throw a rock at a bird at some time in their youth."

Michael responds as though it is silly and says, "I was forgiven for that too, but I can't recommend it, as it takes a while to be processed. Though, not exactly a sin, it moves slowly as such and I don't want to go back there."

Gary Coleman asks, "So, why are we constantly punished?"

Michael says, "Because, we are protected in darkness and any secrets kept in darkness are not allowed to be told. Any smart white person should know that. Also, my father says I should be proud of my name and now I know why! Actually, all that is left when we die is our name inscribed on a tombstone; to wait until sins are no more."

Gary Coleman asks further, "So, what makes one person good and another person bad?"

Michael responds, "I think it is a choice?"

"I am not taking any chances, I am Saturn Man!" says Gary Coleman.

"Yes, I tried to disassociate with reality too; it worked out well for me, but may not work out well for you?" Michael as "ghost," infers…

"Hey, let's go to a party tonight, we will spook some girls?" Gary Coleman asks Michael as though now ghost.

"Okay, sure, why not?" Ghost replies.

"But, first, I must make a pact with God, never to reveal the secrets kept in the dark." Gary Coleman evokes a truth.

"You already started something bad, well you didn't refer to the mediators as the darkness," Michael implores

"Oh, right, I am sorry." Gary Coleman feverishly complies with the notion thereafter.

"Why are you apologizing to me?" Ghost asks.

"Oh, I am sorry that I am sorry, whatever?" Gary Coleman closes the sentiment as though a prayer too. "Hey, have you ever been with a white woman?" he adds as a question.

"Yea, she was sort of a prostitute, but I did not like it, it seemed like she was treating me like her child, really strange?" Michael responds.

"Hey, let's dress up as Gilbert and George for the party?" Gary Coleman makes a pitch.

"Yea, right, how are you going to pull that off?" Ghost infers and adds, "So, how long does it take to get to Saturn?"

"Oh, for me it takes just a flash, I am Saturn Man!" Gary Coleman affirms what seems so obvious to him.

The Ghost asks, "What do you do then?"

Gary Coleman is "Saturn Man," and responds, "You know, collect cans and go to parties."

Ghost asks, "How do you get to Saturn?"

Saturn Man as Gary Coleman again says, "You know, tap your shoe three times and say there is no place like home, there is no place like home. No, I am just kidding; I guess you have to do good things and then you arrive and nothing will harm you? No, like I said, I am Saturn Man! There is someone hitting their kid and I go up to them and say do not hurt this person, we are all children of God."

Ghost asks Saturn Man, "So, what is the difference between heaven and hell?"

Saturn Man replies, "Heaven is knowing that you are loved and hell is a punishment. Actually, in my previous life, I was a celebrity and, as a child, I would be punished for other kids' wrongdoings and this made me stronger and eventually led me out of the darkness."

Ghost asks, "Would you go back?"

Saturn Man says, "No, but I am thankful anyway. Some persons confront me and want me to be their child's plaything, and I am not that thankful. I think that they get the wrong idea."

Ghost says, "Why?"

Saturn Man infers, "Well, I am definitely directed by higher powers and sometimes people assume this power as themselves and this is obviously wrong and it is sort of embarrassing."

Ghost asks solemnly, "What would you tell kids who want to be successful like you?"

Saturn Man ponders, "I would tell them to do the right thing and don't believe everything that you are told."

Ghost envisions the notion, "Are children innocent or guilty?"

Saturn Man confirms, "Children are guilty as a general premise, and their parents will make it worse by assuming their innocence. They are falsely accused by such a scenario, even though they are guilty and should repent and be responsible like everyone else. The parents just make things worse and you ask why I won't go back? Well, I do not sit in judgment of them, truly, that is not my job. However, their parents would rather blame me for their kids' problems and sometimes, like I said, they think of me as to do favors or be nice or something. I feel exploited at such times if not worse."

Ghost inquires further, "Do you forgive them?"

Saturn Man retorts, "Yes, I forgive them, but I am not writing this, this is someone else's words, right?'

Ghost is curious and asks, "So, what do you have on Saturn?"

Saturn Man sits back and embraces the question as though saying like, "Well, we have a lot of old tires. My dad has an old Buick and someday, we hope to have a thriving metropolis there. Ghost, let's go. We don't want to be late to the party."

Ghost is slightly afraid and inquires, "What kind of party is this going to be?"

Saturn Man calmly replies, "You know, it is a mixed party as one of different means may assemble and have a good time as we are all assessable to God and in this light, we are able to communicate somewhat even from Saturn. That does not make us gods or anything, but we just have a good time."

"So where is this party?" Ghost must know like talking to his own muse, it may be himself.

Saturn Man coughs slightly as though fictitious. "Kooklyn, where else?"

Not knowing, Ghost asks plainly, "Do you think they will mind if I come?"

Saturn Man evokes, confidently saying, "Just pretend you are a walking coat rack and no one will notice you are hardly there."

Ghost says, "Okay."

"You know ghosts are sometimes a bit scary," someone says as though anonymously out of the blue.

Saturn Man ignores the comment and just says, "Don't worry. Besides, they can't see you, and just stick with me. I wonder if we will see anyone from *Different Strokes*? I think that their parties are usually impartial to race and this is Brooklyn, you know?"

Someone at the door says, "Hey, what's happening?"

Saturn Man states the obvious, "Hi, I am Saturn Man and this is 'Ghost.'"

"Right, Ghost, come on in." The man at the door hardly notices anyway.

Saturn Man interrupts the pause, "Oh, they are watching Wheel of Fortune. Let's watch on a flat screen TV. I wondered where all the money from *Different Strokes* went? It says, 'something that is not usually said in public' oh, don't turn over the 'd' Vanna, 'undress yourself,'" Saturn Man further chuckles to himself.

"That is really funny…" Ghost infers further.

Saturn Man makes the statement, "Everyone is watching to see what Vanna is wearing, at least the good people, and that is pretty much the whole story?"

Ghost asks, "So, where do you live?"

Saturn Man responds, "Oh, I live in California, mainly, but maintain an apartment in Brooklyn as well. My roommate is named Elsie and she is from Guiana, but stays nearby as she is scared that people are trying to put her into the darkness from which she has already left. Do you want to meet her? You know, I was just kidding about being poor? Actually, I collect tin cans as something to clear my head. We may take my Porsche and pick up two prostitutes on the way." On the boulevard he would add, "Hello, we would like the company of two female escorts."

One of the prostitutes responds, "Hey, baby, aren't you a little young to be driving around in your dad's Porsche?"

Saturn Man as though Gary Coleman would rather pee in his pants and responds to Ghost, "I get this all the time."

"So, what does Saturn Man do?" Ghost asks.

"I travel around in the sky, looking for injustice and those eloquently said are in darkness and bring them into the light," Saturn Man replies resolutely.

"Man, that's deep!" Ghost does not need to mention.

"Yea, I am pretty good at what I do. Sometimes, someone is having a bad dream and other times the person is scared or something. There is a typical case over there, a zombie and some kid hitched him some heroin, figuring he is homeless and needs another ride and so I penetrate his world and feed him some good old black medicine. I tell him that I once was like him and not to be scared as you will come out of it. You remember how you are not suppose to bury rocks in the earth as you said metaphor or whatever?" Saturn Man envisions while Ghost quickly gestures, "Yea?"

Saturn Man continues, "Well, a zombie is like that, someone living, but buried in complete darkness. They are not dangerous, but extremely sensitive to harm, so they don't show their faces often out of fear."

Ghost asks, "Do you do black magic?"

Saturn Man responds as though asleep in the moment saying in a low voice, "Yes, I do, but it really is powerless. It is a sort of way of passing time and others exclaim in the light, how it is weak and love stronger. These sorts of magicians are just that, but I do not think anyone really believes in it? Sometimes, one does it to fulfill the voids that are inflicted in bad intentions, like when someone says black people are bad. Otherwise, the magic is a way of communicating with higher powers without offending them as to say we are better than you."

"Did you ever do something bad as a kid?" Ghost is curious to ask.

"Yea, I once found a caterpillar, one of those long slimy things that turn into a butterfly and I put it into a jar as a pet. And though I would feed it ants and leaves, a few days later it died. I couldn't hide my guilt and you could say it stuck with me as I looked guilty and that was enough for me to get spanked once or twice. I couldn't pull anything over on my parents. They seemed to want to seem like that they knew everything." Saturn Man reminisces about his previous life.

"Man, that seems pretty innocent?" Ghost confides in him.

"Yea, but it still sticks; what bad thing did you do as a kid?" Saturn Man injects a further inquiry.

Ghost bitterly remembers this one time that is more like a dream but says, "Oh, yea, I told my father that my sister bit me. Actually, it is the other way around, she said that I bit her and man was I spanked! I guess it stuck with me as it has bridged a gap from those who want to harm me and I have been good ever since."

Saturn Man asks, "Do you think that was wrong?"

"Yea, it was wrong as I do not remember ever doing it, but it is not unlike how black people show love sometimes; it is very discombobulated." Ghost as Michael thinks that is enough said, but asks anyway, "Do you have any pets?"

Saturn Man says, "Yes, I have two pit bulls named Jerry and Mike."

Ghost asks, "What do you feed them?"

Saturn Man responds, "Oh, I feed them steak bones, sometimes, that I find at the dump. They enjoy a steak from time to time as well."

Ghost mildly continues the conversation and asks further, "Did you learn anything in school?"

Saturn Man responds, "Well, actually, I was home schooled mostly while on TV and, as a consequence, I missed out somewhat, but I did learn that the people around me were good, should our paths cross, which didn't happen often."

Ghost asks all of a sudden, "So, what is the difference between black and white people?"

Saturn Man wisely confesses, "Black people are white people's history and white people are the face of God to black people, no matter how scary." Ghost is intrigued and adds, "That's interesting, you mean when a black person sees the face of a white person, it reminds them of God?"

Saturn Man explains, "Actually, it resounds more to do with the fear God evokes in black people are resonate on the face of white people."

Ghost whimsically invites, "What is the nicest thing someone white has ever said to you?"

Saturn Man clarifies in a response, "Actually, it was a young kid, who came up to me, the way innocent white kids always do and asked me what it was like to be a superstar? I know what he meant, but it seemed a little confusing, as it is not as easy as it appears on TV, but I took it as a compliment anyway."

Ghost is still curious and asks further, "Tell me what Saturn is like?"

Saturn Man reflects "Okay, on Saturn, there is a drum beat that follows you from the outside always and it reverberates that one day you will be a part of the drum that only black people hear. Here, man assumed strength over nature, we are far from it, but it gives hope anyway. It is not a bad place, but if you do not like black people, you probably would not like being there."

Ghost then asks Saturn Man, "What is the worst thing you have ever said to a white person?"

Saturn Man replies, "Well, I didn't say anything really, but I thought it and that is the same thing. I guess I may tell it to you. I told a white girl that she was white, and that, I suppose is taboo and it has stuck with me anyway and the fact that I feel sorry reminds me that we are all God's children, but that is the worse thing I ever said really."

Ghost asks, "Hey, do you want to go to Africa and see what it is like there?"

Saturn Man is pleasantly intrigued and says, "Okay, but you will have to hold onto me tight, as I am supersonic."

Ghost says, "Man, those fools are doing things that we never did, I guess we are different now in some way?"

"Hey, speak for yourself, I am my own person if you want to know," he envisions further.

Ghost says plainly, "I am just saying we are blessed in a world that we do not have to make a play for the sun; we are free and they are not."

"It is different in Africa and America, not better or worse. They care about their children just like we do. And the drum sound is loud and may be heard in any corner of Africa too. Hey, let's go to the Congo and check it out?"

Saturn Man confirms, "Okay, let's takeoff."

Ghost exclaims, "Damn, there is a white person beating a drum in the Congo, how bizarre?"

"What do you mean about being bad and such?" Saturn Man turns the table as though to ask Ghost now.

Ghost infers, "I guess I swallowed my fear and that was what came out. I guess it is sort of a defense mechanism."

Gary Coleman now asks, "Yea, and I suppose you marrying America's darling and you know what that instills in white people? So what did you do to your face?"

Ghost just says, "This is what I feel I look like inside; I keep on hearing a voice like I don't want to be seen or something. It is my inner child and I feel apt to protect it."

Saturn Man as Gary Coleman asks seriously, "So, what happened with the kid at your ranch?"

Ghost implodes, quietly, "Oh, that is long history, anyway, some kid asked if he could touch me and I said okay and I guess that is wrong or something."

Saturn Man wants to ask now ,"Have you ever wanted to get married again?"

Ghost jokes, "Yea, there was a girl named Billie Jean; no I am just kidding…"

Saturn Man breaks in to say, "Hey, there is the Starlight Express, let's hop on?"

"Okay." Ghost complies with the injunction.

Saturn Man says, "They are headed, with the trash, for Uranus and will send us to Brooklyn when we get there. Let's go to church there, you know, a black church where the preacher will be saying something like, 'Do you know where you are my friends? You are in the big apple pie in the sky. I am talking about salvation.' People believe everything they hear and I suppose they are happier as a result."

"Yea, I use to be spanked silly when I skipped on Sunday school. Ghost intercedes as though just a memory.

"So, what happens when you die?" Saturn Man asks.

"Nothing, really, you just become a brother or a sister like now or even better," Ghost answers the prolonged question then says, "if I could be any animal, I would be a mouse, because they do not do anything to anyone."

Saturn Man complies further as though a joke and says, "You wouldn't make it very far; I would be a cat and you know what that means."

Ghost complies the notion saying, "I would be a mighty mouse and you are a fool to think that cats may fly!"

"Yea, but eventually you would get tired and come down and that would be the end of it." Saturn Man injects finality, and adds the question, "So, what are you scared of?"

Ghost says, "I am scared that the things that I don't do and are blamed for are real, even though I take full responsibility."

Saturn Man says, "I guess you are like me, and you would rather disassociate in a state of spectrophobia. Let's go to Neverland Ranch and have a chance to meet Michael Jackson?"

Ghost says like a child, "Yea, it is a fun place and I do not discriminate, you know. Yes, I was brought up in a world where I may now claim my inner child."

Saturn Man asks Ghost as though now a child, "What's your favorite ride?"

"I do not know, but the Ferris wheel is fun, not too scary, but a thrill. I love to watch the kids all having fun and not being scared either. Race is not an issue at my ranch!" Ghost stipulates further.

"What is the best thing about America?" Saturn Man asks Ghost.

"It is not knowing you are any different than anyone else," Ghost confirms.

"So, what is the best thing about Saturn?" Ghost asks Saturn Man.

"It is giving yourself to the greater good. We may fly over the Neverland Ranch to see what it looks like from above?"

"Okay, here is a question, why do you think God made us different colors?" Ghost says in a serious tone.

"I don't know?" Saturn Man must admit.

Ghost adds, "What is deliverance then?"

Saturn Man envisions, "It is when white people return us to our native land, better than we were when we came."

Ghost retaliates, "I disagree, I think it is when Christ is absolved of all blame in the world and children are free to play together no matter what color."

231

Saturn Man says, "Anyway, it sounds like a fair trade, but I am going to hang out here on Saturn, just in case. So, what is a ghost anyway?"

Ghost responds, "I think a ghost is someone who is caught between two worlds, between the physical and the spiritual."

Saturn Man says, "Oh, that's deep."

"The only difference is that there is no pain and you get to see a lot of cool things. Rap, is to me like sunshine is to an orange," Ghost infers gently.

"That's cool, did you write that?" Saturn Man inquires.

"No, I heard some kid say it and I wrote it down," Ghost confirms.

"So, you hear things too?" Saturn Man must know.

Ghost replies, "Not, really, but I could read his lips and anyway, it does not make any sense. Do you know what he was saying?"

"No," Saturn Man says.

"Me either," Ghost lost his train of thought and adds, "Anyway, I think in my former life I was a white kid living in a big house with two sisters and a loving mom and dad."

"Where was this?" Saturn Man must know again.

"It was in Washington, D.C. or Baltimore, I don't know which? Anyway, in this life, I had a meal at breakfast, lunch, and dinner. My sisters would tease me because it was obvious I was the favorite. My best friend Will and I played football in the backyard and sometimes hand hockey with a small marble on the entrance to the house. On weekends, we would camp out in the backyard and catch fireflies, when it got dark. The Pac-Man machine on the third floor was especially fun; I could go on for hours on it. Anyway, my dad was a big person in politics there, a wealthy Democrat who did not mind using his persona to influence politicians and my mom hardly ever came out of her room." This must seem somewhat discombobulated Ghost says.

Saturn Man asks, "What was it like being a white person, Ghost?"

Ghost responds, "Maybe, I wasn't white, but it was definitely privileged, but I sort of felt sorry for them."

Saturn Man retaliates, "That is funny, because, I once lived in a penthouse with a white father, a white sister, a white maid and a black brother who is talking like you now!"

Ghost adds, "Anyway, my parents got divorced and the love was so great that I became what was the ghostly stepmother and I am here now."

In shock, Saturn Man says, "Now, that is weird," but to continue a strange inquiry he asks, "Do you think cows are black or white?"

Ghost says, "I know for a fact that cows are black, white, and sometimes brown or even mixed black and white for that matter."

Saturn Man says, "That is not what I mean."

Ghost says, "Then, what do you mean?"

"I mean, do cows belong to white people or black people; are they in essence black or white?" Saturn Man would infer meaning where there is none.

"I wouldn't even know, but I would guess the right answer resounds in not knowing." Ghost presumes like a question in a test at school.

Saturn Man says, "Thanks, that is what I wanted to hear. So, what happened when you became a ghost?"

Ghost replies, "I thanked my family and said farewell."

"Why did you not stay longer?" Saturn Man asks.

"I guess when it was time to leave, I left." It's as if Ghost is blowing smoke in the air and responds to the question not knowing how to answer either.

Saturn Man confirms the previous notion, "So, you told me that when you threw the rock at the bird, what was it, a robin, and did you hit it?"

Ghost affirms, "Yes, I may have hit it and it was a blue jay."

Saturn Man asks most inquisitively, "So, what was your punishment?"

Ghost injects as though slightly disturbed, "Nothing. It came down from the sky as a white woman, Audrey Hepburn, and she freed my soul in Africa."

"So, you are freed then?" Saturn Man injects as though throwing a curve ball calculatingly to the catcher."

"No, I told you, I am a ghost," he intercedes.

"Maybe it freed all of Africa?" Saturn Man reflects in an interested manner.

"Yes, it may have freed all of Africa and yes I am responsible for my actions and yes, I think this feels good." Ghost exonerates the masses.

"So, you being a pop star was just a ploy for escape?" Saturn Man asks Ghost most resolutely.

"I guess it was destiny," Ghost responds.

"I think I am going to head off to Italy and ask them why they eat so much and Africans eat so little?" Saturn Man imposes the notion.

"Hey, I am really popular there, and may I come?" Ghost intercedes.

"Yes, you may come too," Saturn Man replies.

In Italy, the children are different, they are taught to not give you the benefit of a doubt. When you arrive, you get the first taste of adulthood and the wine is more flavorful and hearty. The people are walking down the street, but it is nearly impossible to approach them. They say that France is worse and don't even bother to translate their demeanor. The first step is Rome and the Coliseum. Imagine the lions attacking the Christians? Does the lion get killed or do they eat another Christian? It would be a strange place to perform, Ghost envisions, with all the history. Rap would be out of the question and opera is closest to the culture. Each stone must represent a Christian who has died in the cause. And don't touch the stone as it is history or you become the stone and it will not allow a release.

That is scary and you ask how to get out of here and the answer is the same way you arrived, unless you are an orator and want to remain here forever. Anyway, that which is old must be respected. Italians are funny about leaving the same way you came and the labyrinth represents the eyes of a thousand flowers before and this becomes something eternal, something that is a hope of a people to which repent their sins and do not wish damnation on others as well. This is history and one easy wrong move finds you at the mercy of lions, as it is not who you are, but how you arrive and leave.

There must be a bat that tasted blood already and it hangs upside down in one of the passageways once sealed as history. It will consume you like a tradition left un-flickering in their candle that blew out a long time ago. Nestled in the center of the Coliseum is that which one cannot touch. It is a passageway, where an old woman will laugh as there is no way out, everything else history, actors in their own play that do not wish this alternative and seek only good.

What appears as a Martian landing becomes something to do with not entering the center, this is the trap and if you are the same person that arrived, then the exit is plausible. However, if you wish harm on the flowers of yesterday, the poison will eat your outside and you will become a different person entirely. Damnation is not a question. It is the outcome of those who seek harm on others. Everyone must drink the blood and only a Coliseum remains to that which a pardon is plausible and only the center is not obtainable.

You see kids on the street playing and you draw a tear as you only see history and, like the Coliseum, you may not touch it. When you leave the coliseum, this is now your history as well. It would be fun to kick a ball and not have it land in the center, where ever that may be?

The next stop is Florence to see Michaelangelo's *David*. Here, too, you may not touch the statue as it is in the center of a ring which makes it vulnerable. A man, in God's eyes, is not approachable and deserves a certain amount of respect, as a result. Actually, a thousand farmers would give their last penny to make this statue a reality? Here, history divides among believers in the past and those who believe in the future. "Benny the fly," may not find a place to land which merits the center, the center of the two factions and therefore maintains a mystery of the mustard seed in its breath. When the fly is no longer needed, the two factions will meet and no longer are they different and find a rather wishful center in which leads to the present, rather than the past or future. Some have actually passed this test and therefore are called Christians. Jews say "shalom" as this is no longer their quest. David represents to Jews their desire to enter the center, God permitting. The mustard seed is trapped inside some plaster statue maybe in India, but do not bother to try to find it. May you kill a bean? I think not? By breathing a sacrament that is good, the statue will not tell you where it is and therefore it is highly unlikely that you will find it. David may find himself in the center to which the pondering is greatest and lead those who are in darkness into the light and not without the price of many poor pennies.

Lastly, the volition to Venice may be a vice in hindsight, where lovers who have received their last tear, boldly confront God to be judged. Meanwhile, a black man walks the earth in repentance and inherits the faith that the mustard seed should fall and then it is as though healing salvation is a possibility?

But lovers who seek judgment are much bolder like eating the fruit of another in sin, could it be blasphemy? Satan may reappear for those who do not pass the test and are offered a tear to meet the water that floats like the other in memory. Should the two tears of the lovers become one and relinquish someone into heaven, then the sin is forgiven. Many a prince would die for this cause and this is an entrance through an exit as those who make it need not leave. I suppose Satan would rather do other. Here lies the mystery of life after death, which should foretell the fate of those so bold?

There are secrets like this hidden all over the world. Sometimes you need the information and sometimes it is in vain. In other words, it may lead to your success or your demise. Once upon a time in Africa, a snake slithered upon a man and, out of fear, he beat the snake to its death. It was not any snake. However, it was the snake of original sin. Unlike the black man, another black man is wandering the earth for the sake of salvation; this man did basically nothing. The man is tall like an apple tree and is innocent. And, like Adam, who instigated the fall of brothers like him, he walks outside the bounds of Africa, an apple tree without a soul. Satan may walk the bounds of which is outside as well, but unlike this man, has no hope of ever returning to Africa. Also, he blesses those in the past, but without a soul, he feels only pain and may not inflict harm on others either.

But, for the things that people do that are bad, others should inherit the curse and blame the less pronounced of the original sin that Satan inherits. Here, in Venice Beach, he rests and children of darkness put coals in the fire by kicking him as they pass. Others, as a holy relic, offer this man expensive sneakers and hand-woven garments, even though he is guilty of a serious crime. There is no mercy for other. Here, it is clear that one black man is good and the other black man, bad. Somewhere in between, there is an African man staying at a motel in L.A. and he shows his craftsmanship to the sky as an offering in the form of wood statues of those who are never seen, places where a movie camera may not penetrate the darkness and God sheds light inducing the rain to come. The first drop that fell from the sky landed in my soda can and from that point I was free.

Though most of you will not reach America, I will maybe give you a tour someday, of my experiences there? You may not see America from Saturn, I think, but one sees my every move likewise. This may be what you call black magic? As it is not the full picture, it is still enough to wonder about? Uranus, which America is its eyes, nose, and mouth, is like Saturn and Africa thereafter. In other words, like the princes who occupy the Earth, they are fertile to the future, hence attractive to Christians, I think? That does not mean that other places are less. Rather, it means that their light is more influential to Christians than the other. Anyway, anyone may join the light where ever you are.

Contradictions

People who have been forgiven of their sins and who continue to sin and stand in judgment of others are those who should embrace Christianity and they don't and singularly face a worse fate as a consequence. Alternatively, in Africa, man is stronger than their sins and, therefore, he is not susceptible to this ill fate. Fortunately, the African masks in the Metropolitan Museum are not their fate and, whether ritual garments or things meant to scare, they do not represent a loss, really, and the persons who made them, are probably bored and happy to get rid of it. They are children of a black rose which does not tell lies like the alternative green rose, which only tells lies if picked?

The game is played out like this, should one take pleasure in being above God, then a curse is bestowed upon this person's soul. It is not the actual physical objects in the Metropolitan, but rather the fact of what is missing abroad and, like giving a contribution to a false god, this is beyond that and acts as a whole like a zombie. To walk through the building and not be absorbed in it is a blessing from all the places it exposes without any modesty. Those who are on the edge of good and bad need not come here, as it will only make the balance within you lean toward the bad. The black security guard who smiles as you leave is the only charity evident in the mammoth structure.

Egyptian art is an exception though, and I find it something that which should be returned as it is part of Africa truly, but resounds as stolen to me. There are also works of art and historical relics of intrigue that seem out of place, maybe a country's history in the Middle East, that dates back before Christ. These pieces are like little secrets that are not to be revealed for a vanity that does not understand it either? Pablo Picasso paintings make the stolen African masks even more significant and sacrilegious, as though time stands still, and it is a token of something like a clue to the mystery that is hidden in the dark continent and never to be revealed. The danger lurks even in a world that seems as perfect as the display and though not physically dangerous, knowing the secrets that are displayed as such makes a person guilty of the likes of original sin. "Too bad for dinosaurs, what if a giant dinosaur bird laid an egg on its roof? What would the people think of that? (Probably looking at each other in shock?)"

Ghost, Saturn Man, and I walk down Fifth Avenue, quite happy that we all passed the test. "Something about the number three is a good thing unless you are Italian."

"Hey, I am an Italian and watch what I say," I intercede, as though it is just a foil for me of not being Russian/English ,which shows my darker heritage which I would rather not subscribe to and therefore call myself more appropriately, I think, as American/Italian. I leave my bodily parts behind me and therefore subscribe to something more true.

"What do you mean the number three is a curse if you are Italian?" Saturn Man asks.

"No, but to see three Italian men talking is like talking to the devil, it is a bad sign," I respond most resolutely.

"So, if the pope was talking to two other Italian men, then he would be in essence the devil?" Ghost eludes.

"The pope is Polish, though, and I think he represents the Trinity and therefore, the number three becomes something very good," I contemplate.

"So, let's go to Little Italy?" Saturn Man beckons a response.

I reply, "Good luck. You have a better chance of drinking all the tears that comprise the Venice channels with a straw, as the sacrosanct people are long gone. But, the neighborhood stays intact after all these years; the people are the sins of others, though Italians are Christians you know? We could go, but you will get a feeling you are talking to dead people."

Ghost invites, "We could walk a little farther and check out Gianni Versace, the clothing store, oh yea, it's on Madison Avenue."

"That guy died?" Saturn Man confirms this as factual.

"Yea, I think he was shot, more wine for us to drink, I guess. I don't mean that in disrespect, it just seems sad that someone would kill a person today as though all the sacrifices people have made are meaningless?"Ghost detests to this notion.

"What do you mean, today?" Saturn Man feels more inclined to the future.

"I don't know. It seems like a lie, like it is not possible; it was just an act; today is not the past and the past, not tomorrow. I can't understand who would deny the passage of time in which God freed us. Behind the false act, who should do this is a false person. Maybe, someone should burn one of his exquisite silk shirts as though the time it took to create it, meaningless? Ghost asks point blank.

"Did you know the witch to man is a Jew?" I find it is time for this injection.

"No, I did not know that," Ghost must admit.

"Yes, Diana was homeless in Central Park when I met her and she blessed Italy, as though her second home," I say , "She represents how there is good in the world, that there is forgiveness for things like the Holocaust, that the knowledge is there if you seek it?"

"Didn't you say some dog belonged to her?" Ghost asks.

"Yes, I was watching him for her," I said with remorse, "I do not know why," and I add, "Forget Gianni Versace. Let's go to this hamburger place on Madison Avenue, between 79th and 80th Streets. It is a cool place, sort of dark though, a lot of ghosts swimming in the air."

"What do all these ghosts think?" Saturn Man wonders as the names are inscribed in wood panels.

I add, "They lived good lives; try the hamburger, you will see?"

"I will not answer the question regarding what they think, but rather what they want instead. They want to be free of damnation, but make a deal instead." Ghost lacks reticence.

Saturn Man asks, "Do you feel the same?"

"Actually, no, it is quite natural for me as I wanted to be a ghost and so the deal was in my favor," Ghost clarifies.

Then Saturn Man says, "I sort of wanted to be Saturn Man as well?"

I say, "Anyway, my aunt's name is written on one of those panels. I wonder which one? No, she is probably one of the winners, I don't think they are all ghosts, they just lived in a different time and mark the other passage that they know and feel comfortable with."

"What was your aunt's name?" asks Ghost.

I reply, "Well, my dad had three sisters, Jane, Susan and Anne, it might as well say Madonna."

"Why do you say that?" Ghost infers.

"Well, my dad's mom was sort of a perfectionist and subscribed to a wealthy lifestyle and none of her daughters could possibly have their name inscribed on the wall of a bar. I guess, if there was a bad one, she would rather not be known?"

Saturn Man asks, "You mean two of the aunts were good and one was sort of an oddball?"

I say, "I don't know? Well, it does not matter, Madonna, you know 'like a virgin' she would be a funky ghost?"

Ghost says, "Don't you ever enter a house and say that there is something else here or were here or whatever?"

"Maybe, ghosts like you?" Saturn Man interjects.

"No, for me, it is more how the passage of time manifests itself in these entities? There is no point in chasing ghosts and slowly time always brings you back to reality," Ghost intercedes.

"Yea, time, I don't know what you mean?" Saturn Man proposes.

"Yea, me either?" I say as though a bit curious.

"Well, forget it then, it doesn't matter," Ghost vents.

"You are right, these hamburgers are good," Saturn Man admits.

"Do you want to go to Tiffany's?" I ask.

"Yea, that is where all the rich ghosts go, wait, I am a rich ghost," Ghost confirms.

"I will go with you, but don't ask me to buy you anything, 'as I don't have a dime, and my sweetheart left me for another man,'" Saturn Man is in his element in a way.

"Hey, what do you think a police officer would say if he went up to one and said he is Saturn Man?" I ask.

"I suppose, I don't know, I do not go up to the police, the force, very often. It's bad karma," Ghost implies.

"Do you dislike cops?" I ask.

"No, I just don't think they play fair and they sometimes do bad things too?" Ghost says, it is just a question and adds, "Everyone is equal in the eyes of God."

Saturn Man says, "Yea, but they think they are above the law sometimes, and besides, even if they are fair, they act like their sins are less than others.

I say, "It is sort of a hoax and don't bother to waste my time unless they want to waste my time, which happens from time to time… but, I would rather not waste my time on bad cops."

Ghost says, "Don't worry about Saturn Man. They would look at him and see a kid going to a costume party; there wouldn't be any question, but you were saying bad and good people?"

"Well, a bad person is not bad because people say he or she is bad. He is bad because he does things that are bad and a good person would rather not participate in it," Saturn Man concludes.

"You are saying bad people are a bunch of losers?" I ask.

"They are losers because they do not respect the life of others." Saturn Man closes the thought like a prayer.

"On to Tiffany's and don't go near the cops," Ghost says.

"I think the bad cop and those others should start a civilization somewhere else and leave those who would rather not, alone, that would be a good solution? Though, good cops should be respected too," I think.

At Tiffany's, it is different entirely; even if you just got out of jail, they would let you look more than the average Joe," I ponder further.

I add, "Money is an objective, but they don't treat you less because you have less money than someone else. They are splendid."

"Good choice of words!" Ghost intercedes, "Yea, splendid!"

"So, who shot Kennedy?" I ask.

"Oswald," says Saturn Man.

"And, who shot Oswald?" Ghost infers.

"Ruby?" says Saturn Man.

"So, if Ruby shot Oswald, how did Oswald shoot Kennedy?" I ask without respect to hindsight in this notion.

"We still can't figure that out?" Ghost says and adds, "If Ruby shot Oswald then how did Oswald shoot Kennedy? A sort of form of reverse psychology, I think?"

"I can't figure it out either?" I say.

"It is kind of strange that in an insane world, that there are sane people?" someone envisions anonymously.

"And, the tigers are let loose at Tiffany's and in a frenzy, go crazy."

"So, what is your father like?" Ghost asks resolutely.

"I don't know my father, maybe? But, I hope he is forgiven of his sins as he is a good person, but the way things are today, it is like putting blame on a scapegoat. Hitler was killed and died, in reality, like the Jews; and so forth, my dad is exonerated, I think. But, I doubt, he will get a fair shot and has otherwise had a really good life," I reply most resolutely.

"Where did he grow up?" Ghost asks.

"He grew up in Greenwich, Connecticut, in the house that Diana Ross now lives in!" I exclaim.

"Hey, I have been there." Ghost replies.

"Yea, me too," says Saturn Man.

"Well, I thought we had something in common," I acknowledge now.

"Yes, it is a big house," Ghost says sincerely.

"Actually, for my father, it is a curse he has gotten use to. I think at this point, he would not care as others do things that we would not do, you know gangs and such and he being a good person, is miserable. There is no way he may wake up from this nightmare and shrugs it off just like a lion would, as though not to care. (Ferocious committed suicide and, as a result, killed the lion, I think.) And, he has three sisters which in a perfect world this would be a blessing?" I state for the record.

"Yea, that house has a lot of ghost energy. Maybe we should call ghost-busters?" Saturn Man interjects.

"It is not important now, but I don't think my dad is a bad person," I say.

"What does your father like to eat?" Ghost asks.

I reply as though it is true that, "Mostly black people. I am just kidding; mostly meat products, but he has a special affection for Vichyssoise soup and dainty sandwiches with the crusts cut off. We have an affection for Southern cuisine as well, like collard greens and hush puppies."

"So, what you are saying is that your dad is a rich kid who never had to confront a black kid, as he is sort of lives in his own element," Ghost asks.

"Yea, sort of and he is tall too," I say, and add, "You would probably think he is scary. I guess he sins and repents too, and therefore does not bother to associate with what he considers something else as his world is confusing enough?"

"So, he stays at home and never goes out?" Ghost asks.

I reply, "No, he just does not associate and rather the fortress he has built around himself is stronger than most people. So, what is Neverland Ranch like?"

"It is sort of a playground for children." Ghost is now Michael for a brief moment.

"Why is it called Neverland?" I ask.

Ghost replies, "I guess, it is a place for kids to fantasize, but not to penetrate. They just have a good time and then leave. I try to provide a good place for kids to play."

"Why do good kids do bad things?" I ask.

"I guess, they don't get the love they need?" Ghost concludes.

"So, Saturn Man, where did you grow up?" I ask.

"I told you, I grew up on Saturn; and I do not know what you two are talking about!"

The Sun, Jesus, and the Holy Ghost

Yes, Jesus delved within the confines of Africa for nearly two thousand years. The sun, however, only has a life span of so much. When Audrey Hepburn went to Africa to facilitate change, she freed him to the body of the other. The alternative of Jesus is Satan who thereafter also left Africa and was expected, by contrast, to never return, however. The heart of Jesus is to thrive forever, until the sun, as we know it, is no more and the Holy Ghost is a metaphor for what is in the past as well.

Africa views the emissions to the plight of what is outside its realm. God watches with bare feet that are flat like his, but first, he must stand in judgment of those on the outside. I think Jesus in the year 2200 (give or take fifty years) will return to judge those on the outside, but this is only a formality to allow God the time to ascend and Africa is a metaphor like the Holy Ghost, thereafter.

Satan, however, is on the outside where children subsist. America is a fortress of solitude for the young at heart. While Satan is forbidden to return to Africa where God's "final act," will unfold, he is also entrusted, Satan, to watch those kids who do not decide to return and partake in the scene to live here otherwise. This "scene" will occur in 1 800 years' time from the present, which is about the time it takes Jesus to judge the living and the dead, and the clock in China slows and those who subsist here will be freed to travel to foreign lands and will be an asset to America as well.

The Indians who are counted in the death camps of Stalin, may return where the brats escape their plight too. Those who remain in America will join hands with others and form a circle, and Satan will be no more. Otherwise, he is entrusted for the pursuit of children here. Satan will fly his spaceship to Neptune and Saturn will have a thriving metropolis on Earth. Likewise, Uranus or America "the land of the birds" will divide him from what was once his native land of Africa, I think. While, no one knows it, Satan will subsist on Neptune, in a trade for the children who want to come inside after all this time. Satan will talk with the dog on Pluto and besides a few wandering Indians, he has no friends.

It is not that Satan sinned. It is the lack of recognition of sins of others that would make him responsible for something. I think the lack of it thereafter is sort of offensive to God and the sacrifice he gave and adhered to? The lover to the moon may not escape the world of man and someone must be blamed for her plight, I think. Remember, to sin may be expected, but when God returns from the ocean or wherever, it is offensive, and this answer is blowing in the wind and there will be no more sin, I think?

Part of God's quest is in time? One who dies, their love must subsist 1,800 years and not less, as there is 200 years that children shed mercy upon you. To be judged by children is also a punishment. Rather than sacrifice his son, Jesus, God will trade this scenario for Satan and Lily, who divide, in a sense, leaving those who still sin behind forever. The sacrifice of his son may have only been a precedence; like Adam and Eve, they are forgiven, but they, lovers, will not meet thereafter as they become the sacrifice of God and the separation of the lovers is a form of redemption. Again, the two hundred years it will take for Jesus to return thereafter year 2000, give or take fifty years becomes a black hole in the confine of 1,600 and 1,800 years thereafter. In the year 2000, Mt. Fuji leaves the ocean in which he hid out of fear of the sun and reminds God where lions swim in its outreaches that it is time to go.

Children will play in his red sun and sinners will be left behind and be at the mercy of children, unless your love is strong enough, however, to strive 1,800 years and subsist within forever. There will be no more sin, as the saints come marching in, and heaven a reward as such. Those who do not make it are alone in time forever, remaining in a box that the devil ponders through Satan's eyes...

(The year 2200 is important as it is when God, through Jesus' love, will manifest for Christians and 1,800 years are counted thereafter year 2000, until the end of time, I think?

The Past?

When I said that you might be a Jew too, it is like saying from God's mouth that Satan is "all" until he returns Jesus, to judge the living and the dead? Religion is innately blasphemous here. When God's son died on a cross for your sins and mine too, I lived in darkness where mushrooms are picked by deer. Mimi had a sister, but I did not know it and I wandered the night, at nature's mercy, which means I was doing pretty well. Somewhere in India, I might eat from a mushroom at her request without actually picking it, in the dark too. The reason I know that the people of Africa are stronger than their sins is that its spirit should lift me from what would become India and I arrived in Africa, where my father took the step for me. A friend left, to return someday to Africa and he stands barefoot, flat like God, but on the boat to America, the tiger is lost at sea.

"Christ?" I may not leave Africa, but was I ever really here? Ferocious's ego divided in three ways and will become Will's mission and he will return to Africa someday. It was not until 1991 that I should meet Mimi again, as she had told me to wander the night and look for mushrooms. Now, in the light, but not really, we are together again. I think to myself, "I have not been here before" as I did not know Mimi has a sister. I told my father that I have not been born yet, which is another way of saying that I seek life in death. I will never meet you, my friend, but remember that I was here and the saints go marching in?

Prior to the death of Jesus, the bookends, my parents, formed an alliance in Africa and for this, the night tendencies subsist thereafter. A snake and a lion, I am not darkness, but my parents are and immaculately, I leave this world with my friends, never to return. The darker tendencies will free me and I leave behind my sisters, who will thereafter tend to the number three like Jesus. The tendencies of darkness will remain in my parents and there is no mercy here! (Big Brother is watching and God and Jesus is one.) Bob Marley said that he shot the sheriff, but was really not him.

Now, a bear remains for those who must believe, (until the end of time). My friend Will and I will never meet, thereafter, and meet up later on instead. My parents are my creation as the dark star and the Star of David, become one. And, remember, you might be a Jew too? God was that formidable picture of a woman, Joan Crawford, as an overbearing mother. A tiger tear is left in the ocean. And, Africa will overcome the sins of the world, left behind, I think, as though stronger than a feeling. Thereafter, sinners will be propelled outward always, I think. And the Garden of Eden heals from the sinners of the past, in the time of the present? Those who are not welcome, may not enter from here. I guess the game is to sin less and this may be good in the eyes of God. In the eyes of God, I think I may represent three points in time, to go inside like the Holy Ghost it represents.

Deliverance

The sun, as we know it, will eventually die. Though, the dinosaurs died a long time ago, it is reminiscent of three lions and a tiger, which will thrive afterward. The number four is a funny number which is like a full gas tank in a car which eventually succumbs to the ringed hubcaps to which the tires adhere. The number three, on the other hand is round, in a way, and will overbear the square three times over, so that four, four, four, as each of the lions will die in a 2 000-year period each, like the twelve suns they represent. Only a tiger remains and the sun dies eventually. In exchange for the sun, there is a deliverance of children who fruitfully compose the land we know now as America too. Eventually, the exchange is made. Children, holding the hands of others, and there is no worry of being different in America? Only a chrome hubcap remains once the sun fades into darkness. In exchange, in Africa, the children find some comfort being protected in a sort of tire that encompasses the children there too.

"Simon Says..."

As for the children of America, it remains to be a choice to adhere to another way of life. The spectacle is immense. A whale named Simon and the force of twenty-four elephants may bring resolution to a prior matter left undetermined. Simon asks the children if they want to leave the land of the birds to travel inward to what is called Africa. They have 200 years to decide, but in the end there is Simon which, like an arc, provides an alternative to life here in America. The games that follow are pending and new beginnings are found here too? A silver fish remains in the brackish waters off St. Simon's Island, Georgia, and he is my father and jumps out of his dimension, to express, he too is home. Meanwhile, a lion sadly must die. Maybe, the sun manifests itself here and a mere fish remains? But, really, the sun will die and

Simon says to jump on the boat back to Africa. "You can't kill that which never was, anyway!" I guess the rain, tomorrow, is pending?

Satan is from Within in Three Parts: "though I do not believe in the devil..."

One: "If not for some damn Black Labrador..." The set comprises of when day becomes night: "Goodnight"

He may be exposed for a while in the light of day, but confesses it is just sex, and goes in to have sex with the maid. Love becomes the glove and night manifests that it is possible to go in without the intoxicating cry of a Black Labrador that waits in the garage instead. He is an African man with a dark complexion and does not want to be stuck in the rain. And a compromise is made in Amsterdam so that I too am a dark entity at night there and I hide the evidence from this one damn Black Labrador.

Two: Voodoo Devil (What is Left?)

Should I eat a pear, someone may be eating a pear too, and this remaining substance is all that is left of me that which is a voodoo devil. I am in a predicament where waste makes surplus, but I am not it and it may be all that is left, a devil without remorse of a substance so offensive. If I am a consenting adult, the flowers in their house demonstrate that there is in fact a history furthermore. I do not know that the flowers picked are his, though?

Three: God's Loss (I was a slave when Satan was born)

Before this voodoo devil that manifested here as waste, "no shit?" I may have been a slave when Satan was born. I ate things like greasy chicken fingers in mustard sauce, French fries or onion rings, a Diet Coke, and a pickle on the side. I was a slave and so is Satan in this light. The kids play at the beach club, and the waste is a timely response to a rendezvous that should be hidden from view. This may be God's creation too, and not mine and I am just a vestibule that separates it from the source which is God, I think?

Crossroad: A memory of a white kid growing up black

God exists also on the outside and the bleachers at the high school in North Carolina, where I was born, rust and the paint chips that expound are the only testament that he is even there.

My dad may be the epitome of growing up white and grew up sometime in the early 1950s. He may be named Biff and drives a Buick convertible with white leather interior and wears his Winstons in his t-shirt sleeve which is white also. In high school, he played on an all-white basketball team of which he is captain as before the black kids infiltrated the scene. On Sunday night in Greenwich, Connecticut, where he grew up, the servants and cook, all black, would prepare the meal. The first course was Vichyssoise soup (always cold.) Then a course of a watercress salad with finely sliced beets, roasted pecans, and cherry tomatoes which squirt in your mouth. Lastly, the main course was lamb which is finely savored in its own juices with a side of mint jelly as a condiment that adds a sweetness to the meat cooked slightly rare. He never leaves the life he knew then. He would run for Congress as an affluent American in North Carolina where we have deep roots, tying him to the tobacco industry there. He would end up a major Gary Hart supporter. He still drives a Buick and into the eighties allows his hair to fly free in the wind in this liberal sentiment.

I would not consider him a racist. He just never had to experience other and is rather well adjusted on a white cloud that he never leaves and would not know other. He finds raccoons rather interesting and, in the back of his head, relays the sentiment as this having to do with black kids, but does not verbalize the gesture as not to know really.

I may have grown up differently. The nanny who raised me as an infant was a Jamaican woman named Elsie. She would jump over the moon for me, but even better was my expression saying something like "got milk?" This was a crossroad that verged and the things that other kids might think they would get away with was terminated at this point. Like Jimi Henderix who may have experienced other, I was now a black kid in a white kid's world. My first friend may be African/American and his name was Neal. We dug up worms at recess and it is my destiny as well. It is kindergarten in Washington, D.C. and Elsie is a memory still. Nevertheless, some kid steals my toy and my expression is reminiscent that I am guilty. I may be punished for someone else's act. I would rather not do anything else bad even though I was innocent.

My past may be deeper than this picture I paint for you, though it still resounds in the color black. It is particularly assumed that I, like the moon's own, would end up a white kid. I may represent three points in time, and the inner trinity is a trade that God may live with. A tie is made with Africa where my dad is an African Jew whose step releases me from the land. I mention that Michael Jackson would become my stepmother, which is to say not the moon's own and resonates a sentiment which is neither man nor woman, but represents the seventh dimension. I know something at this juncture and God's people may be other. The children are present in darkness. The moon does not claim a color here either.

There are dark places in Africa whose people subsist without this knowledge. In exchange for the inner trinity, I may paint a picture of myself. These may be pictures in time and I encourage you to do the same if so inspired and this will free you as well as me. God leaves a light on at the kitchen door, and this is your heritage too.

Dark Star in Nine Parts
who are you? Seven: America
(Matt Harrison)

*Uranus is the land of the birds and liberty
for all. A child's tear is ok, to be free and smile
in sunlight. At night, each child holds on the
hand of another and there are no worries of
being different than everyone else.*

Part Seven: Tales from the Beer Spider

"The color of gold"

It may be difficult to bargain for white and get gold instead. It has a relapse when trinkets sold for the blood of others should ponder a silver aspiration, but die in the sweat of the moon, and the sun it once represented is now gone for a while. Really, gold speaks many languages and is fitting to virgins who taste champagne or even beer for that matter, for the first time. And the realization that gold may be assessable to all as the moon is alone and panders to silver questions, its own malaise of what may become you if you try. One teardrop of the phoenix should beckon the rise of a new sun and ants in crevices on street asphalt subscribe to a new day. A teardrop lies in wait for a time when in this still life time fades with the moon so that a new breed of golden nuances will emerge.

But, like the Indians who died and were not present, no one will see the teardrop land maybe out of a callous reminder of one tired girl and her love for her father. Here is where Van Morrison's "Poetic Champions Compose," begins and the sun dies to songs of the Bee Gees so a new sun will emerge. Their record of an apple torn from a tree branch, rather the spectacle endears children and other to saunter why the moon is all alone in the sky as well? Not of bravado, but rather the sweat and tears of an other and he emerges from the darkness without the memory of those who do not remain. Silver aspirations will rather endear them in their flight and girls wonder why the moon rises and the sun fades? Actually, in pure darkness is where you will meet me, as though a verse in a poem which does not know the answers, but leaves you in a safe place anyway. It foretells the ripeness of bread at church while after church sinners must drink the blood of another as wine and not presume why?

The children are guided so that the gold bracelet their mother wears escapes the presumptions of time and church service is a ritual that allows believers to foster it further when you die, that there is a god who does not surrender trust like the gold cross the pope carries in this journey, but alone for a time sadly. Maybe the mint tears of the devil lead to an entirely different end all together. Jim Morrison then walks a path to where Indians once trekked in the light of a silver moon. He finds a home there even though he keeps walking farther and never returns home entirely. He said there was a car crash, but still has fond memories of his childhood. The cross is not the instrument of his demise, but rather represents the retardataire pain felt once. The Indians are no longer present and subscribe to linear equations which only means anything to themselves and maybe a few others.

They are but ants that build castles in the sky, "let them be not lost as that is where they should be, now put the foundation under them…" so Thoreau mocks prodigies of himself, in Walden Pound. While children are ever present and compose questions of blood for sweat, and sweat for blood, and may not know why the two relate at this juncture? Rather, the devil composes his own poetry at such times and shares this with children who do not recollect anything at all really. Still, they stare at microbes in jars which ferment a passion of why ask why, not? And it is really something intriguing of that which is trapped in a jar at science class. Witches may compose a dimension that is different entirely, but leave a light on in a room so that they may prepare the swath for the sun's tears for the following day.

Meanwhile, the children do not remember why one does not ask why not? For those who are welcome, the scenario is quite sufficient if not impenetrable to those who would know otherwise at such times. Each child holds the hands of another at night and there are no worries of being any different here, and forever more. When they grow older, the children will learn that believing is respect to God. Whether the swath of witches' toil is natural or not no longer matters. The leopard sits in a tree protecting her flock from those who would want to cause harm. The ocean otherwise is not penetrable like glass tear drops from blue soldiers eyes. She speaks of this in mourning of those who do not make it, to see the scenario when the sun and moon parts. The golden bear remains away from harm and never returns to where the poetic champions compose, and it rather eats the honey from beehives as a sort of compromise.

But not really, the coffee is the earth, and the cleft milk, the moon, and everything else is left unsubstantiated like fire which is the devil's only tool. Chimpanzees do a dance to remember those from a world in the past, while the past has no future, which is the present. We should all join together someday and this is the heaven that the poetic champions compose. The earth will be flat, where horses cross the wind's eternal plain and goldfish cry tears so pure in ponds that dispel notions of what is fire here, and bees explore the desert of sand fearful of the dimension of a half life eternally. What will become of this wish of life in death? Meanwhile, a heavyset man with a red beard sits by a lake and dries his socks on sticks by the fire, while the sun fades just one more time…and the children play and play. I guess gold at such times is busy with other responsibilities.

"My silver aspiration…"

In the beginning, there are three blue devils who work on the sky. It may be a compromise for God to create all from a mishap that leads to me throwing a rock at the sun, and we arrive at his door to summon the ants to predict the light of the next day. We may have really split the night, but it is not time to enter here and we remain in the dark still, and this may give God the time to make creation. As meanwhile, my spiritual mother, Mimi, tells me to look for mushrooms and we do not touch in this process; though I need not know that she has a sister. It turned on me, the creek in Central Park, where I kneeled to drink from its natural resource. Even though it is sort of not pure, I think thank you just the same not knowing otherwise at the time. As God forsakes others to not eat from his tree of knowledge, now it does not matter, nor so pure either, I think. Still, we would remain in the realm of darkness, for the time being and I wonder why?

The step of my father which he would take for me, would not penetrate his world either. But my tail is separated in the process, in hindsight, and she would rather guard the tree instead as my birth mother. Before this, I travel from a distant land and eat ripe mushrooms like insects that are small enough to do so like an atomic equation in hindsight. Here, deer frame man, to pick the mushrooms and deny it in the process. The lie lifts me and delivers me in another land, but was never really there? I can hear Simon and Garfunkel's medley "Homeward Bound" then suddenly there was light, and life is a gift which pondered man's future as something vulnerable, but good still. So when Lily claims her flower, the ocean drowns in a lie which for Eve is a similar crime as to eat the fruit which is not hers, as well. God may have said "Let there be light…" but it is a paradox really for a Paradise Lost, as the sun would eventually subside.

My birth father may have eaten his soup with a silver spoon, but he too, like the lion he represents, would only subside in spirit, though. The Jews who would die under his diction are the many faces of Jesus, whom God sacrificed in the process, and my father is not he, but a lover in a previous life, he wonders, but not God in the process. The ocean parts but for a young girl who inspects the remains of a boy who is tempted to pick a forbidden fruit, while my mother will claim this primal sin as her own, even though she is innocent.

Then, Abraham may have offered his son in sacrifice like a lamb "of God." Eve may have bargained for something less, but her guilt still blooms in her cheeks. The apple that she aspires to will not land in the world she adopts for the time being. It is the beginning when a sky is broken and a family exists to live by God's law in India. However, Jesus dies before the Jews, and God is not man! And Bob Marley sings a redemption song from afar. And redemption is accessible to those who seek, I think. Adam will pick an apple for Eve and he is not God either. The apple that falls will eventually land in God's hand while Mimi's flower is picked somewhere else too. Her sister is an alibi for a crime she did not commit. She remains a virgin despite Lily's tempestuous affair that would resound. Meanwhile, Satan remains in a corner of the ocean that is considered separate. I think it is ironic that Lily is alone. Hitler and I share the same spiritual mother while Alison hides in the womb of a female zebra and Ilona claims the sins of the father is bearable. Satan does not claim a right to the "brats of doom." If the deer deny their right, then what is God?

With the light that should happen, the three blue devils should avoid judgment by God. Still, three entities exist in the future; the remain of a lion is Bob Marley, while Michael Jackson lives his life as a ghost, and represents my three points in time, that would later reminisce my dog as in life as well as in death. There is a queen in Africa, so far away as Mozambique, and she waits to unify the good forces of three warring tribes in Africa, to be one at last. (Nelson Mandela walks to freedom while Queen Latifah sings hip hop somewhere else too.) Should I throw a rock at the moon seems pointless now anyway. Satan is separate from God and Africa as well and sees through the devil's eyes. Lily loves a boy who is not God and remains in the ocean as a punishment. She does not socialize with Satan, but remains in the ocean as well.

"The Lost Generation"

The sixties came fast and left in such a way that my generation hardly knew the splendor the zeitgeist professed prior. Furthermore, I knew that Guns N' Roses was not part of it all and by my second year in boarding school, "hippie" meant that you listened to the Grateful Dead to carry on hopes of a brother who grew up in the seventies, thereafter. It had been a culture of love, but drugs played a role in the new generation's life and the prophets prior was pre-disposed as to have little meaning in 1987. Though, my class is not entirely lost, the display of further conservative sixties' innuendo meant the end was near. They recognized the demeanor while swimming in an ocean with a loveless attitude toward life in general.

The world of the WASP is most eloquently professed in the characterization of three other students I would come to know while at St. George's boarding school in the year 1986 to 1988. I guess I was expecting something else and it seemed money aspirations had over shadowed the growth of character that was evoked prior in chatter by my father when he went to boarding school in the 1950s as well. I guess the money in families became a token more valuable today and, though not poor, most students' lack of having more of it compelled them to contest the day further and to meet the ends of greater wealth later, I think. A WASP to me meant that you may be from the upper crust and in my dad's generation, which was the 1950s. It also meant that if you worked hard and attended a good college, the opportunities would seek you out. The difference, now, on a grand scale is that the lesson taught is not about character, but rather, one is to create their own destiny. One is not suppose to wait and allow opportunities to seek you. You must go out and seek it for yourself. This is a major difference between my father's and my generation. Though I came from a wealthy family and never had to think like that, I am introduced to the pre-disposition the moment I met my freshman year roommate, Ham. As soon as our introduction had occurred, he was out the door professing opportunities right and left that may or may not help him later on in his life. The WASP lifestyle had been demoted to a fly slapped on the neck of a hyper-intensive boy whose father instilled fear.

"Split Ego in Three Parts" (Reference is to Ferocious)

"Ham"

I guess it was easy to tell by my laidback composure (the moment Ham walked in the door) that I was a love child. For some reason, Ham felt it necessary to fight this characterization that he saw as a flaw in myself. While I would not compliment any of the students as to go so far to say that he or she was a Nixon Republican, but rather a dark cloud of conservatism overshadowed most to the point that they did not even know why they stood for what I think? There were a few students who showed some point of view and for those I was slightly impressed, even though I embraced the other side of the political spectrum. Being "lost" is when fear becomes more important than love on how you interact and, when lost, this makes you act in such a way which was unbecoming in my dad's generation.

I guess Ham had aspirations of being a banker like his father. His father probably worked hard, but the competition professed that one wrong move might leave him in a disease that he saw someone like me to possess. He was a sailor in Ducksbury, Massachusetts, and attempted to surpass the wind in his sails. Ham was bi-polar, I think? Either he was fighting cultural disease like notions of love and so on, or he was racing sailboats, just to go faster and faster. A sane person would tell him he is already going fast enough, but he would not listen. I think he saw me like a tick that desired his blood and he constantly fought reason as his father professed "to make your own destiny."

The generation is lost when secret societies manifest like rap is to an inner city kid and the fear of both entities is formidable. Either Ham will not have enough money or to an inner city kid, he may conclude that he might not have any at all? When everyone becomes partial to only money, the generation is lost. As long as he does not fall on graduation day while walking on the stage for his diploma, everything would fall into place. Ham may have sat in the back, listening to Guns N' Roses on a walkman and that was a sign the sixties was over. A cat may be his only friend, as he enters the world of fanged hounds from hell and I admire his tenacity. But, I was not at the graduation; rather I find myself driving a taxi cab in New York City at nineteen. If Ham had known this, he would fear me even more, I think. I am sure he finds success very rewarding, but gets lost on his way home and does not care anyway.

A lost generation is more compelling than driving a taxi cab and he thinks his father was right that the pieces would fall into place as a result of his strife. While he is eating shrimp salad at the country club, I find myself at Tiffany's admiring everything and our worlds part for better or worse. He probably married a girl even more tenacious than himself?

"Jamie"

Jamie's guitar compels the ego of giants to divide in three parts furthermore. Unlike Dean, my sophomore year roommate, Jamie had little if no ego. His father attended St George's like when my father professed the character of WASPS seen obscurely in the movie *The Graduate* (character always comes first before money.) While Jamie's father was like my father, Jamie did not admire him at all and wished mainly just to be different. To him, his father was a sell-out; his mother is maybe someone who compromised love for money, to have a comfortable life; and his sister is a snooty little tattle tale, whom he further finds a waste of time.

He strums his guitar, professing the greatness of Bob Dylan in his voice, which is sort of respected from every direction. His family is a sacrifice he can live with, and his guitar is a way not to care either. Jamie wore plain brown corduroys, a red plaid wool shirt and, of course, and a pair of understated Docksiders, which like the Beatles was a remnant of his family's past that he could live with. While the Beatles were passé, Bob Dylan was God to Jamie. In his freshman year, Jamie talked verbosely about how he was against drugs. By sophomore year, like Bob Dylan exchanging his acoustic guitar for electric, he thereafter becomes obsessed with the psychedelic experience and we still do not know why? All we know about Jamie is that within the time frame of sophomore year, Jamie took three double-dosed globes of L.S.D. and his life at St. George's was history thereafter.

I guess some of us resented that his roommate, Morgan turned him in, as he was catatonic on his bed and could have died. Morgan probably saved Jamie's life, but we were all sorry to see him go. Jamie later died in a car crash and I do not know if I could have prevented this. The last time I saw him, he was visiting me at Simon's Rock College and I noticed he was not acting right. I embarked in a tirade one night, alone where I lived, and tried to call Jamie as I felt something bad was going to happen to him. I guess, I felt more sorry for myself as I was the friend he left behind. The sixties are remembered here as he died in this fashion. Where ever he ended up, I feel sorry he got lost on the way.

"Dean"

Dean was an arrogant display of Dead Head conservative values. He followed his older brother and was on a mission to make conservative values "cool" in the eighties. Ronald Reagan was president and he need not try hard to make this his reality. He went even further to make Jerry Garcia his god. What is cool to Dean is to make the sixties converted to conservatism and he professed such values while listening to the Grateful Dead. I guess I did not like him after returning from a marine biology expedition on St. George's

Geronimo program. I find that some of my coveted clay pieces I bought in Ecuador that summer, were broken? I guess I knew that it was going to be a rocky road. I think Dean knew why he was conservative, but never mentioned the Republican Party, I guess he was hardcore. His family professed a dream, the sixties would be overshadowed by the Ronald Reagan era. He did not debate politics as he didn't really attempt to go there. He knew what he stood for, but what was his beliefs?

I think for Dean, the term "belief" is still too liberal and, rather, he collects bootlegs and laughs at the wind for being lost. This is too egotistical even for "the beer spider" and she shunned to think what insult this professed for her sister, I think? Dean was the "king" of cool conservatism. I regret that I did not listen to my African American friend Kevin, that he was a bigot too? The zazen zeal he eludes leaves him at a loss too.

"At age thirty-six"

I am sitting by the pool at the beach club at Sea Island and think to myself that there are vaginas in every direction. This is my spizzerinctum. I say this, to set the tone for how in my late teens, I should become a yellow taxicab driver in NYC? The answer is twofold. First, I expected to someday become a photo journalist, since winning the camera prize at St. George's my freshman year? The mistake I made was not to make it "tangible" as a goal. It rather invaded my subconscious and never manifested itself in reality like a state of Torschlusspanik. The other reason I became a cab driver is that I did not think I could get any other job. Even a rich kid has to pay the bills somehow.

I had several opportunities to make my goal a reality; I spent vacations traveling to Eastern Kentucky and Eastern Tennessee through Save the Children. Furthermore, I went to live with poor black families in Mississippi through MACE Mississippi Action for Community Education, and documented families in both places at age sixteen and thereafter. I would spend weekends in NYC with my mom where there are even greater opportunities in photojournalism. But, Ham was right that I did not make my goals, my destiny and ended up a cab driver in NYC at age nineteen. Though, I was not lost entirely, I guess time should pass like sand through an hour glass?

You might ask yourself where did I go wrong as I am single and thirty-six and thinking about vaginas at the pool at the beach club at Sea Island? I guess

I thought that masturbation could be a way of life? Though, like other straight protégés like myself, I sought sex early, but eventually I gave up in the cause and found myself somewhere else, living in New York City on the Upper East Side while attending Hunter College and driving a yellow cab to pay my bills. It is not that I am lost, but I do not live up to the aspirations of other students while attending St. George's before that. I guess I am a loser, but I am proud still of what I have done. Meeting a homeless woman named Diana here in NYC was a pivotal point in my life and I do not regret the turn it would lead in my life thereafter. Her dog, that of the good witch to man, became three points in time, that my three friends should adhere to like a split ego.

Tales from the beer spider (continued)

The Glass Menagerie

"Kevin"

Kevin is the oldest and carries a charm that cannot be anything other than his father. The younger sisters, with the exception of Elizabeth, find him regal, with blond hair and a modest complexion which girls at school find attractive. But, not as far to say "pretty," he carries a gift from the father that does not allow for his image to ever go there. Furthermore, he has his own room and his varsity jacket that sits posed on his bed over the wooden frame is easily visible to the door that is slightly open for any spectators.

Actually, he is somewhat modest, but pretends when Elizabeth is around to be dominant as he is older than her by eleven months. Still, Kevin knows that playing guard on the varsity basketball team will not pay for his future college and he works hard at his schoolwork to keep the doors open. It is assumed, in the Frawley household, that he would become a lawyer like his father and that would make all the difference, leaving Elizabeth more in the dark as a domestic goddess.

Kevin is unaware of the competition and does his algebra homework, hardly noticing the fly that keeps on buzzing around his ear. In this household, there have to be many options as its survival is based on societal qualms. The number eight seems to be taboo in the crystal menagerie downstairs and it reflects the light of something not reflected or missed, but in actuality there are eight children in all. Mrs. Frawley thought it appropriate that both Kevin and Elizabeth share the family secret and did at first set a gloom on the other children that was difficult to rectify. Actually, it wasn't really a secret at all, and knowing was taboo like the number eight; it became a perpetuity, a challenge to say the least. Anyway, the permutation should pass and eight is a good sign maybe in Buddhism. Meanwhile, Elizabeth seems slightly pernicious in her intent on Kevin as a whole. On the other hand, world religions may have been an interest while girls too seemed a little more accessible at school in which seemed a bit risky to the oldest of eight in an Irish Catholic family in a small town in Upstate New York.

He mildly met their acquaintance and thought of religion as a means to sidetrack his demeanor toward girls as well as a prophecy of what was to come. He knew the one Jewish girl in the high school and sort of felt sorry for her being all alone all the time. In Elmira, time plays a trick on its residents, although it is in the late sixties, it feels like the fifties as though when Kennedy was shot it did not penetrate and rather induced lethargy as well as the hope for a sunny day from time to time. The people did not notice the time slowing as they were actors in the confine of Elmira; if anything, the residents felt protected from the outside and any change was quite noticeable.

The only change Kevin notices is his younger brother now playing basketball at his capacity if not better, and this sort of swamps Kevin with self-doubt, he being older by two or three years, not having experienced this before. It is clear that the tides are turning somewhat, but mother's glass menagerie becomes the focus, as it protects the family from harm. In the corner of the living room, there is a wooden and glass cupboard that wedges itself on the far side, welcoming one who should come forth to see it. There, Kevin stares openly at the figures and counts nine pieces, including a crystal cross. That is it, religion, Kevin thinks. What could be a stronger force in this household? Therefore, Kevin makes a concerted effort to be honest and this would increase his faith as a Catholic and, consequently, lead him in the right direction. It is a turning point because it could only happen in this one house and this one family in Elmira.

Kevin embraces Christ as a demeanor to being a worse basketball player than Brian, but it is the right path anyway and Elizabeth might demur his effort as something less than how scrupulous Christians should act. In a sense, Kevin is receiving objection from two siblings at the same time, but he feels it would make him better in the long run and father Frawley makes a sign that he was on the right path, and Brian eventually apologizes for showing off on the basketball court.

"Elizabeth"

By the time she entered the eleventh grade in the high school, the Jewish girl that Kevin felt sorry for was more a figment of his mind as they never talked. She had left the school and must have moved with her parents to another school in another town. Elizabeth never met her; I guess their paths never crossed really. Elizabeth was now gaining popularity at a peculiar pace and seemed to be literate in most areas of school curriculum. There may have been some insecurity among less popular girl schoolmates. She chose her friends carefully as to be slightly better than her associates and religion was important too, as it made her feel safe like a bodyguard that blocked from view those she did not want to meet.

She would talk to her friends as though reciting a prayer at church. At age fifteen, she thought she could be a nun, if not better. She assumed religion as an outlet and did not have to testify her faith as long as she was moving upward in the hierarchy. It is strange how Rosemary, the second-oldest daughter by a few years, would follow her around to denote a certain caring that she was not use to, always playing with the boys and trying to be better than them. Furthermore, her ambitions outside of home seemed to compete with a male persona in general, and this might include something on the level of a priest as she is a devout Catholic and this serves a purpose in finding her identity. Elizabeth wants to be better and this seems not to be her fault entirely. The rebellious climate of the sixties may have blown some air in which defied the air to which her life was repugnant.

By age seventeen, Elizabeth brought her first boyfriend into the house. She did not know him well, but the act made a statement like "I am on my own" and "I don't need you anymore." Who knew from what family he came? Step by step, she was becoming a person of influence and she knew this meant more power. I guess it made her feel good that she would be exonerated for her sins in the end. Since then, maybe, she regrets her ups and downs. Being Catholic meant to her teaching others about what is right and what is wrong and this made her a vice to be dealt with. Little does she know that Rowie, who was still following her around, meant well, but her disparaging words were to leave me alone.

This is still a respectful household with problems like every other family. When she does not attend an Ivy League school, as her grades are redeemable as such, she is repressed. When she chooses a Catholic School that is in the budget of her father, a judge, she is neglected. One way or another, her life is not suitable for her aspirations and this is blamed on her older brother and father as well. Her right as a Catholic and a human being requires the repudiation of someone else's rights. The question of what is natural is apparent to me.

By the time my stepmother married my father, Elizabeth made a score and this should serve him as an aperitif and that is all, but not the scorn that was left him. Rowie still calls Elizabeth, Elizabeth, but their lives are parted still.

"Brian"

It is Brian's room and in this room which he shares with his younger brother Terry, there is a dresser and mirror that each day after school and basketball practice, he takes his shirt off to stare down at his crucifix hanging from his neck, so sanguine and unfaltering just like the church, he thinks. The flowers that absorb the grounds are particularly beautiful and the smell of roses is like his mom, especially on a chilly spring morning. He coughs to show God the pain he feels for the son that is lost on a cross like flowers maybe. Brian continues to keep his cough in his chest as a ritual of what may be despoils of the Virgin Mary's own tear. There is a slight degree of uranomania here. With the pain that inhibited his throat from clearing, he dispels the notion of pain, what pain may symbolize from a mother's point of view.

As the third oldest child and second oldest son, Brian feels a special responsibility to serve the family, but even more to serve the church. The family is already developing like a rose bud, with many petals. An Irish Catholic mosaic headed by father Don Frawley, and with eight children – five girls and three boys – from his loins he may pronounce their faith in Elmira, New York. On the other hand, from Hunter College, their mother travels a distance to live away from her own town, New York City and she ends up in the small town of Elmira. She may be like a foreigner to what seems like as "A Wonderful Life."

The father attended Columbia Law School and, as families go, they should unite as a force to be reckoned with. The children do not understand pain, the pain a mother feels when losing one of her own at birth. In the early days that began to develop, their father's pride that shed from a large family and the pain is a little difficult in understanding. The family seems a close-knit circus of faces, all of whom are loved. Yet, even at early stages of the family,

Brian distinguished him as slightly closer to his mother than his father, and after the loss of one child at birth, the pain and further shame this involved became a puzzle for Brian. He began to reflect on what this pain involved, naturally cohered by his mother's image and this picture superimposed as Jesus dying on the cross.

One day, Brian found a wool poncho of many colors and made the association to Joseph and he put it on even despite it being somewhat dirty and felt like light had penetrated his darkness. It was normal to feel such thoughts and maybe he too, like Joseph, was special in some way. On the other hand, Brian was popular with the girls and knew he must repent his sins as well. What was so amazing about the poncho was how it made the bible real, like it was living and not just a history book. To Brian, it took on the form of life itself and this felt good as well. He felt sorry he never talked with someone outside his religion and he did not cast a damn on them either. He just wanted them to feel as good as he felt on that day. He kept a penny in his pocket to remind him that he would take on a poor person's life for the sake of Jesus.

The family was very understanding of what seemed like a good path and I feel somewhat resonant of the gesture as well. Brian continued to ponder sin which he painstakingly tried to avoid, but became a fickle matter when it came time to confess. Brian felt he was making up things as though he were a sinner. As a Christian, but more as a Catholic, one is supposed to confess their sins and, if you don't, than it is a lonely world. Brian would do something innocent like not finishing all his food on his dinner plate and try to count this as a sin. Really, it was much deeper than that because it may be not what you do, but what you don't do which is a sin and, with this knowledge, the world is something intensely more complicated. And Brian then felt an emotion of helplessness; it was a bad feeling and he wished it would let him go. His father asked him how his grades were going and Brian responded as though slightly better than he implied – it was the helpless nakedness that Brian feared most. He would talk to his girlfriend and she would tell him how perfect he was and he did not like this either. From which angle may he approach God, he thought without being offensive, and it would be a long road from there.

"Terry"

Terry is the most daring member of the family and, though also he shows a good time, he may have brought everyone into the sixties and out of the rain. His charm is knowing he is a sinner, but sins that are not bad, but rather edible and something to talk about. And, others, seem a magnet to this carefree existence and feel their sins less when around him. You could say he is a role model for the younger sisters of how to be when outside the confines of the family, which was sometimes a serious matter. He would talk about music and sports and wait for someone to say something bad about someone. Then he assumes the person in question sins and does not fall into the trap of judging others which he does not like. The best way to go about this is telling a joke and, with the laughter, change will come in the Frawley household. Terry likes gadgets as well, and is able to buy a car with what he saved from different money prospects he calls jobs. Otherwise, materialism is not an issue; he is truly interested in the advancement of technology and will further discuss with his mother how amazing the new blender is or how much larger the new refrigerator is and this simply manifests itself in a used car he will eventually buy. And his mother thinks the wonder is helpful to bring the four younger girls to school and other events as they are quickly maturing into young adults. Peguine asks, what are you going to call your car and Terry replies "the tin can" as a joke and the age discrimination of the older siblings do not harness their contempt here and rather may form a line to which Terry is mainly in the middle as well as Rowie, who still makes an effort to be Elizabeth's friend when issues of the older siblings are at hand.

Meanwhile, Terry listens to Jimi Hendrix and is amazed by the riffs he sounds on the guitar. Terry feels more at ease in this new generation. This is something the older kids will never understand as Ellen, the youngest sister, thinks he is funny and that is about it. A conspiracy formed as a result of Jimi Hendrix and the older siblings think it their duty to try to circumspect Terry's influence on the younger kids and, of course, this alienates even Rowie from Terry, though she is in the center too. Kevin shows some interest out of kindness to Terry's new vision and listens to Hendrix, replying that it is really neat, Terry, and Terry appreciates that instead of feeling alienated.

"Rosemary"

Within Rowie lies the mystery of the family. Rowie knows it is her duty to keep these secrets her mother confided in her. It is not a matter of knowing though, it is rather the understanding of another that this household seems somewhat vulnerable at the time? Maybe Terry's enthusiasm would be enough to forget about a tragedy that is to a Catholic family a preponderance to make those involved feel guilty. The problem, here, is the wall built does not necessarily heal over so well. This is an Irish American family and knowledge of this secret would become gossip to an unwelcome neighbor.

In Ireland, people know how to avoid the hindrances that may divulge itself in what is timely of an Irish Catholic family. But, this is not Ireland, and the taboo, far greater than suspicion, may fester a problem in itself and Mrs. Frawley would rather not address it in such a way. I guess I am to them what their pains are to this matter and, consequently they decide to plot a course of revenge for the pain they feel. This, of course, is a dangerous matter in itself, let alone hate, for others who don't particularly have anything to do with the matter. The countdown to the end of the world resonates in the last three daughters, but this will come later.

An ultimatum is a good word to describe the Frawley household right now. The family would take sides and though even united, the disease will fall in their court and eventually lead to its demise. It is then not a matter of who was good or bad, but rather not facing reality became something unruly. Rowie knows how to talk to her mom by telling her, as she would later become a nurse, how things like this would heal and not to make things worse by harboring injustice on others.

Years have passed since my stepmother married my mom's husband and I feel a hostage of their secret throughout. Now, a darker side is foretold. Rowie will later be the only one to escape the stigma that manifested itself in this family and, maybe, be the hope for others who find themselves here as well. I think union was their downfall. Otherwise, Don Frawley, who will be hailed as a great father in another world, goes to court as the judge and must put one more kid who is good or bad away somewhere for now. He may have risen over his pride, but at what cost to his family and, in hindsight, this accomplishment is mainly unnoticed. The beginning of the problem is a hoax where somehow a family makes itself believe that they are in control of food chains and therefore others should be thankful to them.

Not all Catholics think like this and, if a cow would rather participate in its distribution and not forsake it? After the preponderant has sealed their fate, the toil is introverted in a way that shies their eyes away from their guilt. Whoever's eyes they meet will likely become a foil in the plot which begs for more participants. Others' respect becomes something more like fear. The dogs are also fearful as it is a plot in which they do not want to participate and hopefully be spared of the fate. I was thinking of converting to Catholicism, weighing the pros and cons, but still an Episcopalian, I would rather not divulge why not.

The truth of the matter is Kevin tied the knot most responsibly and Elizabeth took it unto herself to steal control of the family by forking him when not looking. It is her responsibility in the decision to marry into someone else's family; she denies the intrusion and must take full responsibility for her actions. It is not fate or even a natural sin. The course of the fate that is bestowed on my family is no longer in her hands and she may deny her responsibility and laugh at another at what meager sins she has committed in this fishbowl. In hindsight, there is no confession and Rowie is now married and living in Boston with her husband and daughter.

"Peguine"

Even at an early age, she was bound to be a mother. What manifests itself as evil to the older children, resonates in a good way to the younger three daughters. Even in Elmira, there is danger that lurks in the eyes of a passing boy even within herself, though she is mostly blessed. The house provides a sanctuary where she may discipline her mind, but she carries a certain flair with her that is ever so slightly sinful and uses this self-defense to ward off those with whom she does not want to associate. She never enters a stage in her faith that makes her think corny thoughts like how some girls do, saying to themselves "only pure thoughts," or at least no one could tell, rather her persona is reserved, but still strong in a motherly way.

She obtains a doll or two and, when it is time that she no longer needs them, she will without any emotion give them to a younger sister and they looked up to her as a leader. Part of her strength is her mind and how she allocates her time. She tries to expose herself to a variety of domestic ways of spending one's time, while going to a dance is a chore. The neighbor looks at her kindly and mentions what a beautiful garment she is wearing and she responds equally saying something nice as well. But, you can tell she means what she says then asking if there is anything she may help out with?

Fortunately for close-knit communities, there is always an angle of fun in whatever she does. Peguine feels she is blessed and, consequently, she never needs to worry about petty things which might depress another person. She never succumbs to an evil thought and addresses it within herself as foolish and indeed she is blessed. She has one or two friends with whom she associates, mildly, in the context of school, who are true friends.

But, at the same time, it does not neglect her will to be a good sister; rather she spreads her time generously in each situation she encounters. The problem that most resonates with Peguine is change. Though she knows it is natural, she does not always like change. There is, over time a certain degree of animosity from other girls at school and, unaware of this, it will often be channeled in such a way to harm her. Furthermore, boys will see their jealousy as weakness on behalf of herself, which is not true. The result is simple, she must be stronger than them while not fostering the impression that feeds their jealousy. At such times, her friends are even more important and the pact they make will block these proponents of harm and, sometimes, to the point where the other should also feel vulnerable and that solves the problem.

One thing that is confusing is how, as her own life improves over each year, Elizabeth seems very disturbed and she cannot confront her without making things worse, seemingly. Elizabeth plays rough like boys and Peguine never enters that domain and, therefore, does not understand it all. Peguine wishes Elizabeth the best and hopes she will get the things that she wants out of life. However, that is the best that she can do. Rather than squabble, Peguine takes on a leading role among the two younger sisters and that is a daring move. Elizabeth might see this as a threat and that will cause animosity which, in this house, is forbidden. Rather, Peguine would use her mind to think of ways to avoid confrontations without being a wimp about being a role model for the two younger sisters.

She invites a certain degree of danger toward harming those she regards as in her protection. She stands for the fact that there are good people in the world. This means in the church as well, but guards herself even in church, knowing there is a bad side too. Actually, religion sometimes causes people to believe in something too much and she guards herself against false icons, which is clearly not good, and conditions her mind to see through these temptations. It seems that the house is divided for a while and, of course, she tries to absolve the others and, being younger, their cancer spreads. And, she never forgives them thereafter while staring resolutely into Rowie's eyes? Not another word is spoken. It is easy to see that Peguine will become a mom, but for those who do not understand her silence, they are not worth talking to. Those who follow her to only seek self-fulfillment will not understand self-sacrifice anyway. From three, the countdown begins with Peguine, her voice never heard.

"Bernadette"

Of all the children, Bernadette is the most closely associated with the father, at least among the girls. It is a spiritual relationship mostly, and Don Frawley thinks of her with care and is aware entirely of the association. He loves all his children, including Bernadette in a special way. Sometimes, nature plays a trick on you and the most distant of children reappears as an ally that means she takes on a role which denotes the father mostly. In a large family, this is not always good, but in this case, it is a bond that is mostly unspoken. Bernadette envisions what her father most needs and tries to be that person. Sure, she plays like a girl, but her ambition is foremost to assimilate good things for her father. And, at the very least, she wishes to free him of pride and all impure attachments and to know he is loved. The pride that a girl may replace a son is often a bad kind of pride as a desire for someone to take on himself in essence. To be that which he lacks, this seems a fortitude between a father and son only and, consequently, there is a certain degree of delusion at hand. Actually, the heart that subscribes to this role may be a son or a daughter. Therefore, in order not to placate her brothers, she keeps a distance and shows up at every dinner like another pretty face. Then, when one of the older brothers is not looking, she weeps slightly with an eye-to-eye glance. She assures her father with this that he will not be dishonored. Maybe in Japanese culture this would be a normal sequence? However, it is not without reward and to not seem awkward, she is sanguine at all times with the matter and thinks like a lawyer, winning or losing each motion she puts forth. In return for a comfort that a father of eight children deserves as well as a mother, she delivers a sort of package that they may accept or decline? They, in return, free her the way only a father's love may.

To do this successfully, one needs unscrupulous tactic and nerve. Facing the father from a girl's point of view is something intimidating, if not downright scary. I suppose the promise is to afford the father with a son in his honor and Bernadette is the closest to accomplish this feat. In return, she acquires a certain confidence in her father, shielding all that is bad from him.

He would offer his love to Bernadette otherwise, but the pact is more secure. If anyone would compete with her for this love, she would win. I suppose, a father's love is worth its weight in gold? She will, in the end, free her soul from any misery and lead a normal life. I suppose, Bernadette seeks out adventure thereafter while questioning if this love is enough? On one hand, Catholic girls often seek out security, I think, while quite opposed to any business agreement with her father as this sounds like a fraud. Should she be Kevin, she might be happier in the end, but the love or agreement persists and that keeps her nose in the air and far from danger. The countdown sounds two and there is a better life lingering on the other side. But, no words are spoken.

"Ellen"

Ellen is the brat they never had, but she is carefree to her end and, in terms of the family, a good final implementation. Ellen would rather be a movie star like Marilyn Monroe, but settles for a rather free life and tries not to mention that she is the youngest of eight children from an Irish Catholic family. As a girl, her knee might bleed and it seems to be a tribute to her somewhat daring approach to men, as she plays rough on the soccer field. As for Ellen, all eyes are on her and she does not know as the last person through the door, she inherits the greatest responsibility not to dishonor anyone in the hierarchy above.

At first, this seems playful to Ellen, but then she finds it as leverage in any whim she schemes that comes to the surface. The family is an entrance with wide open eyes;. She is alive and this makes her special, in a way, that could cause great harm as well as goodness for the family? You might say the family comprises parents who give life to seven ghosts and Ellen. At this point, the parents are in some sort of free-spirited love and the brothers and sisters are staring from all angles at the dinner table the way only ghosts can. The secret is torment and well-wishers as well as enemies enter the arena as though to determine the fate of the family? Should the secret be divulged to Ellen, then they no longer have an outlet to live further, as their family is dishonored forever. Mr. and Mrs. Frawley now gain the respect they want and find it in themselves to be rather neutral. They know the trials and where their love will lead?

Ellen is totally unaware and pretends to be playing Scrabble at the dinner table. It is not the secret, but rather all the fantasies that she confides in the family that makes them seem vulnerable. A chill drapes the dinner table and someone screams in horror that "not to drink the wine." All the sacrifice and work to create a family is hanging in a decimal of sound slightly echoing in Ellen's wine glass, though she does not hear it. Whatever she is wearing seems to be so loud, she thinks. In this chessboard of life, she has a boyfriend and that is enough for all the pieces to be put back in the box. The end.

Tales from the beer spider (continued)

"Broken Sky"

Diana sits on a park bench in the entrance to Central Park one fine autumn morning in 1987. I seek out a rugose homeless woman and she embraces me likewise, as I have a camera and prepare to shoot. She is not any woman, but represents the mercy God would evoke for Adam and Eve, if there was such mercy anyway? She is the witch to man and her Jewish faith seems the least of the proponents that would diagnose her character. In fact, I have a plan and maybe in such a scheme, she waits for me and prepares for my arrival, I think. What I may say for the witch to man is that she does not like charity and further, in her early seventies, she sleeps in some hidden doorway, but will not tell me where. I think she is more an Indian than a Jew, and my plan is to photograph her from below, in a trash bin, where my camera is rested inside it and facing the sky. I use a shutter release cable to snap the shot as she reaches into the trash bin. I did not know prior that the sky is broken. Otherwise, her claim to fame is being on a poster in my real estate office, which jokes that a homeless woman is shopping at Bloomingdales, a bag lady as such. The broken sky occurred in such a time when Jews were more than persecuted in Germany and, further, Stalin foresaw the rape of his daughter, or may it be his homeland Russia, I do not know. The fact that the tally of mushrooms lost in the blood of Indians over there would be too much and she embarked on a vision where she could claim a tolerance for the sins of others? To be friends is an honorable act and she shares the food she would find with another homeless man and the sky is broken for a time. She does not know if it will rain later and reads the New York Times that also blows in the wind at such times. She reaches for it as though a banana that is half eaten. She made a pact with God and it foretells a life of opulence which will come later, she thinks?

She does not believe in reincarnation, but rather she exists with a responsibility she rarely shares with a complete stranger. At some point, she disappears like the clouds dissipating after a storm. Man waits to hear the verdict she would foretell. The witch to man has a dog she has never met, still the dog searches the horizon for a sign that his mother still loves him. Rain is forecasted, she said, for tomorrow, and she never sheds a tear for another as it is a waste of time. She thinks the sky will heal and this is enough for her to carry on. If the witch had a family, they would say she was never here. God foretells a storm and she relinquishes the authority he administers. I think the banana, half eaten, may be her lost child that will return to face God someday?

"poem..."

Tables Turned

I found this poem by the side of the road,
It was crumpled, the piece of paper, I mean,
On an orange, steel-grated trashcan.
The person who wrote it must have left in a hurry,
Because next to it there was a banana,
Which I ate, of course, in a hurry too,
In case she or he came back.
So, here, I stand on the corner with this crumpled piece of paper,
On this upside down trashcan.
Actually, wait, this is all a lie.
I wrote the poem.
And, to tell you the truth, that banana,
Was not really a banana, it was my baby.

"Paradise Lost"

She asks, what do you sell here besides beer, as though a feast of ants in the rainforest? But, we may settle for serendipity instead. Will was there at such times and she would never return to her earlier home in Brazil's Amazon region. She calls this bar home and it is enough to try to forget about the loss while the wild pig is fattening anyway? The checker tile floor is more faded now and the Rolls Royce, once a tad outdated is from a time the pub stood so ephemeral and now like a shibboleth and a token of good luck. Now, the most questionable object is the fancy-shaped broom in the corner and maybe the checker board already clashes with the floor. Now, it is just a set in a pop stand nightmare.

When you are drunk, it is easy to forget your problems. She just likes to watch from the corner as people wobble about in their less-provoked demeanors, though through the viaducts of her eyes she is a savant to Betty Davis's façade. Here, the specialty is beer spiked with orange juice with a cherry or a cork. The bar is so outdated that drinks become more objects of cursing conundrum like the wheel of a car sounding so inverted as it rolls away and screeching at a once-bratty princess. The presence of the milk of a spider in spring lace is upon us and then it absorbs the split substance to dry the table in it and leave?

She thinks the table is square and so outdated. Still, the language truly has not changed much from this premise and is it at odds with this accomplishment where a person may feel pretty relaxed and at home here. The door does not creek too much and music is still chanted by the occasional wave of spirit. She says, though, there are no ghosts allowed in her bar. In this room lives someone who cannot find the exit, but has been here so long no one bothers to question for what reason it remains? Really, a beer spider may be a Toulouse-Lautrec painting then fade to the music of the Beatles, *Abbey Road*, and awaken to an early morning rain. All the aspects of the living may transpire in the web that mourns the sun better than a word spoken in life.

She loves the sound of the rain pounding "tidder tat" with the screaming of drunk friends, all male, and a woman about to take them on. It is a rest from the sericulture that denotes some time wasted. The edge is much sharper in the oasis here, where all the benefactors must bow to the woman who catches a ride at any time of night, having a cab to go home to her nest somewhere.

Actually, she will stay for Irish coffee with bourbon, but it is too late for the midnight horseman and the boys of the bar have a thing for all-male surroundings, like the old west, but somewhat dignified. There is one boy who always sits in the corner with a beer. She likes him because he never drinks with company and never goes home alone. Somehow, this person sits in this fashion long enough for some wandering female to feel sorry for him. Something is missing from the picture tonight and Mimi stares across the channels to watch a news station reporting a death of a cop in a drug bust in a Queens neighborhood. Suddenly, it becomes apparent that his name is Tim Marceloni, and she thinks without putting forth a muse in the light and thinks of all her friends, realizing that she does not know him, but how unfortunate. More importantly, the assailant is Italian, which always means good harvest or something dear to the ambiance of this bar.

Maybe, the name, Tim, of the police officer, is a coincidence, as it is one of her favorite names, which she reminisces is what she would name her own child if she had any sadly. Actually, to look across the bar one sees hardly anything besides the bartender,

"I think his name is Frank," replies Mimi then forfeits a little black book in her pocket, just to make sure his name is not listed. This time between six and seven o'clock is a good time to appear here as no one notices that she is not wearing any antiperspirant and confidently hesitates at this, but does not know how she would answer should someone ask?

Her favorite question is "what time is it?" as she always thinks this is a come-on and always makes up some time without checking she says, "quarter past nine."

"Poor fool," she thinks. "I do not look down for strangers." The watch she wears, though, is a Tiffany sterling silver watch with, "To Mimi with love, Brett," engraved on it, a gift from me.

This charade may go on forever if not for a mutual friend, Will. But, one understands the cankered sore lining the jaw of a person prescribed by a love doctor, and know to say her name in this space is to hear the other hollow sound it conduces at this place. At times it sounds so lost and eternal, repeating in the halls like an echo, "Mimi, Mimi, Mimi." No one knows why it sounds so funny. When someone spends a great deal of time somewhere, it is difficult for this entity to part with the surroundings.

"No, really, dear, I think a white carnation is too dressy for the bar."

"But, what if I might wear a yellow tie?"

Mimi responds, "It might clash with me, dear? Oh, so worrisome, what a trifle, not even a worker at the car park may conceive of such an idiocy. Please, really, wear a red tie and no carnation tonight, I will be wearing something pink."

"Very well!"

"Very well, you repeat what I say, dear?"

"What is the point?"

"I know not any point, it is my birthday."

And he stands to the rhythm of uncertainty to recognize the humor then loyally embracing the second crowd with not a smile or a faint scent of a flower to carry along just to fade into the...

"Now, I must decide what to wear..." Mimi thinks to herself. Talking to a canary and I must think twice, "Is it me? Is it me?..." Again, she takes her question and exits the building unmolested, but alone. Not harassed, but everyone else must reach the most solemn note with a handkerchief to exit, she thinks. "Oh, I almost forgot to meet William, after all it's Friday night."

As she leaves, she is in another space, so no object or person may be sacrificed to meet the imposition of her mundane trifle with Will. No flowers smell so ripe, Will should say, and Mimi never knows to answer, but is thankful for those who are drinking plenty at the time. Will enters the room and looks at his watch, seeing he is ten minutes late which may be five minutes more than he is allowed, just kidding.

"Oh, Will, what is it you said, an interview for a business associate, something mundane really, oh, on Wall Street, you say."

"That is right," Will replies with a smile and says that they pay a six-figure salary, "if only I weren't so available and maybe a promotion in two or three years!"

"What are you working for anyway, so you don't have to say, 'I don't work.' Isn't that what you are afraid someone will ask like it is their business, 'Oh, what do you do?'"

"Tonight, I am only reciting works by the late Edgar Allen Poe, no I mean Milton."

"Paradise Lost?" Mimi serenades such notions as though shooting a ball calculatingly funny in a pool game. "That is right."

And Will confirms further, "Milton, Paradise Lost."

Dr. Shark Knife

We embarked on a journey to tag sharks on my school's marine biology vessel named *Geronimo*. Josh leads the senary to make an incision so that this shark would bleed like Jesus Christ once did and be freed back in the ocean again. There are six students on board; three boys including myself, and three girls. It is curious that the girls and, in particular Sarah, treated the captain as a father figure. For the blood this one shark bleeds is a paradox that would expose it to the sky and be a crime scene too. She is in a nervous frenzy so that another shark, this time a mako, is caught on the line to diagnose her guilt and how to eat the evidence. Josh is exonerated to the point as he is acting in subordination to the captain and Jesus already bleeds in the past anyway. My friend Kevin reminds me of the notion that may act as a double entendre and I am free as well as him. Kevin is African American and all of those in this heritage are freed in the process.

"Fujimora"

They do not wish harm on their enemy, but for those who seek the alternative lifestyle; it is the end of the world really, the last opportunity for what is now the only mercy conceivable. For a culture that has been backward since the beginning of time, or vice versa, they assume it only brings about bad results for those who embrace a darkness to which they are just slaves in the process. Their culture is thriving, in fact, and their toil is simple, not to cause harm to the children of the sun. That is not a problem, and they survive mostly on seafood, which is available after the energy line was broken by another and were well aware of the crime invoked, but are not blamed as a result. Their heritage is like Abraham in darkness, offering their son to God and God replying, it is not necessary. At such a time, Mt. Fuji plays birdcalls, on the beach, where he practices a peaceful rendition of martial arts to lions occupying a distant land. In fact, their culture is much like America and, despite the bombings, they are strangely affectionate to those they should hate otherwise.

I am a timely reminder to an accomplice to it, who is innocent really? Seaweed grows out of the sea and provides broccoli and other vegetables to eat. I suppose this secret lies in their history, which with all the suicides etcetera, it is hard if not impossible to retrace. They cook food with corn and sesame oils while erect "hotdog-like entities," decompose in the sun on a set which seems to me like the Brady Bunch.

Otherwise, the sea will last long enough for them to subsist to when their world should become else and hell is the least of their concerns. Their grace is creating children who feel jealousy of their privacy in the eastern world, but need not touch those who become like America, but something else entirely. I think the mercy they provide for disturbed youth is genuine. And the games they play, though, rough, are eventually a fantasy world that often ends up as a stalemate with the other, more serious one, who does not know it is just a game. I guess it is not like the lies one tells oneself, but rather if you want to be liked or not liked or neither.

There is a camera store with a one-hour photo service in most communities throughout America. Photography is quite popular to families and children as well. One aspect is taking the photograph as not to see anything in particular; rather it is much better to trust the camera as a truth in context of what is seen through the microcosm the ocean offers. Everything else falls into place. (The Eskimo leaves the camera store only to buy a Klondike Bar in which he eats obsessively.) The pictures turn out all black but this does not mean they are bad, really. It may be an alternative lifestyle to which photography adheres and Andy Warhol says to paint it black.

"Vietnam"

The children of a black rose live in foreign lands abroad. I am sitting in my car thinking if Salman Rushdie may write this crap then so may I. It is like driving a fine automobile, which (I have never,) except my dad's overpriced American luxury car which he trades in for a new one every three years. I wonder if I will ever get my hands on a car like that; I doubt it, but I am just kidding, it is not that important. I remember, though, one car was sort of special. It was a maroon Buick convertible, and it evokes only good memories. I think it rocked, so to speak, and my dad always seemed carefree when driving it. It is strange to have affection for a car?

Actually, there are many ways to be a patriot without going to war. Anyone who says otherwise is probably a liar. Sure, I have been in fights on one or two occasions, a quest to show my brawn, of which there is little, and I chicken out at the last moment. It does not take me long to realize that the other guy is probably trying to smash my head in and my head would rather not endure this, I think. Still, ironically, I have never lost a fight either. Then, there is peer pressure and things such as nationalism. You wonder why so many go to war and why so few return? I think, here in America, we are fighting "the Good War." This does not mean I would die for you, per se, but if you read history books you will find lots of answers. Then, fiddling my thumbs long enough, I would think, what am I doing here and, sure enough, my best friend sits back in cruise position, a life ended short as though an excuse of which there are many. I am alone again and all I may say is what one calls the good war? So, it is me, minus one person, now. Jamie was a friend, but I do not know the circumstances of his death really? All I heard was that he died in a car accident and now he calls himself an American in a foreign land.

"God Bless the Great American Hypocrisy: Part Seven"

Recently, a fellow photographer invited me to his studio to see some of his work. The idea of us putting together a photography show comes up in our conversation. Some of his work is an observation of parts of the female body. I acknowledge that my work is different. I attempt to convey spiritually in the subject from a holistic point of view. In a show, the contrast between our styles is exciting, his work tangible, while my work is spiritual.

I attempt to conceptualize for him, art, in my perception. I tell him that art is the subjective expanding of the objective. On this premise, I argue that the attempt to convey total objectivity is futile because human beings have a limited point of view when conveying meaning through art.

However, by accepting that one perspective is equal to another, then the combination of these individuals, but equal subjective views, is in reality, the expanding of the objective. In saying objective, I mean more or less objective, like two perspectives is better than one. Therefore, the combined meaning creates greater artistic substance and improves the quality of what is art.

My acquaintance does not see my way. Instead, he switches my conception that art is the subjective expanding of the objective, and says to create art is the objective expanding of the subjective. This is difficult for me to swallow at first. However, not compromising my initial conviction, I cannot prove him wrong. Even though I do not want to see from his point of view, I step over the line to take a glimpse. This makes me insecure because his view contradicts what I believe. It is not that I want to prove him wrong. I just want to prove that I am more right than he is. This creates a healthy mental war. Ideas must be challenged and I realize our opposing views, in which we both strongly believe, only strengthen each other because neither of us is wrong. It is just different ways of looking at art. I suppose there is one thing in favor of his argument. If total objectivity applies relative to solely oneself, then objectivity does exist.

Another way of conveying this conception is if one is to say, "I try my hardest." The statement may be prone to argument and debate. However, if the person is truly sincere, you cannot win this argument. You may go your separate ways and disagree, but the final outcome is that person still believes he tries his or her hardest. One weakness in his argument is if one was to say, "the sky is green." Of course, I object to this ludicrous statement, unless you are a rap artist and speak metaphorically. You probably have met someone like this before; when you attempt to argue the obvious truth, the person hides in his or her right to an opinion. However, the problem here is that the sky is not green. The sky is blue. I might understand justifiably if a person tells me that the sky is gray. Yet, the danger in this perspective becomes apparent to me. What if this person manages to convince an isolated group of people, for instance Indians in the rainforest of Brazil, the sky is in fact green. To some, this might seem like a warped sense of reality. To denote the former statement which is a lie, this may be a fascist concept? Once you cross the line, you may think you are God too. The only good in it is to dream on clouds with blue sky of what the concept might entail? Clearly, here, one argument is right and the other wrong, in reality. In life, one may not disclaim that which is right from that which is wrong, I think. You might say that "blue is empty of all color, that it is an illusion" then neither of us is right. God gave us a way of seeing, but he may see differently and thereby argue us both wrong in the end. Maybe the blue sky is just an illusion, I think? Similarly, men do not see the same as the way a woman sees and therefore, from a man's point of view, there is a blind spot.

Therefore, I may not deny women the right to an abortion, even if it is wrong? However, what if a prominent person declares that Jews are sub-human and deserve to die? This person assumes the position of total objectivity and convinces many others that what he says is true. Where is the evil in a fascist revelation? The reaction of Americans is that what he says is wrong.

However, in Ted's conception, art is the objective expanding of the subjective, and it clearly implies that the perception consists of an expanding, which might just be a metaphor for Santa's expanding belly? This means an increase and, further, they cannot overlap. No two human beings may measure accurately the degree to which one believes? No, at least not numerically unless one is to say one point of view is equal to an other, and this is subjectivity? It is not possible to trap an emotion in a bottle without contriving superficial meaning through words with average meaning? Therefore, the subjective has no definite contours if defining the subjective here as a degree of belief. Though, each perspective is unique and, when applied to a geometric form, one might argue each point of view, is different, however? On the other hand, there is an assembling of units, each equaling one, in my scenario? One may speculate intensely, but there is no real mathematical translation in an individual's belief represented in a coinciding whole. Then, where is the evil?

Someone once tells me that the Nazi Germans of the Third Reich were not individuals. However, the metaphoric American blanket sweeps over Germany, imposing that they are wrong; does anyone bother to consider, despite the soldiers dress alike, that maybe these people have individualistic views? I realize the historical implications and agree it is horrific that six million Jews have to die in the process. However, is Hitler any different than a wimpy kid in a schoolyard declaring that all girls have cooties? One may argue yes, because he enacts what people, today, consider a great evil in the delusions of young minds.

Yet, if one isolates Hitler to a simple premise and speculates he is an unpopular kid in the schoolyard, maybe he defends himself by saying he has a right to an opinion. Maybe, a denial of someone's individuality is a similar evil in denoting a denial of the premise. When it applies to two different people, it may be threatening with the prospect to do great evil. But, also, it may seem insignificant. And, on this level, hidden in the shallow cracks in old school buildings in America is a fascist perception. The danger may be that we do not even know it is there. Maybe, you question "are they really the same thing?" So, America looks abroad, playing the role of arbitrator of morality of what is right and what is wrong. However, may we see ourselves?

Is there a real threat of hidden fascism in America? Probably not, at least not in the way we perceive the fascist Nazi Germany in World War Two? Our country strays away from extremes politically, to the point where fascism and communism seems to lose their historical meaning when they manifest or apply here. Once the topics are debated here in the center, America's political arena, it begins to take the form of mediocrity. Do fascism and communism, in a pure theoretical sense, exist in America, without applying historical representation? I argue yes. Are they dangerous? I argue, that depends. Ted's perception is that art is the objective expanding of the subjective. In this scenario, one must consider that even the Nazis, who in every respect, challenge the idea that they are, in fact, individuals must be heard too. The danger in America is that there is communism and fascism in our central political arena. However, few if any politicians will admit being in favor of either side. Essentially, our politicians, despite the talk and debate, are really straddling the fence. Why? Because, Americans fear that the evil we apply to others, also exists in ourselves.

The second part of this fear involves denial. In denial, one refuses to associate with either side of the world's broad political spectrum. Consequently, America makes an effort, which is good, to balance the two so-called evils. The flip side of this is to not take any significant stand. We, as our political system, are to a degree a product of fear. Our journalists, however, do a good job exposing Neo-Nazi groups in America and, more importantly, allow the members to speak for themselves as individuals. Here, though, I must take sides, because I think it is better to make a stand than straddle the fence, between two negatives or positives. They say indifference is the opposite of love. Furthermore, a mental war is always good unless you are God.

So, I say again, art is the subjective expanding of the objective. My dad tells me once that I speak like I am a communist. Carefully, I do not deny it without acknowledging it too. I find myself, like many politicians, in a balancing act between destructing accusations. Politicians have a tough job. Why do I believe in my conception, which may or may not be a form of communist philosophy? By expanding the objective with more equal views as though one laborer is equal to another laborer, in ideal speculation, the objective view expands accordingly, greater or less objective, not total objectivity. However, if truth theoretically, not in literal translation, has no defined contours, communism may only exist without borders. Isolated communism may be dangerous. So, for now, I am not a communist.

However, if it were only God, he may see a lot like the way Hitler sees. Ted is right, it being "the objective expanding of the subjective. God, in this sense, is a fascist concept which has no end. You would not deny God this point of view and therefore, you may be a fascist too. Good people will not assume they are God in this scenario. I need not judge you either. Let's meet later somewhere in the middle. My dad is Catholic and I am Episcopalian.

"Jupiter Bear"

Outside of Pasadena, a young man stops his car and picks me up from the highway along which I walk, as my car has broken down. I leave Ferocious in the car and attempt to walk to the next exit. It is not hot out and the window in the car is left open. But, the person is not like everyone else, and, in fact, he drives as though inside a bumble bee. It is a odd experience and bears do like honey, anyway. The brief intermission, when I met this person, lasted only a minute, but the fear I felt from this other, seemed like an eternity. I wonder from what corner of the earth, a person with what seemed like a bear temperament imposed? The radio is on, but only evokes a sense of being lost and static is heard. He does not talk, and though not dangerous really, the person I hardly know seems fearful of me. I wondered if he did not smell my dog of whom I was his travel partner over the last several weeks? All I can say about Jupiter and a bear that lives there is that it is very different than what you will find here on earth. The missionaries will try to convert him before long.

"Transformation"

Once you leave your second stint at education and find yourself driving a cab in New York City, it is evident that there would be a transformation rendered. From innocence, there is only one path and that is to less innocence. I would find myself somewhere safe, but I guess Mike foretold this path would lead me somewhere else. My transformation from innocence was not bad, but definitely was not easy either. My advantage, here, was in not knowing that I was innocent and this made things easier as I did not know where I came from, or where I was going either. It has been a long time since a woman and man conspired to eat from the tree of knowledge and, as time passed, like a Chris Isaac video of "Wicked Game," I hardly noticed it.

By now, God had forgiven them of their sins, but to sin again would lead them down a dark path in which mine would not cross again. Though, times had changed and my family formed a swastika that its ends had fallen off, leaving only a black cross. You could say we were a close family and my stepmother is the slash in the letter "Q" and this did not deter our strength. Innocence is being happy and not knowing it. Now, Adam and Eve have moved on and the apple tree which was once forsaken to them, is still here. I guess, you could say, I am the same person as before, but transformed to somewhere else.

Like two blue moons in any given month, you are the same, but it feels like you have journeyed from point "A" to point "B." I guess the loss of innocence came to me when I discovered New York City was now my home and I do not think I could leave even if I tried. The dark star and the star of David, became one and Mike yells from a place in time when dinosaurs walked the Earth. I knew he was a friend as he said not to enter his domain and he will not tell me why not? As long as devils walk the earth, Mike will be my friend and his twelfth sun died when going to a "red" McDonald's drive thru when I ordered a fish sandwich which tasted like cardboard? He says dinosaurs are still roaming the Earth and I guess he never left and, therefore, remains the king of his domain, forever more. I am now less innocent than Mike and I talk from this end with other taxi drivers about olden times. Time plays a minor role in the dimensions that placate my reality. I walk down Broadway and remember what Mike said to never enter his domain, and I still do not know why not? Mike claims he can see three perfect suns on Earth, which belong to that of a lion, tiger, and bear.

Maybe, a lizard does not know from where, while hiding under a Kleenex tissue in the shade? I leave from time to time, and it does not seem to matter. I can tell Mike is smiling at such times.

"Four Chinese Laundry Devils"

Four Chinese laundry devils is a good sign that implies that "the devil," is at bay and he should not cross the line with good Christians across the land. While it is true that the devil lives within as though looking from the outside with the exception of just a few friends, he does not spread his evil among those who would rather not. In other words, he is inactive for at least eighteen hundred years and waits for the clock to cease ticking. Time overtakes sinners to live in a distant land and walks with good Christians somewhere on the Chinese/Russian border, for the cause at hand? To meet the devil, which I am sure you will, is a blessing! He stares in four different directions and smiles in the tenth dimension and rather is intangible to sinners who do not make it like a long distance runner. He leaves behind his friend, "Puff, the Magic Dragon" and walks always in mourning as he crosses the land bridge from Asia to North America, to re-populate those once lost in a legitimate homestead where we live today in America. Maybe, this has already happened though?

The devil is a formality which crosses with such saints to their new home. There are no drugs here and children left by Satan to forego the transition which, in time will meet here; later is better than never? The shepherd walks with him and asks what to call him and he replies that his name is Steve. He smiles as the flies of that which sticks to Satan's excretion from yesterdays becomes something good hereafter. The children play and play and Steve, like four Chinese laundry devils, smiles at four different directions at the same time, and they are accessible to him in this land. Evil is only to placate those in the past and this land holds a bright future and children smile not to worry about being any different than anyone else. I just hope the bison will survive the transition. But, I really do not believe in the devil anyway, as though to take over responsibility here and Satan sleeps in the ocean as his shift is now over.

"Tattoo U"

Even at age ten, I was an avid Rolling Stones fan. In the backwoods of Aspen, Colorado, I spent part of a summer with my mom, my sister, and a friend, Matt. We got lost hiking on Ajax and found ourselves among the wolves. This landscape is most formidable . Once Satan left Africa, it was not until later that I found myself among wild dogs and an occasional lion. I then must confront a piercing shot to my chin from another. And this is what is left of tattoos you inherit from the sacrifice of a good man who returns to his homeland Mozambique? He died there and shunned the thought to cross the border into South Africa. And a cross still remains as a reminder of the tattoos you foster in the blood of another, you have never met, but the Christian cross remains there and very far away.

The blood I shed in NYC might be his sacrifice and the sign says thank you at Howard Johnson's in Times Square. On Tattoo U, "Start me up," is a song about sacrifice and others embark on a journey with every new tattoo that you color the land with, and God thinks this is good. As for the wolves I left behind in New York City, they still roam the mountains in the outback of Aspen, Colorado, but most have moved to Canada. Meanwhile, my friend Matt lives in L.A. and reads his L.A. Times to smile and remember the time we were at the mercy of wolves and survived the ordeal without a scrape. You will find certain Native Americans in the North West have a special pattern that resonates a design that nature adhered to and though we were lost in the wilderness, we were also found. London may be an oasis for these entities we call wolves and I think Mick Jagger sings on the last track from my cassette, "Waiting on a friend." He was a friend, though Mick is calling long distance to his new friend from Africa and drinks cherry cola while smiling at wild dogs who need a lift.

"Stew was a racehorse"

I was stuck in the picture, the cover of Cat Steven's *Tea For the Tillerman* and here there is a person who hangs onto the balls of a great horse. Whether Stalin should walk on the earth once, it is a horse that in its grandness should be sacrificed and his eyes forebode a fire stronger than any tiger and would be put down in a chamber where the oil's emissions emits and really it is his own. While it is difficult to understand this distant faith of Hinduism in India, one aspect of this culture and religion that harnesses the past allegiance of Indians in America is for them this perfect specimen of a horse and, in memory, we share a common legacy here. The children inherited a horse in time, but I think they had some help too.

Lenny Babboo

Lenny Babboo represents a cross at ground zero. Prior to the ordeal, I am an Indian version of the swastika. My family represents the arms cut off, leaving behind a black cross in the back country around Mozambique. The difference between Lenny Babboo and myself is that 9/11 does not provide hope for those involved. I am my own creation and the cross that is designed from a swastika unites us. My dad is united with me prior to his death on January the second, 2010. You may not recognize my cross, which includes my two sisters. Nancy is on the left and Nicole is on the right. My dad represents the upper tier of the cross while my mother is the lower tier. I understand that a swastika may represent a sentiment of good luck too.

On the other hand, Lenny Babboo is evidence that the holocaust did occur. Where the cross remains at ground zero, there is little hope for those who remain. His cross, which is a manifestation of "love lost" does redeem that there are bad people who may participate in the ordeal. I will not reveal the steps leading to his cross. All I may say is that neither of us flinch prior to the goings on. This is to say that neither of us knew what was to come before it. I will say that sometimes there are tipping points when bad things occur and I do not know why? Do these occurrences manifest into human form is the question at hand?

"Polish Peace" is a metaphor for good things that still remain. I relate to the Jews who died in the holocaust through this guise.

"Adam and Eve Re-Examined"

The sin for Adam and Eve is not picking the apple nor the temptation prior, but rather the presumption that what belongs to God could be theirs as well. They still cling to one another and they have learned their lesson. Really, the occurrence gave God the time to inspect his creation and decide who should merit the reward of continuing in his world. Adam and Eve are not only dispelled from the garden, but this is a metaphor for being outside his love as well. Two lovers hope that they will be able to return, but in the play of life there are winners and losers. The lovers are not allowed in and though they may not return, their bond foretells a downfall, even after all this time. Mike Tyson might chew the ear of his opponent and Lily still claims that she loves a boy who does not love her in return. A calla lily once clung to the earth with all the splendor in the world and now it is shamed as a disgrace. Meanwhile, God eats the apple from his tree and smiles for a brief moment.

"Something in the woods..."

When I first met the Faulkners, I was living with a family, the Lays, in Eastern, Tennessee. David Lay said that there was someone he wanted me to meet. George Faulkner lived in the woods of Jelicho Mountain with his wife and three kids. George is also known as "Caveman George." He was a three-time Vietnam veteran and carried this medal on his shoulders, but otherwise had lost his sanity years before after leaving his third tour of duty there. It did not seem like "the Heart of Darkness," but he was lost and his kids otherwise played on the mountain.

The kids swung on a rope into the river that metaphorically separated them from the reality outside. No one would know what delved within their oasis? While Susan and Charlie played, Chris, the oldest, showed me his collection of pornographic magazines in a cave that harbored the family. Though, the Faulkners squatted on this land, George would not leave without a fight and owned an assortment of nine or ten pit bulls for protection. George believed that from the sky, the mountain they lived on was in the form of an Indian lying on its back, and George thought it would be nice to color it with different trees. He did not get far, as his wife and three kids left and moved to Kansas. This was a hard blow for George as he loved his family. When I visited him for the second time, he was living in a housing project. But, before leaving the Faulkners and after sleeping one night there, there was a picture that Susan took. She asked me the next morning if she could use my camera and take a picture. Years later, I saw the negative that she took and I noticed that there was something in the woods. I still have this photograph in case you too want to see it. It looks like a carcass hanging from a tree. Surely, there is something darker about this family? The kids would cross the river on planks, each morning, to catch the school bus, to go to school and none of the other kids know either what is in the woods. George likes this mystery to persist, though he does miss his kids and wife.

"Of mice and men"

I guess I was being inspected to see if I really did have a mental illness? Brian and I went camping and hiking on the Appalachian Trail in the autumn of 1989. I did not know I would not return the same person that I was, when I left. From Great Barrington, Brian and I hiked about seven to eight miles each day and made it to the Vermont border. We had a good time and brought a bottle of gin and drank it at night getting thoroughly drunk. I had a hat that was special to me and somewhere along the way, it fell out of my backpack and I knew it would be hard to replace it. It was light tan color and bent around the rim in all directions. I was now a man, as I did not cry and tried thereafter not to. The thing that divides men from mice is not to be afraid of expressing what you feel either. The foliage on the trail was truly splendid as I crossed the line from adolescence to manhood.

Brian was smart and declined to share the apples I picked from the wilds, but I think he eventually succumbed to the temptation and ate one or two? The problem of men is that once you cross the line and become a man, you can't go back and mice might be your best friends at such times?

"Easter"

The color green is not hers, but it is her milk that the cows should eat its harvest and which came first, the grass or the milk is not important? Only the Emerald Princess, she who wears the ring, knows the answer, which I will not foretell. Still, the grass around about Musgrove is beautiful, and it is cut from time to time and she knows, at the least, it is not hers. The woman, a common green garden snake is not her daughter and Mimi throws a rock at the sun and the moon must seem very large to the rest of us at such times. Around Easter, the Virgin Mary may be a spider, a green garden snake, or a cow at any given time. Like the trinity is for man, so it is for woman. (From the spoils of the sacrifice for man is the assortment of Easter eggs in many different colors.) The Emerald Princess harbors the milk of a cow, which is not hers in the end! A green garden snake is always present, knowing the milk harbored by the cow, belongs to a spider which falters from a tear in her eye, and the emerald princess or cow may not claim a right to it in the imposition. She resonates what is the cow's anatomy in the beginning and the end and she is both. She washes down dinner with a glass of red wine and the sun will not escape the web of the beer spider from where she is perched in the negative of that which is the night.

"Autumn in New York"

Perfection in death is a hard task to be. She forgives those in her past who, in the spring of life, picked her flower at such a time. I would not know this, as I have not even been born yet. Still, I admire the autumn as it expresses that every leaf that falls is slightly different and has a past all its own. As the leave falls from the tree in its own way, and always different; it tells a story of that which is perfection. While in France you will find spring, and the Incas of Peru harbor summer, and Japan knows its role only in autumn. Japanese men find women of their later years in life as beautiful. Personally, I enjoy the winter months that lead from December to January. Autumn in New York may be beautiful from this point of view too but it is an esoteric few, I think.

"A desert in the ocean"

The reason that I know children are guilty the moment they enter the world is that a girl should be born from the flower picked. And she does not know the fertility endowed in Mimi, her feminine connection, but she persists in the ocean as there is a desert there surmised in infertility for the past. She shares this with someone else she has never met; who she will call her father. It is not a bad life, yet she inherits the sins of the father. Abortion, in this light, seems wrong as if you are fertile to the future, why would you want to kill your harvest? Furthermore, it is wrong not because of a choice, it simply is not your choice to make!

In the desert, there are few things that will survive and it is a desolate place. There is a desert in the ocean where she lives and it is the opposite of the flower once picked. Sierra is happy wherever she is and considers this is a blessing. The sin of the father is endowed to the children thereafter.

My father drives a tow truck in Malibu and he knows it is not his battle to win, anyway? As for marijuana leaves and raspberries picked in summer, Sierra does not know there is a world outside her domain, and this is a blessing. Her father is exonerated and Sierra's brother takes up karate, which is not far from where he stands. A desert in the ocean might seem like a paradise for some (as a place you have not been to yet.) There is Sierra and she, like a travel agent, will tell you how to get there, and with a smile too. (Otherwise, Lily remains in the ocean, at her mercy, after the fact. Lily tempts the gardener to pick a flower, which did not belong to her either. The gardener is Mt. Fuji and he inherits some of the gold of an Inca king, which is a blessing. Lily found affection for a young boy, and denies her past with love of another who is not God.) The flower, which is picked was a sign of fertility and maybe respect too. The Rasta man smokes cannabis in the park, and this is the next best thing to where it grows in patches of a somewhat fertile malaise, which they inherit in Libya? Like Sierra, there is a maternal connection here that grows out of its own disposition.

There may be more to Sierra, as the Valley, in air conditioned accommodations, melts with memories of fertility like a Chipwich, which is her fruit as it returns to the ocean with the sun always at their back.

"The Fourth Dimension"

From where Will stands, he can remember the great ones, who lived here even before the settlers flocked to this land. I have described them earlier in this book, as "tree entities" and would not go so far to patronize them with titles like Native Americans, and Will may be one of them?

Will is not from Mars really, but calls a place destitute as such, home, because he may escape his past. He lives on Earth as though never here, but this is far from the truth. Will does have a past. Rather than be a great redwood tree and its musky smell is his cologne (to remind others of his existence) he swallows his own seed as a grand red-headed woodpecker and rested in death as a goldfish pond, where he may exist in negative space only. He is a reminder of when "tree entities" walked on Earth, but it is difficult to meet him too as he is in his own element and this world is difficult to penetrate. He is a red-headed kid with whom I grew up and occupies what one might call the fourth dimension. If Will did ever sin, he would be the type of person who would be proud of it, if not long enough for a free meal. A tiger outlives three lions and this is where you will find Will.

Otherwise, he might be playing tennis in the park and no one knows of this past as "they" are all now gone and a mere song sheds light of his existence here, where there was much life and many tears as well. May it be a lesson too? Will lives in NYC and there is much in his future even still. I warn you to beware of the fourth dimension as Will will not tell you whether you are welcome and you will find out sooner or later? For those who would rather not, there are more of you out there and that is good. I call Will "Half Moon with Red Tide," and someday he will stand with flat feet like his, I think? Mick Jagger drinks "cherry cola" and kisses Will smack on the cheek, even though Mick is busy on a long distance call to Mozambique? Stronger than a feeling is an enigma where Will is a square and the dragon enters it as to return to the sea? From here Satan will never escape the home he adopts there. His home now belongs to Will too and his feet are flat like God. As Stew the racehorse may not find the sky and it is just a metaphor for the millions who die under Stalin, "Christ," this is Will too. He now stands on feet that are flat like his...(The past is the past,) and it dissipates like sand in the ocean. He may now claim the fourth dimension.

"Musgrove Maid"

The Musgrove Maid would be my grandmother or my father's mother. She stands strigine in vanity for the "owl rock" she possesses and that which I inherited really. A hawk, in Thousand Oaks, where I had lived for a while in Juliana's care, brought it to me through the guise of a neighbor who witnessed it falling from the sky. My walk in the desert should foresee it and I left it there with an imprint of the owl of what is left of the sun. It is difficult to exclaim such a vanity as her and all I may say Musgrove is a beautiful place. So beautiful it is that she would call herself the maid destined to abhorring its fruit. She would not leave such a place without making her mark first. As thirty million blacks live in shanty towns throughout the South Africa landscape, she allows the breeze to blow through her hair where she lives alone. She would go so far to vainly call herself the maid too?

"Texas for sale and world peace"

Don't get me wrong, the Lone Star state is a beautiful place, but I pity the cowboy who thinks "time" and "good will" are the same thing. I traveled through Texas one summer and found it to be a most formidable place, though it is not California either. Like black jack, the longer you play, the greater chance you will lose in the end. I think Texas should be a country in its own right, and the higher bidder might give the respect it deserves. Otherwise, America needs a buffer zone with Mexico and I think you are strong enough to take on this mission I sublimely call "world peace." Thank you just the same and I bought, outside of Austin, two Cairn Terrier puppies I would call "Ferocious Two" and "Texas Caldwell." They called Georgia their home for a little while, but my dad told the caretaker to give them away. They probably hitch hiked back to Texas?

"Silver Spring"

My dad was born with a silver spoon in his mouth. Little did he know that silver is also the metal of diamonds. Elvis Presley may have been the protégé in himself that his dad would not know and the Beatles would soon after invade America as well. "She," asks either you like Elvis or the Beatles and a silver spring divides the two. My dad may have been fed food with a silver spoon, but he plays games where he lives in Africa and does not know either that he is the only white kid there? The chief tells him that you have to be so tall to play and he surpassed this line by far and is accepted as such. My dad does not want to be disinclined in the games and he takes this business very seriously. When Elvis and Priscilla married, I was soon born thereafter, and I guess I never really knew him, my father, very well?

"Into the Slipstream..."

The slipstream is a period between 1945 and 1952, a period of time when America was actually conceived, I think. There were people here first, this is true. But, to be here really is to come after and those who do not recognize the slipstream may not participate here. Eventually, those who "do not, do not " so to speak, will die out. It is very clear that this seven-year period will produce an offspring that sheds the beginning of time in 1952 and the death of the past prior to it in 1945. The point here is that you make a choice if you want to stay here and eventually, to be courteous, you must leave if you are "not wanted" to say most eloquently. It will take eighteen hundred years to decipher those who are welcome guests and the clock will cease to tick in China, thereafter. The sun will fade into darkness eventually, but this is in the distant future.

"The Devil Within Goes Outside"

The devil or Steve as I call him lives in China and he will never leave the plight he shares with them. Though, he walks there too with flat feet like God, he lives somewhere outside his domain and sleeps while looking inward too, I think. In a jade garden with giant rock statues and a common garden snake and small springs with goldfish that share a forest of pine (he may call this his home,) but very far way from here. But, someday, he might visit America as he hears the Chicago Cubs are worth seeing and he hasn't decided if he will make the trip someday?

"Stalin's Daughter"

It is sad to think that children grow up in poverty in every corner of the world! But Stalin's daughter, like anyone, should be born in the third world and, even in distant melodies of the once-great Bob Marley, they may not penetrate her world. What is already broken will not be broken again. The third world claims her wherever she is and the sins of the father are collected by God only. As it is a sin to kill a whale, likewise, it is the same sin to save it too? (In the eyes of God.) She lives in the past from which she may not escape nor the father either?

"Madame George"

One of my favorite songs is *Madame George* in Van Morrison's *Astral Weeks*, which came out the year I was born in 1971. It seems to embrace my earliest inhibitions of what is good in the world. The "Cypress Avenue" must exist in some void that shuns notions of what is bad versus what is good. While Van wrote the exquisite expression, a spider sits on his shoulder and he drinks a mug of beer, which you may only find in Ireland. The Irish are not, not bold, and the expression eclipses the wake of an ocean which carries the mysteries it does not want you to know. A woman is old, but still she has time to love and the void she feels becomes a glove that may be enough to consider it as a metaphor for this love that does exist.

"L.A. Lady"

What is a L.A. lady to me? Sexual promiscuity has transgressed in women here, and their natural tendencies forebode their inner inhibitions like the confidence of a Madame named Heidi Fleis. It is not a question of sex, as there is plenty of it; it is a question of when and where? Women find sex rewarding and the demand seems greater than the supply to the men that haunt a L.A. diner and "Pulp Fiction," becomes the reality of the terrain here. Here, lies the mystery of who likes sex more, man or woman? Meanwhile, a Mexican woman is selling tamales and such on the boulevard and her daughter may be poor, but invites an illusion that she may be sophisticated too and sex becomes a way of life. California relays a starting point that inherits the gold of an Incan King to detest that God is present too. From here, "no sex," is an option as though Robert Frost's "Road Less Traveled." Some of the gold may foster the imagination of Mt. Fuji as an alternative point of view which there are many. God is not present, but the exchange is made real like a flower once picked. California is a sort of paradise for some, and "no sex," is not an option.

"The runners from Germany"

Someone must take responsibility for the Holocaust that took place in Germany and I think they do. (With responsibility there are opportunities too.) The runners from Germany are "pretty paupers" and cover magazines such as Vogue and Harper's Bazaar, and are inclined toward a look that could kill. The expression is that a woman may be strong and a man, beautiful? They do not have to decipher, as the father figure they seek, died as though a Jew too, (I think) and they are left behind to figure things out for themselves. With each death there is a picture taken of their soul. As for the Jews, I think it is good that they prosper in another dimension entirely. And I do think Israel is a good thing, and it might not be far from the sky of modern people the sky demands? There are 10 000 maniacs and the "three" runners from Germany that cross over this void from time to time in this sequacious demeanor. Annie Lennox may not know her father really, but if looks could kill like a winter's long cold edge over a witch made dumb? They, males and females, harness each other as one, at least until time should stop and the children left behind, play with prodigies of a different world entirely. The Jews are separate from Mimi's palate where 10,000 maniacs exist in the sky. The sky reflects the ground and Mimi paints a picture of the lightness of her sister.

"Rocky Raccoon is dead is a lie!"

I think raccoons find France to be a desirable place to live. Whether he is not Jewish, he blends in well with the surroundings and women like him at the cabarets too. Rocky Raccoon lives in Texas and challenged the Mustangs that inhabit the countryside to a race and picks up a hitch hiker to drive part of his way to school in Great Barrington, Massachusetts. He is on a mission to death and thinks that his complexion in the vanity mirror fair, like a Mediterranean Jew, he says. The old blue Buick he drives runs over a raccoon on the road? But, he landed a job in San Francisco, California, and lives there with his wife and children. He left his dead carcass on the side of the road.

"Nancy Got Married"

You know the type of person who brings light to the oddest of situations is Nancy? She is my oldest sister, but does not hesitate to have her share of fun when she wants to. I suppose, like the cartoon, we are wonder twins, I being some sort of ice patch, and she is an airplane riding through the sky over Cuba and waving as to say hi to Fidel Castro. She does not assume truth in politicians like so many, but is vulnerable just the same. She rather looks at life as a game and the more exciting and daring, the better? When someone is in danger, she will show up with her fun-loving and innocent appeal and dares the person to play the game one step further.

Most of the time, the perpetrator, whether good or bad, will decline as there is something about her that even the worst of cops relate to. So, as though the other knows her already, as quick as a flash, she feeds into their subliminal and they will usually walk away from something bad with a smile on their face. Someone will recognize Nancy all too well, as though he or she knows Nancy already, "of course, she is a celebrity and in all the magazines." In other words, whether good or bad, there is something irresistible about Nancy and she may walk into the most dangerous of situations and walk out as though fearless and, what do you expect, she spies a glance at a passerby, as though to say, "I do this all the time."

The problem is knowing, like when a lion is playing, when she is having too much fun and she, in a trance, which may be dangerous? I don't mean she would pull a gun on someone, but rather she is having fun and this may not be true for all the entities involved in a situation. Usually, she recognizes my face and she may go to sleep peacefully that night. The last thing you say to her is that she is a girl, which is an insult as she knows things that not even the most seasoned adults understand. It has a reverse effect and, though Nancy is stronger than it, she might walk away, maybe upset and not knowing why? One has totally misread her then maybe and everyone knows not to do that.

Hopefully, they play into the fun that most people feel guilty about having; and she just provokes some magic that only she knows how to do. She does well in the world that she creates; it does not matter if you like her or not, she does well anyway. Her most profound skill is making people feel sorry for her just slightly, but not really. The emotion at hand, if one is rude, it becomes a dark cloud above suddenly and she laughs later at how scared people bigger than her may be, being much smaller than the average male.

She, a female, plays in a male world and this is impressive, but she may just have you around her finger. Females do not conspire with other females. They share information, which is much more deadly than even a gang could possibly be, knock on wood, she does not mean harm on others. She is both innocent and sometimes dangerous. One relates to her like a younger sister and plays into it well, knowing all the things you do not. At such times, she will play more than one role and this seems complicated to most male brains and this shows her to be stronger (even in their world) what ever the perception may be? On the other hand, she is very gracious to meet you halfway when one is in need of a friend. As my sister, and as the years pass by, I assume the role of that of an older brother. Although, I don't think she is ever hurt in her shenanigans, she plays pretty roughly and I want to watch out for her better interests.

I guess I know something she does not, and so I am sucked into the game occasionally, although I do not always like it. Sometimes, adults may want to mediate something, but they do not know Nancy and so I am there. There is another side of Nancy, the sister who plays with the cousin's children and Nancy, who is an adult and is looked up to very much, but without being out of reach to the kids which adults sometimes are. You cannot quite put a finger on the fun and she manages to escape from a weird situation. She is reading an article about the Hutus and Tutsis fighting a civil war in Africa. She may well be thousands of miles away during her coffee break at work and some bizarre, brain-washed person and so far away, has to smile all of sudden as though

293

Nancy is going to war as well and she stands out to everyone like a flower they just can't touch. As she passes, she asks, "Are you having fun, yet?" And if you are part of a world religion, you may feel sort of funny like the dull, serious side of life has passed your life away, and the children play and play.

"Vaughan"

Vaughan sits on the pedestal of the life she was given. My mom speaks to her through me, and for me, we were never really introduced. What is more important is what one may fool from a fool's game. A child that would like to negate all that is evil, but who should judge the other anyway? We watched her grow up, though the luxuries she would receive turned into fire, in hindsight.

She is somewhere between Catholicism and last week's tea session with her mom. They request both as company to fight amenities and so forth. And if charity is shared, it is met with a slap in the face; we may not reach her. The love that is usual is only physical and is and was too late to do anything about. I guess a bad mother blames her daughter for her own flaws and protecting this fire of vanity requires grave secrets in which Vaughan would rather be the first person to share this, but is unable to escape the fate anyway. Among the other children, she is quite tall, especially for a girl, and they would be safe with her, for only which a father's love knows how? How should a mother bear a cow on a hill and this token of love manifests itself with a betrayal. She, my stepmother, should at her own demise have children with someone else's husband, so to speak. It is ironic that Vaughan is innocent in some way, yet she cannot escape the children of doom. In an incestuous falling, she would rather point the finger at another, but it is not her fault really and I think other. To have the devil's children in this manner, is a laugh as he does not show his face at all. It is an act of betrayal too great for punishment.

I suppose the Germans were not ready for each other when the Jews were killed at their hand under Hitler. They may not have known that the Jews were in the second house which is death and therefore, maybe the Germans were only following the orders of a higher power, not my father, and should be commended for freeing them? Without their cause, the Jews would not have survived anyway, as they had all drunk blood already, so to speak?

In the eyes of God, there is a short passing of forgiveness only by surrendering to such a plight and some of them may have known this and surrendered peacefully. It was to my knowledge that Hitler did not commit any crime, but was rather an orator for the Jews, I think. He did not, I believe, commit suicide. But, rather, he was killed like the Jews in a way and is innocent like bread for wine? I did not know the curse of these lies could awaken Hitler, in the form of my father, a face of darkness that encourages hate as a lifestyle, but not really, I think. This knowledge may have freed many kids tempted to hate which are trapped in it and assume lies to be true, especially of those they know nothing about. It must have been explained to her, an incestuous relationship is not me, nor I a Jew and we go to church like any family does? However, my stepmother ate the fruit of which somehow tells her this though me. Her hate is calculatingly and she must be proud of it. Hate compels it further for no reason.

She feels betrayed by those who are energized in the spectacle and abandoned by her nest which at least allowed her own hatred to fester more. I guess, she sees me as a Jew like the ones in the Holocaust and is way too far gone to reach for. My father's hate is forgiven as he does not know why he hates and it is as natural to him and too far gone as well? I guess Elizabeth's marriage to my father affords her a lifestyle that allows her a respect to draw others into it. It is a disease in which I could have freed her, but she enjoyed being the wife of my mother's husband and in this vain? Fortunately for her, my hospitalization may fester a curse and I do not wish this upon her, really. She may be an exception and I do not recommend hate, as a way of life. She may fornicate her hate in another and there is nothing I may do, really. She may of given her life for me, though it seems superfluous in the end. Still, there is Vaughan, who, may or may not know what is love? Anyway, she is becoming to the younger sect and this seems unavoidable. Elizabeth wished her own fate on her daughter and this does not seem natural in hindsight! (Good Christians of the world unite and for those not yet in the light, it is worth its weight in gold!)

"Original Sin"

The Virgin Mary has an affront to waste that perpetuates its pause further. If all things (including food) are represented by a dynamic of human form that allows for God to create further, then waste is its alter ego in a game to perpetuate further a carrot or tomato to breathe like this. God created a cigarette just like a pear and to waste the meat growing on a steak bone is disease itself that manifests itself in original sin from the first kill. Waste has many forms, whether fat in excess of one's own body, food that escapes consumption and even excrements of tobacco shunned to be not necessary, but is very necessary in its further production.

If not for the Virgin Mary's affront to waste there may be no surplus, which excels further when confronted with this scenario. The chef who prepares a dish must add an element of oneself in order to escape the diagnosis of disease that which perpetuates otherwise, I think. Eve may eat a bland form of cuisine, while fish in the ocean absorb the poisons in the moon that transforms the form of what is edible thereafter. Otherwise, a chip of chocolate remains either as waste in one form or another, and represents a time tested display of production in this form, but not entirely edible.

Really, the chef is key in isolation that allows one to know where and what to eat, but fast food may be another thing altogether. And, no one really knows which came first the chicken or the egg? A young boy stands in a field next to his excrement, and this is not proof that he may well not be welcome, while meanwhile Eve eats the forbidden fruit out of shear vanity, which is not far off from original sin. As far as tobacco is concerned, a certain degree of excess creates surplus in this scenario. The farmer, like religion, may be obsolete in this scenario. Tobacco will grow naturally otherwise. Like water for wine, they are the same thing really! Meanwhile, we eat the meat on a chicken bone to get rid of the evidence of that which is original sin; this perpetuates waste, which creates further surplus!

The Indians of North America may shoot an arrow at oneself, which forfeits a great bison and they are forgiven of the destiny of that which to others might seem wasteful. It is a deal designed in heaven and they are not convicted of any crime. God may well be an alternative lifestyle while the Japanese eat seaweed and this seems quite natural in this light. Otherwise, God's bloodline may not cross over with his, but the lion the tribes of the African plain will eat, adds to their strength and I call this respect. The disease of fried chicken at a fast food restaurant in Georgia manifests itself as waste, somewhere else entirely. Without the waste that this will entail there would be no surplus. I eat grapes on a vine as though the blood of Christ fermented as wine, and this represents something good. But, this is necessary to create other waste in this scenario. God offered his only son to die on a cross for the sins of others, and this is really the beginning, and perpetuates life further in this fashion, I think. She may well bear the blood of Christ every month and the clothes she wears is a fashion statement that expresses a shame that she is not responsible for at all. She eats a hamburger, fries, and a Diet Coke at McDonalds and does not show a blush at such times. It is forgiveness through repentance that she provokes, but she is innocent. And the animals die for original sin, which is not hers. We may all be mechanisms of that which is food without a beginning too! Meanwhile, animals are heathen displays of God in which he will forgive from the first kill. The fact that waste in all its forms is an affront to the Virgin Mary is not an issue?

"The Color Green"

The snake slithers from a tree, but the exchange is like the color black for the color green, and further the viridity as it is no longer dangerous. It forms on the outreaches of a head of lettuce and manifests itself as far away as foam forming at the mouth of the ocean, as it crashes as waves to the shore. Like a thousand points of light it may well represent the end of the ruby's chivalrous conquest over that which is the emerald. She was beaten to death and represents a loss that will never be accounted for thereafter and represents a fire that will not be put out either.

The Trinity does form here in the form of a woman. The green in the grass is not hers, and manifests itself in the form of that which is milk, which belongs to the spider thereafter. The otherwise cow wears leather vainly, which is hers knowing like water for wine, the milk is not hers otherwise. She might eat Häagen-Dazs ice cream and truly believes at such a juncture. A cow, a green snake, and a spider are her own creation and represents a loss and original sin is still another's, a memory of the loss she should adhere to prior still. Jesus's spine is this green snake, while the black snake allies with another to provoke dark tendencies. A spider remains good despite another's alliance and a cow jumping over the moon every month.

A black snake represents the good in the worst of people and she is master of the fourth dimension. This is a deal with which she may live. She is perpetuating the milk of another, but still manages to sell her offerings for the money she will inherit over time from my father, a deal made in the dark and she promises to be friend to God and man while in this lifetime. She would buy all of Africa if she could with cheap jewelry that affords this situation too. She is bitter that she does not represent the Trinity, and finds some solace in an alliance with my father (made in the dark) and really does not care anymore, either. She maintains the luxury of fake jewelry and some Chanel No. 5 perfume. The spine of Christ in the form of the number three is no more and will prosper somewhere else as sequential mathematics like the number five as far away as South Africa really?

This becomes important to the end Jesus will entail into the future. He aligns with God in someone else's heart, the inner circle being the Jews and the outer is Stalin's millions. My sisters represent eight, eight, three and the other three transcends three, two, four, and where the threes meet, the door may be opened here that which is Musgrove. The doors open and meet at three, which is his spine. A cow claims others for her offerings and milk from the water of the spider, is not hers. It is a spider's own tear and she is fertile despite her offering as a desert in the ocean does expound? The grass expounds to an assortment of tiny yellow flowers and this is her offspring in the end, that of a spider which is not her mother either. She negates the cause of who is my mother's mother as a mystery unspoken to who should claim the daughter instead? Mimi's sister is freed in the conquest as well as the color green. Mimi does not claim a daughter either. The children of the sun remain like little yellow flowers near where baby cactus grow near the overpass to the ramp in Pasadena. Cars whiz by to scathing demur their scatological mission. Mike, as a lizard, sits in the shade of one of his cactus patches to master the light of the preponderates ordeal. Mike's evil son Jim Morrison and the doors are now open? My sisters are the gatekeepers to Musgrove, but do not claim to know him either. Meanwhile, the red light on the backs of cars passing by are reminders of Mike's friends from the past. The exchange is made so that the color green is freed in the process. I claim the ruby instead and the color is freed as well.

The cow would rather sell her wares to others and carries the title of the Emerald Princess at such times. The common green snake is not dangerous, but opens the doors who are my sisters for those who seek out Jesus in the end. My sisters will represent sequential equations to help out in her functioning well; once a year it happens at Easter Sunday when the grass is cut to remind us of another's loss. At such times my mother sits on clouds too far off to reach, really. She is a reminder to those who forsake her and they do not make it in the end. She listens to a distant drum that may not be penetrated anymore. Otherwise, the milk of a spider denies the color green and the cow may be envious of the tear someone else shed, but unprovoked by leather she vainly wears upon her feet. Matt's finds her fate bearable, but the green flower is not picked in the process. Jim Morrison recognizes the fire that absorbs him in the sky.

"Diamond Light"

When we arrived here, there was only darkness. Could a black snake, another, find repentance through her own strife, is the question at hand? Otherwise, Mimi's left hand is in the form of a gold ring with eight diamonds or four sets of two, and she does not penetrate God's world, but this is thereafter heaven still. When the rock is thrown at the moon (this may be before Battery Jack) which is attested to thereafter as our sun in God's light, and I throw a rock at it as well. An alignment is formed that sheds dead cockroaches into strands of her hair composed in the DNA and provokes further the stars that compose. a map of what is there. The dark star would subsist thereafter. Upon her epidermis that may only be subject to light now that God is present, he will use us as in his greater plan for us to meet in heaven, thereafter. In the beginning, there may be only darkness. I guess someone must be tested and the poetic champions compose.

The configuration of a "Dark Star," may be seen from Earth in nine sequential motions that do exist. There are many dark entities here too, and they may see the stars too, like a map of consequence read on her epidermis, but hidden from view. NOVA exclaims that hydrogen atoms may be smashed, where a lack of gravitons appear signifying that particles, like God do resound. The Jews believe in the Star of David instead. We all represents universes in dark matter, which may connect us through varying worm holes that manifest here. God is on the outside looking in, like a labyrinth detested by the devil, of what is there, like the darkness the night permits? The stars seem so close when seen from this venue. After "Battery Jack," fades as though our sun and seen by Aborigines in Australia, the Dark Star and the Star of David will become one. This is Christianity as it is dispelled to thereafter. The Andromeda Galaxy and the Milky Way Galaxy may become one too.

"The Bear"

She need not pander to black stars, dark in the infrastructure of Africa where a play is fostered for the dying sun, as she is free of the disease they administer. A spike is made on his chin as he entered H and H bagels on the Upper East Side of Manhattan in New York City. Entities such as my chin administer the blood she will shed as a destiny of sorts as well. The Playboy bunnies serve her chocolate molds still, and Hugh Heffner requests a glass of bourbon, but he has no answer why it must be like such? He inspects the register as though his own creation, but not God's. She has pink blood and exposes such at this time, and only once. The bear bleeds also at this time, but does not foresee its future, and may be sacrificed like blood for wine, a hindrance that is created from its own inherent disposition. God could not penetrate the fortress she will endure. Jennifer Lopez may carry the cross farther still? Three perfect suns may appear from here in the sky and belongs to a lion, tiger, and bear. This may be my creation too as I bleed for her just once and she escapes a lesser fate. The bear is her creation as well which stares back at her from a window less understood.

"Pink Bunny Champagne"

She drinks water from the fountain that is exposed to bird callings in the garden of the mansion, which he inhabits. They excrete a sparkling bath in which the pink bunnies absorb as their own. Where do sparkling wine and the urine of others unite?

She is not subject to any anger from God and she composes something in which merits a respect of sorts. She is diagnosed as a participant in this play, which is really a practice run for others to participate as well. Wine tastes like blood, strawberry fields forever. It reflects the DNA of cockroaches in her hair is insane and lives onward like this forever. I think, from this point of view, everything is accounted for? She may excrete a pink bath from this point of no return.

The African Man trades his wares so that their light will last forever and her path will not cross theirs like the devil propelled outward. God may allow some of the statues to be returned in the future too.

The dress rehearsal leaves her naked at such times and as she puts her clothes back on, her lover drinks her offspring with a subjective disposition, which does not allow one to conspire at such times. The nectar of bees absorbs it even though she is still only half-dressed at such times. He exposes his loins to the nightmare he will inherit and his chin protrudes, showing that he is still playing the game despite the pause the play would foster and plunder.

The quest arrives and champagne is served at the door. Andy Warhol will not eat the chocolate molds in which they serve as well. The pink bunnies find the protruding subject matter obscene. The bawdy scene could not be foreseen, as he is gay. The red wine tastes familiar to Mr. Heffner at such times as he is living the life of another and the wine is expelled here as blood.

Another man backs away from the door as a dog barks before entering and he fears the destiny that is not his either. Yet, he sheds a protective stance to the animal that is more instinct than fear. A bear stares back at him through the bowl of that which is another's life still. "Mille Fleur" belongs to my dad at such times! Pink bunnies guide him along a path that was gone long ago. I shed the blood he will foster as "a step" made once upon a time and for me only, I think. He sings to "a spiritual," in Georgia and says "That's alright," too.

My dad created his own destiny as a bird bath that protrudes with the pink it represents. Pink Bunnies serve champagne at the door to his house called "Mille Fleurs," and Mimi takes a picture of him as "the Pink Panther," in this light that resounds. He will not escape the fate of a lion that will die in three implements thereafter.

My sister Nancy drinks pink champagne as though the door once closed, and Nicole opens the door so that Bob Marley may re-enter. Peter Tosh denies my sister's right to this light. It is all that is left of our dad despite the picture Mimi takes, not to mention his baseballs he leaves me as well. A fountain remains in his backyard and he drinks pink champagne from its natural resource, once upon a time, that Mimi provides. Note: if gold had a compass, it my be a Corona with a lime in Mexico. At such times, a lion drinks a beer as though drinking from a forbidden fountain. My dad may be this lion in hindsight. Leonardo DiCaprio dispels the notion of blood for wine. The pink bunny champagne propels from my chin that will bleed and the bear is separate. The Virgin Mary maintains an innate psyche that allows Satan and God to be separate as well. Her blood may not be sacrificed as to drink from a fountain that pink bunny now claims. Also, pink champagne may be tasted now like a call from her sister. Yes, my dad drinks a beer as well as though from its natural resource. Meanwhile, pink bunny champagne is trapped in bottles in the exchange so that birds from a fountain as well. They excrete a bath that may be tasted like blood as wine. I do not understand how pink bunny champagne and the urine of others may be tasted? My dad asks his wife for a different point of view. Mimi and Renata hold hands leading into the sky to tolerate such a junction.

"Bob Marley Died"

My dad is buried in a cemetery reserved prior for only African Americans, but is honored to be the first other to participate. Bob Marley may live onward in his memory. Chocolate may be reserved for others as either

301

may be re-born at such times; the worlds part only to unite at a later time. What is fish food for some is redemption for others and a lion swims to shore in a distant Africa, but he is not my dad really, and Bob Marley is not my father either! Three lions will die at his conquest to a different sun, which will rise out of a darkness that will allow him to remember his past as well. Bob Marley unites with the past and asks could this be love?

Xander is not welcome at the door, but smokes a joint before the storm dies down and six thousand years wasted, being not his legacy. Darkness protrudes and no one is any different than everyone else. Slavery was just a teardrop in the ocean "so far away!" A zombie rises from the periphery of the ocean to manifest itself in a new beginning and the past is forgiven as such. He stares down at 10 000 souls and he sees this is good too. And the children will at least know themselves. Six thousand years is the time it takes for three lions to be sacrificed for this spectacle at hand. As we count back from 2 000, it will begin again and the children play and play. Each lion is in Einstein's creation of "a square," and will die within two thousand year intervals as such. Three tribes here will unite all as one.

Meanwhile, God sits in the back left corner and is married to an African queen here who wears diamonds on the soles of her shoes. Jesus will rise as his calling manifests him in heaven only; all subjects present are welcome. Meanwhile, Will stands in the center with flat feet that are like his... As they rise to this place in the heavens, Cat Stevens sings some melody and everything else here is propelled outward as though not to care. God wears K-Swiss tennis shoes and closes to the spiritual "All things are possible..." which is true. I hear in the back the Beatles sing that all you need is love. Stew, the horse, is a sacrifice to this notion and the door to Japan is sort of closed? All I remember is a dead shark on the beach as its natural resources will draw it back into the ocean through its mouth,

What the children do not see will not hurt them, I think. They are given a white horse instead. Stew remains black in the night sky of a Raven's eye and could not find the sky on that day.

Bob Marley may be spared from the death of three lions and my sister will die for a sin which is not his either. God winks at my sister and smiles at Bob Marley too. God's face is as stolid as the sun that does not shine? He orders a gin and tonic and accounts his creation that detests the waste of a lion as his own creation too. It will not die like a tiger lost at sea. Will stares at the stage from which Bob Marley stands. Now, the intermission occurs and dancing bears cross the threshold of the life my sister is given. Meanwhile, Michael Jackson plays with Ferocious , in the shade, behind the bleachers.

Queen Latifah sings spirituals with hip hop motifs from the venue of Africa from which she stands too.

The Painter's Palette (in eight parts)

1. Maroon Buick
2. Green Izod
3. Pink Flamingo
4. Yellow Swimtrunks
5. Red McDonalds
6. Purple Egg
7. Blue Tattoo
8. Orange Gummy Bear

*

There are ten thousand maniacs detached from her palette. In the sky, a black bird elopes with white linen and forages in the past that which is the gray in the turning pages of the New York Times. Her sister affirms that a touch of gray does not hinder the palette at hand, nor a silver tree blowing in the wind from this perspective is just memories of past lovers whom she no longer holds dear. They will envision paper cut outs of dancing bears that may compose the music into the future.

They pause to feed their goldfish that inspire these slogans rising into the sky, but still confined to a simple glass bowl. A black cat jumps on the ledge to stare into the infrastructure, which is now torn like black jeans, and Mimi says to get dressed so it is not confused with a belated task. The cat is well aware of what is for dinner at such times. The goldfish glow back to inform the preponderance that they will not meet and gray is a neutral color that detests that rain is falling outside and be aware of nuts walking on the streets of New York City.

In fact, it is the last emotion to embrace Mimi and she would rather make birdcalls with her sister and calls long distance to Sweden. The key is jammed in the door and her birds keep the time that it is past midnight. The birds turn into snakes while she is sleeping. A small black pebble falls to Earth from a shooting star and is just a reminder to us to keep secrets that are conceived in the dark. We are vestibules of God in his creation, that is all.

Steve Jobs may have created a simple silver apple and, in exchange it pays the bills so that a man pan handling outside a Seven Eleven may dream of becoming rich playing the roulette table at some fancy casino. The men with blue glass eyes have no tolerance for the mockery, and give him a quarter instead. He will inherit the color black in some distant land. Still, the dream festers further as raccoons huddle around at slot machines and spends God's money; the winnings are at least enough to buy a roast beef sandwich at Arby's. The man finds this to be enough and the night befriends this man so that he may not seem ashamed either.

Meanwhile, I trade my gold watch for a black pen and a silver half-dollar with an arrow sticking through an eagle's skull, and the gypsies tell me it is quite rare. My dad cracks almond shells at the Plaza's Oak Room and manages to stay inside out of the rain most of the time. He likes that his money is always accepted there. My mom wears turquoise scuba gear and cuts the ocean's wake backward in time that stipulates as a sort of an adventure in Bermuda. They are now divorced, but find the time to take me to the Red Lobster which is a belated task that seems to me odd. I still believe that they were in love at one point in time. They go their separate ways. My dad has a blue umbrella and my mom has a green pen. Otherwise, the air between them seems distant and the ocean divides them so that the wind may not hear a bad joke at this juncture. The seagulls tease that Santa Claus may not get it up anymore and he wears pink polka dot boxer shorts that he buys at Macy's because he is too poor to go to Bloomingdales.

Further, they say that he sometimes loses control of his bowel motions while sleeping, which transpires as a sort of orgasm too. Santa is so poor that he buys at Kmart cheap Duracell imitations to charge Rudolph's nose.

"Enough," and the wake that now separates my parents is distant like Santa's belly. Despite being Caucasian, they subscribe to a sort of dark humor, but I would not know this. Someone else intercedes that ebony is so black that God scratches his balls with it…

"Enough!" A man sleeps in the corner of the street with a few nickels and dimes that seem to pay the electric bill despite the menacing circumstances. We may be distant relatives, but the world is divided so much that such humor is significant relative to the dynamic at hand. We may still learn from the children in the future. Santa Claus hires a black maid to clean the underwear he so vehemently soiled. Someone in Mozambique speaks Belgian and says "enough."

Now the ocean will divide even more. And her sister may not hear bad jokes and she goes out on a date instead. Her date asks if she knows what are "Depends?" No, really, you will not see the love as though a black glove left at the crime scene.

She lives in Scandinavia and Santa lives not far from here, ten thousand maniacs in the sky. Rudolph is sold at the butcher shop and Mrs. Claus does not want for Santa to be seen with his pants off either. The black maid helps out enough. Dark humor is on the outer fringes of society, but may reflect a sentiment heard on the dark soil of Africa and God may live not far from here. There is a sign saying, "Crocodiles are not welcome." Though his predicament is poor like the homeless man outside a Seven Eleven in NYC, he does manage to save enough to buy a used Volvo. Still, he is rich in spirit. Real black panthers live on the fringes of the estate where sharks do not tread. He calls Africa home, and the homeless man says he is welcome in New York City any time he wants to visit? Meanwhile, Santa is in the kitchen making a sort of potluck stew with Rudolph's remains. God will not see this and is rich in spirit, instead. Despite the night sky, you still will not see God. His love is a glove and so dark too.

1. Maroon Buick

His friends are dinosaurs in the past whose remains are used as fossil fuels burned in cars. Mike blames the cars for this preponderance while one car in particular is damned in a scenario where it creates pollution. It may be healing agents to the stars despite being convicted of old testaments to the enigma that a diamond is saved in their spirit's demise. A sort of contest remains to which flowers adhere and the nicer the car the greater its guilt, which will not deter its quest.

Godzilla and King Kong fight in the transmission of my car and it ends up as a stalemate as the tow truck arrives and leaves it at a space in the shade in Malibu. There is no winner and the car is blamed for the crime, which merits us as cavemen without the grace mercy sheds on the person driving the car. The car talks to Mike through its tailpipe. They consider the contraption to be guilty and may side with the devil in its conviction. There is a magenta van in Jamaica and the ganga smells intense and heals its user so that diamonds in the sky are freed by its stipulation. The intensity of the fire seen through the façade of a diamond is so great and the pollution intrudes their space and feels healed and much better.

Lucy may sympathize with their plight and stares at stars that would rather share a joint with leopards that smile on trees as you leave the savannah. It is a way out to feel high as though a black Labrador smelling the butt of a white Poodle is offensive. Mike laughs at this juncture and his friend's radiator needs more water too. The car stipulates time that has no meaning to God anymore. They say a maroon Buick my dad once drove is guilty of some obscure crime and Mike has a museum of these contraptions and this is also hell, I think? Women are sometimes mistaken as other and blamed to be guilty too. Lucy looks away as diamonds in the sky find there is mercy here too. The devil will not penetrate her domain in Africa. Mike rides my dad's maroon Buick with its top down and is inclined to consider it is his girlfriend, which finds the compromise tolerable where dinosaurs still tread in its wake. It is a compromise he can live with… He calls the car Lucy, but my Blue Eagle Summit is out of reach. The devil drives a white Volkswagen Rabbit and blames the Jews for his plight.

2. Green Izod

Cotton is as white as clouds caught in the eye of God near a resort under which the Seychelles converges and may belong to him too. At the resort, there is an assortment of his friends who serve Pina Coladas wearing green Izod shirts and the infrastructure where he lives in a rainforest in Mozambique seems to adhere to be separate like a bill remaining unsubstantiated. Gorillas converge here and God may remember a time when distant suns that die are reborn in this form. The real devil abides by God's wishes and the green in the leaves torn from a branch calls in the wind that the bill is separate and money subsists in its lesser form at such a juncture.

My dad will use the urinal in the back and the bartender serves a beer at God's request. Otherwise, another man drinks a Pina Colada spiked with a cherry and asks why seagulls are mistaken as clouds in the outer fringes of the sky? God says that he does not know. At the bar, they play a game of backgammon and pretzels are free in a bowl as though not to care why the waitress scratches at her bra that is attached in the back.

His friend smiles like my dad once did, but I may not make out what is blocked from view as the waitress passes. He says that he once knew a boy who thought he was a cat. God laughs and we will meet much later, I think. My dad offers him a fine Cuban cigar and I may make out his expression as though good. He has a deck of cards where I am the "Blackjack," and my dad "the King of Spades."

A woman arrives in a black bikini and hugs God so that he seems somewhat vulnerable and she is his acquaintance, so you do not get the wrong idea. She speaks Swahili and says "Jambo" and relays her top as inconsequential to the picture at hand. The women of Barbados may detest that her breasts are more than the equation of being lost on an island with tropical splendor? Her name is Roxanne. The moon's own disdain for the situation at hand may be seen, but is hidden as it complies a jealousy that does not know why it feels such emotions to this one isolated woman? It is not welcome at the casino and God plays roulette with black chips instead. His favorite number is five.

Raccoons play craps in Monte Carlo and accept the mirage as charity with which they can live. I give my sister Nicole a gold coin in the exchange. She serves God a gin and tonic, and collects shells on the beach in her spare time. Roxanne sits under a gondola on the beach while topless and says she is pretty. Nicole says the same. They are now friends. The clouds will converge in a dangerous fashion and Roxanne offers her a Camel Light which Nicole declines. God meets a new friend named Kyle and play gin in the back of a bar that does not know why the sun shines either.

3. Pink Flamingo

Pirates assemble on the beaches of Martha's Vineyard as though vestibules of Paradise Lost. They drink a sort of rum punch in pineapples that have a plastic pink flamingo stir that fathoms concepts of Satan entering Brazil, which may be God's waste too. Without hammock or parrot, they sit around a fire on the beach in which their shed shares the company. They are not related to God in any way and rather tell stories of Blackbeard instead. They may be like children staring into the abyss of the fire and dare one another to dream of tropical islands in the distant oasis of their imagination.

Mimi is here too and she tells them that there is a grand island far away and the people live without the cold Budweisers they share on the beach? They would rather play Risk inside and consent that they have not been there either. Donny claims that Charlie Manson may get out of jail soon, but would not know that he may know of such places too, dumbfounded in a place where they may pretend to be pirates and such too. There is no knowledge of other in this scope. Mimi is the closest thing to be an authority figure and they respect her enough and rather play a board game inside and may be slightly tipsy too. They all laugh and next to lost paradises; this is the next best thing.

Alex intercedes that sharks in the ocean are aware of which way the wind blows, but protect Blackbeard too at the bottom of the ocean, but this is just a story. They do not know that Mimi has a sister in a faraway place? Sharks form a circle in an eating frenzy and a shaggy dog sits on a beach tearing a skull and bones flag with pink undertones. Out of Africa, they are ignorant to the cause to dominate the world at hand. Mimi does not reveal to the children that this has already happened in the past. The last domain is the ocean where pink flamingoes protect its periphery and otherwise the conquest is lost deep in the rainforest.

Darwin will profess that evolution is the law. With the exception of Ferocious, it rains so that no one may enter and the Jews are not welcome here either. Fidel Castro's chauffeur drives, while black panthers fall like rain from the sky. His girlfriend kicks him out and he has respect for those savages that still remain. He is Catholic and will convert them when the rain subsides too. Mimi will not infiltrate their oasis and rather allow them to subsist in a brave new world as though nothing has changed. Pink flamingoes maintain the secret of the ordeal. At such times, Mimi poses for a picture as one of the birds that stand on beaches on one leg, while her sister is a blue-footed booby and sheds a tear for her sister at such times. The children continue the dream as pirates in their imagination and may not leave the fire that they sit around on a beach in Martha's Vineyard. Mimi confounds a secret in Conor, and he plays with the others knowing something the others do not. He is invited to play Blackjack at God's table, but leaves the others without their presumption otherwise.

4. Yellow Swimtrunks

Simon wears yellow swimtrunks to the beach on Coney Island. His kids suck down more than one hot dog at Nathan's and dispense it outward on the Cyclone as a metaphor for a once-whale that will travel like an arch to journey with child protégés who participate in the ordeal. The kids are Catherine, Susan, Michael, and Anne. The arch that a whale is inverted in the past to embark on a voyage that reins the force of twenty-four elephants. Other kids who are willing will ride it from here to the coast of western Africa as though they have been on vacation to return with America being a memory. Like they never left, they take a picture with a disposable Kodak camera on the boardwalk. They will know themselves; that is the gift.

The ocean has a way of absorbing them in the wake of a whale's tailfin and dispensing them to land somewhere else. Mike sits on the dock before the arch sets a sail and requires in payment a smile for the thirteenth sun he represents. Meanwhile, Arnold Schwarzenegger will act as one of the chaperones whose mission it is to repopulate Africa with these displaced kids. Will is on the deck with sunglasses on and tells stories of the spirituals sung by ancestors who came before off the coast of Georgia. Simon says he had been there before.

Will's son, Nathan, and Jamal are now best friends. The color of one's skin becomes subordinate to the cause at hand and the rainbow joins them as though everyone may see it in a void of the blue sky. Seahorses ride the wake of the craft to join forces in the cause. A dolphin crests the wave and says farewell as it remains in the gulfstream that he presses against off the coast of Florida. The seagulls that subsist here will meet them when the children feel like a dream only separates them from the dynamic at hand. They will not return, but maintain the dream that fosters their spirit further. The Statue of Liberty will shed a tear and waits for the blue sky to join with ocean currents as though one and always has been. The moon falls into the ocean and the sun rises like a magenta sky that is their mother. They are now home! Meanwhile, the ocean divides like Japan it now represents. Simon ,as a whale, is now free and some of the children return to Africa too. It was just a dream.

5. Red McDonalds

A Red McDonalds is when China becomes possessed by the cage it represents and manifests further to rather envision a predicament that is less than heaven too. China does not know that it is confined to a microcosm that will not free those within at its onslaught that is a cage with a black panther is like a vision they represent? In Chinatown, the cage has iron bars, which leave children's imaginations stolid with perplexing equations and will not free the animals either. The scaffolding begins to meld a disposition of a sort of a sticky sap that is detested in the mouth of the beast at hand. The children will further meld with the substance and will not allow the participants to be free either. It is a sticky substance and a spider web is formed in the configuration of a sun and the dark entity takes a picture that will not allow them to be free either.The brats of doom remain on the outside and inside too. They share Hitler's private island and stay inside, out of the rain, and will not penetrate this fortress that is China.

The Owl Rock detests that the sun of old once existed, but the Red McDonalds is still less inviting. The spider leaves the children's remains stuck in its web's interior where a black and white picture is all that detests their existence prior, the Big Mac only half-eaten. In the time span at hand, some lovers will be freed after an 1800 year interval and does not know that we will leave behind petrified remains of French fries in a dump in New Jersey too? Those who will remain find the scenario less than inviting and the devil erases any trace of tears that are shed in the past and otherwise the rain will not penetrate their oasis either.

Each child will inherit a pine tree and are freed by the devil as it will comply with a deal that would diagnose others with shear damnation and God does not seem to notice. The Owl Rock is an imprint of the sun of yesterday and China (the Red McDonalds represents) is a photo negative that may forgive the children who remain.

Will makes a deal in heaven and escapes their fate too. Those who enter the door to which is a deal made with the devil will not leave either. They become preoccupied by the slime of a spider's green mustard and the cage of the Iron Man then toasts with champagne in crystal migraine palaces in the sky. There is no way out. The children shed the only mercy while crying like "Purple Rain," at the Red McDonalds in Chinatown.

The black panther is caged at the center of the stage and will not deter the children's quest. My sister works at the Red McDonald's from where I will see a perfect white sun depleted of all color and I order a fish sandwich. Though, she does not recognize me either. She does not know that a black panther lives within and she is freed from the notion that she would be other. The body builder's muscular façade is a cage like China is to such preponderances and the meek will inherit the Earth. Otherwise, the Chinaman serves like a computer chip to nature's mathematical equations and be free like the devil to walk back to America sometime in the future.

The dog is an entity like the number "33," that will free them from their plight and they say the Chicago Cubs are worth seeing too. Snow leopards and a black panther remain in their homeland of yesterday and is only a picture of the sun. The Dalia Lama will shed mercy here too. Ronald McDonald will fall with the diagnosis of a heart attack in my arms and turns into the Joker in my mind. This is a bad joke to an end of a movie thereafter in Colorado as memories of the rain too? The door of the past is now closed and everyone remaining will prosper into the future.

6. Purple Egg

On the plain of Africa that is flat like God's feet, 10 000 maniacs in the sky (all women) reflect 10 000 men on the ground and there is a show to remember the sun of the past and leaves a purple egg that is vulnerable like God which may serve as a rain muse too. At a seedy motel in LA, the first rain drop lands in my Diet Coke can and meanwhile God's friend sells African wood statues and does not know the tear may be for him too. The purple egg is a perfect spectacle and may reflect a universe that may captivate the ends on the outside too. We may not penetrate God's world either. We settle for reflections of him as the egg falls from a tree and we speak with others that represent the universes we represent where wormholes join us designating that God is there too. He is rather on the outside looking in and an art deco Oreo remains for those who still are less than believing in the scenario. The purple egg is a rain muse and she tends to be sort of regular anyway. I will represent three squares. The sun of the past invites a vision of a perfect plain from where you may meet God as well. Unlike the apple that falls into God's hand, the egg lands on the ground and a vulture arrives to eat its remains. God is bothered by the spectacle and walks on this island to collect shells that stipulates as some time wasted.

A leopard in the tree is the culprit in the egg falling from grace and smiles sort of farfetched while on a tree and transgresses it is sorry in this scenario. God will not meet the outer fringes of what is space. God may not conspire with the animals at such times and rather cooks zebra meat without menacing circumstances on a grill for friends and such. The light blinds too and he says he will not leave Africa until his darker tendencies are redeemed in the dark where poetic champions compose. The zebra meat tastes sort of dry and is an enigma to that which is Eve before the fall. Someone must be responsible for the purple egg falling from grace. Meanwhile, I sit in this motel room in LA watching Oprah, while the tear is for Satan and caught in a can that will not allow him to escape. The laws of nature are now dispelled outward for those who want to ponder further. Satan is caught in his own nightmare, but he says that it is better than hell too. God will leave the barbecue while forgiving Eve of her crime and squats somewhere and it will not land as though it is Satan lost in the past. His friends will join him in heaven later. Ten thousand maniacs escape the rain in the sky and he is our baby too. The purple egg will not dispel secrets made in the dark. The devil sees from within and purple rain falls in Germany, for exchange of this lion that will be sacrificed.

7. Blue Tattoo

Jesus may have been born on the outside. While color is not an issue, I may be a dark entity and a dark man reveals its manifestation as a blue tattoo embossed in a sentiment that I may be born again within. It is somewhat overcast on the boardwalk in Atlantic City, but the sun sheds light for a short time that exposes this like a memory of an existence that once was, and I am not ashamed at this juncture. Jesus here has sort of thick woven dreadlocks and resembles a bear in this dark configuration. Though nothing is left of tears that a blue devil sheds except for this one tattoo and the scar that a bear once stood on African soil too. He may be my friend and is welcome to remain on the outside and racists enter within without this grace. The gangs do not know that the game we were playing is now over. Satan may tread from the ocean on Venice Beach and is now in his element too. I watch VH1 on TV and it may be a testament to Mariah Carey's video of *Honey*. In a trance too,` it claims "peace" is the answer. Still, the darker tendencies of death persist further and I walk downtown from my Upper West Side apartment to the World Trade Center as though knowing something that should not happen. Ferocious has not left me yet, but remains in the apartment and talks to a bird to further spread the word of peace and tolerance. "The woodpecker," in Malibu closes in prayer and takes Ferocious home. The blue tattoo remains to detest that I was here once too. I stand in the rain as though isolated in my spiritual mother's tear that will not fall either.

8. Orange Gummy Bear

Yes, God screwed a bear which is seen as only as self-defense in this light. I may be one of the animals, and trade the picture I take for him as he leaves for a picture of a cheetah. This is God's creation despite the ants that work tirelessly somewhere else. China seems so far away and he will not leave his domain in Africa on a voyage until the show begins to redeem the sun that will die. Darkness is his forte and will envelope notions of love like in the spirit of Adam and Eve, but in a different light as well. Out of Africa, they walk while the air of the light still separates them. Eve picks mushrooms without consequence of God's grace shed, while Jesus dies on a cross somewhere else too. A child in America eats the picked mushroom's harvest. It is an orange gummy bear. Food may seem so boring and the children will not penetrate the ocean that persists. Gummy bears dance in the sky so that the door to other may be Mt. Fuji's home and may be closed to them as well. That which the children do not see will not harm them. The kids sit in a circle while my mom reads them a book. God pauses and smiles for a short time, at this juncture. Mimi paints a picture of herself and she is smiling too. She holds hands with her sister where poetic champions compose. I am forgiven for "nothing," and my dad is forgiven too. Ten thousand maniacs rise into the sky and represent those on the ground as well in God's creation.

Dark Star in Nine Parts
who are you? Eight: India
(Xander Pomgarten)

*India is eight… but to go further in Hindu
by the holy rivers; to clean the dirt from one's
skin. Such a trivial crime like picking
mushrooms in the dark. They, such man,
innocent, and framed by deer who deny it.*

Part Eight: Doctor, Doctor and the Rebellious Jew

"The Bronze Thing"

She embraces the statue like a piece of art always. Actually, it may be a wake-up call for princes and good-natured entities of her liking… Without this invocation, she would be out a job, but she takes her work seriously, turning the circus of cockroaches into remains that exist like this manifestation forever. The dog barks at it, as though it once represented its master. Then the number twenty-one plays a role in her creative venue similar to how the number one repeats itself as the number thirteen. Similarly, twenty-one may have a relationship to the number forty-two. Here, my dad stands in the rain in New York City once with a red umbrella near Forty-Second Street on Fifth Avenue of course. He may well discover life after death, in her invocation of him as a viceroy. While I walk to Scarborough Fair, he waits in the rain not knowing what the latter implies really. He may well stand backwards at such times and sits at the Oak Room grabbing a handful of salted nuts, where his money is always accepted and he likes this. Like the pine trees that conspire around Christmas time, he is the "king of umbrellas," as a lion if you will?

Though he does not know where he is going, he can keep a secret while walking down corridors meant for kings. It would be a dive for such a man to wear blue jeans and he buys his suits at Brooks Brothers specially made for his large stature, being six feet six and a half. He leaves behind a tear in the lake he previously called home. Instead of invading the space of the future he looks back and hands the doorman at the Plaza, the Carlyle, the Waldorf Astoria, and even the St. Regis a five spot and buys his place in heaven at such times, like disparaging the different-colored ties he harbors in his closet. A man of such stature as his may buy clouds in the sky and finds himself in a esoteric club reserved for the few who also may do so. He converted to

Catholicism from Episcopalian, but I know him only as "the African Jew," and he parts as my father, though we only met once so to say the least.

Growing up in Greenwich, Connecticut, he was acclimated to the metal silver, which served up fancy dinners including lamb with mint jelly, watercress salads and vichyssoise soup, his favorite. Lunch at the pool includes iced tea and sandwiches with the crusts cut off. However, when it was time to pay the bill, I think he forgot to leave a tip and left the bill unsubstantiated. And his friends would rap before rap was ever popular and they were like old-timer Jews like my grandfather, who brightens his great stature at such times. He drank a glass of water before going out with his friends to play, and forgot things like the holocaust as he is a Jew too and as a right, he may do so.

While memories may be bought and sold; this is not true for women, and I inherit a silver tray from my grandmother instead. This may be like a misnomer that plays into his adult life much later. I guess money only goes so far, and when it was time to leave, he is unable to escape this conundrum which leaves the other sex at a lost for words. His six children play as though the tally is an illusion and he is just a bronze statue in the park. The step backward leaves him in an awkward position yet he finds some peace here. His mother left me the "Owl Rock," while my dad's saving grace is his baseball collection which he leaves me, with no depravity to mention yet, just memories of dead heroes that live on in this scenario. I think he tells me he has 1950s Yankees autographs. I learned my lesson not to sell his soul at a pawn shop as this is all that is left of him, and he may dream on forever in this state.

He pretends the cab driver is an old-timey Jew and this satisfies his ego even though a dog commits suicide and leaves him in a state that may only be described as a semi-charmed kind of life. He thinks this dog is way below him as he has a stature much like a lion. If not to say he has been through enough torment, his third wife would leave him crucified and steal all his money, which she did not deserve. He lies in urns at three different locations as memories of God's tears in an ocean so far away. As not to pay the bill of your existence, I guess it is some sort of punishment, though the tear is his. I hope he finds his way home, despite his statue is unable to get out of the rain. He finds some peace here, a vindictive one though, which will never forget his tormentors, either.

So, what is a rebellious Jew really? To ask such a question is like asking Mike what a dinosaur is or at such times Ferocious finds himself catching a flyball in the park, and the lion ignores the bee that is bothering him where he lies in sunlight, sort of free from any torment that she may feel compelled to direct at him, the man who gives so much, though. Yet, some calculated errors leave him only half blessed; his life is that of ten men and this is not always a good thing? To dream a better dream, he may do so now and his sins may be reconciled now that there is no danger around that would threaten the cloud he shares with my mom in heaven, I think. This concept may or may not be true, but I think, she being only his second wife, and the other is a bit jealous that he did not pick her, and he rather goes back to my mom, is not entirely false either. Rarely, do bronze statues smile at sunlight in the rain and this is such a time.

He is a slave like his son to bygones that of friends he has never met. Still, he talks to the taxicab driver just the same and this is when we meet. I can't say, therefore that my dad hates Jews, but she, the evil stepmother, may be an other story, really. I guess she thought she might buy a cloud in heaven too, but this is not the case and now she is subservient to lesser beings and cleans the mess of others in houses where once she was the queen. All I may say is that greed is one of the seven deadly sins. Otherwise, my dad escapes the torment she administered in his life. Vaughan may be a testament to this fact and Conor otherwise does well in school. I wonder if my stepmother will give me back the baseball collection I inherited from my father. Otherwise, my father loved all of his kids though he had difficulty expressing pain; that should foreshadow his existence. In this scenario, Hitler is his alter ego and was killed cosmically speaking.

My dad is sand raked up by the ocean and died as a Jew and will not feel tormented any longer, and his mother rings the bell where he lives as it is time for supper. My dad may well have memories as such but mine are totally different. This is when my dad separates from mom and this is one of the few times I feel a true tear leave my eye and my dad moves into the other side of the house we lived in, and I am maybe nine or ten. Now, Neil Diamond is king, and my dad may have acquired a collection of eight tracks and it may be a sort of an escape, too. My dad could be said to be living in the moment, so I can't say it was a waste of time, and he kisses me on the head after driving me to school each morning. It may have been a curious thing for me to see him in the light of where he is going, rather than the step back he shared with my sisters.

The present temperament is a sort of an escape. He listens to lounge singers in his den on fancy leather sofas while Mike serves him a scotch on the rocks, he would say, and Mike at such times would serve as a gondola from the sun and he stays inside mostly. While Nemo the dog may provide other brats enough reason to stay indoors too at such times? My dad is different; he may be sort of a leader and being captain of the high school basketball team is proof of this. His friends may have died an untimely death, but they survive in his memory anyway. In the end, he did love my mother. Meanwhile, the money he leaves my stepmother could not buy a ticket into heaven. Even though I am powerless to alter this scenario, I think she did learn to love my dad despite the money, really.

The debt my dad leaves me may not be paid for in his tears. Fortunately, he had friends who looked out for his better interest at such times. Still, he pays me back in the lessons he learned in his life that seems so foreign to me still. This resonates in the realization that you do not touch flowers, but rather it is a lesson to appreciate them from afar and I think this may be the lesson that he taught me.

I regret the tears I made him cry, still he does not forsake me for this as I did not falter a tear later in this tantalizing scenario. At such times, Sierra's desert in the ocean seems so dry and the oceans part for a man so great. Mimi served him his favorite vichyssoise soup and did not ask for anything in return. His three sisters remind him like in death, like in life that he is still loved beyond the toils of life, that should plunder him in dismay after the fact that he is a Jew, and Hitler died as such. Diamonds dispel this notion and he leaves me a gold cufflink with sapphires that is engraved his initials as a step backward, even though he feels free to swim in the ocean at such times too. Time attests that there is more still and his natural cycle makes me ponder if our paths will cross again, as I do not know. Still, I will not recognize him later, I think.

Somewhere, he flaunts the elegance of the matter like a pink lion at a cabaret show in Paris and leaves behind to one of the black boys a pink Volkswagen Rabbit, in which someone drives on the freeways of LA. Otherwise, Ferocious coaches Dr. Emory on how my dad may be a better dad even though there is not much room for shame in this scenario. My dad does find time to throw with me the K2 Jr. football in the backyard after school. His coffee otherwise on the way to school is shear vanity for such a man, I think. But, I think he would rather entertain for presidents with a glass of champagne in hand, and this denotes that he has lived a good life. You have to love Paris!

Doctor, Doctor and the Rebellious Jew

The body of Christ was reborn in this form. Jesus is a dark entity on the third day, but left Africa so that no one might see his tears. Three persons represent the Father, Son, and Holy Ghost. They are my dad, Steve Shiffman, and Xander. Within a triangle hovering above the savannah of Africa; a tear is isolated in the sky and will not land. Otherwise, my friend Will is Christ and represents the fourth dimension. I am the Holy Ghost and escape the fate of the Jews, with three points in time. I foresee God rising from the ground and will not leave until the interjection occurs. It is a sort of hell I can live with, but I do not know he is my father until we meet. My dad may be a Jew, but I detest that I am not. Who is a Jew is the question at hand? Will breaks through to the other side and gains a respect like a tear drop isolated in the sky. A gorilla in the Congo exists in the outer reaches of a pentagon and I will not allow it to land.

When Eve tempts Adam to pick the apple from the tree of knowledge, I am hidden from view. I am my own creation like one of the animals that remain. God recognizes this scenario as I need not ask for his approval as I rise into the sky. Satan represents an apple tree without a soul. Adam and Eve leave the garden to tread where God may lay waste to it in this scenario. A bear remains for those who must believe and is a metaphor for a soul that is lost in the process. Lily tempts Mt. Fuji to pick a calla lily which does not belong to her. As Satan enters the ocean, Mt. Fuji is forgiven as a man who does not understand why many men must depart from Africa too. Kyle plays Trivial Pursuit with God as the Jews will be judged by God too. He asks that those who are not welcome to leave through the door in the back. South Africa revolves from the play at hand. Those dark entities that leave Africa are forgiven like God who does not know why the wind blows?

What is a Jew? I ask this question to locate the redemption they seek and the wind does cry Mary from four different directions. Also, Bob Dylan sings that the answer is blowing in the wind. The trinity asks who are you and religion should be obsolete by now, I think. Will is Christ and I am not. The Jews cross the path of the devil and are freed so that his tear will not land. The devil may be like a Jew too. My father is exonerated in the process.

"Doctor, doctor and the rebellious Jew" continued:

Though I am not a Jew, I will pretend to be one for now. The cow on the hill is my stepmother, and I think the lines crossed at some schemozzle where her relationship with my dad is incestuous. I also think that I am a sane person in an insane world, but I go along with the accusations so to draw the least amount of attention to myself. I have my friends and my family and the rest of my life is a juggling act. The black man at the hospital is gay and I think this is like standing in front of a wall and not being able to turn around. Really, the hospitals in which I have stayed are not bad and I would compare them to a Holiday Inn maybe. Still, the doctor out in California, not Dr. Emory, was a pervert, I must say. I watched some movie there called *Willow*, and this is not far from my mindset either. I am worried for my sister Nicole as she is out of range for my protection, though I can see her every move. She is not put here on earth for the sake of life, but exists otherwise and it does not seem to matter. I ask, cautiously, if she just put a mint in her mouth? And, she would sense my psychotic tone and not bravado, but replies "no" as I do not want to hear other. I am really scared as I know it is the devil's and not mine. Mints might seem like a guilty pleasure to some, but to me it is a decision, which I would rather her not. "Look at me, look at me!" I would say, "I am a Jew! Look at me."

The doctor asks me questions like "How do you feel?" but deeper and I touch myself and think this is weird. Meanwhile, I have friends here and Marvin walks on walls as though a child of the moon. While in the garden enclosed on all sides within the hospital, I call out, "Nicole is here," but it is soundproof and I think no one can hear me. I think Nicole has an odd resemblance to Marvin, the cool black kid and I wonder if he is not somehow related to Nicole? Eventually, I would forfeit my shoes, as it is not very Christian like, I think.

Instead, I tie National Geographics to the bottom of my feet with shoelaces and someone must have though this to be kind of odd? I swallow the "ruby" pearl before I leave and fight off a nuclear disaster and my stepmother would not know that I am not only acting crazy, but judging by the four workers it takes to tie me to the mobile bed and ship me on a plane back to Georgia, I am crazy! The first sign of this illness is when in seventh grade I felt up a girl in a movie theater. Though I did not want to harm her, this was not normal behavior. Otherwise, to diagnose the sanity I play in the insanity of others, one must shed light on my parents' divorce at age nine or ten; and though I have denied this in the past, I had some sort of schizophrenia ever since.

My parents gave me enough tools then that I may reclaim my sanity now, otherwise, you might simply call me "other." Before leaving California, I swore I could see Dr. Martelli's face on the TV screen as though he were a lounge singer and performing for an array of lizards who want to cool off and get out of the hot sun. Mike's friends all look alike and the Jewish mafia would not leave me alone even though I pleaded with them, "But I come from a really nice family!" The sanest element of this diagnosis in which according to Dr. Martelli, I am psychotic, is that I would rather claim American/Italian lineage, rather than my bloodline that is sort of English on my dad's side and Russian/Polish Jewish on my mom's side.

I am fighting the whole world at such a time when leaving the hospital in California and no longer want to leave. The fond memory of being with my grandfather outside the wax museum in London seems useful at such times. Girls in bikinis mock me, and the Jewish kid inside me in which I do not know, at such times. You would not know that he considers his mom a full-fledged Christian and I was baptized in the Episcopalian church as well. I would not conspire or make a deal thereafter and Mike promised he would let me go in the end. I think, then, I will meet his son, Jim Morrison, and he may well be the lizard king.

"A picture of hell..."

The palm trees at the beach club have no coconuts. The pools have children that scream like sirens of yesterdays that will never meet the horizon, as it is too far away. The emaciated stewardess lies in the sun chewing her Wrigley's double mint gum as though a shark biting more than its share from an ocean that will exclaim God is dead, at such times. Paris Hilton had just committed suicide and a man reads US magazine and walks to the restroom, then leans at the bar with a black tight bathing suit and he shows his package without any modesty. And, Tom Cruise has proclaimed he is gay. There is an orange juice vending machine that all the kids flock to and it tastes more like Hi-C, which the kids like better anyway.

The kids' moms hide Ritalin in their tuna fish sandwiches, but they still refuse to eat it and hot dogs are more to their liking. The lounge singer leaves the penthouse of an older lady with whom he shared the night. And he, a gigolo, thoroughly enjoyed the experience and is singing a medley slightly overheard by me, as he passes? Something about the red-headed kid says he needs more sun block, but refuses his mom, saying it smells funny. The crows are fighting over the Ritalin in the kids' uneaten tuna fish sandwiches. My dad shows up and I actually think he is "cool" compared to everyone else in this place. I sit like a couch potato in New York watching CNN only to arrive in paradise and sit some more, and the flowers mock the girls who dream of someday being a life guard here. Fortunately, for my sisters, they did not and married well.

The boys of summer, on the other hand, grow up to be gigolos like their fathers until I realize bingo that night was really a Klu Klux Klan convention. The little boy with blond hair is crying hysterically that he may not have soda as it is past eight o'clock in the evening. He may well be a stockbroker someday? I am, meanwhile, listening to The Who's *Meaty, Beaty, Big and Bouncy* and a track *The Kids are Alright*, is playing on my walkman, and I hope for a better tomorrow. (Just kidding that the kids will grow up to be gigolos like their father.) But, the notion is like playing ACDC's *Back in Black* and the French girl at the grill asks if she could have escargot? Anne Bancroft makes an appearance at the beach club and she still smokes a lot! And the kids cry more, thinking Starbursts are a good substitute for carrot and celery sticks. In the corner, Conor plays with his Gameboy and acts like a well-adjusted protégé for other kids to follow. My father calls him a chip off the old block like he use to say to me. Somewhere, someone throws, uneaten McDonald's French fries in the dump and they would become petrified relics of a past I do not hold anymore.

"Inertia"

My mom sits at the pool in West Hollywood and never meets my dad there, as it is my destiny that I was never born then and there. My sister Nancy is born to another father who is Mike, and works as a waitress in a café in Connecticut. Nicole would become a dancer in one of Prince's videos. My best friend Will and I never meet and he works as a dance instructor at a summer retreat in upstate New York. (He married the first girl who felt sorry for him.) As for my dad, he inherited a lot of money and made a lot more on his own, playing in the stock market. He lives in a lavish home in Montauk, Long Island, and never married again, but had a girl, besides his son Walker, there prior. He holds season tickets to the Jets, of which he is an avid fan.

Doctor, doctor, continued:

I ask my doctor, "How do you kill a bean?" and ask this solemnly as I really can't figure out how something tangible like a bean may become nothingness? It is more important that I take my medicine now and I respond only as I do not like this.

Really, he never actually asks me "How are you feeling?" and otherwise my friends from Sweden tell me I should get a second opinion. Still, I feel trapped and stopped fighting the doctor long ago. What is more important to him is that I act normal and it does not matter if I feel normal? The whole point about medicine is to balance out that which is a chemical imbalance in your brain.

My argument, on the other hand, is that I always am aware of what I am doing whether right or wrong? Insanity is a lot like table tennis, always fighting what seems outside, which is yourself. I will claim at such times, that I am not bothered by this. What is more important to me is that one does not interfere with what is on the outside, that which I call my business. As you apologize later for penetrating this reality, I will tell you I will not forgive you as I too am at a loss and am not able to heal from such acts. I might pity the fool who tries to help me at such times. I appreciate good people and that is all.

The number games I play in my mind is my business and not yours and from my point of view, it makes a lot of sense. In fact, it would not have happened as such if not for you, and I do not think this is a good thing or a bad thing either. What is more important to me is that you do not move in the still life that which is my life.

"We are from after the dinosaurs and before the stars," I tell anyone who wants to ask, but usually I am shunned as though not to care anyway. Sanity may be the ability to recognize when someone harms you and act in such a way that is forgiving so that it makes you stronger, in case it happens again. For me, I must admit, there is little of this and I usually tend to hide my eyes while looking at the pretty flowers and do not even know why not?

Sanity is the ability to recognize what is good and bad, and emulate that which appeals to you? I, on the other hand, do not bother to see anything and assumes God will judge them in the end, anyway? I may have come from darkness, but I like the world God provides and do not plan to leave anytime soon. I live a life that most could only dream of, but still I want more. I do not know why, and my mom would claim this is a sign of being a character flaw, that I am shallow in nature. She may not like me, but is usually thoroughly entertained by the book she is reading. I do not know what it would be like to create your own destiny, but there may be some of this here as well.

In my life, I have learned two things about God. His favorite kind of pizza is pepperoni and, on rainy days, he will invite you inside too play a game of pool, which he enjoys thoroughly. You should know that he loves my sister Nancy immensely, but hardly notices my other sister, Nicole, and says she seems sort of introverted. When he kicked Adam and Eve out of the Garden of Eden, he was just playing, but thought it would be a good lesson for them anyway. When I drove a taxicab in NYC, his friends were looking out for my better interest, just the same. Someday, he will return to the world, which is you and me, and maybe thereafter call himself Jesus?

Jesus is his son who died on a cross for our sins. But, I think he will eventually forgive those who seek it, in the end. Ferocious waits in line at the Tower Records just to get the new Maroon Five CD, which is his favorite band, I think. It is important to note that in the web of life, though man is his creation, this does not make man, God as well. Also, remember to be nice to Mimi as she is like you and me, but is special and I will not say why anyway. Will likes raspberry ice cream as does God, and Will is a friend too. Will and I once hid marijuana in the closet where we stayed in "the cabin" of Musgrove Plantation, and God does not know this. As for my mom, he does not know her, but she sleeps on clouds too far to reach anyway. So, Dr. Martelli, what was it you wanted to ask me if I am crazy? God writes me from time to time, in between the lines of my father's pen. But, I do not consider this crazy, really.

"Positively Fourth Street": (Reliving the Holocaust)

The Jews are reborn at a time while meanwhile others must die too. For those who are an ingrown toe nail, of time, time will seem like a punishment and Bob Dylan sings to those who want to explore the outer fringes of that which is this time. The holocaust will still heal over and with this re-birth, there will be no memory of it thereafter. Those outside of Africa are united as one. Bob Dylan's lyrics are no longer obsolete and people like Peter, Paul and Mary, are present too. All is one and one is all and the poetic champions compose outward forever. The children may keep a secret and they play and play.

"The Yellow Whale"

"We all live in the yellow submarine," and propels the life inward, outward, where children sit on sandy beaches off the coast of places such as England and Ireland, is now one. Somewhere here in the northern light, lies a special garden where the paradise lost is reborn. Children's excrement is forgiven as such in the ocean of a once tear, which is dissolved there as no longer. Like the queen's jewels, it is sacrificed here as well, for the greater good for who are present. A whale carries the children on a ride, which they will free as though Stew, the race horse, who once could not find the sky. The ocean remains a playground where it, the whale, swims in it forever. God remains inside at such times and plays pool, calculatingly hitting the eight ball into the corner pocket. Musgrove is a playground for his friends and the Garden of Eden is re-born; that is like the Jews who died so long ago. Before the show begins, the children will make a journey inside this whale which is harnessed by twenty-four elephants. The ship leaves from Saint Simon's Island, Georgia, and arrives at a later date off the coast of West Africa.

"Five Gay Indians" and Gandhi

One: The Bonfire of the Vanities: "Bite off more than you can chew!"

The *The Bonfire of the Vanities* is a book written, and survives the transition as though sand composed to make the pyramids in Egypt. The pharaohs' vision of eternal plays, plays out here and Nancy flies in the sky so that the rain will return here. Mimi's sister returned here just once to collect the salt left here in a tear that remained. She turned the light off after leaving and said her name is Siaom, which is an acronym for "sand is afraid of me." This to say that each grain of sand has a half-life that is less than her. Mimi will forgive me for stroking her hair, which was not cockroach's quest for eternal life and her past is mine as well. The ocean divides and we become one, once again as though to bite off more than you can chew becomes better now that sin is obsolete. And the whale is free like the sun it may have stood for, and Chinamen walk with Steve to distant lands, and we are one too. I am not a Jew I am not a Jew, but Steve is adopted as such as a diamond in the rough that cannot escape darkness like Satan.

Two: Paradise Lost

Milton's *Paradise Lost* may not be pertinent anymore; now that sin is a passing that does not know which way the wind blows. Libya is Xander's paradise and a large Rastafarian society exists here, and Qaddafi becomes subject to their way of life. He is now a pig farmer which is a lowly pursuit which does not entail any dead animals in the end. Otherwise, when the animals die, they create a material that is used in the production of clothes. The desert is sometimes cold at night. Lions no longer shed others as scapegoats in the sacrifice they once administered. A popular dish with their remains is a sort of pig skin snack food as well, though some decline consumption due to religious dogma. American football becomes acclimated to this new land and Rastafarians find it a fun passing of time. To say cannabis is déjà vu is true as it grows in certain outreaches of Libya and it is no longer *Paradise Lost.* They foster "sweats" like native brethren to the land they never knew either, but was acquainted to it thereafter, though. They will sit in the desert of Libya and meditate in vented domiciles made from camel hide and enter it here through an eye of a pin.. The fired rocks burn sweet scents of rosemary, and is really a way of life.Sage is also burned to ward off those unwelcome, and may maintain a wisdom that is also God. If God is a vegetarian than I am one too.

Three: "Harry Potter's Secret"

The fire, a goblet in Tunisia is put out and reborn here. The secret is that fire without impurities like a carrot in the wind, will not cause pain here when in its own element, though. Rather, it becomes a vestibule to those who want to experience it thereafter like a volcano. The sense of fire is here and in its own element so pure does not cause any harm and vegetarians without the sin of animals might adhere to this alternative lifestyle.

"Conor may be transcendent of 'love,' itself? He burns forever for a love he never knew, which is the next best thing. He sits in Will's Casino and Bar drinking fine brandy and enjoying mesmerizing cigars as he likes roulette, and finds the number 24 does well.

Four: "Satanic Verses: Algeria"

Satan left a brother in this dark land. There is a mystery here as we have never met too! When dark forces from abroad reach a tipping point then something bad happens on the outside, though this blessed land is immune, and he is just a reminder of such forces on the outside, do exist. He is the lesser of two evils, but chants his brother's song in a sort of coma zoo, and his drum is respected as something good that exists.

Five: "The Unbearable Lightness of Being"

It is my dad's favorite book in his favorite city, Casablanca in Morocco. There is no doubting that my dad was alive, but he had three sons who spread him out sort of thin as well. He, an African Jew, may have escaped the holocaust, but died like the stature of a lion which he was. The plane flew him away to America, and I remained somewhere safe as well. He visited his childhood home in Greenwich, Connecticut if only to speak briefly with his mother whom he loved dearly. My dad lived a different kind of life, like this book possessed, but you can't say that he was not here either.

Doctor , Doctor and the Rebellious Jew

Steve Shiffman should sneak through the cracks and proclaim his innocence as though it does not matter that it should not matter that my sister should die for his sin. Girls find Xander attractive like an Adonis, but he is more of a Jim Morrison than a Kurt Cobain. Lastly, my dad showed up for the show's zenith, where his son is killed to spare his own life. Elizabeth appears again to proclaim the offering of her son so as to maybe receive retribution against all her flaws. Conor does not have a voice and, therefore, his fate is written in stone, whether it be a good or a bad fate. The play should forgo in the office of Dr. Emory where I am treated for something in regard to one of the above. Their solicitous voice will speak through me to determine which one is the real Jew, if any at all? Their identity is spoken through the viper in this stolen light.

I would not consider myself a Jew, unless it were medicine for the blind? It is true, though, I believe that some people find it therapeutic to overcome their hate. Steve thinks he may alter his destiny and I offer him a hug and he declines, as he is well aware of his destiny. He rambles around the hospital muttering things such as "psychosis is dangerous." I still do not know what he meant. Then, all of a sudden, he comes through his crazy front and smiles at me saying, "I get out tomorrow."

Next, Xander is an androgynous male, though shows a bit of his mother in his composure. He would rather not recognize this side and takes the side of the father and, if he wanted, Jews find him attractive. Unlike myself, of whom I am not a good liar, they would accept him as their own. My dad is a brat from a privileged upbringing in Connecticut. Though much like a caveman in reality, he is use to getting what he wants and occasionally uses me as a scapegoat to meet such ends. I do not think he really means harm.

It is curious that Elizabeth is still in the picture and looks into her emerald ring and now truly believes she is a Jew too. Conor is on his own and though his friend might never believe it, he is a prime target as a sacrificial lamb in a volcano that in Chile has his name on it. This may be a joke if not that Will is inside him without the immaculate part, without the history of suffering and struggle that Will would endure for others.

Will embodies the red of a tiger and is late for his own emancipation of the color entirely, I think. And, I suppose Conor just a blank page that must go somewhere. They think it is an honor and would find a fitting life in the contours of the fire that would absorb him. Otherwise, this information is confidential and may seem outdated as well for Conor at least. To this end, it is uncertain and the Japanese without access to him, have a role in the endeavor, and maybe they should look away as though it is his fate possibly. The offering would free Elizabeth and, actually, Conor may suffer a worse fate if not. Conor is totally unaware of the imposition and plays his Gameboy. I must give him credit for being strong enough to stand like a man against such a fate as such a young boy. Besides being born with Will inside him like a carrot that he will digest is a question; he is otherwise innocent?

The better of two, Will may just be a carrot in the wind, yet it is not possible to deny his existence and bequest him in his own fire like the other would hope. Should someone become an incestuous fire, it would redeem Will, though not innocent or guilty, not to have to toil with such a situation. It is an objective that exposes different lights of the dove as not pure and rather not heavenly compared to his long struggle in which all the Jews are witness and makes a long legal bout, not worth very much in the end. His role, which merits respect among the Jews, is shrugged off as his destiny and is one that he had to fight for. He is no longer playing the game, but pretends to anyway. If there is some delusion, making Will into a bad person, it is not Will. He never thinks to scapegoat any individual and, though he is recognized by God, he never feared hell either. His strength is through forgiveness; he need not shed a tear on the past and the ghosts are long gone.

I suppose there is a sort of hate that is rightly his as his past is not gone, yet he still manages to be objective. Even against the scorn he endeared, walking from Mercury to somewhere else as the Jews through their native son, the sun, beat down on the skin on his back and he knows and remembers the pain he endured in his struggle. If he were the first Protestant and I suppose maybe I was the first Catholic, we would still manage to be friends? Furthermore, he knows and understands God's love better than anyone I know. Though, God is untouchable. Will is obviously a favorite and may have the opportunity to continue the relationship, which is unusual, when it comes to the physical world. In respect to God, I think he is all spiritual. Maybe, it is hope for others too, who do not think they may cross over the barrier that Will may prove false and provide such hope. Will need not respect or loathe the Jews, as he is in his own element and otherwise forgiveness is much better than hate.

"Doctor, doctor," Steve is like Jack Nicholson in *One Flew Over the Cookoo's Nest* and he is aware of his fate to escape at the last minute and I warn him not to go as there is nothing there. Hey, Will, he thinks in Dr. Emory's office, I want to join you as you made it to heaven. But, I am here, and not stronger than them. Steve is a boxer in the ring absolved by his own sweat. I call for him and say I love you Steve like forgiveness and security, but he is freaked out by some of the nurses and wants to run away. They just want to take my brain, he thinks. Earlier, in the ward, Steve tries to pretend he is a bird, and thinks it might prevent the nurses from doing something, maybe to feel sorry for him. Dr. Emory asks what he meant by it and he simply says, "I want to get out of here!" It is not his insanity, but rather convincing them he is incurable.

If Steve were a Jew, he does not seem vulnerable and I think church would be a good thing if he gets out. Around the other doctors, Steve is a perfect gentleman and acts to charm the other two, who are both female, and she says that we have done all we can for you and he gets out like that. Steve has a persona like he is going out to fight dinosaurs and probably will accept that world as his fate as he does not want to come back here, as though everyone wants to harm him. If someone in the real world approaches him along the way, he will fiercely push the homeless guy against the wall. He is that destitute. Steve is still on the defensive, but his mind provokes a world that is not there, whether sane or insane. It seems Steve is not a Jew, but he continues to walk in the spirit of previous cavemen and does not understand when a girl touches his head and says he is cute. He will look at her like a dinosaur about to eat him and there is no way to penetrate his darkness, as it is natural and I was the only hope to bring him out onto the other side. He does not see the Indians in his head either and he relives the past with no end. Should he go to church and request a meal, they would feed him open heartedly as he isn't trying to harm anyone, and though not a Jew, isolated as such. He seems to be the counterpart of a female who has a soft butt like a cushion. He is all male and quite an oddity to see someone, a man, yet still in the land of the lost. I guess the Jews nourished him for all time and when it was time for them to go, left him behind as to determine he is not one of them. If my sister did die for his sin, that makes him a free man and this is all he wanted, maybe. Picking a purple flower, he walks away anyway, and eventually he will realize he is no longer somewhere during the dinosaur age and as he still has his brain in tact; may survive after all. It is good trade-off and my sister accepts her new life readily.

Steve may still hear the dinosaurs and talks to himself in his new sports car, which he buys with an inheritance of an uncle who dies rather timely. And, he mumbles to himself the way someone who has been isolated like an animal frozen in time in the Arctic would only know. The first thing I will do is find a prostitute, he thinks. Actually, retracing his past, he may think Mary Magdalene as his mother and oddly recounts back to his origin which is rare and stays away from ones who reminds him of what his mother would look like if he could see her. He picks up a girl in South Beach and talks to her the way cavemen confess their sins, and she tells him her name is Maggie. He can tell she is Irish and likes that as he likes Irish girls and says, "Maggie, you wouldn't believe where I have been," and they drive to the nearest motel and make love like there is no tomorrow.

Xander might be my brother if there was any part of the mother in me as there may not be much? I still hold an allegiance to my spiritual mother Mimi, but we should never touch either. Her sister represents that I am related to God in the distant past. The Jews would rather consider him as their own, though, they, like I, have a completely different bloodline. Still, he is an attractive male and they would approach him as though to steal his "manliness" as their own. They consider it charity, as he is destined to end up at the devil's doorstep, eventually, they think. The Jews were a vain sect and consider people sometimes like pets and Xander would be a lion in such a case and high on the totem pole to mix blood in their own. I suppose the Jews are also opportunistic, in this way. I think I am sometimes mistaken for

Xander in such cases as, however, I am not available. Meanwhile, Xander is usually in a pack of other males in order to defend against the other. I feel sorry for him, still, as girls would like to get a piece of him and put him on a pedestal. He is use to this though as he seeks someone better than himself, which in his world is negated and he flips through a magazine at the library, curious about what it would be like to be with such a woman. The rocky road behind might scare off the deer and be a warning for the type of women who should taste a forbidden fruit. When someone of the children of doom should enter her, she will feel a pain like no other. The girls tease such a woman, as they know that their worlds should not cross.

My dad checks into hospitals for sport, but actually it is really just a short visit to his deranged son. He knows he has lived a blessed existence and tempts a doctor to try figure out what is wrong with him and, when the deal is made, he would rather blame what he feels on me. Really, the hospitals are more often with a fancy concierge, who bring his continental breakfast up, with his coffee and is rather refreshed like this. He does not really understand why he needs me and this is his illness. I remember when our paths crossed and he does not, still, he would over time become this step, so to speak, and then become my father and bring me out of the world of darkness.

Though, it was certainly my step and I am responsible as such, it was no sin like the other in Xander's case. Unlike Xander, my dad is like a horse that has only tasted wine. But, this is not my dad and the fire bequest is proof. My dad checked in a hospital for an ailment like gallbladder problems and I never saw him again. So, this person may well be like any other person you meet and his charm just a ploy to escape the fate given to him. He stares you down like a lion looking for dinner and he may not remember his childhood at all. He is an African Jew which sort makes him an individual among the other Jews, to say the least. Having not tasted blood, this person, who was my father, has a natural cycle and is revered somewhere like in China, as "The Last Emperor" I think. It was a deal made in heaven and, consequently, he has lived the life of twenty men and likewise dies just the same. However, his inner child, in which no one has ever confronted, escaped and therefore it is like a lion without the threat of danger. He rather finds in his time to be a predator to those who are un-expecting. I am a reminder of the life he once lived and therefore a third existence, and I guess he does not like me very much, but does not know why as he is safe in his own world.

There is no question that Elizabeth has lived a sinful existence and angels smell her out and, in return, she makes them well aware that it is true. On the other hand, she tends to my father like a good shepherd, but does not know that he is long gone and only a shadow in the dark remains, and she, an easy meal, though his wife. As a person, she "may" have hated Jews and I do not know this, and she has become someone who has changed and now wishes to be a Jew herself. It is an odd transformation, which I do not really understand. She pretends as if my father is there anyway and they have two children, which is actually even more of a lonely existence? She knew that she may have made some ethical mistakes, by marrying my father, but is too far gone to go back.

Rather, now the opportunity to free herself from her sins did not work in the case of Vaughan and Conor, and being a Jew would be desirable to her in a strange way. This does not make her not a Catholic, it just shows her vulnerability and I rather not watch as she has denied herself of love. She does not know where her fate will lead. I feel helpless, of course, as she arrives and I give her a kiss on the cheek, though it will not help her fight materialism though and her problems seem apparent to friends who may not do anything either. Others in the church have suffered real hardships and the suffering would heal naturally most of the time, but Elizabeth has created a world of hardships for herself and at the expense of others. I do not know how other Catholics look at her as a result. They might kiss her on the cheek and do nothing as well.

Conor is the most innocent. He has the capacity to keep a secret even when not told to. His fate seems bleak even though it embodies the best of intentions in the world. Barbara Streisand, who I do not know personally, visits Mille Fleurs, which is their house in Georgetown they named as such. I do not know why either, but she arrives at the house and reaches down to Conor, a young boy, which is neither good or bad, and gives him a hug and this may only be a blessing. Conor lives a protected, but normal life. The life he is given and he will follow as his destiny regardless of what it is probably is a better life unsaid, as it is not what it seems really, in one way or another. He does not know a father I knew, but my dad still finds the time to play with him and proves he is not entirely gone, my dad or Conor. My stepmother really loves Conor dearly, the way she only knows to and I guess he is a gift, though he is not accessible to "Christian Goodness," as he is sheltered and in their family of four, looks at outside forces as mostly bad. In contrast, I was born out of my own resources and inhibitions, and will be born in death as well, if I was ever here? God is still accessible to me, though.

"Doctor, doctor?" Steve may not address the doctor as such.

"Yes, Steve, what is the matter?" he replies but only fictitious in truth.

"Nothing is the matter, everything is great! I met a girl who likes me for who I am and plus we have great sex!" Steve implodes.

"Why is that so important to you?" the doctor continues. "You know, she really likes me, we might really get married, the whole shebang. Do you believe that? Me, with a beautiful woman. I am over forty and the only women I have ever known have been prostitutes. She is real wholesome, full woman and finds me incredibly interesting, and I know it is not the money as I do not have much, but she has money anyway!" Steve is enamored by the moment too.

"Suppose she finds out that you have a mental illness?" the doctor projects in what seems sort of cruel.

"What does it matter, she is in love with me and I am too with her. I could never imagined this happening; I think I will take up golf," Steve says, while ignoring the doctor's previous line of questioning.

"Well, you have been fully diagnosed and you are mostly bald, so I suppose you are a lucky man. Will you have kids?"

Again Steve ignores the inquiry, as though taking a small jab in the boxing ring.

"No kids, don't even say that, there may be no kids. Imagine those little people looking up to me saying feed me and I want this and besides I had a rocky childhood and would not wish it on anyone," Steve says most resolutely.

"How old is she?" The doctor says as though that is important.

"Oh, she is just two years older than me and with no kids either. It is perfect!" Steve is still energized in the moment.

"I just thought kids were in the picture?" the doctor infers as though an annoying fly too.

"No, no kids, I can't stand being subservient to a lesser and, anyway, we will take luxurious vacations to Europe, read books late in the evening, everything I would not afford myself as a bachelor," Steve envisions and this does not seem like weakness either.

"Have you told your mother?" the doctor inquires as this question.

"Actually, as far as I know she is dead. I ran away from home when I was sixteen and really never looked back. I use to get in lots of fights with other kids and my parents were austere in punishing me, like locking me into my room. I thought it was cruel, like they did not care," Steve responds as though doing a psychiatric evaluation, which he hardly notices either.

"You mean, they punished you sometimes, and you did not know why?" The doctor seems somewhat sympathetic now.

"Yes, it was that sort of household. If I didn't finish my milk, I was punished, if I listened to the radio in the basement instead of doing my homework, I was punished." Steve is cautious not to reveal too much.

"So, you have undergone a transformation, a metamorphosis if you will?" The doctor acts intrinsically ephemeral.

"Yes, and God is a large part of it," Steve concedes the notion, as though finally a question he may answer.

"Yes, I believe it to be," Doctor Emory mocks divinity while showing some compassion.

"Thank you for listening to me, I really appreciate it!" Steve closes the dialogue like a prayer.

Steve goes to meet his future wife, he thinks, and in a sort of manic frenzy, then arrives at her door. It is open, but he knocks anyway.

"Dear," she says, "would you like some guacamole I made?" and he looks at her deeply in the eyes and gives her a kiss like she is everything. A week passes and she asks him about his family. Steve tells her that his father was Jewish and his mother Irish Catholic. The modern woman must know when the relationship will go no further. He brings up the idea of getting a dog and she shrugs, knowing it will never happen. She just does not want him to know yet that she is not interested and tells him so anyway.

He asks, "You are not interested in getting a dog?" and she replies, "not, the relationship." Steve finds solace, leaving through the same door, thinking it seemed too much like a dream. Anyway, he is use to this and finds a job as a non-socialized member of society and that is it.

Xander arrives at Dr. Martelli's's door having thrown a stone through a store window, while drunk and high. He and his friends ran off and oddly he is the only one caught. Xander is usually the lucky one and the other friends know this and so when the judge fines him five hundred dollars and counseling, he feels in a weird place that he did not know before or even how to confront. The other guys he hangs out with wait in Dr. Martelli's lobby downstairs and wonder what fate this will lead to, to the group as a whole, as they always do things together and are rarely isolated from the others.

"So, what is this problem?" Dr. Martelli asks.

"Okay, we are walking down the street and a girl gives me the eye, you know, and so we follow her, me and the boys. She says something like go to hell and tells a traffic cop that we are harassing her anyway, and she lectures us for a while and says basically to go somewhere where we are not a bother and so this leads to throwing the stone through the glass window." Xander is intelligent and may be quite coherent even if high, but is a male and has to be stronger than the opposite sex. "It seems girls only like me for sex and I am tired of it and that is not all, older women would rather treat me for dinner and bring me back to their apartment where we have sex and that is a problem too as my buddies feel alienated."

"So, what do you think of women?" Doctor Martelli asks point blank.

"I do not know what I think. I am not doing anything to harm them, still they try to come up to me anyway and I feel violated," Xander replies earnestly.

"What is your relationship with your mom?" The doctor furthers the line of inquiry.

"It is great, she never tells me I can't go out and prepares a meal in the fridge, when I get home." He implies that things are good there.

"How about your father?" The doctor asks to assume a line of balanced inquiry.

Xander replies, "He is great too, and he took my brother and me to Venezuela last Christmas."

"So, you are saying women find you attractive, but not the kind you like?" The doctor seems mostly benevolent in his line of questioning.

"I suppose so, I never really met one that really cares, and I can tell the ones looking for a one-night stand. It was fun the first one or two times, but now I feel violated. I don't know, I have my world and they have theirs, yet still the paths cross and then what ever happens, happens, and I go home with a bad taste in my mouth. I would rather go out with my buddies and this is like taboo among girls, whatever that is and so can you help me find the right girl?" Xander pleads as though the door he enters is not his to enter anymore in this perplexing dynamic.

"I do not know how to help you there, but you might try going to church or talk to girls who seem shy as they are usually the nice ones." Doctor Martelli envisions something else.

"Well, sometimes people look up to me because I am attractive to women, so I suppose I use women as well," Xander admits.

"That is decisive, cognitive thought, very good! You need to not think of only yourself and you will find someone who likes you for who you are." Doctor Martelli is off-balanced and seems slightly smug.

"So, women may not know the real me and I have to open up so that they may see me for who I really am?" Xander speaks as though at a crossroads too.

"Why don't you take a class at the community college. Women seeking careers tend to be more mature and searching for a soul mate." Doctor Martelli is inventive with such a response.

"That's right, soul mate and I can't hang out with the guys forever, yea, but we are tight and they will have to be in the wedding." Xander is slightly reticent.

"It is not like you have to wait for the sun to fall from the sky. There are opportunities here. Anyway, I will tell the judge you are fit to be in society and your father should really tell you this, but grow up, as. excuses only go so far." Doctor Martelli seems to exceed the notion.

My father enters Dr. Kraus's office with his entourage, which includes Elizabeth and their son Conor. Dr. Kraus says to sit down and asks, "What seems to be the problem?"

My dad then tells him that my son, a different son, "Brett," will not go on the trip to Hawaii, "and so I told him that I wanted him there with the family and he responds 'no,' and he will not listen to me."

"Anyway, the problem is that he decides to go somewhere and then changes his mind?" Doctor Kraus vaguely sums up…

My dad continues, "We just want him to be with us and so I told him I was going to talk with you."

"You feel sort of powerless that one of your sons, 'Brett,' who is way past adulthood now and how many sons do you have?" Doctor Kraus pauses his line of questioning slightly.

My dad responds that he has three sons from three marriages, but that his two sisters do not act like this.

So Doctor Kraus continues, "Maybe Brett is not telling you something. Maybe he has moved on and would rather not be a problem? Anyway, I can tell you are upset, but Brett is perfectly healthy and he takes his medicine, should there ever be a problem? I heard what you said on the phone. You were worried the medicine was not doing the job, but I am sure something else is wrong. If it were Brett like you say, he would not go along with some ten years of therapy and he takes his medicine like clockwork."

"I just think it is wrong for me to have to pay all this money and he does not appreciate it at all," my dad says, as though a sane person in an insane world. My dad might be my mother at such times. (Elizabeth closes in prayer, "We are always there if you needed us.")

My dad is an African Jew yet he is not God. He used God's sperm and conceived me through my tail, which is black, and severed once from me as my mom was once immaculately connected to me as though a cow on a hill. She bears me as such, and bears me too so that all that is left of our parting is the umbilical cord. Once connected to her, and twice departed, I am free only to be a slave again. My dad was a Jew who took the first step for me and I am exonerated from Africa as though to never be there. I am innocent in the eyes of God and the apple picked is someone else's crime entirely. In this sense my mother is her own creator, but she is friend to man so that God may do the rest. She may ponder a natural sin and, primal as her own, and she will inherit the color green which is envy to hide her jealous disposition at least and she will not stand naked in front of the sins of others. She holds onto primal sin like a dog does a bone, and may sympathize with the animal's disposition. It may be a sin that is not hers, but still God may not forgive it as it surfaces after the fact and transcends the realm of four corners to that which is Satan and this is much too close to home; a decision is made that to which is not God.

Even the most wicked of witches knows not to oppose the word of God. My mom is unique as she actually envies the absorption of the sin, but rather reads a book instead. It is unusual for the snake to be jealous of a sin, but she may retire soon on her own cloud, and this is much better than the alternative. The deal is made in heaven with God, as she may not remain on this land that is flat like God's feet. The horse's hoofs fear her primal disposition and her abuse makes her blush that she denotes that much respect. Too close to home for those who do not believe in God, and this is essentially a warning to Jews of the crime and my mom is not a Jew, but free to create her own world, not mine but still it is an honor as such. Culturally, she may be a second-generation Jew, and she ponders their culture as something interesting, like her mother a pointed girl who is once removed but a point of reference, which like Jews, she finds interesting.

Really, it is my dad who is an African Jew, something different; he lives in his own realm like a lion in a C.S. Lewis novel. He may leave in his own time, but feels slightly at a loss as it is really not his own decision, yet he leaves the domain without the hesitation to ask why. He may be Hitler's alter ego and, for those who keep faith, will join as one with other Jews in heaven, and he feels sorry for himself only once and I think this is good. God warns that one should not pick the fruit from the Tree of Knowledge. Those blood that bleeds through from the primal sin, and my mom bears me as within a cow on a hill; she harbors only once in hindsight. My older sisters understand the sin, as does my mother. However, I am left in the dark and am lifted here, but I instinctually know there is a bad element here not unlike the animals.

Mimi tells me what to believe and that is all, and that is faith. She is my spiritual mother. Either way, we are friends and I am lonely and their watchful eyes free me in a sense of misery, particularly loneliness, as my dog lost in space commits suicide and I suffer, but more over this is a warning to Jews (the last warning) not to take the fruit of knowledge, otherwise what if it should bleed over? But, that is in the past anyway? We came from before the stars and after the dinosaurs. Though I am not a Jew, I will be one for you if it helps. I think a choice is made of which path to take, but at the very least a warning is made, and Christ died on a cross for our sins. Why should God be raped and the evidence killed in the process? I ask this as though my own too.

For my mom, having nothing is worse than being poor. Things such as leather and skin moisturizers will be her points of trade, not to mention the guacamole she prepares is better than anything you will find in Mexico. Though, not guilty of any crime; she remains good in the eyes of God.

(Doctor , doctor, and the Rebellious Jew)

"What do you call it?" my dad asks, as though scrupulously unimportant.
"Sir?" the waiter asks.
"You know, bring the tablet," he says like a caveman with somewhat caveman sensibilities.
"What?" the waiter scoffs, but only slightly.
"What do you call it?" my dad pleads.
"A menu?" the waiter invites what seems to him the obvious.
"I must be losing my mind, right a menu…" my dad says as though at a lost for breath and exasperated.

*

When you party all night and night becomes day, he stays at the Carlyle and wears the tight white socks into the shower, while the robe is disbarred so that he awakens to two roosters playing ping pong in the rain. It was a very long night and he sort of awakens to them, roosters pecking at his toes, though he hardly feels anything as he is just sleep walking.

He sees himself as more of an outlaw than a Jew. Still, he holds hands with a Jew and hopes for the best anyway. At such times, he complains to his wife that the shades are not blocking the light from the sun and it is flickering in his eye as he tries to sleep. He tries not to notice, and turns his head so that the moon would eclipse his imposition. The pillow is his best friend at such a juncture and the maid is the devil, who asks what he wants for breakfast? Surely, he is above this and stares down at scrambled eggs, toast with butter and jam, and a glass of orange juice. The moon will rise another day, so that a party turns dumb in the witch's broth.

The maid considers the wife to be evil, and does not know any animosity to other shall he be my father or muse? Either or otherwise, his friend Tommy calls and asks how he is doing? Meanwhile, Lily makes his bed and the moon may rest for a while in an emerald broth that claims rights to trading on the floor of the New York Stock Exchange. From here, the plastic contours of green contact lenses seem sort of without purpose. In the game, she raises more money for her cause, which she shall play the poodle at backgammon and win more often than not. Tommy hangs up the phone with my dad and feels sort of sorry for him. The coldness of her imposition shall not allow him to breathe and I guess this is why and I will not follow this path, though Tommy is a good acquaintance still. My sister will come by later to raise some light into the dark hovel and the curtains may stretch into Rembrandt's smile. This is a sign my dad can keep a secret and he does.

Every day passes like this, and the number 13 becomes the same as the number 1, and the maid Lily tries to befriend my dad, though he already made a deal with the devil, so that conversation is pointless at this juncture. Nicole and Nancy become a question for an answer to which I confound myself in. I told Tommy that he would make a good father too.

The deal is made at the restaurant "21," which is half of the number 42. It is not that he fears hell, but rather looks forward to heaven instead. The waiter assumes the usual and my father buys me a thirty-dollar hamburger that is pretty good. My dad is a lion and demands a certain degree of respect! The waiter can tell that he had been there before. Still, he hates the thought that a dog commits suicide and kills him in the process. He makes his bed and sleeps in it too, and orders the chicken hash, which is sort of hearty, but not without dignity either.

My dad drives to see my doctor and hesitates to turn on his windshield wipers as it is raining and it reminded him of Germany, though he has never been there. Actually, his home away from home is the Galapagos, and this fulfills the promise of Darwin that a man may evolve and prosper, and that is all, I think. I visited the Galapagos and I think my dad drove me to the airport and it may have been raining then too. He waved goodbye through the glass partition, too. He may have liked to see the blue-footed boobies, though he thought that I did not appreciate the experience maybe, but I did. So, why are you here, Dr. Kraus interrupts the thought?

The Lion, Lettuce, and an Umbrella

Hitler died in between the lines of C.S. Lewis, which makes me wonder who he was really, or maybe instead of an evil dictator he may be a loving family man of whom is an African Jew, never to leave. But, still, the oceans eventually subside like he does, I think. He definitely leaves a mark on existence. Lettuce is money, living money, which is good while my dad is alive. The heart of lettuce is a Christmas tree which has an alter ego too, like Hitler as my father. An umbrella may be denoted as a Christmas tree and maybe you can call it as other, while still planted in soil, you try to get inside out of the rain?

Mostly, my dad is good, but the temptation to be God is great and unfortunately money, like living lettuce or a salad at Howard Johnson's in Times Square, becomes a curse thereafter. My dad was killed in a cosmic sense like the good that he offered while alive, he is similar to God still. To say that a lion is killed as a result of a dog committing suicide and then comparing this to God, who was in a guise of a gorilla that screws a bear in self-defense, all is good. However, sin is not and my dad tried to warn those remaining that danger lurks for those who continue sin after his passing. I will say that umbrellas are Mike's way of getting back at his existence as the thirteenth sun, which he represents. Still, my dad takes responsibility for this, it is God and the contraption makes money, which is more malevolent after Madame George leaves Central Park for good. God forgives himself for his predicament and my dad buys a plane ticket to heaven and a dog trades his third and last life for a seat in the bleachers of Shea Stadium; a hot dog is a sort of funny pun, and he too has a good view of those watching.

Bob Marley is next to my dog who looks sort of dark in complexion, but fair too like Michael Jackson is his ghost, I think, and not my stepmother? Bob Marley represents the death of a lion in three implements but not my dad, though. Anyway, he is part of the display when the show starts 2000 years from now; a metaphor for three lions will die in the form of Einstein's square dimension, or even the pyramids in Egypt the squares represent, each lasting 2000 year periods and he is not my dad. Meanwhile, my mom sells her seat to Queen Latifah for a cloud far away where she can read and be left alone. She offers her recipe for the best guacamole to render to the worst of witches. Will is at the center of the participants and eventually divorces her and is free. Will divorcing the evil witch is proof that God is merciful from where he stands in the audience in the far left. My dad still complains that his view is not the best. Even Donald Trump's view is better. Anyway, my dad says that I do not appreciate him. I retaliate and say we are not one.

Ferocious is once the good witch to man's dog and they part as well after I eat her dried leaf on a branch in the parking lot of the beach in Malibu. An umbrella seems to always keep him out of the rain. My dad is still angry at the poor dog, and forgives him to a degree by throwing him a ball in the park. This is not God, but pretty close anyway. My dad will exist on his own cloud as well, and you may call it cloud number forty-two which is not far from the serpent that owns the sky, though she traded all of Africa for it in this guise. Money is now worthless, but like the Jews it subsists as a tradition that merits some respect still. The wicked witch with my mom's recipe for guacamole may never enter Africa or maybe rarely. The stage is set and Will is at the center down below. The witch is "cursed," like Satan who remains in the ocean, I think.

You may wonder where those who believe in false gods then go? Madame George closes her umbrella and lets me enter heaven in the end and, in return, she is not blamed for the death of Christ, and for those who do not make it, it is an enigma. She says thanks for watching my dog. The dried leaf inside me will grow a new seed and the wicked witch otherwise will have no home in the end. My dad now goes to the doctor and has a dialogue with Ferocious, but is broke from both sides, so that therapy is free. I pay for his existence like a salad at Howard Johnson's in Times Square; a false God which is also money. From this venue, I say farewell. But, my dog remains still. My dad has a gallbladder problem and has the balls to face God like this despite his sins that resound. I compare him to Stalin, but he is more like Jesus.

"Ferocious Intercedes"

Dr.Kraus: "Why do you resent your son?"
Dad: "He does not appreciate what I do for him."
Ferocious: "I had a dream last night that I was at a spa with naked women all around and Marilyn Monroe reaches down and touches my collar."
Dad: "What can I do for him to respect me?"
Dr. Kraus: "He has moved on…"

Ferocious: "I am Joe Dimaggio, I am a Jew."

Dad: "No, you are not. You were baptized and I converted to Catholicism; my son is just being controversial."

Ferocious: "I am not your son!"

Dr. Kraus: "So I was saying that your real son, Brett, has moved on, what is left is like a ghost."

Ferocious: "Yes I am a Jew, yes I am Joe Dimaggio..." as though also Italian and is reborn as such.

Dr. Kraus: "Why do you think your son hates you?"

Dad: "Like I said he does not appreciate what I do for him."

Dr. Kraus: "He has moved on…"

Dad: "But, what about the trip to Hawaii. He could of come if he wanted to…"

Ferocious: "I remember hitting my fifty-second home run out of the park…"

Dad: "Yes, I remember that too…I think I will check in if you do not mind."

(My stepmother intercedes again that we are there for you if you need us.) In some movie, my dad takes on an opportunistic flaw as Jack Nicholson to say he never had eight hours sleep which is a lie.

Saturday Night

The sky was darker than a raven's eye. We were behind the veil here, as we left a tiger lost at sea and a lie that he would not return that which is my father… Otherwise, my father took a step for me and it is a metaphor for the lion that would die thereafter. He is Hitler's alter ego and the door is open, an African Jew, as he never left! So I was never really there. The sacrifice is a horse in some distant land, so that children may stroke its mane; a window that will remain open for a time, maybe 2000 years back inward. And Christians join hands that one should have faith in God and Christ's death on a cross should be enough to believe.

The Jewish Phenomenon

The Jews are reborn and those who die in the holocaust, including myself, though I am not a Jew, I think. And I will not return to their world as I think we have never met. God asked us to believe and that is all, and Jesus is reborn in their world and it may only be thought as a curse as though his prior death and the belief in the cause do not matter, I think not. If I do not see you again as though we have never met, this would be a blessing, as faith in the cause is all God asked. Should he be born in another, it is a curse, and for this I do not like Jews. They will be validated by the struggle they endure. The Jews still remind me that my father did exist. Like his Jewish counterparts, he is forgiven in time.

The garden once closed will never be re-opened for their cause of such proponents. My mother still watches over the garden but from a distance. For the Jews, death might be better than being denied God's love. Waste left is an affront to the Virgin Mary, born to, if she had a child really? His fruit is left behind, so it does not protrude and remind him of a lost, now tallied as though never before, a bear screwed by a gorilla; though. He thinks it is natural but somewhere else. It may be natural, but protrudes as though ugly in this guise. The door is closed to unwelcome guests; except the animals that remain for all time, I think. The Jews who died before the blood of sin should bleed over may be blessed in a way, anyway. They, not proponents of their demise, leave behind a horse and the children play and play. Should the Jews subsist in their world, I may give up religion as a Christian, so that it is clear that Jesus never left. Religion may be futile then, but I think the other. I fear that the blood of sin will bleed over to some Jews and the curse will not allow the guilty ones to enter where they left, as though all of Christianity is in vain.

The hate I feel may be more than the fire of a pool where goldfish cry and are witness to the crime; an animal should never cross the line to that which is God; and I am neither. Still, Will is at the center of the audience with feet that are flat like his and is witness to their fall, though only actors in a play which is man. I do not think it is a sin to believe either. Maybe the Jews represent the many faces of Jesus in this conundrum? I think this will be a blessing for most, and I will shake your hand, but not from behind; the prophet anoints the cause further I am told…and most will survive the blast in the past as though never again, I think.

Sorry

Why I should ponder Eve and the fall of man, thereafter I do not know? But, I express sorrow anyway and the snake leaves the crime scene to have faith anyway, as it may be in fashion now. She may be in hindsight my tail as an animal I leave their world, and I am not African American or man but may be a straight male in my new world and I apologize for their lost anyway. I remain here for a while to let the children know that they may return if they want.

Children have a choice to be good or bad. For those who are bad, there is no reason to understand the path it should foreshadow, as there are no answers for such questions, I think. Otherwise, it is as easy as a choice and return in the wake of a whale remaining in the ocean but good, near to the evil that God pardons as bad in another vestibule, but always farther away, I think. I am sorry my mom is left behind in Africa, as though children are not accepted and she loves them anyway, and the abuse she feels for that of another prescribes that she is innocent and Will feeds Eve food and there are no other questions from here. The rock I pick up is in the form of a heart that relinquishes the kids from this great land America and I am here, finally, for a while but bring it from India. Meanwhile, the Owl Rock which I inherit is a remnant from Stalin. He seems good in this light, as though a fruit of the innocent many who die in the process.

Kurt Cobain joins God in someone else's heart, in the process, that which is a swastika in hindsight, but not really God, though. I leave the Owl Rock in a backwoods place in Thousand Oaks, California. As it should remain there, otherwise the other heart-shaped rock is now a magnet to another heart-felt rock, joining the two and it belongs to Mimi, now. I note, though, that there is only one moon, and should you have any further questions now, and that should answer most of these issues, I think.

Half-Moon with Red Tide and the Fisherman

Will ate his own seed and landed in a goldfish bowl. Although I have vivid memories of a seahorse staring into my eyes through the glass while God ponders lost love while sitting in his boat. Memories of lost friends, but don't rock his boat, I think!

There are three dimensions in his realm and, though Will is four, there are three entities left behind that allow Will to ponder further. There is a lion as Bob Marley; a dog who conspires with death to be Michael Jackson next to him; and there is Queen Latifah who stares at children the way a giraffe cares in this distant land, Africa, and represents the realm of a black panther too. She exists where God is born very soon in Mozambique. Otherwise, there is Will, who exists in the center though not God, but escapes the bowl that once enslaved his brethren as I should not go back there as though I was ever there really?

The black panthers may return there if they want to, but this may comply with God's wishes? The queen will pardon those 10 000 disciples who stand with God in a grid as though "stronger than a feeling," though there was never really ever a doubt. This may reflect the sky too. Eve remains there in the womb of a zebra as it kicks to remind those who will not see this that the earth is still fertile anyway. Lily and Ilona will be forgiven for their crimes against man. All that is left in the ocean is Satan, who washes up like sinners onto the beach in Venice Beach, California, time to time?

Children are left behind in his watch, though. Children do not know why, but he remains behind anyway. He is a fly caught in a sin representing a plastic ice cube which stares at infidels at high society parties on the Upper West Side. Otherwise, I would rather be a Jackson Pollock painting than kangaroo shit. I choose to be good instead and the foam from the ocean barely touches my bare foot as I stand on the beach in Malibu. But, it does not touch and sharks patrol the ocean so the children do not wake from this dream. Satan is what is left of God that is bad. I choose to be good and sharks patrol the ocean like the police which are better than the alternative, children wandering into his realm and waking while drowning in this dream. They should never touch I think.

Instead, a beautiful horse is given to those who do not know either, and it is a reminder of those lost in this dream that many should die in the guise of religion prior to 1952. Many millions would die in vain at the hands of Stalin. The horse is a reminder to children that God is good, though. Benny the fly, flies around feces, in general? It may be a metaphor for that which is the plastic ice cube or the next best thing is kangaroo shit? Benny is a post in the desert of Australia, which reminds the Aborigines brethren there that they are halfway there. They begin to walk inward from this venue which will take 2000 years, and time will revoke the past, then. Like a picture from the album *Tea for the Tillerman*, the children play and play; though he is not God either. The fisherman is a fading picture of God and the deficiencies man inherits as a result. Will remains in the center of the audience on flat feet like his for a time as the play should be rendered too. Half-moon with red tide may be a picture of a tiger as it is stuck in the past. A deal is made in heaven, and he subsists into the future.

Doctor, Doctor and the Rebellious Jew

From where the thirteenth sun divides dark space is where one may find the Indians of yesterday. From here, Jews must believe in a colossal sacrifice that they claim is not theirs. Its efflorescence in heaven may not be redeemed now and for some it is too late. The air that separates their belief from the very Virgin Mary becomes a disease that indicts those non-believers in a cause that once was smitten with laughter on the soil they walked upon. My sister may be Mary Magdalene in hindsight and she may forgive herself for a sin that is not hers. Rather, The Police seek her out where Sting penetrates the realm of the Jews with little forgiveness of other who may be just my dog. I guess Mike knew the blood of sin would bleed over and the thirteenth sun he represents exonerates most that pass on its display. (But, not his evil son Jim Morrison of whom he will not forgive Jew or not?) And he prays to another God now. Meanwhile, Simon remains a whale in the ocean and forgives those who seek him out. Mike is his brother and denies this right to others for a cause there is in a dying sun, where there may be no mercy. The Jews who are hindered by the past will be responsible for his fate in the end. Mike and the thirteenth sun he represents is at the mercy of children. The brats of doom now comply that they are now separate? Meanwhile, Hitler's private island will not be penetrated again. Indians remain in the sky without the mercy he sheds upon the brats. The rain passes like the clouds like the mirage that does exist there while the sun is shining too.

All God asked was to believe. The death of Christ, though real, may be a mirage for what may not happen as a result. They may be responsible for a crime of a sin they did not commit and sinners walk on a path to heaven that is now yours. Though, Jim Morrison now prays to another God. The children believe he is innocent too, and the Jews who remain in vain must tolerate what they will inherit as a result. To "not believe," is a crime in the heart of God, I think. Jim Morrison waits at Tower Records and says he is friends with Ferocious should the two meet?

I may not be my mother's father, Stalin, and the person who dropped the bomb, but my sister Nancy, like the photo from a negative, represents everything else. Sting and the police seek Nicole out so that others may have a future too. She looks inward here at the children, but from the viewpoint of California. Here, she offers her gold coin in exchange of the children of the sun and their freedom. Mt. Fuji stands with back to them. And Germany , where Purple Rain alludes those participating and so far away too? (While

Jim Morrison is not Jesus and Sting not God either?) Nicole wears modest pearls and may be my sister, but we have never met. She and my other sister, Nancy, inherit Bill Gates's fortune for her strife anyway. The revolving door is where some enter and some leave too. It is possible to love someone you have never met. I watch from afar and she has a life now too.

"The Holy Ghost"

I represent three points in time, yet I have not been born. Meanwhile, Michael Jackson is part of the inner trinity and represents my dog and he is a ghost as well. Ferocious is freed as a result. I have a picture of God that is so dark like glistening of waste in the sun somewhere in Australia. I look twice at the phenomenon to note now that Ferocious is gone. But, something remains still that is bad too. A sun will die in the process though he is still scared of the dark. Satan says he will abide in God so that God may be born in another. It provides enough light so that I may see his face once, and I trade this picture for a picture of a cheetah that may be an open door to Africa, should I enter?

God will not touch the ground really thereafter like an apple that does not land either. It is just reflections of his pride as 10,000 maniacs are born in the sky (all women) and represents the ground he may not stand upon. He sees through Renata's eyes and her oasis is Australia, and such dark entities do exist there. Benny the fly complies with a split ego that recognizes that I did exist once. Satan may enter any of three doors here and may not return to Africa and is separate from God now forever. God is born in another there so that Satan may not penetrate the domain. It remains as something so bad that he does not have a name either. It is so dark that it provides light in the night sky in a reversal of fortune somewhere like Australia. But, Renata will walk somewhere else even though Australia is her domain, as she sees for God as though there is light in blinding darkness too. There is no negative to the picture Will takes in this light. His existence is a sequential equation that exponentially declares the earth is crazy from four different points of view. From here, there is a fire that absorbs it too? Meanwhile, the Holy Ghost represents three points in time. There is light in complete darkness. I am a ghost that complies with this notion, and in this light God lives forever, virtually.

One: "Bear"

The bear would return to NYC and be in passing at a crossroads as the remaining of two bombs that invaded another land foreign to him (with the tremble that which is the witch's dog.) A man, through his eyes, is always created equal. Although I am not present, he remains as a token of their demise which also frees them as well. All that is left of the reckoning are two urns that should not leave NYC. However, it is too late and the bear enters the void that is NYC without regard to the viaducts of her blue eyes. I am a powerless vestibule to feed a blueberry to a dog, representing the blood of the earth of which she will not partake. And she frees man instead and Annie Lennox grips the blueberry through me to offer the sacrifice and I escape a worse fate here too.

The bear through Paulina Porizkova may witness the freak turn of events though not her fruit either. While Heidi Klum denies the lesser fate of a dog and brings it to a land that he craves in the ordeal. He may be one again with his father who is God too. I am powerless to the sacrifice at hand and do the walk from west 80th street between Columbus and Amsterdam; with bear shackles on my feet and walk alone down town all the way to the towers. I think my fate is written in the stars. The lesser denies the right to a light that will absorb them later on, a staircase to heaven. And God absolves their existence as his own like a square window in the sky. God is not me, but exists in this hierarchy forever as the number five.

Ferocious, in the reckoning, plays ball in the park with me one more time. Before going to make a sacrifice, he will leave me, he knows later on. I accept his fate though not my own. At the crossroads, the dog chose heaven and the bear does not pat its backside out of respect. He will be walked by Heidi Klum on a leash and joins God instead. It is not my choice that he should find another home and the urns remain somewhere else too. The dog wears the Star of David for me and frees man that acknowledges Israel through his sacrifice. South Africa seems too far away, but finds a home in Africa anyway. I will not transcend the square that frees me and Conor eats the carrot blowing in the wind, while mocking such divinities at such times.

Unlike the brats who claim allegiance to the Virgin Mary, Ferocious is without the bloodline and may have an adopted mother instead which is a sacrifice with which he can live with. The bear absorbs the sky on that day and transcends a sacrifice that may transcend three days. Jesus dies on a cross and rises to heaven on the third day. The children inherit a horse in another land which is white or black depending if it is night or day? I can still hear them chant in the verse of "the Wiz," in a land that is flat like his feet and they say instead "lions, tigers, and bears…" I still feel somewhat responsible for the dog anyway. Diana is my soul at such times! (She does not forsake me.)

Yes, a bear remains for those who must believe. It seems difficult to understand its light, which sort of demands a certain degree of respect too. The goldfish that sheds some light makes the bear seem dark in the toilet bowl it transcends out of this perplexing dilemma. Sometimes nature will repeat itself and it looks away as it is penetrated by God so that the Virgin Mary is no longer responsible. It is a living manifestation of what is waste that glistens like red coffee beans that will embark on a journey and provides light to which its sun adheres perfectly. Whether the ground reflects the sky is not important. The lie compels me to ask Satan if he needs any change? The devil's sojourn will not be paid in money made by man as he is broke anyway. Overcoming his plight in Africa will not access any money in the exchange either. He now lives in China and is provided with what he needs like condensation of the rain that falls. The African man stands on flat ground and will not forage a loss like money is to the devil.

Two: "Tiger Ghost"

Where did the Jews go? Someone might ask this question on a pilgrimage to Mecca. At this time, Muhammad may be accessible to the children for a short time. He is their stepfather and is born out of a compromise for a tiger that should begin a journey inward at such a time. In the rainforest, the black panthers remain, but no tiger. Rather, a ghost exists which foreshadows the red in the beans of coffee that still grows wild. The laws of nature manifest themselves like a computer chip and are returned to her as though the cost and strife of her existence will compensate her demeanor now. Nature overshadows their struggle to grow wild and may lose its independence and it is regained somewhere else.

She tells the manager at Starbucks in Los Angeles to pay her back. Like a computer that tells its future, coffee like "Paradise Lost," does not grow the same way it once did and she knows this. There is some solace to her as Paul Simon smokes a joint from time to time and this shows her the respect she deserves. But, the Jews are now gone, and a tiger ghost is all that remains. Will makes it to heaven and that is enough. Meanwhile, Muhammad envisions a city in the desert and he heads inside so as to not disrespect the moon either, which seems out of place like a dorky kid at the high school dance in the corner alone. The children born to a faraway land such as America enlist in the military and he knows peace is the answer.

"What the children do not understand, they will never understand," I think. The children inherit a horse and head inside as well. Africa draws the others in too, and Will may see the sky in full like no other place. He stands on ground that is flat like his… A picture of God is given up and I see the cheetah instead. My mom still watches over a garden, but like a square box that which is the Kaaba, I tell Muhammad that I hope we may be friends. An inner trinity exists and I wait for the show to begin. A square may not be entered and that is God. I think the Jews are watching from a distance too. The grapes of wrath show an odd pity so that he chooses eternal life.

Three: "Mike Tyson #43"

I felt his hand reach into my pocket one more time. He knows Morgan Stanley complies with the exchange as a pentagon exists in the rainforest of the Congo. An entity exists here, but it has no pocket and he carries naked money for him. God participates in an exchange that seems limitless like bread for wine. Still the environment is vulnerable, just like the green oasis he calls home, to the east and it will become stronger. If it should plunder or falter, so would he. I think it is appropriate that Mike Tyson represents that all men are created equal, but his journey inward represents a quest for mental health that would not exist without him, I think. It is the recognition that man's civilizations may be good too. Nancy may be his opposite and stays in touch with God at such times. Mike Tyson comes to Earth from Mars and carries God's money as a figment of the imagination that Mike (Simon's brother) is a lizard and is naked too. A lion will be sacrificed in heaven for a slight indignation that merits what is God's.

"Gold in India"

Gold is no longer a disturbance when once in India a black cat absorbs the miniscule bit of a mushroom like an insect. The golden apple it represents does not see the fall of man in hindsight. Though, man is framed by deer that deny it; the apple is picked somewhere else and the nation will reap the harvest which is gold too. Without this knowledge, there may not be three blue devils that worked on the sky. The sun transcends this realm as it bleeds the color blue into darkness. Gold provides a certain light that there is mercy here too. God asks, who ate the fruit? Satan is a manifestation of this and the devil denies God by claiming his innocence. I am neither.

"No shit," I hear a toad echo from the sun that does not exist except from a child's point of view, who remembers a time that is in transition like a storybook without a beginning too. A mother, father, and a child join hands in India and gold joins them further. They may be part of Satan otherwise. They are otherwise forgiven of what is God's plight. The insects chant that they are home now too. If I were not so poor, I would give my mom a gold watch which she inherits anyway.

"Domain of Australia"

Australia to Renata is an inverted swimming pool. The fish surround its contours (long and lanky) like a drug that is a joint and reminds her of her sister. The blue sky is her eyes and meets the water in a compromise that an eel lives on the outside forever. Satan's dark intentions may not penetrate what is her domain. Madagascar is my domain, which is something else entirely.

"Out of Brazil..."

Even before God, Mimi and I meet in the rainforest of Brazil. I may be only a ghost in hindsight, and the three points it represents may not be purchased in money made by man. I may represent three points in time, yet I have not been born yet either. Like "Paradise Lost" the oasis may not be penetrated by man until its wound heals from a time which made God seem vulnerable too, and we bring him into the light. He is our baby too. God does not pick her flower in a distant land, but given the stellar splendor of the dilemma, he is the only entity that may claim a relationship to it in hindsight. I think Japan will claim responsibility out of Brazil in this perplexing dilemma that sounds like the doves crying in sunlight, that which is so pure too.

"Age of Aquarius"

There is nothing so dark as the fabric of a garment the woman wears in the desert of Kuwait. It is strange that her voice evokes woman's liberation in the tumultuous times in the 1960s in the USA. She lives on in this form. It is a voice that need not be spoken in the 1990s. She still drives a taxi in this small town (a car that coughs like a camel on a dry desert excursion and is made by Fiat too.) She leaves the window open to feel the wind so far away as it pauses like something really good does exist here. She represents a small black rock one of us once possessed. Here is a mirage in the night sky of a black horse that the stars confounds in its contours like diamonds but so dark too? Japan's red sun will not penetrate its domain. The black horse is real, though, only in the night sky, and Yoko Ono is like a sister who possesses such a notion here.

"What you do not see, will not hurt you," someone echoes my voice in a dream on a visit to Woodstock, New York, and they will not meet either. In the daylight, a white horse dissipates in the clouds that the children will inherit the beast. Stew remains somewhere else.

"Black Shoes"

I may not be Obama's father, but the sentiment is taken kindly. Yes, I was here for a while then left. Similarly, I was a dark entity, but not really anymore. I wear black shoes and dream what it would be like to be a father? In the house in which I grew up, in Washington, D.C., I remain in the dark and dream a better dream. I am not really scared of the dark but look under my bed to check if there is something there and I guess this is progress.

(Roland)

Roland complies with the Gestapo. He escaped the holocaust by hiding in a wine container in Tuscany, where he had a lover too. He was promised a flight to America if he would reveal the people who were fighting against the Nazis in Italy, which was sort of an underground railroad out of Malta. He kisses his lover and flies from Florence to Casablanca then on to Los Angeles; though his lover considered him more of a gigolo as he kisses her on the cheek out of respect. Actually, he began revealing his sources as a form of retribution to the cause so that should they die in the gas chambers, God would redeem them as a blessing in rebirth. Somehow, he got caught in a web and he had to choose whether he would die or live; and he chooses to escape.

The husband says, "You are such a Jew," as they said farewell, and Roland does not look her in the eyes as he walks away from them and gets in the plane, instead.

"Again..."

The runners from Germany take on the form of all women, yet they are not lesbians either. They relay messages from the ground where God stands, but not really; as it rises into the heavens. I tell a friend that the past should not repeat itself, which is a bad joke, which I curse from this perspective.

"Half-moon with Red Tide, 'again'"

So, I ask Will, what it was like to die on a cross as though his reality merits this respect? His previous life may be pretty similar to this in the end. He says it is like crying and not being able to get inside from the shame you feel, while it is raining outside too. Stew, the horse, on that day could not find the sky and this should never repeat itself.

I think God is rich like the color black that will not forsake him. He may not be touched like a counterpoint in a square dance. He may not have a son, but adopts Africa as his home instead. His seed seems dangerous and Kyle is the next best thing. Religion should be obsolete by now? I still believe Jesus died on a cross for our sins! I sing the spiritual, "All things are possible..." and feel a slight tremble in the wind.

Dark Star in Nine Parts
who are you? Nine: China
(Colin Barker)

The children are beyond Mimi's ring here,
"stronger than a feeling," he swings with its
neighboring Neptune, beauty and Pluto
in the dark. But, the people will be free to
settle the lands afar and wait for the clock
to cease to tick. The sun fades into darkness,
redemption recognizable.

Part Nine: Blood on Pluto...

Prelude...

"The Great Sphinx"

I think if I was around back then I would be a slave. At such a time, David fights the nemesis to good as a sheepherder and does not confront the pharaoh to whom he is a slave. He is part of the tenth tribe and does not leave Africa until all are vindicated and Moses walks on water or so it seemed. The true nature of dogs is revealed now and they bark at the Jews to win approval of their masters, who lack the emotion of compassion and the Jews would not return. They see a sea of benevolence somewhere else, I guess. The dogs with ivory fangs remain and cross over a line to betray the pharaoh and a falcon flies and lands in a more remote and dark corner of Africa. The Passover of something else remains. But, they do not understand their plight and rather compose the sand and three pyramids that remain for an "other" cause. The bird carries me from somewhere else; it could be India. I land where my father takes the first step for me, if I ever was there?

In modern days, a boy in Kansas remains in detention and solves the mystery of the sphinx as he reaches for the three small cartons of apple juice in his coat pocket that he steals from the school cafeteria. He may be only in sixth grade but determines that these apple juice cartons represent the three pyramids which each represent periods of two thousand years. In the past, much is taken from Africa and, as compensation, so will much be returned, he thinks. The Great Sphinx watches over this land just in case.

At gym class, the children form a circle clasping a parachute and the moon may be visited by man, as though retribution to his cause that seems plausible now. The Jews leave Africa through a circle and wolves pay homage to their plight by barking at the moon, never to return again. Israel may be retribution to their cause and someone says that it is a nice place to visit. The wolves have no master, but the boy whose name is David comes pretty close. Their plight is rectified in the tears of animals who do not understand why they formerly acted so badly? The Jews will never confront a nemesis so dark again.

Meanwhile, from where I stand, the tears of the Great Sphinx are dry forever more. My grandfather flies over Big Ben with fashionable beige raincoat and umbrella in hand, and remains out of the rain like this. Just the same, the "David" as Michelangelo's statue is compensation for the exchange and many a child's two cents pays for this prophecy to be real again. Satan wears dark glasses and walks on the boardwalk of Venice Beach, California, and watches over the kids now while all that is good is exchanged in the cause. The soul of Africa or an apple tree remains alone wandering and is outside it until the exchange is made in the near future. From Africa, God ponders his loss and it would seem like an apple tree without a soul of that which is good too. He asks that some of his wooden statues from deep within be returned too as some sort of compensation. I drink African rooibos red tea and am quite happy now in the exchange, being out of the rain… Only a fake tear from Sierra's eye remains too.

While 6,000,000 Jews are not present, it is true that God's blood and the blood of animals should not mix. Sherry should swallow the bug so that those on Pluto remain good and Indians are dispensed outward in darkness. The loss is tallied in mushrooms picked that freed them beyond Pluto. Nine animals will sponsor each and they will not penetrate God's domain or each other. The brats have some sort of allegiance to them as well as the very Virgin Mary! The Jews passover as I had done prior and I am not Christ! They will prosper like this as though Christ on the cross and are not responsible for other people's sins either.

"Tea for the Tillerman"

Though I may be extinct, it only means that I am out of Africa, a sort of black cat that may represent a treasure map in the dreams of small children forevermore. Never to go there and a treasure map remains in places as far away as Madagascar. The children are safe here in dreams so far away. In this concept, some children are extinct in the same way. They inherit a white horse like Stew who was all black though and he could not find the sky on a dark and gloomy afternoon. The 13th sun remains too for children to stay in and dream outside of the rain. I may be witness to some sort of exchange as though bread for wine. The tillerman with red hair and beard watches the children play and play and it could be called somewhere else. This storybook has no end either. Just a cross remains in Mozambique where a friend of mine once stood. Will reads the story now to the children which does not reveal Satan entering the ocean. He shows some demure as this book is now replaced by the Bible.

"The Lesbian Cause"

I know I mentioned before how an entity may represent three points in time. All at once a flash of light marks the beginning of time in the year 1952. I may be guided by good forces outside this dark land. It appears to me that three women remain to confirm that there is another side to this story. I do not know Annie Lennox to be a lesbian, but her calculated ploy to the coldest venue allows for her to escape the fate that these three women will inherit after the fact so to speak. Meanwhile, Hillary Clinton is an actor in this play and will not cross the line so far as though not to return either. Instead, Alison is the first point. She lives now in the womb of a female zebra and calls for man to fall with no way to land either. The zebra kicks as though to confirm that she may have been fertile at one time too. She had thought that what belonged to God in the form of an apple tree was hers too for the taking. She may have tempted a boy to pick it and is admonished to a plight that envisions a world without man. She became a metaphor for an apple that falls, but does not land and such is man in hindsight. God does not understand a greed farfetched as Eve in the garden too. Eventually man is forgiven as is Adam, but it continues to fall like an apple that his plight represents. She kisses another girl and likes it. She dines alone at "Chez William" and she considers this retribution for a crime she commits that she only understands why she did it. Only a bear remains for those who must believe. God holds the apple in his hand as a lesson to all as a farce so farfetched? I call New York City, "Adam and Eve Hotel Theater Productions." Meanwhile, the play "The Gay Quarter Show," is prep work to a show in the future, a play for a dying sun in Africa. It will not impede God's greater plan in any way. The apple does land eventually in God's hand and such is man. Alison as Eve does not know what crime she commits, but is punished to show a slight indignation to what God claims as his own. She is forgiven in the end and Adam is considered weak by God.

The second point is Lily. She carries her blue leather luggage to the airport in Lima and steals the seat reserved for an Incan king so long ago that her tears actually feel good to her. She lusted for a boy who she claimed raped her and a perfect white Lily is picked simultaneously in a distant land which is not hers either. She thought she might betray the sun as an Incan king represented and fly away in a jealous rage somewhere else. To wherever it may lead, only her name remains in case she might find some sort of benediction in time too. Instead, she will remain in the ocean just in case God will forgive her. She is now a female tiger shark and cries in the ocean which is not hers either for a lover who is Fidel Castro. He fears the ocean as a result, and remains isolated while Christ dies on a cross a long time ago. It manifested itself in the death of millions in the former Soviet Union under the wrath of Stalin. Fidel Castro is a sign that Adam is eventually forgiven for picking the apple for Eve. Lily has bent teeth and represents the second point in time. Meanwhile, the sharks comply with notions of burning effigies of God's waste deep in the rainforest of Brazil. The sharks swim away on their backs in a circle and will not socialize with Lily and her crooked teeth and her lack of disposition to the ocean that she now claims as her home. The gold may not belong to her nor a flower picked either.

Ilona is the third point in time and she was jealous of Mt. Fuji and his perfect symmetry so much that she thought to love Hitler as though God. In exchange, a Polish boy is killed, to be sacrificed in the holocaust as though he was a Jew too. Poland may be where the umbilical chord to his true mother was broken like the ocean. Her love of Hitler made her think of power synonymous with the ocean. She sought Hitler as a lover out of revenge of her hatred of her father. The Jews who died as of a result of this phenomenon are reborn as the many faces of Jesus, but not this one Polish boy that she disgraced. She harnessed (for a short time) the milk that is in a cow in this act of betrayal, which does not belong to Ilona really. She is not welcome in Israel and Hitler would die like a Jew and is forgiven by God who sympathizes with the plight which he does not understand either. The Polish boy is separated from his spiritual mother, like Ilona from the ocean and the riches there she sought. Ilona may have been jealous of her father. I claim three crosses to bear in the process here, while you too may have a cross to bear as well.

"Stalin's Menace"

Who is responsible? My dog commits suicide and killed the lion in the process. From the blast of an atomic bomb in the early 1950s, it extends out farther, farther than the German police dare to go. The TV shows for a time Mickey Mouse seen with his pants off. Stalin reaches to as far as South Africa and holds hands with Nelson Mandela, knowing full well that the Oklahoma City bombing was not necessary (any way you look at it.) Stalin may be forgiven like a dog forsaken by its father and God may have fought off a bear in self-defense too. In modern day, it was like betraying your dog and going to the drive-thru to Jack in the Box to eat the evidence. Brian Williams goes to Shea Stadium and eats a hot dog in the shade. It is not Ferocious's fault and Brian Williams may be acclimated to the cause and appear attractive to Jews and this is not his fault either. Brian Williams did not forsake Ferocious and the hot dog he eats becomes a crime in present times from which he exonerates himself. It is a power trip as someone thought that Jesus would be an attractive specimen to another and, though Ziggy is the next best thing. It seems easier to not take responsibility for the death of Christ in the process? Joe Dimaggio hits a ball into the stands and no one is near by to catch it. Brian Williams may have eaten the evidence in the form of a hot dog, but he did not reach for the ball, and it is not his fault. He may seem attractive to Zion? God is raped and someone killed the evidence? A nun may be a plight that is a metaphor for the very Virgin Mary and she is doing well in modern days. No one will point the finger at me and I would rather not now too? Really, Christ on the cross is an enigma to me. I am not sure how this happened?

"A Picture in the Garden..."

I took a picture of God's excrement from where a little boy stands in the garden before the fall. I was there then and before, but God walked past me as though to say I am responsible to clarify that the boy is another and God should enter his domain in heaven. There is a short pause, as though Japanese tourists loading film into their camera and seeing the Washington Monument in Washington, D.C. for the first time. The garden is beautiful but the confusion of this little boy's excrement causes God to seem vulnerable for the first time and the body of Satan should take the form of an apple lying on the ground and is raw and the fruit from this one tree should not be eaten.

It was a short passing before it was too late and the window to the fall of man was open for a time as a temptation that God forbade as a test and the serpent is neither good nor bad. This is a lesson in time that would lead to a mission to believe in God, as he would later offer his son for the sins that grew out of this dilemma. The garden is no more and I see God leave through the door in the back. The picture I took with the blink of an eye is dark and, instead of binding to their cause, I enter a doorway that should not be crossed by mankind. I may be an animal, a sort of black cat that detests the vulnerability that God will inherit. I am from before the fall and will invoke faith in others there after so no one will taste the fruit. The Jews may be God's chosen people, but the lesson of the ordeal runs much deeper. Where poetic champions compose there is a test of spirit and Satan is ousted from the garden. The black cat that I am is extinct, which is to say I do not exist there anymore, but I am good just the same. Meanwhile, the picture of what was a little boy's excrement remains somewhere, and God forgives those who seek redemption. The tree is not evil, but the act of denying God's word is a sin and for this God will not forgive like time that invades his space. Satan may be God's excrement as he is vanquished in time and I am just a slave temporarily. Those who existed prior are forgiven too. The tree will not foster indignation again. After Stalin's millions, the apple will be accessible to me as well as you.

"The Slave"

I may have been a slave once and twice I confronted my spiritual mother and I ate my fruit to shed what is God's excrement in the form of what is Satan. A fig tree now grows in his back yard and it is like pineapple or papaya and like a placebo causes no harm now. I walked like a slave in America and the land likewise need not hide from the sins of yesterday. The path leads into the sky and birds fly free. I am exonerated as you are too. There is no apology for the tribulations that no one understands anyway.

"33s and the doors to Musgrove..."

The door has two venues, and one leads to Africa and the other leads to America. There is no way at any given moment to decipher the final result and a choice is still made here. The door leading to Africa forgives your past and in compensation, you will know yourself. America's door forgives the Jews who inherit the two cents every child is given and do not ask me if I think this is fair? They buy "the David" and the children are given a horse instead. David lives in Israel in case you ever want to visit. Where eight-eight-three and the three in three-two-four meet is where you will find the entrance to Musgrove too. Those who are not welcome need not try to enter.

"883" Watching from a distance...

China is a negative of the composition of the sun of yesterday. Prior to 1952, when Will ruled New York City, it is now old and Nancy watches from where she is perched like a snow leopard in the highlands of the Himalayas. When God takes a photograph which is a blink in time, he may be delegated from any perspective on earth. The witches of China represent the ninth house where beauty resides and a tap may be felt on the head of Indian witches. This may be a way to tally a sin in anonymity in Africa of who is no longer welcome. Maybe a statue is made of the specimen and he may or may not be invited back. It is foolish to think that witches do not have a function in the cosmic reality of the universe. The Indian witch represents unnatural sins such as rape, and the devil may be a living manifestation of these unforgiveable acts. After God judges mankind, the door to America will be open forever thereafter. Nancy and Steve walk back from China to America.

"324" Purple Rain in Germany

Purple rain is forgiveness of man outside of Africa. She need not fear bad things as she is stronger than them and rather foresees good deeds and rewards the proponents offering a purple popsicle for those of merit. They make movies of these specimens which may be why Steven Spielberg made *Schindler's List*. South Africa is curiously considered in her realm or "out of Africa" and the Nobel committee makes notes dealing with her work. She is also an innovator as God did not include women in such a competition and she retaliated and includes women in such a task. She is my sister Nicole and saying so does not deter her strength either. When the sun does not shine, "purple rain in Germany will be her final act. Africa may overcome the sins of the devil and this is redemption. Those who do not make it are remembered in prayer.

"Three Lion Statues in Tunis"

There is a protected land in Africa where three statues tarnish with a green film on their surface and wait for three lions to be free and get out of the rain. It may seem like a sacrifice, but the sun will live on for the sake of these three lions that a square represents. The Virgin Mary will not be touched in the process. I ask, if God does not recognize Lily or Satan, then how does Mt. Fuji escape their fate? The Japanese live in a microcosm which denies their relationship to God and the devil! They are masters of their own destiny and little remains on the outside of their culture except for these three lion statues that cannot get out of the rain. They are aware of Hitler's desert island where "the brats of doom," subsist. They are spared the fate of a lion which is as close to a father figure they detest in themselves.

Meanwhile, Brent conveys the number five as his family; and he swims at the pool at Musgrove Plantation, and claims the number seventeen as his own which is much like God.

"Sugar cookies, ice cream, and popcorn..."

There are three of us who came from the sky. After the dinosaurs and before the stars, I know. In the process, we would bring riches to God. In the sound of silence, the night split the sky and, for a time, the sun would be adopted as our own. The eternal power of our cause is in the form of an eel, a spider, and a black cat. God is severed from the dark and we wait to bring him into his light. On arrival, one of us may have thrown a rock at the sun or moon. God may not survive otherwise and may not be touched by mankind in the process. He does represent the fifth dimension, and lives on forever in our embrace. The midnight express shall float and at the given moment he will be lifted so that he may not perish. The sun is a clock and the alarm denotes a time to lift him into heaven. We are one when the social fabric may be claimed. It is true that there is light in darkness, but this may not be the case of Satan and the nemesis threatens the cause. There is a wall in Africa where God resides and Satan may not penetrate his fortress. This is why?

"John Lennon on the cross"

The death of John Lennon may only be a distraction. The children love him anyway. They sit in the dark and hold each others' hands and there are no worries of being different from anyone else. Yoko Ono leads a procession to sing, "this land is your land," and it is an anthem to their cause too. Native Americans watch from the sky and see a constellation of a purple zebra, which may be their mother too? They do not maintain a relationship to God, but are distant cousins once removed.

Satan lives in the confine of a tire and the children form a configuration in a circle around him. This is the third dimension and children sleep upright and dream that three perfect suns shed light but only from within. The sky absorbs their smiles in darkness, while the sun sheds inspiration for the time being. Benny the fly zips around kangaroo shit in Australia while all that is left of Satan is petrified remnants in a museum in Tulsa. John Lennon was crucified on a cross too, while the devil claims he is a Jew. Satan slips into the ocean and the fish will absorb his waste that dissipates. The fish bark back as though Ferocious is now a soldier in Hitler's army of the Third Reich and is misguided like this with no sound to speak of. In the museum, there is a remnant of the dinosaurs and that is all that is left. The children transcend the realm of animals and they are now good as they float into heaven. Rocky Raccoon said he saw Satan leave. He was singing the Beatles song *All you need is Love*. The owl perches on a tree somewhere and watches the children from afar now. The bomb that resounds is not my creation, should you ask as to say once again, "Do not cross the line," and my back is turned away from you too. I will live on in your dreams.

John Lennon remains as what children see as love from a father's point of view. Otherwise, Stalin seems a bit intimidating and Satan is long gone. Stalin is intimidating like a picture of Christ on the cross. The Hindus in India recognize him like a grand black stallion and they see its constellation in the night sky without a past too. Satan does not dispel waste in the ocean really, but remembers a time when the children knew what darkness meant. The storybook God reads to the children is a beginning without an end. Obama says, "I got your back," which is Japan. Though, "they," would rather not...even Stew the horse could not find the sky on that day. He sleeps quietly in the night that subsists. The image of Christ will fade like the ocean which is divided in two equal parts.

"My Mac Book Pro Incident: 'computer resurrected'"

Sometime after the death of Steve Jobs, my computer died too. I called Apple and was told that there was nothing that they could do. On the third day, the computer rose again and somehow was resurrected. This is a true story. The laws of nature may be told like the confines of a computer chip, but I did not see Steve Jobs rise too. I think it was a sign, though I do not know how to interpret the incident. Someone may have entered heaven, but I may not confirm this either?

"The Internal Revenue Service and the realm of God 'Chanel #5'"

God's witch in England wears Chanel #5. Simon and Garfunkel sing "me and Julio down by the schoolyard." The Jews want to know more about you and they are disguised as the IRS while children go to the Martin Luther King Jr. Library in Washington D.C. and this is a distraction. Ziggy is a Jew and I am a young American. (God will live forever.) Bob Dylan says to watch the parking meters too. The children are M and M's melting in his mouth and they are offered two cents as retribution to the cause too. The children are asked by them if you have seen this man in the picture and they lie and say no.

"Where the apple lands?"

Japan has suffered a tumultuous history. They are united in this past and divides prior to 1952. Someone will point their finger at them and this is good. I could not prevent the bombs from falling, but this may only be considered a suicide and I do not know if this is good too? Children may not penetrate their realm and Mt. Fuji practices a sort of martial arts to which lions on the plains of Africa may adhere. John Lennon's death is not in vain and the raven's eye is dark from where Stew the horse will adopt it as his home. Meanwhile, Satan remains somewhere else entirely…and Yoko Ono sings folk songs to children around the campfire in Santa Fe, New Mexico. They will not know her heritage and *Lemon Tree* is my favorite. I know something that you do not. Man, like the apple, falls for 2000 years and there may be some redemption here too. Like Stew the horse who could not find the sky, the door to Japan is closed forever. Satan and Lily are divided in the ocean for all time and for Japan this is a compromise in which they can live.

"Satan's Box: 1600 Years"

Blood on Pluto is the next best thing. I sit in the train from Goteborg to Oslo and stare into the eyes of a man across from me and God asks are you good or bad? I am good but for those who time conquers their souls, there may be no forgiveness, and anything may penetrate the box which tests the spirit in 1600 years counting backward from around the 1980s too. Rather than to point the finger at any subject, time may be the judge instead. The serpent in the ocean will absorb them in time and this is called "Satan's Box."

Satan betrays his longing to do bad things and washes to shore in Venice Beach from time to time. Though, the ocean is his home he is a slave to a box where good children stare into the abyss which forms a sort of cage with their eyes. I will not judge you and Jesus finds redemption tolerable and enters God's heart instead. After the clock in China ceases to tick, he will judge man in Africa as well. Prior to this, outside of Africa, man be judged in time and if love will conquer their demeanor and last 1,800 years inward, then there soul will be set free.

"Shepherd Smith and Steve in China"

Steve is a human being without a soul. On the good hand, he inherits my dad's natural cycle which counts backward for two thousand years. Meanwhile, he is like an apple tree that wanders without a soul. Shepherd Smith will embrace him and walk with him like vagabonds on the border of what is China and Russia today. The sun will be eclipsed by the moon and he calls an inverted "Stanley Morgan," as an investment in children and this is not good or bad. The clock revolves backward and he may join the children in the Americas and this is a long journey too. Tibetan monks remain and say he was a good person. The Dalai Lama remains too and sheds light on what is the cruelty of the sun. There is no mercy in this situation.

"Meeting the devil on the subway..."

To meet the devil all one must do is take the subway. He will not harm you nor may he escape the torment he feels. His predicament is in darkness. To understand how he feels one must look into the eyes of a black panther and, at the same time, feel what is inside oneself. As for the devil, there is nothing; a void of darkness that he may not escape either. He sort of likes the poster on the wall of the Marlboro Man and relays this with "14 Outlaws" of America's old west. They represent all the faces of mankind. In this way, he knows you before you know this and he will not harm you. I am not Stalin, my mother's father, or the person who dropped the bomb. This is not his tool, and princes resound in the process. As for Satan, there is only darkness. As you shake hands with the devil, you will feel his pain as well.

"Black Enigma"

Satan is the epitome of black. The truth kills and he is sometimes mistaken as good and he is not in this case. Woman may not be his alter ego; for that which bleeds is considered good. He reads the New York Times, and one "L," represents a good witch and two "L's," represent a bad witch, or vice versa; I really do not know as the sentiment may be taken to bed with the children too? Death may be a better fate than confronting his wrath. He blames God for his predicament, but God is innocent. Jesus Christ is his son and Satan is jealous of this too. Satan may stare through the devil's eyes at such times, or vice versa? I think Satan is scared of the dark and the devil sheds light that transcends his realm where there is very little mercy.

"The apple tree that wanders...out of Africa"

Satan is blamed for this phenomenon and kids kick him from where he sleeps on the boardwalk of Venice Beach in Los Angeles. There is a stench where other homeless people urinate on the trees nearby. But, they must obey his word, which seems like a resentful demeanor. He may have a satchel with a gold pen. The other has nothing and it is not fair that Satan wears fancy Air Jordan sneakers that mock grandiose ends of which he may epitomize. God said that it is easier for a camel to enter the eye of a needle than a rich man to enter the kingdom of heaven. The homeless people wait in line at the soup kitchen and ascend into heaven here. Satan may be like other and he does not care either. Satan is an actor in his own play and calls this "Adam and Eve Hotel Theater Production." Like the devil, he has no soul either. Diana may represent my soul for the time being; and Satan may be a rich man in the eyes of God. Animals represent one sin only and Satan's domain in the ocean should not cross my path either.

"No shit, the devil and Jon Stewart..."

It is not that I think TV is evil, but it seems from this perspective that seagull waste is edible from where he speaks. The color of white jeans is pages of his book and food is better than nothing too. The TV electrifies her waste and the children are told not to ask what it is that which they eat. They eat with a fork and knife that which is on the plate and there is "no shit" to confuse it with either. The children somehow adhere to the white jeans she wears. Jon Stewart says this is not his responsibility. The devil eats edible seagull waste too. I look into the bowl of his demise as he calls himself Steve too. The implication of voodoo here merits a slight degree of respect. I eat and the children eat and we do not know what it is really? The remains of Satan subsist in the ocean forevermore. And the kids heat up dinner in the microwave. God's son, in which he does not know, is lost in the process; but remains good despite his fate leading into heaven, and I say, "we are all God's children."

Ferocious is on Jon Stewart and intercedes rather smugly, as though he has already been to heaven. In his rather demure attire, he thinks Australia would be a nice place to visit in the future. The devil looks inward at the darkness that should foreshadow his life too, and the tv is left on for what ever reason? Ferocious says that supper should be served at eight and no later. His petrified remains remain behind the glass partition in a museum in Tulsa. The dog transcends little notice by God; like the t.v. that is left on. Ferocious would rather check into the mental ward at Mount Sinai and he thinks this is better than heaven. In a dream, he thinks he saw a giant dinosaur bird lay an egg on the roof of the Metropolitan Museum of Art. Ferocious fears light the same way Satan fears darkness and their worlds part like this. Meanwhile, the devil does not ask for reparations…and it displays only a minimal amount of affection whether it be a man or a woman. (He says his work is for free.) Africa pardons those not caught in his web of lies. A woman may be strong and a man beautiful! The devil remains in a dream that which voodoo attests in hindsight as true. The display shows God as a woman petting Ferocious and while wearing his white jeans too. The devil must make a note of this and he will forebode a memory of the reign she administers, and this may be like a dream to Ferocious, despite that the t.v. is left on. Ferocious has a symbiotic relationship to the devil, but his dreams are free. We left the devil only a picture of us in Santa Monica, while on the beach; standing together like a family. The devil remains outside of Africa and Japan's door is forbidden as well.

"A pear tree in China"

The pear tree in China is a still life of a garden that once existed somewhere else. When someone picks a calla lily somewhere else, a picture is taken of this and will remain for all time. At this crossroad, I may have blinked once and time elopes the guilty ones. And I do not blame the Chinese as those who harness this picture move outside of view, I think? My life is a still life and in this picture, in time, mankind is judged and God may not be blamed too.

"Communion on Pluto too..."

There is communion on Pluto too. For those who do not believe here, they will taste the wrath of grapes and being poor here is not preferred. It may be why the Irish fear poverty suffered as a result of a potato famine? God offers them riches in exchange for their plight and this is within the still life too. They pretend to enjoy red wine with dinner at a restaurant on the Upper West Side in NYC. New... "New York" is not their realm either anymore. Instead, communion on Pluto too is sort of a blessing. The pope in the Vatican may seem lavish to some, but this is not the case. It is the opposite. Gold is a modest end to their means. The Irish remain indoors and this is good.

"200 years to Graceland"

My parents are a picture of Elvis and Pricilla's union. They will perish in darkness, but remain good. They wait for Jesus to return and the children wait too. In 200 years, Jesus will return and embrace them... The sharks protect them from all bad things. His name will be Alex, though. There are five letters in his prior name J-E-S-U-S, and this denotes that he has some connection to God, I think. The Jews will be responsible for his predicament too. Even in Japan, love will conquer their disposition. For those who find love, it may be redeemed in time too? In India, there is a father, mother and child and sin will not conquer their domain either. Could this be love?

"Redemption Song"

Bob Marley is part of the trinity in Africa. His test is to forgive Conor for his sin. The children will follow him thereafter to where three lion statues in Tunisia may not get out of the rain. Likewise, Dr. Kraus will free the children in the Americas and some still fear going into the ocean. The cruise ship is not a pleasure, but represents the whale in which Simon is acclimated and its engine is composed of the power of 24 elephants too. Michael Jackson is reincarnated as my stepmother and he plays with the kids. From a distance, Queen Latifah administers a rein and bathes in Lake Victoria, and they sing the redemption song. The play continues for six thousand years; thereafter time is forgotten and everyone is accounted for. The leopard in a tree smiles at me when I leave.

"500 gay Indians and the devil within... 'A bear in a polka dot room...'"

There are those who remain inward and this is a choice. Some people just think it is more fun. From their demeanor, I make 500 pictures that you might render as gay Indians. It is not that they are bad, but love is blind and so is this domain, (but I do not recommend it.) The first picture is "a bear in a polka dot room." It is part of the design and she drinks a peach daiquiri with a pink umbrella and spiked with a cherry too. The song they are singing is Neil Diamond's *Sweet Caroline*. And he wears blue suede shoes that belonged to Elvis. Meanwhile, the radio blasts the Bee Gees *Staying Alive* while he works out on a exercise bike and the disco ball clashes with the already polka dot walls. The white cat sits on an orange couch someone picked up at Ikea. The bear is the negative space and is invisible to its surroundings. You can tell he is naked by the way a cigar is lit and still burns in the ashtray underneath a Richard Hamilton print in the corner by a large window.

"The Journey Inward and Stanley Morgan..."

Everything seems in reverse, but you will eventually get use to it like driving in Great Britain. The time lapse seems faster too and before the maid is able to pick carrots from the garden, the children seem to eat them out of the fridge and the demand seems to make surplus. "She," not the maid; invests her money at Morgan Stanley and purchases Apple and Berkshire Hathaway and is doing very well except that the bathroom in the McDonalds stinks and she is happy to go outside. Instead, the devil makes a deal with the stockbroker and she goes to the ATM to reap the harvest. She goes to the Dunkin Donuts instead and buys a turkey sandwich with Swiss cheese on a croissant and a little mayonnaise. She drinks diet Seven Up, walks to the subway and goes down the steps then leaves at Grand Central Station. She walks diagonally through the building that echoes with each step with stilettos on. She goes to an anonymous location somewhere else.

"Prince in the rain"

Prince rides a yellow-checkered cab to Upton Street in Minneapolis and gets out with a purple umbrella in the rain. It is a vagrant expression of conceit and the rats that hide in crevices on the street seem to retract his steps for him maybe out of respect. From here, newspapers provide shelter to them and form at gutters that trap the water and it sort of floods the streets. He wears high-rising black leather boots. He walks over the water, step by step and arrives at his loft without regard to the Chinese restaurant downstairs. He does not really know why it rains and takes a bath instead. The newspaper says something about a store in the neighborhood getting robbed and she may not get out of the rain at such times.

"The death of Christ... (Will is reborn)"

Lucy puts Noxzema on Will's burns, as he is orange with the blisters that form from this sunburn. He was outside too long and the pain he feels makes him want to go home. Christ dies on a cross and Will is reborn to a tiger sun and the stars feel too far away to Will now. He envisions a world when the sun abides to the needs of the earth and the stars seem too far off too. Will visits San Francisco where he buys a bong that he sees through a window; one that he likes. Actually, Will is not far off from a tiger that lost his way. It seems so psychedelic that he as a red-headed woodpecker eats his own seed of that which is a redwood tree and like a goldfish in a bowl, dies on a cross there. This represents the fourth dimension.

"Parallel Universe and Mormons"

In Salt Lake City, there is no salt in the tears of lions falling from the sky. It is so pure that the very Virgin Mary may mistake it for her own. In the night, black panthers will fall as well. A child is born while the plain of Africa is the ground that reflects the sky, and lions do not play in the rain at such times. The umbilical chord is cut from their baby, which is a Mormon and cries like rain in the savannah of Africa. The parallel universe rising into the sky is separate. A Norwegian couple visits Utah and ski on powder there. The sky is raining in Africa, but may not penetrate their world either. The devil may be at a crossroad and he trades bread for wine, in this scenario. Hitler invites "the brats of doom" to his doorstep and leaves the Mormons behind. In this microcosm that Mimi inherits, the Mormons rise in the sky like cats falling as well. The Jews form rain from her eye like a dark cloud hovering somewhere near Hitler's private island retreat. The umbilical cord is cut from father to son, and purple rain sheds some mercy in Germany as well. They will not be denied the love of a brother to his sister of whom he does not know either. They say the blood of Christ may be tasted like wine.

"10 000 maniacs in the sky"

Should a Jew's bloodline cross over with the Virgin Mary an entity exists like my father reflecting her desire to reflect a son she does not recognize which otherwise complies immaculately. Her design allows only room for perfection. She does not harbor the brats of doom where her Jewish brethren may reside. Instead she colors the sky with "tangerine diamonds" and "purple globes." 10 000 maniacs would claim the children born into the sky and not hers sadly. She paints a picture of her sister's lightness in this way.

"Hitler's Natural Oasis: (two thousand layers inward)"

Whenever a rape occurs in the sky, there is born a child in the sky too. This expression initiates the fruit of six million Jews who may only be sand raked up by the ocean where tears fall into the abyss and escape fates unattractive to the sky. Hitler lives on a deserted island in the Indian Ocean and claims "the brats of doom" as his children. He is far away and may not transcend 2000 layers of sharks that guard his island from anyone who might want to visit. For those who remain here, it does not rain except for those tears that develop out of the phenomenon, and the brats remain inside most of the time anyway, as it may be raining outside? But, no one would know and the sun shines constantly in a distant mirage of what is there…

"The Jews are reborn: "John Lennon on Waverly Place and catching a cab in the rain"

Really, the Jews are reborn in time and John Lennon at any given time is hailing a cab in the rain in New York City. He has an alternative identity and tells the cab driver that his name is Dudley Smith. He does not desire to relive the life he once led and someone said, "Let it be!"

"God: 'Five Donuts on a silver tray'"

My dad served him five donuts on a silver tray. It is not that he does not deserve gold as he does, but you might say that the discrepancy merits a matter of taste. Creation is two lines merging into one, and the art deco feel and the design is his own intention. I may eat an orange in full and, like the sun that will reincarnate in other the test is to eat five donuts, (without skipping a beat to the drum that beats in a dark and distant corner of Africa.) He shares the space with friends who died before and is a spectator from within and need not participate with the show either. Yes, the donuts must be digested as one and repelled like this.

"My dad and the African Jew Phenomenon"

My dad has a natural cycle which means that the two lines that merge and God created as one design is like an art deco Oreo? He may be the cream in the center. The journey out and inward represent the cookies on either side. He is good and a silver fish that swims in the ocean confirms that he ever was here. He left Africa as though he never left, and such a grace confirms that he was even there. He left Africa when it was time for him to leave. He bought a cloud in the sky and watches from a not so far distance.

"Skittles: taste the rainbow"

A rainbow jets out of the sky from South Africa to somewhere like Australia or New Zealand, and proves that light has color. It forms a bridge where people seem to inherit a common heritage, which may have began with Abraham. I may not claim the same heritage, and watch as it is a beautiful sight. Clyde claims he has a certain allegiance to the Jewish faith too. I do not understand what he meant?

"The bars that separate in a South African Prison: Hitler's Nightmare"

God may have been conceived out of the sweat of two South Africas. Nelson Mandela knew this South Africa all too well. The European Africans claimed the land and divided the people according to color, which was not what God may have intended. For now it is a cause of convenience, but some cross the line and this courage is respected by some. The bars of the prison that Nelson Mandela called home for too long to remember was the only mercy he shared. I do not envy him, but respect him just the same. I think Hitler knew somehow he was not God and still he asked for mercy.

"So, a dog committed suicide and killed the lion in the process..."

The wrath of Hitler may be in the form of a lion. It is divided in three 2000-year periods and embodies one lion. Though, it has three faces which are photographed from three different angles, it appears to be three different identities. You may say that three lions are sacrificed ,that which is one. Inside of it, there is a sort of black cat that is spared its fate.

"Mike, the 13th sun and the evil director..."

God may not approve of the promiscuous behavior of other and Mike (as a lizard) sees their vanity and complies to reveal their flaw in the film with wretched disregard to the beauty of the body's form with few exceptions. He represents the 13th sun and his wrath is directed at everyone if no one. He is already on a journey out of time. Lizards assemble at his house in the Hollywood Hills where they sit by the pool under gondolas sipping margaritas. Really, he blames the car for burning fossil fuels and directs his wrath on others and his son, but they have never met. He may consider the car as evidence of the crime committed and goes to the local Starbucks to plan a film he is directing which is way too raunchy for kids.

"We are from before the stars and after the dinosaurs..."

It felt like we arrived, but I do not remember exactly when in hindsight? I was in a mental hospital in California and was fighting off notions of nuclear war as we passed the moon on arrival. It seems like we have been here for a long time, but I did not know Mimi's sister and someone died on a cross for our sins and I did not know this until Mimi would intercede and this is faith. It is like we wrote our destiny in the stars that would come later, but the dinosaurs existed oddly before. I have faith in God because I am told that is right, but we have never met, like in hindsight. There was a man of dark complexion who worked in the hospital and I told him I could touch him, but I do not think he was God.

"The sound of silence: Playing Parcheesi in space and the children remain with an unopened bag of gummy bears..."

We may see you from afar, but really never intercedes God's greater plan and splendor. You may play Parcheesi in space, but not actually be here. I remember the sound of silence, but am not still part of the darkness. The children inherit a white horse that appears black in the night sky. We are like that? The children remain with an unopened bag of gummy bears.

"The trash dump on Earth..."

It is a pity that future valued objects of the earth are a burden today, and designated as what we call "trash." It may form an island in the sky with memories of rich soiled ends and that is enough. It is not what they are, but the very fact they exist like memories make them valuable in the future, if only an old banana peel, it has a story. There is a flat plane and I think it is sad that some people are homeless too.

"The Gay Quarter Show"

The gay quarter show is prep work for a show in the future. This work may fall under a theater production which I encourage you to do yourself. Some may consider one, as having two halves that represent the whole, but like the moon there is more and the gay quarter which with one becomes a whole. I would like some of this work to be performed on a stage too! The crimes against the sun may be performed later too. It will subsist further through my eyes. It is true that the Swedish sisters are beautiful and are denied responsibility of the plight of the sun that Mike evokes. The show is performed along the East River north of Dykman street in Manhattan and is produced under the title of "Adam and Eve Hotel Theater Productions." Despite the sins of the father, it may recognize that man is good too.

"Blood on Pluto"

What is left of the children is road kills on the highways that make up America. I am taking a bus from Providence to New York City, as I attended boarding school near Providence in Newport, Rhode Island. I knew the devil not I and the time elapsed so that I would leave after three years. Jamie Earl is my traveling companion, he with guitar and I, are visiting my mother in New York City and will stay at her apartment on 80th Street and Park Avenue. She is tolerant of my friends, but most of the time, locks herself in her bedroom while reading a book. Years later, Jamie will die in a car crash, but is first expelled from boarding school after taking an overdose of LSD.

I used to enjoy listening to him play Bob Dylan songs on his guitar after study hall each evening. The first year in boarding school went well, as I did not smoke yet. The sophomore year, however, went by fast, as I attended a marine biology exposition on the school's sailboat vessel called *Geronimo*. By the time I returned, Jamie would seem distant and eventually was expelled from school. I had started to smoke cigarettes that summer in Ecuador, and I thank my father for providing this opportunity. It was not that I was rebelling by smoking, but it found me somehow and thereafter it was difficult to stop. I went to a place called Otivallo, which I forget how to spell and took the pictures of a group of Indians there, that was missing here.

So, I found myself in Washington Square Park with Jamie and listen to him play his guitar singing the one and only Bob Dylan to a small audience; and the sun there felt like when in Ecuador. After returning from the marine biology expedition, I was excited to print the pictures I had taken in Ecuador. It was disappointing that some of the clay sculpture figurines I purchased in Ecuador were partially broken. The year would pass like this, my sophomore year, and after Jamie was expelled, I spent most of my free time in the darkroom. Furthermore, my grades plummeted decisively. I thought it bold that the new students who attended this year actually thought they were equal to those who had already spent a year here, though we still occupied the same dorm as I remember it to be Achincloss.

That year was the first time when someone would call me "you are such a Jew" for not letting him ride my bicycle. I guess it was the first time I had heard this and really, I did not know this to be a bad thing. I had fun, however, spending the summer thereafter in New York with friend Bill. We both smoked and would jump the turnstiles in the subway to go to a bar called Mondo Cane Blues Bar, in the village, to spend what miniscule money we had and we knew the manager named Adolf. He was from South Africa and did not like Jews, but he was cool to us anyway. Also, both Bill and I were photographers and this made us have a lot in common. The blood would come much later!

My junior year was the same as my sophomore year, no better and no worse. I developed a program in the school called "The inner city building project" and if it succeeded I would have probably have stayed for my senior year, but it did not. Otherwise, I wanted students to get an experience working for Habitat for Humanity and a soup kitchen in the Bowery as well. We stayed in a church in Hell's Kitchen and I arranged this as being the same church in which Jimmy Carter had stayed. I guess the other students were not impressed to keep this project going after our first visit. Thank you for allowing me to do such, if not for only one visit. I was becoming more and more isolated and when I heard, a friend, Geoff was not asked back, I too decided not to return. He was one of the few friends who remained by junior year. I was at the coffee shop, a few blocks from the hill in which was St. George's campus. I think I called my dad collect and told him I would not return. I think he cried and for this I am sorry.

The only regret is that I did not graduate for the sake of my photographer teacher, Philip Dickinson. He had been in Vietnam and lost a leg there, and I admired him a lot. I think sophomore year "Bisline" became head of the art program which included photography. I did not like his authoritative disposition either. Otherwise, I would have offered Musgrove as a perfect place to have the graduation retreat? I guess the rest, who were not friendly anyway, missed out on this opportunity. At this time, I was listening to Louis Armstrong play his trumpet and was thinking of this one girl, Eliza, who I sort of liked while sitting at the pool at Musgrove. Louis sings, "Hello Dolly," while Eliza playfully blows his horn too.

Blood on Pluto (continued)

I told you about Ilius, my homeless friend from Mozambique? He slept in Tompskin's Square Park before the community there united and kicked out all the homeless people and we would play soccer in the daytime in Washington Square Park. We were friends for a time, I guess you could say. But, to be from Africa it is an insult to shed blood at the hands of a lesser, may it be an animal or whatever. This is important to note, as I would eventually shed blood instead, for his sake.

"Summer of 1988"

Even though I was destitute, the summer began by getting a ride from boarding school with Bill's stepmother and she dropped me off in front of Lily's apartment building in Riverdale in the Bronx. I truly, at this moment, felt free at last. Lily allowed me to stay at her apartment there while she stayed with her boyfriend. I had a job as a coffee tender at Figaro Café on Bleeker and MacDougal streets in the village. I should not have any animosity for Lily at this point as she did her best despite a past she would rather deny. I found the workers at Figaro Café as eclectic to say the least. I was impressed by Kenny, a funny black guy who was dating an Italian girl. He allowed me and Steve Heinz, another tender to the coffee bar (he was an actor from Holland being mulatto, half-black and half-Jewish), to stay at his apartment on 102nd Street between Manhattan Avenue and near Central Park West.

Meanwhile, Kenny chased some girl he liked and we paid rent for a nestle and shared the apartment with three French persons, two males and a girl as well. Though I was working everyday, the pay was minimum wage. I got the job at seventeen because I was having a show there with the money I borrowed from my sister Nicole, and was able to frame all the pictures in the show. Steve, the owner of the café, had warned me about not being late. As I was late twice and eventually would be fired for being late a third time, I tried my utmost to do a good job. I relied on the one meal I would receive each shift, which always was a Figaro Club and a bowl of Gazpacho soup, which was really good and I guess Steve was generous like that. I tried working another shift at a poster shop down the street. I would go as far as sleeping in the park or in the basement in at Figaro Café. I thought, sort of conceited, that I was doing a damn good job and you can imagine I was shocked when I got fired.

Thereafter, the French people sharing the apartment upstairs and I would drink alcohol that they mostly provided, in the backyard that was a sort of a fenced concrete terrace. I guess when you are down and out, you become desperate in ways, I did not know before. The "bodegas" as this is past the good area of town on the west side of the park, would sell individual cigarettes which they would call "loose" in reference to individual cigarettes, as I became quite addicted. I do not even remember if I went so far to pick half-smoked ones from ashtrays as I could hardly afford them now that I was fired. The whole experience was liberating to say the least, and I lived with older people and felt special as such. One day, my dad showed up in a limousine and said we were going. As I was more than broke and sort of wasting time thereafter, buying a bagel with butter as a meal which only cost fifty cents at the time, to get by; the option to go to Nantucket was tempting anyway? I guess my dad sort of bailed me out of the situation. Though I would never see Kenny again, I would have liked to thank him for allowing Steve Heinz and me rent his apartment even though I stayed two months and only paid one month, I guess I owe you? My dad would tell me to get a job at Marty's landscaping business on Nantucket and only worked a few weeks, but, still, I paid back Nicole for what she had lent me

"After Simon's Rock"

The shark that would bleed for all our sins as Jesus did before, would eventually become my responsibility. I guess the crime was covering it up under someone else's direction by eating it, which was a mako shark and tasted like swordfish. The proof here that I am not a Jew is that I would be blamed by others for the act. Even though innocent, people saw the guilt in my face and what was to come, I could not avoid and all the Jews were relinquished of the responsibility. It happened just as it did before on the school's marine biology vessel. After driving a yellow cab in New York City for two years, I was twenty-one and this kid, who looked Puerto Rican and a Rastafarian black man told me to leave the corner across the street where I lived in a small apartment that I could barely afford. But, I would not leave that night, maybe ten thirty PM. I was pummeled with light blows by the kid and the Rasta man just implied physical abuse. Eventually, I would ask the kid in my expression, why he wanted me to leave the corner where there was a thrift shop at the time on 80th Street and 2nd Avenue.

I had enjoyed looking at their window displays, which would be changed every month. He did not respond amiably and still, I felt like I chased them away. Then, suddenly, the young kid appeared "to tag the shark" so to speak and in front of the H and H Bagels, he cut my chin with what was either a piece of glass or a syringe for heroin. They were hiding in the store doorway and would later administer the blow; he was acting alone now. The people in the bagel shop stared at my chin as I was bleeding profusely. I soon went back to my hovel and I tried to forget what just happened. The killing of the mako came several years earlier. Something in the sky that day told me the confrontation would be unavoidable.

After driving a cab for two years in New York City, I returned some years later. I come eye to eye with a black kid at Musgrove Plantation in Georgia. He thought I was crazy, and I told someone on a bulldozer to leave. I do not believe there should be financial concessions to African Americans, but pose it in a different way, which implies that they should have a choice whether to work. Unlike my dad, I think they are guilty about being slaves in this country, and should not have to work if they don't want to which is another way of taking the devil's advocate, as these kids are far from innocent.

However, it is true they once were forced to leave their land and work for nothing, I think they should be proud of their heritage still. The question is, does their experience, and I am talking to the children, here, are they better than when their heritage should indoctrinate themselves here and I would argue yes. As I eyeballed this kid, I ask the question in my recalcitrance, implying, "Do you want to stay or go?"

They are children of a "silver spring" and I bury a fish at Musgrove, a magnolia tree leaf and a banana peel in the memory of those in their lineage who do not make it here as a result of oppression. It may be a sepulcher observance where a Septuagint body bare witness to it. A young black kid today has no more reason to be angry than Native Americans who persist, yet something still makes them angry inside and I must make a note of this as to ask why? I do not know why, but at such a time I am listening intently. I am not proud of their past and I am not, not proud of my own, as I know things happen for a reason and God has been on the watch for sometime now, and he would not allow something like slavery to happen without a reason.

So, I am living in New York City, Soho actually, after being diagnosed, though falsely, as mentally ill. I will not fight this notion as years have passed and I am tired of fighting. Anyway, a large black man is standing in my way at a gourmet supermarket there and this is the first time I felt this anger that I thought might be God. A few days have passed and I am standing on West

Broadway in front of my loft rental and attempt to photograph the World Trade Center with a four by five view camera with a tripod. I plead with a lady with wrinkled skin beyond her years for a napkin and am mocked by the owner of the European deli that was once there. My heart begins to pound and I can hear someone loud with each step on the pavement "like a hundred lesbian women passing the man in an Armani suit" and he, a black man appears as I had returned to my camera set on a tripod on the sidewalk, on the eastern side of the street. What happens then I can not avoid. He appears and asks me if I want a woman and I reply "Do you understand no thank you," and like a boxing match he pummels me with one blow to my head and I bleed for Ilius that day as I fall to the ground, on top of the camera which falls too.

"Blood on Pluto"

What you may not see will not hurt you; the orphic message blows in the wind. This is especially true of a blessed land like America. Committing a sin is visible to all and those who should part from the security blanket and in a state of reluctance they may find themselves outside of Pluto. Otherwise, children should play with other children and this secures their place where they should be, especially girls, as they tend to disassociate with bad kids often of the other sex. This causes the other kids of other races to be freed of judgment and assumption, and is a natural phenomenon. Sins are like Indians' trail of blood, as no one on the inside will prevent you from falling from the sky. I suppose, therefore, to not see black people is a good thing as they are in a different element and dimension and to blame them of someone else's sin just makes your situation worse.

There are three police officers near my home in Georgia. I am driving from seeing my girlfriend in Jacksonville, Florida, and am quite tired. I am going thirty-five miles an hour in a forty-mile-an-hour zone. When I make a complaint the next day, the police officer assured, on the phone, that it was perfectly legal. Anyway, they were concerned and frisked me and put me in the back of a police car. Over the years, my trust in police officers has declined considerably. They do not know how to approach, but often their intentions are bad and I feel provoked to expose the injustice, even though it seems their ill-fate is more like their own confession with which I may live.

I guess "the force" as they sometimes refer to themselves, tries to provoke one of the officers to do something and then the others sweep up the fish in the ocean as a score. Never has one dared to cross the line of justice, I would want to say, but this has occurred before really, in my blind site; this is such an incident. The female officer who stopped me is definitely agitated by something and the other two are just doing their job. I would comply with their wish to search my van, but already feel convicted and therefore, the disrespect puts me on guard. You may say, I have seen bad things before and often it is something dealing with police officers, who use their job as an opportunity to do such. I watch her bring a dog to smell the van and basically search every corner of it, hitting the plastic interior with some sort of rod which I had never seen. The dog finds one of my t-shirts in the back of the van and this merits their assumption of guilt, and I do not know why they don't arrest me, as I know there are no narcotics in my van, dog or no dog.

I think they just want to talk. This is a conviction of words and behavior and it is offensive. I would rather be arrested for something that would lead to my innocence, but as long as they manage to stay in control, it would feed their sick paranoia, with someone else's arrest. Anyway, I am let out of the police car maybe after twenty minutes and the presumption is that I will reach my hand into the air where she is, no different than subordination of some guy at work in regard to their boss. She holds this pose, you may say vogue, as she is a female cop and without any question, she is vain in the spectacle and may be special. She accuses me that she is sure I have narcotics and, without giving the license and registration back, eventually allows me to reach in the air for my things. I suppose she has already committed another crime somewhere else and let me go to detain someone else whom I am sure she is guilty of. I think this is the way she thought, something gets out of hand and suddenly she is on the bad side and for that she is a victim and must use her power against tolerance or whatever really, as I don't quite understand it. I could not see her nametag, as I do not think she wants me to see it. All cops are not bad, but those who are bad see me as a threat.

Blood on Pluto is the next worse thing than hell. It is when blood passes through, out in space, and your blood and the scared blood of Indians meet, there is no mercy here and you are at the mercy of someone else. I do not really understand the theory and feel safe that my blood will not cross the line, so to speak. You go to a nightclub where the music is throbbing and it is a strange place, like that where time should pass at a different speed, the heart of Pluto maybe and when the music stops that which is not natural is passed out into space, leaving those who are part of the ritual unharmed and still on Pluto.

They have a dog here too, but it does not do anything really and may in token save another dog's fate that was en route inward, it is a sacrifice, but maintains a balance from which is good from the bad and also a receptor like an antenna. As to be able to track their location from another point, it is a network where Pluto is on Earth, but is only visible to those who have access to Pluto like going to a private nightclub. He would seem like a stray dog and, if killed by someone who knows it is not theirs (I don't know if this is even possible), yet it does not find remorse and another dog takes its place, so that the balance of power remains intact. There should not be sin in this world, but as the order changes into that which is heaven, there is no reason now to sin anyhow. But, it makes those on Pluto laugh at the imposition that finds losers outside themselves, and themselves winners. Falling from the sky is judgment in itself. Here, you may find yourself at the mercy of children. The wandering indians, like a thousand points of light, is an exception.

I feel obliged to share my point of view, but wish you not to find it as truth as it does not necessarily help in getting you where you want to be. Anyone who attempts to project a greater truth should be commended and therefore I commend myself, but I am sorry if it does not cohere with your beliefs etc. as it is just theory and does not even represent my own beliefs necessarily. I am a Christian and you may think of me as a different point of view if you want? There is blood on Pluto and I am not subject to any punishment either. Like the indians, my blood does not cross over to the blood of any animals and to the dog on Pluto, this is a blessing too. God feels sorry for this dog who should not impede Satan's life on neighboring Neptune. The dog sheds a tear in the ocean as no one knows why either? It is good but cannot escape the agents of darkness from where he stands on Pluto.

Mimi was blind to all bad things and therefore vulnerable. Her oasis is the Amazon rainforest. The spiral in China formed a perfect formation and the sun was created from darkness; it is a Jew. The fate is that a rape would bring bad things here and the only way to defend oneself would be to offer her only redemption, so others might see the light and those bad things consequently, would not break the fortitude. I became her eyes and she would tell me one day in the darkness that forbade to go search for mushrooms. This was not a problem, as I could go to a distant place and eat the mushrooms without picking a single one similar to how insects would extract a little bit from it and I am only like a "little black cat."

A deer should pick it what is today India and by day the person might be blamed by deer who deny it. God should pick her flower immaculately as he was guilty of screwing a bear that is all seen as self-defense.God, nor his forte, Mt.Fuji may be blamed for this act. It is the denial of God's word that makes someone responsible and sin resounds outside of Pluto. I being a sort of cat with a long tail and it is now extinct, but its closest resemblance is to what people see as a black cat and though the infringements of God's creation showed to be a test at best? Where my dad stands in the dark in Africa, (Satan is scared of the dark) and I leave behind my tail, in which was separated from me, she is with my dad there and may or may not be good? In the light there is darkness still and we felt compelled in the light to bring those innocent of sin out of the darkness. The sky that had been leaked in the color blue manifested itself in what were three blue devils who worked in the sky (different to the phrase in reference to the cops on the LA freeway) and the sun meanwhile felt left out for not being accepted as a Christian.

The ordeal of repairing the sky after the incident with the bear made for an opportunity of the sun to escape and it was jealous, like a child who wanted to play with the others, but could not then. I think the devil is adopted as a Jew, but has no relation to Mike who represents the thirteenth sun and may be a Jew too. It has grown into a deal that will eventually free Ferocious from its plight, like the gorillas of distant suns that occupy the Congo, of this array of suns that have died. The sun penetrated not God whose eyes were delved as one of the blue devils which is pure and the other two would be infected by the sun of yesterday and healed into what is now my eyes. It was after the dinosaurs and before the stars. After the bear incident with God, God may have shed a tear too, that leaked blue like this in the sky. Mimi sheds a tear too, and it is for her sister and not me. We assume a bond which is a compromise I may live with too. God may seem vulnerable and I plead for us forgiveness. I am "Empty Blue," and we are forgiven like that. We leave a white horse to the children instead.

While looking for mushrooms out in space, it was easy to avoid human contact where ever I was on Earth; they could not see me and I wandered here a long time only through animals' knowledge of their sin may anyone detest I was here at all. The animals were a bloodline that crossed over to what were Indians or Native Americans today, and within each mushroom picked, nine animals sponsored each Indian's freedom and were sort of a people without God and a weird sort of blessing as they are not subjugated or responsible for other's sins either. They shared a space with animals that are forgiven for their sins as long as their blood does not cross over. God forgives me for other's sins which grow out of this dynamic that diagnoses God is not one of the animals. A bear remains for those who must believe. God's blood should not mix with theirs and, as a precaution, many Indians are sacrificed at the hands of Stalin. If the sickness confounds in a single body, he or she may not be blamed, but this is less than heaven as well. To compensate the demeanor, the children will inherit a white horse that looks black in the night sky. Children are the remains of roadkills on highways and wander outside of Pluto and the sun seems very distant too.

The Indians are now where I once was, but their bloodline remains here and if consumed, would then lead to a fate that is not familiar to them if not detestable, but definitely different. God offered his own son instead and that makes the world divided according to their sins in the greater ordeal. The world should come to an end in a flash and this made all sinners equal in the eyes of God and their sins prone to repenting and forgiven. Why should not the blood of another not go outside is not clear and I suppose that it is the same reason God's blood and animal blood should not be shared. I guess a good witch is a sin that nature has redeemed. Diana, the good witch to man, may offer her dog as a gift and leaving the sky slightly open as though a warning not to harm it. Meanwhile, a good witch commits or is responsible for natural sins thereafter and, consequently, good and bad is a puzzle that merits even in the most humble abode, the opportunity for heaven and the risk of hell. The two "Ls" in hell may represent a bad witch which nature does not redeem, while one "L" is good as a sin redeemed in heaven, I think.

Though Indians are where I once was wandering the earth, invisible to those who could not see and though a fate of not a blessing, but less than damnation, they subsist on the outside. The bug that should remain to taste the blood that does not leave, should it penetrate the bounds as blood on Pluto causes a chant that is not protected by light and those susceptible to hell are even in more danger? You may call me Geronimo if you want, but I prefer "Empty Blue," and once on a boat tagging sharks, a line was released to catch a mako. I did not want to kill it except there was no choice and therefore I ate it as though my own blood, but more as a token of respect. Kevin Barton was a friend and, while there, told me everything that happened. However, the year I left after spending three years at St. George's and my junior year, it became clear that I could not penetrate the bounds of three African American princes and must retract now to know what happened after I left. The brats of doom must have done something bad to get leverage over these three princes and I suppose I knew this when I left that there was not anything I could do about it.

A bug is left behind to absorb the blood that remains on Pluto. There is no longer any danger, and God is now separate. I may go outside as the rain will not escape those inside at the time. I recognize my spiritual mother , Mimi and the tear that fell from her eye. I smile as though it may be the sun's own remorse. We, in air-conditioned accommodations at the Grove House, play backgammon and the sun is shining outside too. The Indians transcend this realm as though a thousand points of light. Like Stew the horse, the indians are redeemed in the night sky. God's blood should not cross over with theirs. A dog finds Pluto a punishment for a crime Satan commits. A bug on Pluto absorbs the blood that remains. I do not think it threatens God's domain.

"Mercedes"

I am detached from "the dark star," but remain inside as though outside as well. I will not judge you either. Meanwhile, the flies caught in Mimi's web in China will share the mercy of the devil and this is judgment.

Even on Pluto, there is a heaven. I will adopt it as my home from time to time, but remain on the outside looking in, for the most part. God sees through the spectacle at hand and may see through my eyes if he wants to. God is really looking at all of his creation from outside, inward and the devil conspires with this notion to recognize heaven is separate and I am neither. The children here have a choice.

While asleep in their beds on Christmas Eve, the children are protected from all bad things that the night may produce. In a distant place, panda bears play in the snow of what is to them paradise. Like Ilius who fears shedding blood to a lesser outside the scope of Africa, panda bears do not like to slide on ice and for this it is taboo for the black rose who is their mother. Mercedes came from Cebu, in the Philippines and was old when she came to my family as a sort of governess after my parents were divorced. I do not think my sisters knew her as well as I did and she tests me on my schoolwork at night. Also, her favorite show was *Dynasty*. She fell one morning on the icy steps on a winter day. It was a step down like how I drove a taxicab when I had greater opportunity and in that sense, she sees me as her equal. We may both experience a degrading situation. Otherwise, it is not possible to look a panda bear straight in the eyes and the children that live in the wilds of America are protected as such. Though Mercedes and I never looked into each other's eyes, we both could keep a secret. A panda bear is when children choose one hole to enter or another. There may be a choice for children even out there in space. I guess I know something that you do not.

Adam and Eve Hotel Theater Productions: The Tenth Dimension

God and the Ocean's Demise

The broth of fish urine mixes in the shallow crevices where sharks hide in layers from above. Mt. Fuji notices a slight altercation of the composition and sees bubbles of hate rise from a shark to note as though it was time to leave. The octopus, which is Will's mom detest the on goings above and releases him as though her own son. Will made it out and climbed on rocks off the coast of Liberia some time ago and now calls Africa home. I never penetrated the ocean's domain as though "a tiger lost at sea," that which is Will and is a warning. He is my friend too. Instead, I end up in Florida, but detached as a whole from its inland composition as though an episode of Baywatch. Pamela Anderson is a nemesis to judge lions as they enter a mirage in the Pacific Ocean. Meanwhile, Satan is not me, and he ends up in the ocean without mercy on the boardwalk of Venice Beach. Lions will not conquer the tear drop from his eye that which he leaves in the ocean to denote in time that God is now separate. God leaves the oasis and Satan remains somewhere that will never meet again like the horizon of the ocean detached from the sky. Like the seals on the rocks, Satan rather calls the ocean home. Lions tread on beaches under palm trees and confirm that one may dream a better dream. They may be homeless in a sense to leave the ocean as though drowning in the reality the parting should diagnose without pause like the waves breaking to shore should free them. The children would not know such a journey but may experience a different fate like a boy becoming a man is as real as the teardrops they leave behind. God is no longer present. But, the children drown and reawaken in this form and forbid the awareness of a lion's journey as it drowns in children's dreams as it leaves the ocean. There is still a dark corner of the ocean where God once resided. On an evening before a full moon you may hear the seahorses chant his name to beckon Satan to God's domain once

385

detached as the waves break on rocks below. Lily is a metaphor for a desert in the ocean and the moon's own shed its harvest in the ocean and it is apparent that she is naked at such times. She may not leave either, but allows Mimi to embrace her sister too like a black silhouette of a mermaid detesting her loss and the fish swim like her children to such a notion. Satan will not leave the darkness this entails. The fish will not taste the chocolate that separates this oasis from the sky above as though Ferocious will not penetrate their domain either. They meet in a mirage of an island out at sea near Malibu and meanwhile the children's eyes are glued to the tv to remind her children that there is mercy here too. Ferocious rides in the car of the Woodpecker and films the on goings within like hate propelled outward from the ocean. I wave to them (in this chocolate paradise) that the children may dream a better dream too...God thinks his sacrifice is worth its weight in gold. Meanwhile, Mt. Fuji leaves the ocean as a suicide is played out in a distant land though. What the children do not see, will not hurt them either. The children ride through the drive thru at Jack in the Box and order fish sandwiches and place exorbitant amounts of ketchup on it and they do not know what this sacrifice entails?

A child throws a French fry into the ocean as its golden embers are eaten by a fish within the confine which is now its oasis too. Otherwise, we have no children really before this farfetched play below the stars and the moon claims them as her own instead. In this play, a lion undergoes a transformation as it leaves the ocean and Satan remains in it and seems a bit obsolete in the play above. Otherwise, God's children swim like fish in the ocean and such a sacrifice is well noted. Like a chocolate surmise to the cause above, the ship blankets the water with oil and there is no mercy here for Satan. On that day, Stew the horse could not find the sky. Ferocious reads from the script as this is not diagnosed as part of the play above? Only, he recognizes the tear that is shed from his eye is real! From this perspective, the devil finds that Hitler's island is unobtainable and he sees inward through Satan's eyes instead. This hate he feels remains somewhere else too. The "brats of doom" would rather not partake in the play anyway and rather watch the t.v. instead. Nemo, the dog, hides on the dark side of the moon and they do not see him either. Only a horse that seems black in this light is sacrificed in a distant land and the children must ask why? This is the beginning of the tenth dimension where Billy Bush puts the children to sleep evoking the square corners of the t.v. set may not be entered except in their dreams however. Meanwhile, BP is attempting to clean the oil spill from the ocean. Ziggy Stardust screams from above and the sharks claim that it is safe to enter the ocean too. A Native

American man in the west holds a bowie knife and caresses the water with it to baptize its fire like the fin of a great shark that should not leave. Meanwhile, I call my friend Forest in China and ask why this should be otherwise and he replies he does not know why either. In Poland, there is a sort of peace, and the dolphin represents the ocean's heart so that it reaches the sky and not ask why either?

Rocky Robin

In China, there are two sisters who stare at Andy Warhol's black façade of a canvas and do not penetrate its darkness. China may be a map of the sun of yesterday in the form of a negative that persists further. I do not know that my sister Nancy will share its destiny? Meanwhile, a Robin and a Blue Jay lift the veil of the curtain that remains. There is a sort of beauty pageant here that unites mankind with nature and this is the highest point to where they seek. The BG's sing that she is "more than a woman," and Australia is her sister that covets long distance calls from other. The children would not deny that sometimes nature repeats itself. It forms a nest in the confines so that a snake should not come upon its eggs? This does happen from time to time, though. Furthermore, the Robin rarely sheds a tear when this happens, nor does she seek revenge. It just continues like the cool and contained transmission of nature and it is her mother in sense too.

Once upon a time in America, a young African/American boy threw a rock at a Robin and missed. Sort out of bravado, he throws another rock at a Blue Jay and this time he hits it. The sisters are slightly impressed by the ordeal, while saddened as well. Nature always redeems those who harm it which is an euphemism meaning revenge. It is rare that two kinds of birds should share the same bloodline? But, as sisters represented in China, this is such a case. The Robin witnessed the ordeal and while Africa is detected for those who deny God too, a Blue Jay in the form of Audrey Hepburn swoops down on the African plain. The children transcend into a different domain; you might even say transformation. However, the culprit now is responsible and the boy is now above looking down like that which the bird once plundered from. There is forgiveness in nature too. She carries the boy into a better world, but the children who are responsible find this to be a punishment at best. Here, there is a consensus among his peers and the children will return someday to a place vacant of the devil's tears, as though never leaving. A boy once stood in Africa and now he is a man that was born out of this dilemma.

He may only now understand what is a mother's love without ever leaving. He will never throw a rock at a bird again and this is redemption. He is free to be born in another without ever dying. The children in the foreign land know this truth and are witness to the transformation which is the tenth dimension. A soul may not be bought or sold. A snake with two heads formed out of spite in Australia so the sister, once as a Blue Jay should not be harmed again either. She feeds her eggs to the snakes and this is nature too. Once in heaven, there is no reason to want to leave either. There is a swimming pool which repels her tear outward from her blue eye and Rocky Robin flies in the sky that leaks the color blue where the sisters meet. This is not always a bad thing either? Children hold hands in the dark and would not know otherwise if you should ask?

Milk (A Desert in the Ocean)

Sierra was born from a flower picked. It is true that the moon bares its children from above, but the Calla Lily once picked no longer finds fertility thereafter sadly. Sierra never knew of a different existence and so for the flower's harvest, it does not seem like a curse. But, the flower once fertile is now to be dishonored so that she must comply with the disgrace. Every child is born as aware of right from wrong? Like a cow on a hill, there is a certain allegiance of earth to a tear that fell from her eye. It, the cow, harbors this knowledge as her milk is conceived out of the dilemma which is not hers either. Somehow, this is transferred from mother to child. The Earth abides by nature's request and this may not be altered by mankind. A desert in the ocean is a paradise for children who do not disgrace the mother it is detached to, but like a flower dishonored it may not be possessed and gold is similar in this vein. The apples from the tree of knowledge may not be taken and the children who seek would know this. There is a certain respect of Mother Nature that God shares with you and I am not the flower once picked either. Jesus must claim to have a mother and similarly one finds solace in respect of their own, I think. Furthermore, once your umbilical chord is cut from you to your mother, it may not be re-entered either. This flower picked conveys this respect too. Like "the desert in the ocean" the milk is her own and this merits respect too. I was searching for mushrooms in the dark when the flower was picked and, may be said not to be there at the time. I will bleed for her and gain this knowledge likewise, a respect and she may be my spiritual mother too. This is a catch-22 which transcends from the third dimension where I live. I know that the Garden of Eden is now no more.

Satan is now gone, as well as the Jews...

I will never know Satan and nor the Jews. It is possible to have been there, but our paths seem to part so vehemently like Jesus dying on the cross or the ocean parting for Moses. I walk with the children on the boardwalk in Venice Beach and they wear his Air Jordan's and denote as witness to the parting. I came and I left, but was not there when he entered the ocean's domain. He watched the children during the turmoil after 9/11. Africa is where he once resided. I was never there really. I ended up in Barbados like the slaves too, but there may not be a connection here. Satan is now gone as I am a witness to his parting. But, the children remain and are forgiven as such for just being, which may be a crime too.

The Jews who died in the holocaust may not have crossed my path in the realm of the present. Like loving someone who does not know you, we part and the warewolves of London will not find me out of darkness. The "brats of doom" remain and there may be a distant connection here too. My mother may have been born Jewish, but is not acclimated as such and I was baptized instead. I am born out of my own resources and the brats deny this and must comply with a crime once committed like the Jews who die in the holocaust are not God either? The Jews, like a camel, enter the eye of a needle, but I do not think we will meet anytime in the future either? Satan lives in darkness of which he is a slave. The children claim to have seen him enter the wake of the ocean too. Stew, the horse, is testament that he was here too, where children form a cage with their eyes. Meanwhile, the brats are footprints in the sand as children leave Pluto on their way into the tenth dimension. As they leave to Prince's anthem "When Doves Cry," the saints go marching in too. They are like the Indians of yesterday and this is their cause as some sort of sacrifice that riddled the sky like a thousand points of light.

Further Speculation on the Calla Lily

Lily is the pun and the flower not hers. She loved a boy and the flagrant attribution to an apple once beseeched from a branch and relay premonitions that nature does repeat itself. She may feel like God and in hindsight the gold is hidden behind a young boy she treats like a gigolo. An Inca King is disrobed so that she may see God's vulnerability and claim the beautiful flower in a distant land which will lead to man's demise. In the process, I am left in a catch-22 as I do not know the gold should belong to me? Mt. Fuji remains in the ocean, while someone picks a beautiful flower which seems like the lesser crime as it is done in temptation. I think he is innocent and God may be his alibi. Man as well as Adam may be forgiven and it is a pre-conceived decision not to participate in his demise that Mimi will partake. Men might of feared her primal order still, and perpetuated the flower which is her endeavor and the children in the tenth dimension find this as a parting as well. Mary Magdalene may be a metaphor for this flower before it is dishonored and that Jesus did in fact exist. She will die for someone else's sin, and may, as a result, be like Jesus as well. I think man and nature parts like this?

I Bear Three Crosses

The children are beyond Mimi's ring here, off a cat's black tail on Pluto. We hold onto a rock to tally mushrooms picked that Indians pass the oasis where animals shed some mercy too. When the weight of the possessed is too much, a tipping point occurs and the trash is dispensed outward. Rocky Raccoon will release the poison like the witch to number thirteen that begins again as number one. There are two white ducks that convey woman as an artwork that may not enter the dark star from the outside. Otherwise, I remain inside and watch the t.v. so not to draw attention to myself in darkness where the animals tread. You would not know that I am watching wheel of fortune with your children and it conveys a sense of a circle that may not be penetrated by the square. But, still, I lift the pentagon that floats above the rainforest in the Congo and God may feel lifted to a point where there is no danger of ever returning here. Nature overpowers the fall of man and gorillas exist there to detest that he was even here? The witch to God is diagnosed in the number five. She lives in England to note that tabloids may be foreseen to merit some truth in the ordeal. Without the penetration of flagrant lies, God will live on in this form forever. God conveys Pink Floyd's "The Dark Side of the Moon," and a picture is not rendered in the darkness yet. In the O.J. trial, the black glove is evidence that he may exist, but the blood is not his and remains so that animals will never cross his path again. It is a warning that death will not bleed from a flower picked. He remains somewhere else.

Otherwise, a bear bleeds for him in darkness and I see him just once as he leaves the garden that envisions the many faces of Jesus too. He may not transcend the realm of man again, though Jesus snaps a picture of him with a tattoo embossed in the refrain of a spiritual while at church. Simon and Garfunkel snap a picture of us as we walk onward on our way to Scarborough Fair. I snap a picture too, but it just looks black and may not be penetrated. His mother and I share a connection here. Lastly, fire sheds light on what is there like a heartbeat in the distance is the forth dimension. A drum in Africa may be heard as Jesus joins hands with God and the sun fades into darkness.

If I was watching the children in the distance, likewise I see from three different directions. Like three perfect suns that denote me out of time, it lives on in the form of a lion, tiger, and bear. I am not present when an apple from the tree is beseeched and my mother as my tail watches instead.

First, there is Adam and Eve. Eve flagrantly lied as I am not God either. She loved an emotion who is not a boy either and rises behind a veil that God may feel vulnerable and private as well. I may be one of the animals at the time and am well aware that she seeks the apple instead. To assume you are God without his grace is a bad emotion.

The trinity I inherit transcends this realm in darkness. God may have done all of creation in the dark, but the crime scene is fragile and Alison is Eve in hindsight, and she hides in the womb of a zebra.

I am a dark entity and God envisions those innocent to walk onto other lands. I was a slave when Satan was born, but end up in Barbados instead. When the children return, God says it will be like they never left. The leopard smiles, on the African plain, as I leave in a slave ship as though I was never there too. This diagnosed my first point of the trinity. America is now free as well as Jesus and the children may return to Africa if they want to?

How the gold of an Inca King belonged to Lily is an oxymoron too. I should not taste the apple in hindsight, but leave the light on at the kitchen door in case Ziggy Stardust decides to return. He claims Mars is his mother and God may claim it now too. I may represent the Inca King that denies things like possession and God likes it this way. I may have tasted the mushroom without picking it and the gold now belongs to him. The possession of gold is a lesser crime and the flower picked is not hers either. Lily loved a boy who is not God either. The Inca King is indignantly killed in a fire of their love. I am born from this second point in time too. The part of the trinity relayed here is the sun. Lily loved a boy who is not God either.

The Holy Ghost represents the trinity as well. I am not a Polish Prince, but the act of killing him in the holocaust relays that I have a connection here too. Ilona loved Hitler in a way that she denied him as relating to his spiritual mother Mimi and milk beneath the moon would belong to her in exchange of their love in the form of a tear. Hitler and I share the same spiritual mother and I am not his lover.

There are three points in time that I detest to in the trinity and I claim to be Jesus (not Christ,) the sun's eternal plane out of darkness, and the Holy Ghost in hindsight. The bear remains for the children who must believe. I think Jesus will return in about two hundred years. However, this seems like a long time to believe.

The Suicide's Eternal Plain: A Door Never to Enter

The Japanese inherit a realm of a horse named Stew and an eternal plain that will remain a separate entity until it is born again in the tenth dimension. The brats deny an association to the horse and the door to their father may never be entered that which is Japan. They reside in places like Seattle and sort of rebuke their birth mother of trust in the ordeal. Ziggy Stardust knew when he blasted off in his spaceship that a suicide was played out and the door may not be re-entered once closed. The Japanese inherit the animalistic instinct of the black horse. Meanwhile, Mt. Fuji keeps a shed on the beach that contains memorabilia of the distant land of America which he has never been to either. His son says that it is a nice place to visit. I may not represent the tenth dimension, that which is Mt. Fuji too?

Jim Morrison after Vietnam and the Doors

Jim Morrison is Mike's son and he represents that the door to the children of Vietnam and the door to the children of America is one. He, for lack of reason, detests brats and leads the children of the tenth dimension out of bondage to the God he recognizes as his father. Simon denies him as a uncle and they say God had played out the connection of Walker to my dad in Vietnam. God said the children should play together. I know him as my father.

Simon at the Doctor's Office

The bomb blasted outward. He goes to the doctor's office in Thousand Oaks, California, to propel this far from where he stares at me from his Mercedes Benz while waiting at the light on Sixth Avenue near Bleeker Street. The blast propels him from this point all the way to California and he waits in Dr. Emory's office. There is complete annihilation in it, but must ask why no one dies in the process? Simon says he feels like he has been here before.

Diana: (The Witch to Man may be a Jew)

What makes a woman jealous of children who are loved by mankind is that man is best observed from the tenth dimension. To a woman of the twelfth dimension her loyalty and even sacrifice for subjects of the first house seems in vain. She will love Hitler instead as it is like a lion and its putrid hate satisfies her bizarre inhibitions. She feels somewhat betrayed by her own children and the lion is the next best thing. When Hitler feels separate from his children, he blamed the Jews and the rest is history. The witch to man may be a Jew too, but she is not a scapegoat to this play. Man is freed in the process like the apple Adam picks for Eve seems like a crime now too? Woman is innocent and she pays for the fate of the Jews for a love of a father to his children.

Lesbian Reunion

Lesbians must seem like a bright light to the Jews who die and are reborn in this form. On the other hand, man feels betrayed by the onslaught where a woman loves another woman. When the hate is too much, two women join as one and are not blamed by God as it is quite natural too. I do not understand this kind of love? I am invited to my boarding school reunion, but do not attend. The children of the tenth dimension do not understand this kind of love either. Jesus represents a different point of view. I guess Hitler is an union with "the brats of doom," that is similar to when lesbians recognize their love of another?

Mike's (4)X: the porno that does not end

I love a woman in a way that includes sex. The devil is naked waste to a cause which is way too physical in nature. Mike finds this sort of tragic union as beautiful as the lovers embrace in heaven and propel emotions outward. This is so the dinosaurs are given another shot at life long after they are gone. The car may be a woman to enter. She likes the affection that denotes her better than a car. Mike is morose at the sacrifice this entails and presses the film to contain erotic imagery as he is at a loss too. The caricatures are not without the grace that sex portends. I pretend that I like it at such times. The tenth dimension should not transgress into a void of love that died so long ago. But, it may survive "after the dinosaurs and before the stars," like a fire you can't put out.

Mike thanks those who understand the love of this erotic imagery and it is transgressed like a linear plain so that it will not die either. Some of Mike's favorite films are "Sophie's Choice" and "Harold and Maude." He finds some inspiration here. Also, he says "When Harry met Sally," is good for the young at heart. Sex is not the possibility of love, it is love that once existed. Kurt Kobain plays Jim Morrison in a future film. He loves art as an expression of this love that once possessed him for that of a grandmother. They become a triad of affection as both grandmothers; on the mother and father's side will become friends. Sex seems so shallow at such times and a girlfriend is introduced to the film he is directing. Otherwise, God is the producer and likes films like "Maid in Manhattan," and what is better is the children that play and play and there is no ending to this film either. I think you serve as inspiration and you will find out about sex, later, though.

Walking to Scarborough Fair with Will

We walk pass the Russian Embassy on Wisconsin Avenue in Washington, D.C. and the rain came falling down. It is late May and the sun finds a way to shine through the clouds which are passing by. We are walking to a spring time fair. We do not mind getting wet and it stoned me to my soul. Children are foolish like this but even more in the case of boys. It is lucky that I have two older sisters that will guide me through the rain. I sort of felt like God was present. The children win goldfish by throwing ping pongs into small glass bowls. We are not quite as daring and some of the older students consumed them like a dare and God shows that the devil is not the only entity that tempts you as such. They ride a sort of spinning machine, and throw up the goldfish and it is not fully digested either. I do not know if God meant us to be vegetarians at such times? My grandfather Jack sits on a cloud and watches too. The Irish Wolfhound smells the butt of a small white poodle and is testament to how far we have come? We cross the avenue where an African/American traffic guard winks as we cross. Time will transgress to years later when entering the Metropolitan Museum of Art in New York City, the guard smiles as we enter. That is what it feels like to walk to Scarborough Fair with Will and the tenth dimension is left behind like an umbrella you forget while sitting in its aura.

Jesus after Steve in 200 years...

I did transgress Steve on Bird Island some time in the late 1980's. There is no reason to fear the devil as it is not what he does, but rather it is a choice to be good and this will not penetrate your soul either. If your will is good, bad things will not leave you somewhere else. You will find with God's love, a question to be bad may not have an answer. Jesus died on a cross for our sins and that is all. To point the finger at other is tallied like mushrooms picked and you may be responsible too. Here, two paths may diverge and I go somewhere as there is no choice and Jesus may return in about two hundred years. A clown smiles at me and I can tell God is smiling too.

Satan in the Ocean

Satan is like a bear that is homeless. It does not feel like man and this is a dangerous tendency when confronted with it outside the forest it once lived in. He lives in God's domain, but feels he must retract his steps to find a way back to where he last slept. His next meal is his mother, while his father is a pair of socks. It does not allow him to enter the nightclub that pounds to blaring music where he does not know him either. I enter the nightclub with Mimi and from here you may hear his heartbeat as a police officer tells him to leave the park. He is not bad, (maybe?!) but can't find a way back home. He fears that this will happen to you as well. It is a dark entity too, and cannot remember committing a crime at least in this lifetime? He may not find a way home if you want to call this bad. The black panther does not know why you fear it, just God is punishing him and this makes you ask why? If you harm him when visiting the aquarium in Baltimore, you will see the negative space and for this man fears him. I think it is not what you do, but what you do not do and Satan is the next best thing. He is unable to leave the ocean and there is no mercy here and I tell Mimi, "let's go?"

There is a place in China where children who tread upon him feel trapped in cages that a sticky sap will not allow it to be free. You may say he is the reincarnation of what manifests as a mother's sense of what is mercy. She does not choose to participate either.

Three Warring Tribes

"Lucky Thirteen" is a game Indians play. The tribes in Africa are diagnosed as one of three entities that persist. A lion, a dog, and a black panther form individual patterns. The pattern "17" complies with the number five (the lion), pattern "18" complies with the number six (the dog) and pattern "16" complies with number four (the black panther). The devil will not penetrate their domain in Africa as God wears his K-Swiss tennis shoes as he walks into heaven. Sex was never an issue as a diamond in the rough remains somewhere else and this is the devil's fruit and it is a curse to assume otherwise. The children will not participate and princes in foreign lands may be born out of the contests as God may not recognize the children either.

Like Bread for Wine...

An African man meets the Pope in Rome and offers bread for wine. The wine may be tasted best while at a café in Vienna. It is neutral ground that does not know its harvest is the blood of Christ too. The Pope humbly breaks bread at communion that this man carried all the way from Sudan. The two holy men make the transaction so money is now obsolete. God eats a meal with his family somewhere else, and the tent where children persist in war torn Bosnia do not claim it is their own, nor are they homeless.

Joseph's Requital in Spain

The shanty towns of South Africa are far from Madrid. The Jews remain inside Einstein's square in Israel and otherwise its contours forbid these dark entities from entering within.

A girl asks Joseph if he might spare some change to buy a roll with butter? He asks her where her parents are? She says her father is a plumber from Russia and he left she and her mother. Joseph asks what her mother does and she replies that her mother is Mary Magdalene. Joseph says, "carry my bag for me and I will give you a dollar." They arrive at his destination and he gives her fifty cents instead.

Obama and the number Forty-Four

If Obama had two sons, one might be sent to boarding school in Bahrain and the other sent to a boarding school in Detroit. He sees his sons as equal. Somehow God pre-determines Bahrain as a desert paradise and Detroit less flamboyant. The boy in Bahrain asks for money and the boy in Detroit pays for some of his expenses by working at the school snack bar. The boy in Detroit feels that he should leave school after three years to get a real job. In this light, the boy in Bahrain who asked for money is considered to have honored his father.

Satan may have done nothing wrong, but I would not have killed Bin Laden either. This is what a catch-22 feels like. God recognizes Obama as the forty-forth president of the United States of America.

The Devil Looks Inside

I travel to Las Vegas and watch the t.v. in my hotel room while staring into the devil's eyes. She stares back at me through this vice. Then, I go down stairs to play roulette. My number is twenty. I feel like it wins more than zero. She is next to me and accepts my dare and places a bet at zero. She wins twice as much as me. The children ask how she knows this I respond that I do not know? I guess if you are bad "zero," is good luck?

The Shark's Last Testament

Will and I witness a dead shark on the beach in Rohoboth Beach. We do not know what steps lead to its death? We may be nine or ten years old at the time. I carry my Nikkomat that was given to me by my mother. It is as much a mystery to me as the shark. I use Kodachrome and snap a shot that fades like a flock of seagulls on the beach. I render itself in this slide. I may have taken my first picture here if not that it belongs to the ocean. I hear the children call me in the distance. The picture belongs to me though. Will and I are witness to what seems so obviously a dead shark. The ocean is resourceful and the tide's voracious appetite will suck it into the serenity of God's stomach like the waves that draw it in on the beach. God smokes a Doral and it seems so natural where he stands on the beach. The children detest that it is his favorite brand. God may be their stepfather in a sense. Otherwise, I name the shark Alex and we will shake hands on the beach in Nantucket. He is witness to the on goings in Japan sometime in the sixteenth century as though we have met already. He says that the children smoke a joint from time to time as well as God. He says it makes you feel like the tranquility of the ocean as the smoke is released; sucking it in as it is released in shear freedom.

Mt. Fuji said that seaweed tastes like lettuce and to be cool is to smoke a cigarette and not hear the ocean cough. Japan serves as a wall which hides those not welcome to share a joint with God. I would rather smoke a cigarette at such times.

The shark died on a cross and on the third day rose again. Jesus died like this too. He said you don't have to smoke a joint to be cool. The seagulls suck in the air and get high too.

Ferocious Naked on a Redwood Stump

The children claim that the dog belonged to them. This is not true, but I consent that they play with him for a while. To eat his remains would be like freeing him, but I eat a dried leaf from Diana's tree instead and this is the next best thing. Before arriving at a truck stop in L.A., I take a picture of him naked on a Redwood stump. He will leave his remains and the sun absorbs it so he may rise into the sky too. He is as naked as when he is born and they say this is the only way to get to where you want to be. The woodpecker frees him at the Wal Mart and he roams about like getting lost in the ocean. He is now transcended to a different domain. They say that dogs are not welcome, but this is an exception to the rule. He says it feels like his mother is embracing him. I tell him to send me a picture when he gets home. Sometimes children get lost at Wal Mart and this is a similar situation. I guess animals sometimes believe in Christ too. He tenses his stance to show he respects the faith that he accepts thereafter. The chance to meet the technician at the one hour photo shop is like meeting Jesus and this is a big deal for such a small dog too. "I am Ferocious," he announces on the speaker there and no one recognizes him really. He thought it was too much like a dream and he plays with the children instead.

A Giraffe that blinked once upon a time...

The savannah of Africa may not be penetrated by the rain. The children play in the distance where a giraffe stands erect. A tear will not escape its eye and the clouds dispense Mormons instead. They do not deter their strength and they join together as they reside on the ground that is flat like God's feet too. Will kicks the football and hopes it does not get frozen in the center, but he is not one of the children either. There is a certain amount of respect for a tiger that resides there. The giraffe is mesmerized by how the ball does not land and rather floats there for a few seconds for the time it takes for it to blink too. Will is welcome to stand in the audience at the center down below. The tear is for America and Africa is his new home. At night, they sit around the campfire and he tells the children stories about his previous home. They will build a stadium there too. The fire dies into the night and they sleep on the ground with blankets. In the early morning light, the giraffe still stands erect in the distance and a bird lands on its head and the children there will not know the rain either. The children that Will sponsors may keep a secret anyway.

Inside a pack of Camel Cigarettes (the devil in China)

I guess tobacco likes fire? I accost the devil as she wears white jeans and may dye her hair red which is like a magnet to my sensibility of that which is heaven. She claims a tiger as a pet, but they are more friends now. When three Italians meet we are drawn to one another like the devil in China which becomes an oasis that is inviting to him. He does not know what sacrifice this might entail? She leaves the rainforest behind and attends Will's church in

Texas instead. She enters a rectangle that is the door and the Lone Star hangs above which actually has five points really. They ride in Will's Blue Buick Convertible and go to Ihop outside of Dallas. Will is sort of a rebel and smokes a Marlboro Red while leaning against his car. He feels trapped in a camel façade and is happy to open the door for Mimi. The dust will not get in his eyes and he wears dark sunglasses. He admits he does not like the dark either. Fire burns within and the sun goes down like this. Somehow Steve remains in China and darkness does not seem to be an issue. I guess the eyelashes of the camel will dry Steve's tears. Ferocious sees for him in some honky tonk dive and he calls his make believe friend "shorty," while a line of cowboys sit at a long polished wood bar. He may only see their backsides as this is not heaven either. The children of a dark star may find peace here too. Steve thinks he has been here before. The fish in the ocean will not penetrate the oil spill above. It is a sort of private night club in Hong Kong and children are not welcome really.

Steve leaves behind a girlfriend from Omaha, Nebraska whom he meets in college. It is a coincidence that she found a job in Dallas as a graphic designer for a publication. In the oasis there, she rides a Red Mustang and passes Will and Mimi on a desert highway into the night.

Darkness: The Venice Beach Sunset

I do not know this kind of darkness really? It may swim in the ocean so deep and stares at his reflection in a mirage of what is there the Pacific Ocean. When you drown in the black water, you see his reflection for a short time until it lifts you into a light that darkness will not penetrate. The sun sets in the west and like a distant mirage of himself, he will see only darkness at such a time. Like a child who drowns in his oasis, he will share with you his last breath. You fly in an airplane to Hawaii and he meets you on the other side. He may be God's hand too, but fears his reflection and consequently is drawn to the light. He says the Venice Beach sunset is obtainable in complete darkness and this makes you special as you leave.

Lily Before the Judge

She says God is her father, but is born in heaven and denies him her love instead. She does not know that the realm she inherits as a tiger shark belongs to Satan and may no longer be God either. Meanwhile, I am at a mental hospital and draw a picture of myself as sort of a combination of a lemur and a black cat, that would leave me "out of Africa," in Madagascar. Something draws herself to his darkness, but remains in darkness not so deep. She goes to a sushi bar in San Francisco where fish are prepared and it is easier to obtain than other. She inherits the fruit of man and drinks a pina colada with the best rum from Puerto Rico. She considers herself of Spanish decent, but really is part native to Lima where she once existed as a princess. She blames God for her predicament that will not allow her to leave the ocean either. The flower picked resides in the tenth dimension where she loved a boy who is not God. In shallow waters off the coast of Peru, there is a replica of the David in Florence and she guards the oasis and he finds this less than bearable. The fish are her lovers and Satan talks to an octopus so that the door to the bar is now closed.

Satan may not penetrate my domain...

Satan does not exist in the tenth dimension. He is as real as kangaroo waste is in Australia? As Stew is a sacrifice in the sky, he remains in his darkness that is left behind. Those who seek the light would not even know that he is there. He is repelled from Australia as the aborigines fear that darkness may be bad too. After the fall of man, there was a statue of him on Easter Island, and legend says that he raped a princess that resided in New Guinea and as a result was born in Africa, but is not native to the land really? My oasis is Madagascar, but there is no way to get there from here.

Ilona and Alison: Periods in the Sky

Those who bleed may be Jesus too. This is an innately peculiar trait of woman. There is a temptation to disgrace the women you bleed for and man is discounted in the contest. The Virgin Mary bears Jesus immaculately who is the son of God. Meanwhile, her sister may not be tarnished even in a spectacle as grand and horrific as the holocaust. She waits so that God may claim his real son. The unbearable lightness of being is a choice. Neither sister would hide behind the blood of someone as already detested as God. Thus is the fall of man. God is now gone and you may claim to be periods in the sky. The children will be born from your sacrifice in the tenth dimension. There are sandcastles in the sky where children play.God, to be real, may not procreate in your world. He denies others in grandiose displays which also is a Catch-

22. He draws the children in to see through his eyes as the sand returns in the ocean. Mimi and Renata are sisters and hold hands on the beach, but do not claim the children that dissipate in the ocean like fish? Man may not penetrate the realm of God either!

Light will not penetrate a black cat's tail...

The children forage the beach in Malibu for its shells. As tangible as the treasure you seek there, you may not touch the night sky. The sun is obtainable like an orange on a tree, but the night does not know it is untouched. It is a space where rocket ships take off in your imagination. Ziggy Stardust may have tried to break through, but his remains decompose and falls to the ground. Where children dream there is a certain amount of respect.

God's Rendezvous with a Pineapple

God may have been in the tenth dimension when he ate the fruit. That which protects children from darkness seems good in hindsight. He leaves his remains behind and will not possess the fruit when consumed either. Mt. Fuji stands on a beach practicing a rare martial arts that draw children inside. Really, he is hypnotizing lions from the ground they walk on. The bee that annoys it as it sits on the savannah, shows it the respect it seeks. The remains of the pineapple rest on the ground and this seems disrespectful as the children rise into the sky too.

Did God offer his son on a cross?

It seems to me that God may be the culprit to his son's demise. But, I was not there either. All I may say is that what I know about the incident, I should learn from my spiritual mother Mimi. She claims that it did happen and therefore it is right to believe. It is as though offering California's fruits to the migrant workers who reap its harvest? This kind of love I do not understand. I think it represents a picture of greater meaning that is less understood really? Something does happen on the day when Adam picks the forbidden fruit for Eve and I may be one of the animals at the time. The apple represents a primal sin that will not allow God to know his son either. The Jews forage out of

Africa while the animals there remain in good standing. The fact that I am not present when Jesus died on a cross for our sins, does not mean it did not happen? It is a Saturday afternoon and I will not return to Africa either. One sin traded for another sin does not seem natural to me. I will wait in heaven in case Jesus wants to come home. God's love for his son is strong and I am enamored by the spectacle and in awe of the gesture and see only white doves on clouds to say instead, "never again." I think religion should be obsolete, but it is a character flaw as my mother is Jewish. The question is did God offer his son on a cross or not? I may be way too far gone in darkness to know otherwise? I believe there is a place where even Jesus may repent for his sins. I think God loves us likes his own son which makes you special too. If God may have made all of creation, maybe it is possible that we are of one body too, that which is Jesus.

The children know the answer to this quagmire, but I will not ask either? By saying that God loves me, makes you special too. I wait in the sky and embrace God as though he is sort of my father too. He did not create me and he is not blamed of any crime here either. I am naked and he feels invisible like this. God is great and our flaws is what makes us unique. I tell Dianne that she is a cunt and this is not a bad thing either. This is a metaphor for that she is watching the children at the time. We do not claim the children as our own!

Pear Tree in China

The children hold hands around a pear tree in China. What is inside does not merit a loss anymore. They do not know what the sacrifice Stew the horse entails? Otherwise, Steve and Shepard Smith walks back to America from where they stand on the border of China and Russia. Snow leopards are his pets. There may be a choice like two dark spots on the eyes of the panda bear? Some of the children decide to walk back too. Cat Stevens remains in China so to be trapped in the cover art to his album "Tea for the Tillerman." Stalin is Queen's nemesis and remains inside while the tillerman dries his socks on sticks by the fire. He says the children play and play. The sacrifice in Russia was too much and the tillerman's red beard is a testament to that something good remains. Otherwise, Cat Stevens sings "On the road to find out," as Steve is now gone.

"You would think..."

I claim to be half-Jewish. Being blond and blue eyed, you would think is a blessing. All I know now is that if it adds to the beauty in the world, it becomes true. Furthermore, you may be anyone you want to be in the dark. The children hold hands with each other in the dark. There are no worries of being different in this light. The truth is that you may be different, but if there is love, that is all that matters in the end. The adults will learn from this revelation.

A bear remains for those who must believe...

There in the forest of Russia, there is a cabin that is hidden from view. A bear hides in the fortitude of his loins that protects the children from bad things when naked so to speak. His wife tends to the children in the form of Paulina Porizkova and she prepares porridge for three little bears who are her children. It seems so far away from children in America who attend an amusement park there. There are children's books that exclaim that places like this does exist. Their oasis may not be penetrated and the bear remains for those who must believe. Simon's Rock is a window to look inside and Ba Win was my advisor too. He said that once you enter, you may not leave. My dictionary does not have a definition for a bear once it leaves the forest it resides? A bear should never do that. Once upon a time a bear exposed its nakedness to God…

Afterword

The fact that anyone may dislike any group of people is a shallow personality trait. I must admit that in the process of writing this book, I see my flaw and want to put out for the record that I no longer dislike Jews, and fear is a waste of time anyway. Thank you, Joseph, for putting me on the right path.

"To conquer anti-Semitism/racism you have to be an anti-Semite/racist."

Racism is wrong, no matter how you look at it. I remain in the dark still about my heritage, as my great-grandfather, RJ Reynolds, may have lived in the time of slavery, which means he may have participated in the awful atrocity. But, I still do not know what my heritage, which I now recognize, really entails.

After reading Corneilia Walker Bailey's novel, *God, Dr. Buzzard, and the Bolito Man*, I began to confront what this legacy may have entailed. It is assumed that it was awful; still I am ignorant to what really happened. So as I recognize my heritage now, and by doing so, I may begin to fathom what African Americans went through. The fact that it is the 21st century and only now I may recognize this past is a shame. It is like my heritage wants to forget it, which is the wrong approach, I think. In a weird sort of way I am both proud and ashamed of my heritage.

I am riding with an African American man who is a driver for the car dealership in Brunswick, where my car is being worked on. He provides a crack into the reality I inherited. Also, he is married to a woman from Sapelo Island, where the book is set. I am proud to make a connection. I am even more proud that the people there sort of maintain a heritage unbroken from Africa (that they are stronger than the history.) I am ashamed that my great uncle lived without the recognition of the struggle this entails. He bought the island maybe in the 1930s (Sapelo) and this is also my heritage. The man driving me recognized that I am somehow related, and for this I am proud. I now feel like I am ashamed and proud, and at the least, that I may be related here is a good feeling. I am sorry if this book offended anyone. I claim ignorance, but I am now less ignorant.

God, Dr. Buzzard, and the Bolito Man, is about life on Sapelo as a saltwater Geechee. It mentions that the "spiritual," that many assume is written by slave descendents, namely *Amazing Grace*, is actually written by an English slave trader in the 18ᵗʰ century. The man's name is John Newton and, in a strange way, it provides hope, a hope that there is good in the world. The notion of "the hag," in the book reveals superstitions on the island that I may relate to as well. Then there is Bilalia. He may not represent the Bolito Man, which is a sentiment of luck on the island. But, the fact that his heritage survives on the platform of his sweat and maybe even tears, he seems like a lucky notion too. He may have been Muslim when he arrived as a slave from Africa, and he may have been an expert at planting crops such as cotton, rice, and tobacco, which he carried from Africa.

But, it represents that there is no break and his descendents like Corneilia, will carry on his legacy and there is no shame in this. Slavery is conquered! When Corneilia returned to Africa, to her heritage, there are mixed emotions. But, she will form a circle which in its calling seems like she never left. *God, Dr. Buzzard, and the Bolito Man* are still there, and the struggle remains, but there is hope that slavery is conquered. She is home, but maybe she never left. She may sing *Amazing Grace*, "the hag" loses in the end, and Bilalia is smiling from a nearby cloud in Africa; she wins and may be even richer now. The legacy of slavery is a memory like Sapelo, which is her home still too.

"The Physics of God's Creationism"

There may be eleven dimensions that science recognizes, but there is more. I watch NOVA on 7/26/12 and the Montauk Project may claim that there is a vortex; that God does exist. The program reveals that when crashing hydrogen atoms together at near to light speed, the gravitons disappear in the process and reveals maybe that God exists, that sparticles are like particles of God may be detected too. Gravity may seem weaker than electro magnetism, but really they are simply different and science makes a connection between God and humankind, which is also his creation. I conclude after watching the program that we may all be universes with vibrating strings, membranes, and dimensions and wormholes connect us as though this is God. God is what connects the universes together. Einstein did not know that science sheds light on love and such a recognition will allow us to move forward.

"The Police"

The police may be our only hope for a civil society in the future. I regret saying that all police officers are bad. I think many police officers are good and will help us transcend into a better world, and even utopia in the future. Think about the children. I am intentionally vague when I say that in the beginning there are three blue devils that worked on the sky. It is an oxymoron to say the sun penetrated my eyes at such a time too. The sky is now broken which will invite the rain like the viaducts of Betty Davis's facade which bleeds the color blue. When the sun claims a rape; I do not know this to be true either? The police will sweep up the fish who are suspected of crimes made in the sky too. God may not be penetrated!

"Final Thoughts on Politics"

The Democratic/progressive philosophy might be flawed, you might even say fiscally wrong, but it is the only hope we have for hope of a better future I think.

I write: "Someone else plays devil's advocate and you should know that religion should be obsolete by now."

"Truth is from where God speaks and the Jewish faith is after the fact and I think Bangladeshis are as chosen as they are…?"

"The truth kills…"

"Whether someone raped God and killed the evidence is not an issue. Maybe it is time to confront your demons. Those who do so after the fact may not be forgiven. So, maybe religion will be obsolete (it does not matter, I think.) Just have faith is all God asked of you."

"Israel"

Devil's advocate is a game some play, but not all. There is good and bad in every religion. But, to play this game in vain is a note worth taking. The devil will lose in the end and those who deny God's plight in the process will lose too."

"The Choice"

The children have a choice. I categorize each option as there are two (maybe three if you include myself.) One being 'mashed potato,' which means you will not be moved and remain on the ground in which you stand. The other choice is in the form of a maple leaf. It falls from a tree like yourself and you leave through the backdoor you once entered."

"The Missing 'u'"

In all of God's greatness, there is still something missing. To recognize this phenomena, whether through religion is to embrace God, which there is no end to his mercy."

"To the children"

Paint the world that you want to live in and make it happen. Personally, I am not against same-sex marriage. Abortion to me seems wrong, but it is true that it is a woman's body and choice. I may make mistakes too, so it is a choice to make the world a better place. Though, I do not think the church or any religion should dictate how we live our lives either."

"Ants in the Crevasses"

I try not to kill ants out of respect. Their work will reflect the coming day. Should one be killed, it may be considered a suicide, I think. The Japanese may know their plight, but not really and they are forgiven for crimes made in the dark, in the end. There is no way to enter from this standpoint too."

"The Leaves of my Despair"

I may represent three points in time which is a heavy cross to bear. More importantly, I attend a church without the grace God offers in the form of a crucifix. Still, I believe and I think this is good enough."

"Like the sand raked up by the ocean, so will the devil dissipate."

"Like the feather that falls, there is hope…"

"9/9/12:" Including the urns, there may have been five warnings of 9/11. The first occurred in 1988 at Saint George's when I first had a premonition that something bad was going to happen. When living in Soho, I tried to take a picture downtown and was pummeled with a blow and this was a sign too. I made two walks to the World Trade Center thereafter and did not know why. There was nothing I could do. I may have had other premonitions that did not come true, but the fact that 9/11 did occur seemed weird in hindsight. This makes me wonder why. I feel a wrong was definitely done, but still do not know how. Bin Laden may be responsible, but we are not so innocent now either. I truly, by writing this, do not want to scratch at wounds that have not yet entirely healed, not to mention the pain of those involved; to have to relive this, but I thought the truth should be told. I had nothing to do with 9/11, still I feel slightly guilty. There is a cross that remains at ground zero for those who want to believe in a better world too. I hope this book helps you get to where you want to be. I would not have killed Bin Laden, though… (This book is a picture I paint of the world in which I live. If you want to participate, it is a choice I think…)

"The Christian Coalition: Mimi's Vision Through My Eyes"

What's going on? The revolution has already begun! As I stated before, I think Christianity, in its rawest sense, is a combination of three entities. These entities include a race, religion, and nationality. They are black, Jewish, and Chinese. Black people seem poor enough and have already experienced in their history a time when they worked for free. The Jews have experienced a horrible genocide, and are smart enough to survive for five thousand years. And the Chinese already work practically for free; still they are becoming the world's leading economy. The transition seems like it has already underway.

A spark of greed somewhere has aligned with the stars and God's plan, "Let there be light!" This is way too early to draw up the plans, but to scope what is to come…let us just say that Russia and the Eastern Bloc may go back to Socialism if they like? Let us just say the Earth will breathe as one and this is just the beginning. I see a time when the world shares its riches responsibly.

Now, the spark is from within. Africans keep creating children who want our candy, and this is the beginning. The hunger is not my creation maybe, and the revolution is natural (and need not be spoken.) It may not be faltered either. To say their society is wrong is a flagrant lie. I note Christianity is without borders and God speaks at the pulpit of what is America too!

Afterword Continued:

"Entering the Night"

When the Soul Calls...

The sky was broken for a time. Diana's tear was suspended in a half-life before 9/11. She is the good witch to man. It evokes memories of Ferocious in the park and she claims him as her own. I experience dual orgasms while entering the park on the Upper West Side. Meanwhile, Ferocious is subordinate to the Japanese cause, which in hindsight, is seen as a suicide. He detests the fire burning in Africa as a tipping point when women feed the pigeons in the park and nature repeats itself. Children dream of faraway places and the door in Japan is now closed.

Yoko Ono says, however, that all you need is love. I drop two bombs on Ferocious and laugh as no one dies in the process. The fact that Ziggy Stardust may penetrate the sky leaves MT. Fuji isolated. Ferocious commits suicide and kills the lion in the process. Diana shares a half-eaten banana with me. Through the wrinkled façade of her face she dreams a better dream. The trappings of leather seem like a vanity that she will not participate in. The sky is broken so that she will float in the sky and man in Africa stands with shoes on the ground without her sacrifice. God claims heaven as his home and Ferocious will not penetrate his domain there until I may claim my innocence too.

Out of Africa (the trinity is Marilyn Monroe, Audrey Hepburn, and James Dean)

After the bomb test in 1952, these three entities formed a union that is witness to Ziggy Stardust penetrating the sky as his remains decompose and fall to the ground. Audrey Hepburn seeks my soul in Africa. Marilyn Monroe forms a veil to the land where man stands on feet that are flat like God. She dies in the four corners of a bed, as a sin there is isolated like a square. James Dean will not visit this land and inherits my red down jacket that I leave behind at a Holiday Inn in West Hollywood. He may be the devil's alter ego "out of Africa." Men there will not relay in the sky until the clock ceases to tick in about two thousand years. This provides God the time to judge the living and the dead as well.

Milk Mother

(Will and I sneak into an R-rated movie in Georgetown, Washington, D.C. at age fourteen.) We are now brothers! He purchases some milk duds that he shares with me and it unites us with my spiritual mother. The tear belongs to her as cows baptize its harvest and the color green is lost forever in the process. Will and I are not blood brothers, but this is the next best thing. The moon now claims me as his son and I deny the holocaust in the process. Meanwhile, Ilona claims Hitler is her father, but the milk is not her offering. My dad uses God's sperm and I am born like that and he may be my father too. There is a cow on a hill and I claim Mimi as my spiritual mother. Hitler claims "the brats of doom," as his own and I am not his lover.

The Devil's Suitcase

Ferocious's blue leather suitcase blends well in the surroundings and encircles the conveyer belt around and around and no one will claim it either. The devil also blends well with his surroundings to the point that you do not even know he is there. His art is reversing time in the form of a guise. Ferocious packs his bag and leaves it behind to denote that he is also homeless. He meets his father in the sky and no one claims the bag at the airport. Instead, the devil flies to China and adopts this as his home. He was formerly adopted by Jewish parents in Omaha, Nebraska and leaves them behind too. The blue leather suitcase remains in a warehouse somewhere so that Ferocious and the devil will part like this, and they will not meet in the future either.

The Fourth World into the Dark

I shake hands with Will as the third world and fourth world will depart. I call Madagascar as home and I will not penetrate the void that is mainland Africa. Will represents the fourth world, which sticks to Aborigines around the world in National Geographic prior to 1952. I should note that I represent the third world and we are entering a period of two thousand years that is the night.

The Check Suicide

I am witness to the darkness through a raven's eye that I will enter as Stew the horse could not find the sky on that day. I may only detest that the land became divided so that a door once closed may not be re-entered. It is not a curse, but a recognition, that this is respect for a nation that the ocean is a door to Mt. Fuji's home that I may not enter either. I write a check for their plight, but it is not worth very much and I salute this door to say farewell to a friend.

Bear

A bear resounds in the darkness that is not God. A bloody black glove is left behind at the crime scene and I may see him in this lightness as he passes. God leaves the outhouse in California and tells a clown to remember to turn off the lights after you leave. The lights on the Ferris wheel provide greater darkness to the opaque sky that resounds. A bear remains for those who must believe. It may be offensive to the very Virgin Mary's and God seems so dark now and the stars shed a minimal amount of light despite my efforts too.

Thirteen Angels and Tennis on Pluto

The thirteenth dimension is important, as it is where the number thirteen begins again as the number one. I am in a sort of catch-22 situation and a cross is formed here where my sister is my only connection to the sport as the eleventh dimension. Like the darkness that divides China and Japan, my sisters play tennis in the dark.

Woman is the Twelve Dimension

A woman is her creation as a lake on Mars exists and two black swans penetrate the night so that she may be commended for her effort. She is the twelfth dimension and her canvas is black so that it may not be penetrated by man in her creative pursuit.

God is born in Mozambique

I will remain in the dark until God is born in another's heart in Mozambique. It is a complicated design and Mimi works on the fabric so that four entities representing the fifth dimension join in one entity. At the firehouse near ground zero, four fireman's helmets hang on a rack that is witness to his conception. He eats five dunkin donuts and it is dispensed outward where sea lions reside on the outer fringes of his home in Africa. There is a post that represents a cross in Mozambique and it represents his son in the past and I think he has a friend named Kyle too.

Love Lost (I will meet you on the other side)

I do not believe in death. Otherwise, I frame my picture on the wall to ask where you go after you die instead? This is another way of recognizing when death is in vain there is a sort of love lost. I tell Will that I will meet you on the other side. He will be born in another as he is the same person as when he is born and I recognize "love lost," as he is innocent too. Mimi placates this dimension at the beginning as well as at the end.

When the sun does not shine...

It is difficult for light to penetrate a black cat's tail. And the children will hold each other's hands with the minimal light this phenomenon offers. There is enough light to know that you are not alone!

Religion should be obsolete by now...

I believe to know anything is to know nothing. Similarly, I am in the dark as I think religion should be obsolete by now? I wrote earlier that religion is like fly fishing in the dark. I mean that you may seek truth, but that does not negate that you are still in the dark.

The End of War?

Another phenomenon of light is that it may blind too? War is the fruit of its demise. You see the enemy before you, but in darkness we are the same!

The Lie, Hitler, and Living Lettuce

It may have been a plunder to deny Hitler his human essence. He may have loved others like anyone else too. Living lettuce is like money, which is a false god. My dad is born from this phenomena and my love for him is great despite Hitler. He may be a Jew too. The lie is to think that two "Ls" is a bad witch and one "L" is a good witch. Some things you are not supposed to know.

Money

Money is a false god and this is not always a bad thing either. As long as you do not worship it, it is capable of great good too. My father is not God, but as a wealthy man is able to do much good too. In memory, I visit Howard Johnson's in Times Square and order a salad there. The Japanese make sushi with seaweed and this is not God either...

A Woman's Tear (the OJ trial)

Alanis Morissette rides a white horse while naked in the dark. The horse looks black and it cannot see the tear from her eye is real? It is a tear for the person guilty of the crime, as the darkness it foreshadows will not find the light. God sees through the bloody glove and only he knows who did it?

Popcorn Peace in the Middle East

People who die from this ordeal are in vain. I am not against Jews or Palestinians, but it seems so obvious that they should live together in peace.

Siaom

Siaom is an acronym for "sand is afraid of me." It just means that Mimi's sister is in her own element and I think every grain of sand has a half-life which is less than her.

Hitler's Alter Ego

I look in my Webster's Dictionary to find the definition of alter ego? It is a noun. The first definition is "an intimate friend." The second definition is "a second self." Clearly, Hitler does not represent my dad's "intimate friend." As a Jew, my dad shares only a dismal display of hate with him. The hate they share is the kind of hate that is not directed at any particular group. In the holocaust, it is misguided and directed at the Jews without any reason really. My dad, like a lion, does not know why he hates? He is definitely not Hitler's intimate friend either. However, I recognize the second definition as having some basis. My dad is born with this affliction and his second self as Hitler is reborn in himself. The emotion of love implodes in this phenomena though he does not know why? In this guise, love and hate are the same thing. I may have partially been a scapegoat to die in this hate and thereafter be reborn in his love.

The Runners from Germany

There are ten thousand entities that persist thereafter. What this means is that you are not God either. With this recognition, the stars light up the sky. At any given time, there are three runners from Germany and they relay messages from God to these points in time. God stands on the ground that is flat like his feet. Like a hot air balloon, he will float from here. He will not land thereafter the Jews who die in the holocaust. Prior to this, should he touch the ground, a girl is born in the sky and overpowers the six million Jews who would die. The runners from Germany are Heidi Klum, Paulina Porizkova, and Annie Lennox. I attest that the Jews who die in the holocaust are reborn.

"Mt. Fuji Rising"

Mt. Fuji may have picked the calla lily through the guise of God. It is a wakeup call and Mt. Fuji's entourage will leave the ocean and head inward. It is an open door to those who escape the fate in Japan. It is a deal they may live with, but the door is closed for a while. Not even Stew the horse could find the sky on that day. Lily is a pun and the flower is not hers. She loves a boy who is not God. They say, despite this, that all you need is love. Mt. Fuji may have feared the sun of yesterday, which Japan adopts like a red star. The Spanish conquistadors seek the wealth of an Incan king and the gold is not theirs.

When the storm recedes, Mt. Fuji expresses to God that it is now safe to leave the ocean. Their devotion leaves "the alternative lifestyle" a wealth in the ocean with which they may comply. Mt. Fuji, with his perfect symmetry, represents a mid-point to a natural cycle, which is my dad too.

The door to enter Japan remains closed until Stew is redeemed in the night sky. God will leave the ocean thereafter and Japan is separate in the ordeal.

Mt. Fuji has a goat and he walks on water so that a lion sun, a tiger sun, and a bear sun are united as one and can thereby be born out of the scenario. Japan is now separate and parts into two halves like the sea that parted for Moses. The 13th sun belongs to Mike as God rises in the sky. Stew the horse protects those from an aura of a red sun and seaweed tastes a lot like lettuce. Satan and Lily remain in the ocean so that a bear does not penetrate God's remaining domain. The dark star is now separate and is in linear form of the reality at hand. You may possess gold, but this does not make it yours. Meanwhile, like the apple, God will not land thereafter. A Polish prince will die in the holocaust and Ilona is denied the riches in the ocean she seeks. Eve, at the same time, eats at Chez William and is forgiven of her sin in the ordeal. Eve hides in the womb of a female zebra until Adam may claim his innocence in temptation to God. Will breaks through to the other side and calls Africa home. We are brothers, but was I ever there?

"Through Satan's Eyes"

The devil may not be guilty of any sin other than the sin of just being. He is a Jew and takes responsibility as such. Meanwhile, he sees through Satan's eyes, which is compliant to God's request as Satan fears his complexion to the point that Stew can't find the sky. He is a dark entity and remains in the ocean forever.

Alex is a shark that claimed to have seen God before leaving the ocean. But it probably was just a kid diving into the abyss and swimming in too deep of water from the shore? If Satan was guilty of anything, it is forgiven by God except for the fact that he is not God. Stew the horse can't find the sky on that day, but he is not Satan either. Steve is the devil and hides in China until God judges the living and the dead, and this is good. I may have been a slave when Satan was born. I eat at Chez William too, like Eve. From the expression of creationism, the children will eat as I do, and the devil is born out of this scenario.

"Witch to Man"

While I claim Ilius and all dark entities as my brethren, Diana is denied access to their land and she is the good witch to man. She is my soul temporarily and her dog is born there and is forgiven for committing suicide just like the Japanese.

For a time, they seem quite divided, but will in the far future join God in heaven, I think. This kind of hope seems so distant and the picture I paint will unite them in time too. Diana's reward, unlike the Jews in the holocaust, will free her, and she will not be judged by God, either.

"Joseph: #7"

Mike Tyson must forgive me for accusing him of stealing my money for God. In general, like the number "43," he is a good person. He too will watch over the children in America and complies with Joseph as the number seven which is also the moon.

"Land of the Seven Suns and Eagle Claw"

I would like to change our nation's flag as the native people were once here and that is respect. Too much blood has spilled over and it is not mine to claim. I respect animals so as to promote these entities to darkness that in the future is more inviting where I once tread. I ask the question, what is an animal to God? Lions, tigers, and bears may not participate in their splendor. Native Americans are tallied from mushrooms picked and rise from those who die under Stalin. I think our flag bleeds the blood of Indians who once tread here. George W. Bush may have made a decision which is not God too? Bush and Putin are Russian brats. I will not judge you either. God is now considered separate. Satan remains in America and this may be good in God's eyes?

Yes, religion should be obsolete by now. The fact that I did not see Jesus die on a cross does not mean it did not happen. What should not happen, should not happen again. I feel I have a relationship to the Jews who died in the holocaust. They may hold a special relationship with God. This opens a door so that it represent the many faces of Jesus too. Pride, I do not think is a good quality. I think my Jewish friends should not deny Jesus. Nor does a simple character flaw that I foresee, make them closed to enter heaven either? Their relationship to Christ just makes their responsibility greater. I think God is Jesus too in hindsight.

It is not my responsibility to judge Christians or Jews. If they joined hands, maybe religion would become obsolete. However, first there are two tests if you will? First, God wants us to believe in Jesus regardless. To enter heaven, I think you must admit you are not God either.

Maybe Jesus is without sin? However, this denies him the right to live. As much as he will die for our sins, he may be human too. I do not think God wants us to deny his human essence either. God and Jesus are the same. I ask my spiritual mother to free me when I die.

Heaven is the recognition of God's greater plan. While hell is denying your relationship to God. We may all be universes that are connected by God's love like wormholes. I may claim three crosses to bear and will join God in heaven when I die. If you deny God in the process, his love will forsake you. Religion is not a factor here? It is not my role to judge you as God will do this in the end. I guess religion just helps you love God more? Jesus died on a cross and this does not deny you or me, despite some character flaws. I love God in this way and hope you do the same. God is inside you and you may be Jesus too?

"Two poems written 8/28/13 at 2:30 pm after the ceremonies of the 50th Anniversary of 'the March on Washington'"

Of Kings and Presidents…

A young African/American girl offers her only smile…as to say:
"everything is going to be alright."
I respond:
"…yes, I am lustful…yes, I am greedy…yes, I am weak."
No, I was not there at the March on Washington…
But, I see the dew on the dandelions in cracks on the street…
Teardrops from heaven.
"Now, I can see."

Of Princes and Jesus…

My father was a great man…
(no doubt…)
He could remember when…
When there was old time religion.
Now, I see "the darkies,"
As a boy seeks lost dreams,
…only to be regained on the other side.
The children may be remnants of the night; in the past…
And God is without color …
…like black is to the night sky?
My dad was not a racist per se…
…but the kids have no memory of him and this is good.
I see a time when Trayvon joins hands with God…
Jesus is in the corner, and he smiles and says…
"…that is alright."

Made in the USA
Columbia, SC
05 August 2018